EVIL

WITHOUT

APOLOGY

Published by Shades of Light Publishing

ISBN: 978-1-7341467-0-7

Cover Design: Cellar Door Creative

Library of Congress Cataloging-in-Publication Data

Woodman, Debs.
Evil Without Apology / Debs Woodman.

1. Narcissism 2. Psychology 3. Social problems
4.   Interpersonal relationships

362.8'292

EVIL

WITHOUT APOLOGY

A NOVEL INSPIRED BY TRUE EVENTS

By Debs Woodman

Dedication

This book is dedicated to the victims and survivors of narcissistic abuse and those who have been falsely accused of rape.

I applaud your courage and strength in overcoming the hardships and chaos placed in your paths.

Acknowledgments:

There are many individuals I'd like to thank for their contributions to my book. Many hours were spent helping me gather information and assisting me with details.

First and foremost, I would like to thank my wonderful husband for his patience and support. He is always there to remind me 'I can do this!'

A special thanks to Shirley Bahlmann for her support and professional guidance as my ghostwriter.

Thanks to my proofreaders, who carefully read my manuscript, and for their excellent suggestions and enthusiasm. Linda Pratt, Lorene Clark, Steven J. Clark, Janet Olsen, Darla Nielson, Rebecca McGarry, and Greg Anderson.

Many thanks to Todd Ellis and Ben Braten, they are definitely, hands down, the most creative photographers I've ever worked with.

Samantha Sorden, my book cover model, offered her time so I could portray the evil works of Ivy Greene. Her make-up was done by the talented Tierra Valdez Engel, make-up artist.

It would have truly been impossible for me to write this book without the heartfelt stories from the victims that helped me understand their pain and suffering caused by narcissistic abuse. To each one of you, "Thank you!"

Narcissist

(noun): polite term for a self-serving, self-centered, arrogant, manipulative, haughty, patronizing, demanding, conceited, boastful, pretentious, envious of others, lack of empathy, sense of entitlement, excessive self admiration, pathological evil person with no soul.

The only way to win with a narcissist is not to play at all.

CHAPTER 1

Laura Greene was determined to escape Pinedale, Wyoming, by sunset. She had no more use for the cruel residents who no longer supported her. Hauling the last two suitcases out of the house without looking back, she called, "Come on, Ivy." Throwing her cases in the back of her classy red Buick Enclave, she slammed the hatch shut and caught a glimpse of herself in the glass.

Oh, no! She looked a mess. Forgetting about Ivy, Laura dug in her purse for a brush, removed the clip from her sagging hairdo, then brushed her dyed blonde hair up in a dramatic twist and gripped it with the clip again. She pulled out a few strands of hair to frame her face, applied shiny lip-gloss, and smoothed her eyebrows with a manicured finger. It was the best she could do without unpacking her cosmetics and going back inside to refresh her makeup.

Should she?

No. Her top priority was to get away from all these small-minded people, her so-called friends who had turned their backs on her. Even Wendy, who'd hung on the longest, had accused Laura last week of lying.

Ridiculous.

Laura climbed in the driver's seat before she noticed that Ivy was nowhere in sight. Honking the horn, she called, "If you don't get in this car right now, I'm leaving you."

Five-year-old Ivy ran from the house with an awkward gait, trying to keep her backpack balanced on one shoulder. Blonde hair wild, her shoelaces flailed as she stumbled to the car. The open door of the house swung on lazy hinges as Ivy fixed worried blue eyes on her mother. "I didn't find my swimsuit," Ivy said, breathless, the small scar over her eyebrow showing whiter than her skin.

"It's not my fault you didn't take care of it."

Tears rose in Ivy's eyes. "But it has Ariel on it."

"I'll buy you another one," Laura snapped. "Now either get in the car or stay here by yourself."

Ivy struggled in through the backdoor and settled into her booster seat. Her mother started the car and roared off into the sunset, leaving Ivy struggling to pull the seat belt over her lap and force the latch plate into the buckle.

At nine o'clock the next morning, after finishing her fifth cup of coffee on the road, Laura finally pulled to a stop in Meridian, Idaho. She liked the looks of the city. It wasn't overwhelming in size, but big enough to blend in.

Ivy woke up and squinted out the window. "Where are we?"

"Our new home," Laura announced.

Ivy checked out the houses. "Which one's ours?"

"Don't know yet, but it will be a nice one," her mother said.

They got out at the Shell station where Laura took Ivy and an overnight bag into the bathroom. Ivy had to look cute for the next part of the plan. Laura combed Ivy's hair, made her change her shirt and tie her shoes, then gave her a pack of gum to keep her occupied so Laura could fix her own makeup and hair. Then Laura made Ivy spit out the gum before taking her adorable little girl by the hand and going out into Meridian to turn on her charm.

Ivy's cute little face and Laura's fashion sense, humor, cleverly twisted falsehoods, and general charisma secured them living accommodations in a townhouse in one of Meridian's luxury gated communities. After signing the rental agreement, Laura drove to her new home and punched in the #1795 code to open the intricate wrought iron gates to her new home. Laura moved her luggage in and dumped Ivy's things in her room for her to put away.

The next order of business was to find a job. Although she had no college degree, working a nine to five job wasn't prestigious enough for Laura. Using notes of other people's accomplishments, she spruced up her resume, generously adding experiences she'd never had. With no prior business experience in the retail world, 29-year-old Laura landed a job as a fashion buyer for a local department store. *A fashion buyer, if they could see me now. Here's my big opportunity! Now I have the professional image everyone will admire.*

Using her glamorous new position and deviously calculating instincts, Laura began networking with successful people she predicted would work to her advantage. She registered Ivy for school as well as dance classes, having learned that if her daughter was in a social activity such as dance, Laura would be viewed as a good mother and held in high esteem.

On Monday, Ivy ran into the dance studio so fast, her jacket hood slid off her silky blonde hair and bounced against her back. Delighted to find an instant audience, she headed toward five other diminutive dance class members crowded on a bench, chatting and laughing as they changed from street shoes to their dancing ones.

"I got new shoes," Ivy announced, pushing her way to the center of the group. "They costed lots of money." She held out a pair of gleaming pink ballet shoes with no creases across the toes.

A couple of girls glanced at her shoes, then looked at each other and shrugged. Two boys who looked alike paid her no attention as they argued over whose clean socks they were using for a game of tug-of-war. Another girl stared at the shoes, then said with a lisp, "I got new shoes before."

"But I have new ones now," Ivy declared, shaking the shoes as if trying to entice a pet dog to come close enough to lick her feet. "And when these get wrinkled, Mommy will buy me brand new ones."

Just then, a slight boy walked in from the hallway across the room. Catching sight of Ivy, he dropped his gaze to the floor and leaned against the wall with his hands behind his back.

Ivy stared with intense interest. "Who's that?"

"Eli," the girl lisped. "He had to go to the bathroom. He's shy."

"Not to me," Ivy announced.

The girl covered her mouth to stifle a laugh. "He's shy to everybody."

"Not me," Ivy declared, and then marched across the room. Sliding her free hand inside her jacket pocket, she fingered the half dozen fancy caramels she'd taken from her mother's secret hiding place. Ivy was planning to eat them all by herself after dance practice. Was it worth giving one up? Maybe two? She'd try one.

"I'm Ivy," she said, planting her feet in front of Eli. "Here," she held out a caramel, the overhead lights gleaming off the shiny golden wrapper tucked around the treat.

Eli glanced at Ivy's face in alarm, then quickly dropped his gaze to the candy in her hand, but made no move to take it.

"Come on," Ivy urged. "I'm gonna' be your friend. Friends with me don't hafta' be shy. I do all the talking." She pushed her hand closer to Eli. "We're gonna' have lotsa' fun."

Eli hesitated for another moment, then slowly reached for the caramel as if afraid it would be snatched away at the last moment. When he finally took the smooth candy from Ivy's hand, his shoulders relaxed.

"You're welcome," Ivy said. She leaned in close and whispered, "And just 'cause I like you, I'm giving you another one after class, just you no one else." She suddenly frowned. "Don't tell, or you never, ever get any more." At the startled look on Eli's face, Ivy softened her voice and added, "Just 'cause you're my special friend."

Eli dared let a faint smile escape.

And with that smile, a formidable force was created, enabling a budding narcissist to begin rampaging through other people's lives without apology.

CHAPTER 2

Laura walked into the dance studio with a saucy sway of her hips, so well practiced that she believed she'd come by it naturally. Seeing two other women sitting on folding chairs against the wall, she gave them her warmest smile. "Hi, I'm Laura."

The woman with the purple flowered leggings spoke first. "I'm Abby. This is Susan."

Susan's curly hair swayed beside her round cheeks as she nodded. "Hi. Your daughter must be the cute little blonde."

"Yes." Laura sat on an empty chair next to Abby and leaned forward so she could see both of them. "Her name's Ivy. Which ones are yours?"

Abby pointed out her twin boys and Susan to her daughter. Laura didn't really care, but knew from experience that it was better to feign interest. "They're so cute! Who's the other little boy?"

"That's Eli. He's rather shy."

"Who's his mother?"

"Claire, but she's not here. She usually sits in her car in the parking lot and works while he's here. She uses every spare minute to working at her own business, and doesn't often come in."

Susan agreed with a nod.

"I'll have to run out and introduce myself after class," Laura said. "How about your kids? Have they been in dance long?"

Both mothers said their children had enrolled within the last year.

"You're so fortunate to get them in so young," Laura said.

"How long has Ivy been dancing?"

Laura laughed. "Since she could walk, I swear, she'd dance to the tune of the refrigerator motor running." Abby and Susan's eyes opened wide. "She had such good rhythm, not to mention an imagination, I just couldn't hold her back from dance classes. But of course, she comes by it naturally."

"Are you a dancer?" Susan asked, eyeing Laura's trim body.

Laura ran her fingers through her hair and said with a smile, "Aren't you kind? I'm not professionally trained by any means, but I had my day for sure. I was head cheerleader all through college, but Ivy's grandmother danced for years as a Rockette at Manhattan's Radio City Music Hall."

Abby pressed a hand to her chest, clearly impressed. "Manhattan!"

"You grew up there?" Susan asked.

Laura nodded, then leaned forward as if sharing a secret. "Until I married, and then everything changed. You just don't really know a man until after you're married, am I right?"

Susan and Abby nodded their full attention on Laura.

"I don't know about your husbands, but mine was a real Jekyll turned Hyde."

"What do you mean?" Abby asked.

"He started out as handsome as James Bond and as clever as Sherlock Holmes, if you know what I mean." Laura's words were full of irony as she spoke her next lie. "At first he told me he was a financial adviser, but you wouldn't believe what he was really doing."

"What?"

A red-haired woman burst through the door and tossed her bangs out of her eyes. "Hey, girls, what's up?"

"Shhh!" Abby said, not turning her gaze away from Laura. "What was he really doing?"

"Take a seat, Leah," Susan said, giving the chair next to her a slight tug.

Laura smiled up at the newcomer. "I'm Laura," she said as Leah sat down and tossed her bangs out of her eyes again.

"She's telling us about her husband," Susan explained.

"He wasn't actually in financing," Abby added for Leah's benefit. "What did he do, Laura?"

With three pairs of eyes riveted on her, Laura lied with practiced ease, "He was security for a New York congressman."

"No!" Susan exclaimed.

Laura felt a twinge of annoyance at the interruption, but carefully kept it from her expression, since her goal for this whole ruse was to entice these women to be her friends. "Yes," she insisted. "He didn't like me to know his business, ever, if you know what I mean." She lowered her voice to a whisper. "I wasn't supposed to know."

"Now he lives here?" Abby asked, scooting to the edge of her seat. All that lady needed was a bucket of popcorn.

"No." Laura made her voice even lower. "I left him and his abuse."

Abby and Susan glanced at each other. Leah tossed her head and asked, "Was it really that bad?

Laura twisted her lips in a parody of sorrow. "I don't know what you consider bad. He...he started abusing me right after Ivy was born." She rubbed her arms as if cold, the movement from tugging one of her sleeves up revealed a three-inch scar on her forearm.

"What's that?" Abby asked, pointing.

"Oh!" Laura let go of her arms and pulled the sleeve down over the burn scar she'd gotten from being careless with an iron in college. "It's...he...you don't really want to know this, do you?"

"Did he do that to you?" Susan asked.

Laura nodded. "But it's the only one I can show you. The rest are too..." Laura pressed a finger to her lips. "Well, anyway, I joined the Martha Graham Dance Company in New York to hide from him. It worked for awhile, but it was too similar to my college cheerleading, and he found me."

"Oh, no," Susan breathed.

"My only option was to run again," Laura lied. "I tried hiding in a traveling troupe performing off-Broadway productions in different theaters in the east. Little Ivy was cast in parts, too, of course, which helped a lot, because everyone offstage helped with babysitting. They all loved her. I thought moving out of state would keep my husband off my trail, but when I saw him in the audience during a production of "Wicked," I realized I still wasn't safe. I had to escape out the stage door with my little girl."

Abby gasped, glanced at the door, and scooted her chair closer to Laura. "Do you think he'll find you here?"

Laura glanced at the door, too. "I don't think so." Laura's eyes widened as if she'd just had a sudden realization. She put her hand on Abby's arm. "But please, you can't tell anyone, in case it gets back to him somehow." She reached over and touched Susan, then made eye contact with Leah when Leah tossed her head again.

The three mothers all shook their heads, agreeing not to tell.

"He has all kinds of ways to listen to conversations from long distances, tap phones, track vehicles, things like that." Laura shot a glance from side to side. "I think I've moved far enough away to buy us a little time." She fixed her gaze on Ivy. "I hope so for her sake."

The three other mothers murmured concerned assent.

"Mommy," one of the twins whined, running up to Abby. "Joey took my juice pouch."

Abby sighed. "Then take his."

"He already drank it."

Abby glanced at Laura as she stood and took her son's hand. "Will you be here next week?" she asked anxiously.

"Yes, of course, unless..." she gave Abby a significant glance.

"Oh, no, he couldn't!" Abby said. Then she let go of her twins' hand and scrambled in her purse for her mobile phone. "Give me your phone number. I'll text you mine, then you can call me if you need help with anything."

"Thank you so much," Laura said with feigned sincerity. "I think we're safe for now and hope he won't find us for awhile." She told Abby her new phone number.

"Here's my number, too," Susan said, texting as her daughter grabbed for her hand. "Just a minute," Susan grumbled. Her daughter got a hold of her arm and Susan got to her feet, her daughter tugging her toward the exit. "See you next week."

"Plan on it," Laura replied with a sly smile.

"Mommy," Ivy said, running up to Laura. "Did you see me dancing better than everyone else?"

"Shush," Laura said, glancing around to see if anyone was listening.

"But I was the best."

"Of course you were," Laura whispered, "but not everyone needs to hear that right now."

"Why not?"

Laura put on a tight smile. "It's better that way since we're new. Just do as I say."

Ivy and Eli put on their backpacks at the same time and followed Laura out into the warm spring sunshine. As soon as Eli appeared, a woman got out of a car and walked toward him, her anxious gaze on Laura.

"Hello," Laura said, holding out her hand. "I'm Laura, and this is my daughter Ivy."

"I'm Claire," the woman said, shaking Laura's hand, then taking hold of Eli's shoulder.

"He's so cute," Laura said. "My Ivy sure took a liking to him."

Claire's countenance relaxed. "Welcome to Meridian...maybe next week I'll have more time to visit." Claire steered Eli to their car while Laura and Ivy walked beside her. Claire opened the back door and Eli climbed into the car. "Make sure you buckle up," Claire said. She glanced at Laura. "Sorry about that, he always forgets."

"I know… if we only had more hands and time, right?"

"Right," Claire agreed. "Nice to meet you."

"You too, Claire."

As Laura and Ivy got into their Buick, Ivy said, "You never got me another Ariel swimsuit yet."

"They don't have them here." Laura turned the key in the ignition.

"Did you look?" Ivy asked over the volume of Laura's music.

"Of course I did," Laura replied, even though she hadn't. "Stop bothering me about it. There are other swimsuits in the world."

Ivy's voice was just a whisper when she replied, "But I wanted Ariel."

Laura pulled into the Wal-Mart parking lot. "I just need to get a few things before we go home."

Ivy unbuckled her booster seat belt.

"If you're coming in, you have to behave," Laura warned.

"Yes, Mommy."

"If you don't, I'll send you out to the car alone."

Ivy followed her mother into the store, her backpack bouncing against her back. Laura grabbed a cart and started down the aisle without looking back. When they passed a display of summer swimsuits, Ivy stopped to stare at Ariel, flipping her red hair through a sparkle-studded spray of water. It was the most beautiful thing she'd ever seen. "Mommy, here's an Ariel swimsuit, and it's just my size! It is! Can I have it? Please?"

"No. I just got you new dance shoes. I'm not made of money. Now come on."

"You said you'd buy me a new one," Ivy shouted, her brow creased. "You're a liar!"

Laura turned, grabbed Ivy's arm, and barked, "I have no time for this nonsense right now! Why do you always do this to me when I'm in a hurry? You sure know how to ruin my day."

Ivy burst into tears.

"You're embarrassing me," Laura hissed. "Do you want to go sit in the car?" When Ivy shook her head, Laura let go of her daughter and stalked off. She was nearly out of sight when Ivy realized that she might be sent to the car if she didn't keep up. She didn't want to sit in the car. She wanted Ariel.

With one last longing glance at the magical swimsuit, Ivy ran to catch up just as her mother turned a corner and stopped at a jewelry display, fingering the necklaces and cards of earrings. "Mommy?"

"What?"

"I hafta go to the bathroom."

"Do you know where it is?"

"Uh-huh. I'll be right back."

Ivy rushed away from her mother and turned the corner to the Ariel swimming suits. She pulled off her backpack, unzipped it, took one of the beautiful swimsuits, and pushed it into her pack. Then she zipped it closed and put in on her back again.

There. She had an Ariel swimsuit prettier than her old one, and she'd gotten it all by herself. Thinking of all the other things she could get for herself, Ivy practically danced her way to the bathroom.

CHAPTER 3

When Eli Cole watched Ivy leave the dance studio, the taste of caramel was still sweet on his tongue. She was so nice and brave, too. She'd talked to everyone on her first day of class. She got a scar by her eyebrow because she saved her friend from a mean dog. He wished he were brave.

If she'd been his friend when he was four, she would have stopped big, 12-year-old Randan from hurting him in his private places. Eli was sure of it. Eli could have been at her house eating caramels instead of playing alone in his backyard where Randan found him.

"Hey, Eli, I've got a surprise for you," Randan promised.

"What is it?" Eli asked, looking up at his neighbor, who seemed to be almost as tall as Dad.

Randan let out a strange, high-pitched laugh. "It's in your pool house. You'll love it," he promised. "Come on, I'll show you." Randan started across the lawn, and Eli followed. He wondered what kind of surprise Randan had for him.

Eli walked into the pool house, wrinkling his nose at the chemical smell, and looked around for the surprise, but he didn't see one. He was confused when Randon closed the door behind him. It was kinda' dark, and made the chlorine smell even stronger.

"I wanta' go outside," Eli said, turning toward the door.

"Not 'til I say so," Randan snarled, grabbing the back of Eli's shirt and shoving him up against the wall.

Eli gasped, then cried, "I want to go in my house!"

"Shut up." With one hand, Randan pushed Eli's head against the wall. "Quit being a cry baby." With his other hand, Randan exposed himself, then yanked Eli's pants down. The force of Randon's thrusts hurt so badly that when it was over; Eli collapsed and laid on the floor, crying until snot ran into his mouth.

"Shut up," Randan growled. "Just shut up, or I'll kill you right now." Randan zipped his fly, then grabbed Eli around the neck and squeezed. "If you tell anyone what happened out here, I'll find out, and I'll kill you."

Eli couldn't get enough air. He grabbed at Randan's hands to pull them apart, but he wasn't strong enough.

"Even if you're in bed, I'll climb in your window and kill you. Do you understand?"

Eli could only make a choking sound.

"Nod your head if you understand," Randan ordered. Eli tried to nod, his head bobbing as much from pain as agreement. He didn't want to die.

Randan let go, and Eli grabbed his neck, sobbing.

"Didn't I tell you to shut up?" Randan snapped, kicking Eli. "If you won't shut up, then maybe you're going to tell. Maybe I should kill you now."

"No!" Eli put a small hand up. "I'm stopping. I won't tell." Fear paralyzed his voice as he stared up at giant, angry Randan.

"You'd better not." Randan pulled the pool house door open a crack, looked both ways, then slipped through the opening and was gone.

Eli lay still for a few more seconds until he imagined Randan never coming back. Then he pushed himself to his feet, pulled up his pants, and tottered across the patio and into his house as quickly as he could.

"Eli?" his mother said. "Why are you walking so strangely?"

He looked up at her with anguish, tears rising in his eyes. He couldn't tell her. It was so scary to not be able to breathe. He didn't want to die.

She bent and gave him a hug. "Did you fall off your bike?"

The familiar scent of his mother's perfume was so comforting that Eli burst into tears and clung to her neck.

"Oh, honey, did you get hurt?"

"Yes!"

"Do you think a warm bath would help you feel better?"

Maybe, but hanging onto his mother was the best thing Eli could think of to do.

"Come on, I'll get the water running for you." Mom pulled his arms off her neck, took his hand, and led him upstairs to the pearl white master bathroom.

"Here, you can soak in mommy's big tub today. It'll make you feel better. You always like the big tub." He stood there shaking, hoping Mommy would stay and put him in the tub, but she closed the door, leaving just a small crack open. When he sat in the warm water, he writhed, trying to get comfortable on his sore bottom. Mommy finally called through the door, "Are you done yet?"

"Yes." Eli sniffled.

"Good. Get in your pajamas, Randan's going to babysit tonight while we go to dinner."

Eli's scared little heart shot up into his throat, and his stomach clenched as if he'd been punched. He retched, and retched again, spilling hot, smelly chewed food and burning bile out into the bathwater.

"Eli?" his mother hurried into the bathroom and knelt by the tub. "What's wrong?" Her glance fell to his blood-spotted underpants on the floor. "What's this?" she asked in a voice full of horror. "Eli?"

Her scared eyes made Eli feel scared, too, but she'd already seen what happened when she looked at his underpants. He hadn't told her. She already knew. That meant it wasn't a secret anymore.

She wrapped him in his towel and sat on the toilet seat, rocking him back and forth in the safety of her arms while he told her what Randan had done. As he finished, he could feel her trembling. If

Mommy was scared, then what would happen to him? "Don't let him kill me," Eli sobbed.

His mother pressed his head against her chest as her anger burned hot toward an older, bigger teen who would take such horrible advantage of a little boy who didn't have the strength to fight back. And it had been her little boy. She should have been there for Eli. Why hadn't she checked on him? Why was deciding between her Armani or Ralph Lauren evening dress more important than her son? The anger circled back from Randan and needled her own heart. Tears slipped down her cheeks as she held her sobbing son. Why hadn't she been aware of his danger? Weren't mothers supposed to have a special sense to know when their children needed them? Why hadn't she been there for him?

In a fierce whisper, she said, "No one's going to kill you." She stroked her son's hair, tears streaming down her face. "I'm sorry this happened," she whispered. "You didn't deserve this. Eli. You know it wasn't your fault, right?" She hugged him tighter. "I love you so much."

Eli's parents stayed home that night. Mommy put Eli to bed and lay beside him, stroking his cheek with her fingers, reading his favorite books until his eyes closed.

It wasn't long before Eli woke to the sound of his parents' curt voices down the hall. He climbed out of bed and quietly peeked out of his bedroom door. *Mommy had told Daddy for sure.*

"Who'd think this kinda' shit could happen in our own damn backyard? I need to talk to him."

Daddy sounded so angry that Eli stood shaking. *Was Daddy angry at him for going in the pool house with Randan?*

"No!" Mommy said, her voice getting louder as footfalls drew closer to Eli's room. "He's asleep. Don't you think I feel badly enough about what I let happen to him? You don't have to wake him up just to put him through more trauma."

Eli ran back to his bed and hid under his covers just before the door opened with a slight creak. Eli trembled beneath his blanket, tears running from the corners of his eyes into his ears and onto his silk pillowcase.

"Son?" his father said.

Eli didn't move. His mattress lowered on one side, and his father pulled the covers off his head. Eli put his hands over his face.

"Your mother says Randan hurt you. Is that right?"

Eli tried to nod.

"Look at me."

Eli peeked through his fingers.

"Why are you hiding?"

Eli's mother spoke up, her voice stiff. "I told you, Randan said he'd kill him if he told."

Daddy's brows creased into his mad look. "Did he say he'd kill you, son?"

Eli nodded.

"Randan's not going to hurt you anymore," Daddy assured Eli in a deep, gentle voice, "I'll make sure of that." Eli slid his hands to either side of his frightened face and made fists.

"What a mess," Daddy mumbled. "Did you think of, I don't know, running, or screaming?"

Eli wondered if he should have run from Randan, or screamed. Would that have stopped it from happening? Was that why Daddy was so angry with him? Eli stared at his father's reddening face, not knowing the right answer.

"It's not his fault," Mommy replied, moving close enough that Eli shifted his scared gaze to her fists clenched together over her chest as if her heart hurt.

"I...don't..." Eli clamped his mouth and eyes shut, tears flowing from beneath his eyelids.

"You gotta' fight back, son," his father said firmly. "Kick, hit, bite. anything. Punch him right in the crotch." Then Daddy bent over and gave Eli one of his bear hugs, patted his arm awkwardly and stood. "Now go to sleep."

Eli's mother bent to give him a hug that was too quick, her tears falling on his cheek in dribbles that made him itch. "Goodnight, Eli. We love you."

As his parents closed the door, but Eli could still hear them talking outside his room. "I could kill that kid," his father said.

Eli's heart seized inside his already trembling body, was Daddy talking about him?

"It wouldn't do any good," his mother said, her voice thick with tears. "You'd only go to jail."

"He's the one who oughta' be in jail," Daddy shouted. "We need to call the police."

"Lower your voice," Mommy said. "I'll never forgive myself, but what good would it do to call in the authorities? It's Eli's word against Randan's. Eli's only four. Who do you think they'll believe? Besides, think how awful it would be if anyone found out what happened. It could ruin Eli. No one would be allowed to play with him."

"Maybe we should just move, the hell with this place"

"I thought of that, but what about your job? Where would you get another one with your current seniority? I don't know if we could even sell our house. It's nearly paid off anyway, and the housing market is down."

"Randan should go back to the rock he crawled out from under."

"This should never have happened," Mommy said, her voice shaking.

Daddy sighed, a heavy sigh that Eli hated. Daddy didn't sound strong, and Eli didn't feel the least bit safe. "It's probably better if we just don't tell anyone."

"Not even my sister?"

"Especially not your sister." Daddy snapped. "You just make sure to keep that cretin away from Eli, alright?"

"I want to, but we're friends with his parents. If we act any differently toward them, they might guess that something's up."

"They should know what kind of crap kid they raised."

When his parents finally walked away from his door, Eli slid out of bed and grabbed his pillow with one hand and his blanket with the other. Hurrying across the floor to his closet, nearly passing out with fear that a hand would grab his heel at any second and drag him out to the pool house to kill him, he darted into the closet and yanked the door shut behind him. He wrapped himself in his blanket in the farthest corner of his closet, curled up into the smallest ball he could, and cried himself to sleep.

Devastated that they hadn't been able to protect their only child from such a horrific ordeal, Eli's parents stayed up late into the night by the pool, wrestling with their tangled emotions.

As the days passed, Eli was scared all the time, especially at night. He'd wake up screaming, sweating, and shaking from severe nightmares. He rarely left his house. The Disneyland trips and over-compensated gestures of buying Eli anything they thought he wanted came at a great cost to his parents, but they couldn't give him what he really wanted - to feel safe.

CHAPTER 4

First grade was a challenge for Eli. He avoided the other kids. They weren't nice anyway. They ignored him, called him names, or made fun of him. Eli believed every single unkind thing they said. If they hit him, he never fought back. He'd fall on the ground and cover his head. Given the chance, he'd run away home to his mother, which is where he wanted to be anyway.

Worried about his social awkwardness, his mother put him in dance class. Eli hated it until Ivy showed up. He imagined Ivy punching his mean neighbor, Randan right in the stomach. No, punching him lower down where it hurt the most, punching him again and again, right in the crotch.

Ivy was so brave, and she was nice to him. He would do anything for her, and he did.

He couldn't be happier that she was in his same school class. He followed her around the classroom and playground. She chose him to be on her team for games, and hurried to stand beside him when they played with a parachute at recess.

Some days, though, she'd tell him to go away. Eli did. He sat at his desk, watching her chat with other kids, wishing he could be beside her, but wanting to make her happy by doing what she asked.

The next year, Eli was ecstatic that they were in the same class again. When a new girl named Celeste moved in, Ivy didn't seem to like her at all. Celeste was pretty, but no one was as pretty as Ivy. When Ivy stated the rules of a game at recess, Celeste didn't agree with her. When Ivy wanted to get in line ahead of Celeste, Celeste wouldn't let her cut in. Adding these incidents to all the attention the teacher and other students paid to the new girl put Ivy into a quiet rage.

Taking the situation into her own hands, Ivy led Eli to a corner of the playground where no one else could hear. "Eli," Ivy said, taking his hand. A thrill ran up Eli's arm at her touch. "I want you to tell the other kids that Celeste picks up dog poop with her fingers and eats it. And she doesn't wash her hands after."

Eli's eyes went wide. "She does?"

Ivy nodded. "Yeah, everyone should know, because her hands are dirty and she has bad dog poop breath."

"Okay," Eli said, unaware he'd become Ivy's "flying monkey" who would do her bidding.

Ivy smiled at him, then dropped his hand and quickly ran off to play with someone else.

It was funny to watch the other kids react when he told them what Ivy said. Once Eli had spread the word, no one wanted to sit by Celeste in reading group or pick her to be on their team.

When it snowed, Eli watched Ivy put gravel in Celeste's pink fur topped boots, which were sitting under the coat rack alongside everyone else's. At the end of the day when Celeste took off her shoes and tried to put on her boots, she yelled, "Ouch!"

"What's going on?" the teacher asked with a mad frown. She lifted a pink boot and shook the gravel inside. "Who did this?" she demanded, her angry glare sweeping the classroom.

Ivy gripped Eli's hand. He could feel her shaking with fear beside him. He didn't want to get in trouble, but she needed him. He had to help her.

"I did," Eli said.

"What?" the teacher's frown deepened, "Speak up Eli, did you see who did this?"

Eli swallowed hard. He saw who'd done it, but he wouldn't give Ivy up for anything. "I did it."

The teacher's eyebrows shot up, disappearing in her bangs, "You?" She didn't sound angry anymore. She sounded shocked.

Ivy still shook beside Eli; her head turned away, her arm up over her face. He couldn't let her get in trouble. Not his Ivy.

"Yes," Eli said. "I did it."

"Well, why ever would you do such a thing?"

"Because...because she eats dog poop."

The teacher was not amused. She made Eli sit at his desk and called his mother.

When Ivy lowered her arm, Eli was shocked to see that she'd actually been laughing. She gave Eli a sympathetic pat on his shoulder and whispered, "You're my best friend."

Eli glowed, completely willing to be under Ivy's control. She was his friend, and worth lying for.

As Ivy skipped out of the classroom, she spared no thought for Eli or the predicament she'd put him in. He was such a sponge, believing she'd fought off a mean dog when she really got her scar from slipping on the wet kitchen floor and hitting her head on the table. In spite of all his expensive clothes and toys, she was better than him. In fact, she was a cut above every other person in the world, even her mother. Stealing was perfectly acceptable in order to get what should rightfully be hers. If it was anyone's fault, it was her mother's for not buying everything Ivy wanted. Lying wasn't wrong. It was necessary to get all the adoration and compliments she deserved. She was also completely justified in executing revenge for any slight against her. It was her role in life to be superior, and since she was superior, she deserved to have all her needs and wants fulfilled.

Even though no one was as smart as she was, Ivy wanted intelligent friends. She surrounded herself with those who showed compassion toward her. If they didn't exhibit enough tenderness, she'd tell them whatever they needed to hear in order to generate their sympathy. Since she was so naturally likeable, she demanded that her peers should be the well-liked, successful "clique" of kids.

In Eli's case, his parents were wealthy, and she could accept his timidity because it worked perfectly for her plans. There was something surprising inside his soft shell, some kind of animal pain and frustration that burst forth with a vengeance when she asked him to help her bully someone. She didn't know where it came from, but she liked it.

By the time they reached junior high school, the trauma bond Eli had formed with Ivy was as strong as cocaine addiction. The push and pull dynamics of love bombing, devaluation, and irregular reinforcement that Ivy dished out created a continuous fight or flight response in Eli, triggering an actual chemical reaction within his brain. High levels of dopamine, serotonin, and adrenaline released over time, making Eli as dependent on the chemical release as he was to food. He could no more stay away from Ivy than starve himself to death. Even though on some level he knew Ivy was manipulating him, nourishing the unhealthy relationship he had with her was much easier and vastly more satisfying than trying to break away from it.

He didn't even want to try.

CHAPTER 5

"Have you seen my new lipstick?" Laura called.

"No." Ivy replied from her bedroom as she zipped the top pocket of her backpack over the new designer lipstick her mother had just bought. It was the perfect shade for Ivy. She needed it for touch ups throughout the school day in order to look her best, so now it was hers.

"It was right here in the kitchen grocery bag," Laura complained. "It's not like it fell out in the parking lot."

"Maybe it did."

"I would have noticed."

"If you weren't busy staring at yourself in the rearview mirror," Ivy mumbled as she bent to shove a battered shoebox of her favorite new cosmetics under her bed.

"What?"

Ivy raised her voice. "You'll find it if you look hard enough."

The only things she kept in her makeup drawer anymore were broken eye shadows, dried mascara wands, and expired stubs of lipstick, decoys to keep her mother from stealing the good stuff that Ivy knew she'd taken in the past. Ivy had learned well from her mother's example, and her counter attacks were increasingly skillful.

Ivy slung her designer backpack over her shoulder and headed out of her room, past her mother still digging through grocery bags in the kitchen. She strode out the door to Mountain View High School, her head held as high as an Alpha of the pack. They'd never lived in one place as long as this before, but Laura's lies were holding well enough that there was no imminent need to move from this community.

The high school combined several junior high schools into an intriguing social puzzle that Ivy had been determined to solve her freshman year. Now that she was a junior, she'd already conquered the challenge of navigating the big school, made some new friends, and to her great satisfaction, was awarded the starring role in the upcoming school musical.

Just last night, Ivy rolled her eyes when she heard Laura talking on the phone about Ivy's role as Laurie in "Oklahoma." "Ivy's first rehearsal went extremely well, and so did the second," Laura gushed. "Ivy performed better than I could have hoped for in my wildest dreams. I told you I performed on Broadway, right? I'm the one who taught her all the professional tips and tricks. It's because of me that she landed the starring role." Laura laughed into the phone. "She's so much like me, we could be twins."

Ivy had nearly gagged at her mother's flagrant expressions of self-love. *Pathetic.* It was Ivy starring in the play, not Laura. Her mother was just an old has-been who might as well admit it.

But she never would.

CHAPTER 6

Ivy strode into her journalism class, her second favorite class besides drama. She made sure to connect with Mr. Atkins by means of a mostly neutral, yet positive glance. Her new teachers had higher academic expectations than the ones in junior high school, but Ivy wasn't worried. She was determined to exceed those standards by fair means or foul.

Journalism not only offered Ivy a comfort zone, but a chance for power and control. Whatever she wrote and printed in the school paper was read as truth. She did everything Mr. Atkins asked, or got someone else to do it for her, then handed it in with a Golden Student smile.

Mr. Atkins had proved to be a very willing project. She wondered if he had any trouble with his wife. He didn't seem averse to Ivy leaning over on his desk while wearing a low cut blouse, nor did he send her to the office for her short skirts. Her classic manipulation made Mr. Atkins fall right in line. She became his Trophy Student, and he gave her all the articles she wanted. He paraded her in front of the school as the most valuable journalist on the staff.

Once class was dismissed, Ivy strutted toward her locker in the crowded hall.

"Congratulations." Ivy looked up to see a tall, brown haired young man smiling down at her.

"Thanks!" she said with a quick smile, readily adapting to the situation.

"What are you going to write about next?"

Oh, he was talking about her top journalist recognition. Lowering her chin, Ivy looked up at the young man from beneath her black mascara-coated eyelashes. "You, if you tell me your name."

He laughed, a nice deep laugh. "I'm Reese."

"I thought I knew all the cute boys here."

"I'm a senior."

Ivy fanned her face with her hand. "If only I could reach your heights."

Reese laughed again. "You're funny."

"In the best way possible," Ivy quipped.

The bell rang, and Ivy scowled. "Don't want to be late," she said, and hurried to her drama class, mentally relegating Reese to the "annoying" category for keeping her standing at her locker for so long.

Mr. Percy, the drama teacher, didn't notice Ivy's entry just one second before the late bell. He strutted from his lavish office just off the drama classroom, wallpapered liberally with double matted and professionally framed photos of his past performances.

"Hello, ladies and gentlemen," he announced in his resonant voice. His breath was tinged with the vague odor of black licorice, the closest replacement he could find for the Sen-Sen breath perfume that some of the iconic actors he revered used in the early 1900's. "Who will be our star today?" Without waiting for a volunteer, he announced, "I'll begin, in order to show you just how it should be done." He opened the book "A Raisin in the Sun," then looked over the tops of his wire rimmed John Lennon glasses at the students. "One of the most famous plays in American Theater explores the agony, hopes, and struggles of a family in the black community of Southern Chicago. The title's from the Langston Hughes poem, 'Harlem,' that begins, 'What happens to a dream deferred? Does it dry up like a raisin in the sun?' There's more, but you can study that for homework."

Mr. Percy read the first page of the play, using his professional acting voice to fill the room with emotion. Then he closed the book over his finger and scanned the students, catching Ivy's worshipful gaze as if she'd enjoyed every single syllable he uttered.

He stood taller, then announced, "Each of you will take three lines, starting with you." He pointed an imperious finger at Chloe Holden sitting at the end of the front row. "We will go around the room."

As the students did their best to inject emotion into their reading, Mr. Percy barely tried to hide his occasional smiles of derision. Yet when Ivy's turn came, he nodded, watching her with undisguised fondness. She was his star student, his prodigy.

Ivy sailed through the school year, getting to know more people, plying her wiles the best she could to raise her social status. In mid-April, she noticed a guy named Trace, a friend of Reese's, walking across campus. She'd seen Trace before, usually in the company of a senior named Ethan Harrison, but she'd never paid either of them too much attention. Ethan was a brainy nerd, and Trace almost always wore a stupid Yankees cap turned backwards, as though he were still in junior high school.

This time, his cap was gone. Instead, he had a beautifully exotic Asian girl on his arm who was also a junior. Ivy was surprised at how appealing Trace appeared beside Tayla Dean. Even though they made a fine looking couple, Ivy knew he'd look much better if he were walking beside her.

Any guy would.

CHAPTER 7

Ivy rushed home after school and hurried inside. She stopped dead in the living room at the sight of her mother bending over to scoop her purse up off the floor. Seeing Laura in a skirt so short that her underwear was a centimeter away from showing made Ivy burst out laughing.

"What's so funny?" Laura straightened and gave a sharp downward tug on the tight spandex shirt that had ridden up beneath her breasts, making them look like two water balloons about to burst.

"What are you wearing?" Ivy asked.

"I'm going out," Laura announced, mincing toward the door on high heels, a dizzying cloud of perfume swirling in her wake, as her butt swayed from side to side. "If you make a mess, you'd better clean it up." Laura gave her daughter a self-satisfied smirk, blinking her eyes lined with bands of black as thick as caterpillars. Her exaggerated hairstyle was ridiculous, since it didn't suit her age at all. "I'll be late, so don't wait up for me, either."

"I'm sure I won't, Mom," Ivy said, her voice dripping with sarcasm.

"I mean it," Laura said, turning to the mirror and touching a finger to the edge of her bottom lip, swiping away an invisible stray speck of lipstick.

"As if that's going to help," Ivy murmured.

Laura turned toward Ivy with a cold smile. "You only wish you looked as good as me." Her mother angled her head to sweep a glance down Ivy's body, and then gave her daughter a sad shake of mock regret. "Nope." She offered Ivy a seductive smile. "You just don't have what I've got," Laura purred, "and you're jealous of your own mother." She clicked her tongue. "Isn't that just too bad? Well, maybe by the time you mature, you might find a few lucky genes in your pool."

Laura slung her purse over her shoulder and sashayed out the door without looking back.

Relieved to be left alone to do whatever she pleased, Ivy showered, put on a spaghetti strapped teddy, and painted her toenails while listening to her favorite music turned up so loud that the neighbors could hear. What did she care? She was doing them a favor.

Then she picked up her phone, tapped on the camera feature, and took a picture of her freshly polished toes, making sure to include plenty of bare leg. Then she posted the picture with the message, *Just painted my toenails. Aren't they adorable? Does anyone want to come and kiss them?*

Then she pushed a strap off her shoulder and turned the camera icon around to face her. Focusing her gaze on the slipped strap, she made a small round "O" of surprise with her lips and snapped a photo. Then she posted it with the text, *I'm falling apart. Who'll come put me back together?*

Ivy's addiction to instant attention from social media had her posting similar photos and messages at least once a day.

Her early morning pouty face of dissatisfaction was expressed. *Its 10:00 in the morning and no one's paid any attention to me yet.*

The expected sexually charged responses from the boys were gratifying, but even the girls replied about how beautiful Ivy was. Ivy basked in their praise, viewing it as acceptance.

She kept herself busy making new connections while holding the strings of useful old connections that could further her causes. She pushed herself into everyone's business, gathering information as a squirrel gathers acorns. She wasn't sure yet how she'd use her stash of knowledge, but she knew she was smart enough to figure out something that would benefit herself when the time came.

CHAPTER 8

Ivy had been somewhat popular while starring in the musical last fall, but it was old news now. When she felt her status sinking as she began her senior year, her calculating gaze focused on Chloe Holden, her new ticket to popularity.

Somehow, Chloe, with her long blonde hair and sincere sky blue gaze, had effortlessly crossed the social strata of students who'd funneled into Mountain View. She was liked by so many of them that Ivy was determined to boost her own social rank by climbing on Chloe's shoulders.

With her practiced skills, Ivy waited one early spring day until Chloe's close friends, Mia and Carrie, walked away. Then she approached Chloe with the greeting, "Hey, Chloe, how are you?"

Chloe gave Ivy a bright smile and asked with all sincerity, "Doing great, how are you?"

Ivy let her features droop. "I don't know what to do."

"What's wrong?" Chloe asked. Even her furrowed brow was attractive.

"I'm having trouble with my car, and I need to get to school a little before the bus tomorrow because I have a journalism deadline. I need a ride, but don't have one."

"Where do you live?" When Ivy told her, Chloe's face brightened. "Oh, I can drive you."

"Really? You're the best!"

During their drive, Ivy engaged Chloe in sparkling conversation sprinkled with compliments. Without any idea that Ivy only saw her as a stepping-stone, Chloe parked, turned to Ivy, and asked, "Do you want a ride tomorrow?"

"I'd love it," Ivy replied.

During their carpools, Ivy gleaned information that Chloe was an only child. The focused attention of two loving parents was lost when her mother died last year, leaving her father, Ted, withdrawn and depressed. Chloe admitted to her sympathetic new friend that lately, she often felt abandoned and alone. "I'm so glad you ride with me," Chloe admitted with tears in her eyes. "It means a lot to have a good friend like you."

"I'm the one who appreciates you being my friend," Ivy said with all the sincerity she could manufacture.

"I'm sure my dad still cares about me," Chloe sighed. "It's just hard, you know? He's so sad without Mom that he's made work his life."

"What does he do?"

"He's an Ada County police officer." Chloe's face lit up with pride. "He even got an award for exemplary service."

Ivy's interest stirred. "He must be in good shape to be a policeman. They have to be able to chase down criminals, don't they?"

Chloe nodded. "He won the highest award at the Academy for physical fitness. It was a matter of pride for him, and he's kept it up ever since." Chloe glanced at Ivy with an impish grin. "My mother called him her GQ model."

"GQ?"

"Gentleman's Quarterly. It's a magazine."

Ivy's eyes widened in appreciation, "Wow, Chloe, no wonder you're so pretty if your dad looks like a magazine model."

Chloe laughed, her cheeks pinking at the compliment. "He just looks like Dad to me."

"My dad's dead," Ivy sighed.

"Oh!" Chloe's hand went to her mouth, her eyes moist. "I know how it feels to lose a parent. It's been awful since my mom died."

"I'm so sorry," Ivy said. "You're one of the few people who understands what it's like."

"Do you want to come over to my house?"

"Are you sure?" Ivy's face brightened as if Chloe had given her a precious gift.

"Of course, Mia thinks my Dad's good looking too, but she's kinda scared of him. I think it's because he's a cop."

"Scared? Don't know why but I think it's cool."

Two days later, Ivy arrived at Chloe's house with a warm peach pie in her hands. Chloe opened the door. "Oh, my goodness, what did you do?"

"I just baked you a pie is all."

"That is so sweet of you! Come on in." Chloe opened the door wide. "Dad, Ivy brought us a pie!"

Ivy stepped inside, the comforting smell of sweet warm peaches and cinnamon surrounding her. "I hope it's good," she said. *It had better be. It was from the bakery.*

Ivy spotted a muscular man in his late 30's sitting in an armchair. At first, she felt a twinge of jealousy. What would it be like to have her own good-looking father sitting in his chair at home? He'd definitely be proud to have Ivy for a daughter. He'd hug her every day, say she was so sweet he couldn't help but love her, and tell her how pretty his girl was. He'd attend all her plays and be the first one to stand and applaud. He'd tell everyone, "That's my girl! That's my daughter up there, the pretty one." He'd take her out for breakfast, just the two of them, and listen to her talk about her teachers, classes, writing, and acting. He'd tell her to be home by 11:00 pm, or he'd come looking for her, and any guy she was with better look out, because her dad was ready to beat him up if he tried anything with his little girl.

Chloe was so lucky.

Then Ted looked up. His tragic blue eyes in a devastatingly handsome face twisted Ivy's thoughts from a protective father to running her hands provocatively over Ted's broad, muscular chest.

"Hey," Ted grunted. Ivy's heart raced as he clicked a remote and the faint sound of a TV program suddenly went silent. Chloe had warned Ivy that Ted's moodiness intimidated most people, but Ivy wasn't intimidated in the least. She saw a challenge, and she liked challenges, especially the kind she had in mind for Ted. She didn't have a dad, so why not just take Chloe's.

When Chloe found some ice cream in the freezer, they all sat at the table to eat Ivy's delicious pie with ice cream melting over the edges. Chloe thanked her again, Ted grunted, and Ivy laughed and asked playful questions that drew Ted out of his shell. She made careful note of the answers as they lingered over their empty plates in lively conversation, mostly between Chloe and Ivy, but with Ted joining in a time or two.

When Chloe finally walked Ivy to the door, she gripped Ivy's hand in both of hers and faced Ivy with shining eyes. "I haven't seen my dad that talkative since Mom died." Without warning, she reached out and gave Ivy a warm hug. "Thank you! You're the best friend ever."

As Ivy walked away, she amended Chloe's statement - Ivy was the best anything ever.

All that summer, Ivy spent lots of time at the Holden's house, paying close attention to Ted and Chloe's likes and dislikes. Her light-hearted antics continued to smooth out Ted's rough edges, teasing him out of his melancholy moods.

"You brought my dad back to me," Chloe confided one day on their way to the local swimming pool. "I can't thank you enough. You're my best friend."

Ivy didn't let on that Chloe's feelings were a one-way street, because Ivy wasn't capable of loyalty, empathy, or the mutually trusting give-and-take necessary for real friendship. Her only goal was getting what she wanted.

And she wanted Ted.

Her next strategy was to let Ted see her crying. She waited until Chloe wasn't nearby before manufacturing tears.

"What's wrong?" Ted asked, leaning in close like a concerned father.

"You are such a good guy," Ivy said, wiping her eyes. She knew they looked even bluer when wet. She'd practiced crying in front of the mirror. "Chloe is so lucky, and doesn't even know it. I would give anything to have a man like you in my life."

Ted listened as Ivy talked about her heartache over missing her father. Then he reached out and pulled her into a hug. "Honey, I'm here anytime you need to talk."

His words thrilled Ivy to the core. She was winning the hunt. "I'm so lucky to have you and Chloe in my life," she whispered against his shirt, breathing in his man scent beneath the clean laundry smell. "I know it must be really hard since your wife passed away."

Ted loosened his hold and sat back on the couch, his gaze focused on something beyond the room. Then his gaze turned to Ivy. "I don't know how you can have so much compassion at your age."

"I'm a prodigy," Ivy said, "mature beyond my years."

"I can see that." Ted's appraising gaze slid over Ivy's body before his eyes shot away as if they'd been burned. "It's still really hard, but keeping busy with work has helped, and having you as Chloe's friend has made a world of difference. You're good for her."

Ivy knew he almost added, "And me," but stopped himself. Instead, he finished with, "I love having you and Chloe here so much of the time. It makes things a lot easier."

Ivy manufactured a single tear to let loose down her cheek. "Don't ever think you're alone, Ted." It was the first time she'd used his given name. "I can be here as much as you guys need me. I just love Chloe, and you. You've both been so nice to me, nicer than anyone else."

It looked as if Ted wanted to reach out and brush her tear away, but restrained himself. Ivy suppressed a grin and continued, "I used to have a good relationship with my mom, but she's too busy now, and is hardly ever home. All we do is fight anyway."

Feeling Ted's defenses weakening, Ivy used her knowledge of the Holden's schedules to show up whenever Ted was alone, feigning surprise at Chloe's absence and using the opportunity to offer Ted a different kind of consolation.

Chloe was happy to share her father with Ivy as a substitute dad because she had no clue of Ivy's real motives.

At Chloe's side, Ivy found herself in the enviable upper class social strata. On the afternoon of the biggest rivalry high school football game of the season, Ivy called to cancel her plans to attend with Chloe. "I'm sick," she said. "I won't be able to go to the game with you."

"Oh, no!" Chloe was genuinely disappointed. The game wouldn't be as much fun without Ivy. "Should I come over? Can I bring you something?"

"No, thanks, I just need to sleep." Ivy yawned, then finished with a cough. "Have fun anyway. Tell me all about it tomorrow."

"Okay," Chloe said. "Get well soon."

"Thanks."

CHAPTER 9

Chloe made some calls and eventually arranged to pick up Mia to go to the game. "I'm so glad you could go with me," Chloe said when Mia climbed in the car. "We haven't seen each other much lately."

"I've been around," Mia said. "You're the one who got busy."

"Yeah, well," Chloe shrugged and gave Mia a hopeful smile. "It's nice to be with you again."

"You, too," Mia admitted. "Carrie misses you, too."

"I called her, but she didn't answer." Chloe sighed. "I'll make more time for you guys from now on, promise."

The girls found seats in the grandstand and watched the game for half an hour, but Chloe couldn't get comfortable. She tried participating in the cheerleader's cheers, but her heart just wasn't in it. For some reason, she couldn't settle down.

Mia asked, "Are you okay?"

"I'm not really into the game," Chloe admitted.

"Do you want to leave? We could go watch a movie at my house instead."

"Yeah," Chloe agreed. "That would be better, but do you mind if I stop at my house first? I want to change out of these jeans."

"Sure."

Before long, they pulled up in front of Chloe's house. She stared out the windshield in disbelief. "What's Ivy's car doing here?"

"I don't know." Mia leaned forward to take a better look. "You said she was sick."

Chloe pushed the car door open. "She said she was sick."

"Maybe she came over for some medicine?" Mia guessed as she let herself out.

"That would be weird," Chloe said.

"Yeah."

The two girls entered the house. "Dad?" Chloe's voice was tentative in the odd stillness of the house.

There was no answering voice, but sounds came from the master bedroom on the second floor. A sick feeling crept up from Chloe's stomach into her throat as she climbed the stairs with Mia at her back. Lightheaded, Chloe swayed when she put her hand on the doorknob to her father's room.

Mia clutched the back of Chloe's shirt. "No," she whispered, "don't open it. Let's just go."

"I have to." Chloe opened the door, then stopped in shock at the sight of various clothing articles strewn across the floor. She fought down the bile burning her throat as she gaped at Ivy, naked on the bed, straddling her father, who was also naked, his eyes closed as he made little upward hip thrusts. Ivy's scent wafted out of the bedroom like poison, sickening Chloe.

When Ivy noticed her audience, she gave Chloe a slow grin with no shame, regret, or apology. It was as if a blonde blue-eyed angel had sprouted blazing red horns, spewing vileness that buried Chloe's soul in stinking trash.

"No!" Chloe howled in anguish.

Ted's eyes flew open as Chloe turned to run. She stumbled into Mia as Ted cried, "Chloe!" and sat up so fast that Ivy fell backwards. "Wait!"

Chloe managed to push past Mia, her vision so blurred by tears that she could scarcely see where she was going.

Glaring at Ivy, Ted growled, "Get dressed and get out!" Then he jumped off the bed and pulled on his pants, calling, "Chloe, please wait!"

Chloe didn't wait. Mia grabbed her arm and helped her down the stairs. Before Ted could get down stairs, he heard a motor and the squeal of tires as his daughter and Mia drove away.

"She'll be okay," Ivy said languidly. "Just give her some time. We can talk to her about us after she's calmed down."

Ted turned toward Ivy standing at the top of the stairs. Face red, he roared, "I told you to get out!" He pointed at the door, the muscles in his arm flexing. "There is no 'us'!" His voice lowered to a hoarse whisper as he gripped his head with his fist. "I don't know what I was thinking."

Ivy pouted. "You said you loved having me here."

"I must have been out of my mind to let you in this house when Chloe wasn't here. How did I let this happen?" Voice thick with pain, his expression grew fierce again. "Get out, Ivy! Go home!"

When Ted stared out the window, watching her drive away, he wondered *how had she plucked his emotional strings and somehow managed to burrow her way into his bed.* It was horrible to think about, but even worse, how was he going to save his relationship with his daughter? How could he ever repair the damage he'd done to her?

Ted sat on the edge of the couch and sobbed, wondering if he should call Chloe. He dialed and hung up over and over, his body shaking from the intensity of his shame and self-loathing.

Ivy made sure to rub it in the next day. It wasn't the first time she'd used her body to get what she wanted. Riding high on the rush of power, desirability, and ultimate control she'd exercised over Ted, Ivy sent him sixty texts full of poisonous blame, rage, and threats about how she wasn't about to let him discard her so easily. She included plenty of reminders about how she had the means to ruin him any time, any day, if she wished.

CHAPTER 10

Eli picked up Ivy for school on Monday and on the way, they swung by the Circle C for their usual cup of coffee but there was no mention of her Friday night conquest.

After parking at the school, they were headed across the parking lot to the crosswalk when Ivy's gaze fell on Tayla Dean. "Eli, I forgot there's something I have to do this morning. I'll catch up to you later." Ivy pranced across the street, but the hustle and chatter outside the school made it hard for Ivy to get Tayla's attention. Ivy tried her best to catch up as Tayla walked toward the high school beside her friend Gwen. "Hey, Tayla!" Ivy called.

Tayla stopped on the walk leading to the high school and turned, sending her long, silky black hair sliding across her shoulders as she gave Ivy a questioning smile. Gwen took a couple more steps before she turned to see what was keeping Tayla. Her friend Becca caught up to her and they both watched as Ivy held up a bracelet with six charms, which she had carefully slipped off her wrist, sparkling in the sunlight.

"You dropped this." Ivy said.

"How pretty!" Tayla exclaimed with a smile of appreciation, "but it's not mine."

"It's not?" Ivy studied the charm bracelet.

"I wish it were mine," Gwen said, her bright blue eyes fastened on the charms.

Ivy ignored her, keeping her gaze on Tayla. "It's certainly beautiful enough to be something you'd wear."

Tayla's expression warmed. "Why, thanks, Ivy."

Trace Aragon interrupted with a friendly call from the front door. "Tayla?" He started down the steps, his Yankees hat turned backward. His best friend, Ethan Harrison, followed him toward the girls.

"Excuse me," Tayla said, giving Ivy a sweet smile before hurrying to catch up to Trace. As Trace put his hat on Tayla's head, Ivy studied him. He was definitely better looking without the stupid hat. Trace's dark hair curled around his ears, and his skin glowed with the appealing perpetual tan of some Hispanic heritage a couple of generations back. He turned to slap hands with Ethan, who trotted away to talk to Gwen and Becca.

Ivy smiled, narrowing her eyes as Trace wrapped a muscular arm around Tayla and led her inside. With those full lips of his, she'd bet her panties that he was a great kisser.

Chloe was a "no show" at school for days. Rumor was she had moved away to live with her aunt. Students gossiped that she'd just missed her mother too much and decided to live with her mother's sister for a while.

Ivy didn't care about Chloe. She was beginning her narcissistic cycle all over again with Tayla as her new target. She'd already begun grooming the tall, willowy girl with dark, liquid eyes.

Ivy sat with Tayla's group at lunch, studying what she ate while hoarding bits of conversation. Ivy laughed with Tayla's friends, even at their stupid jokes. She had a great fake laugh. She enjoyed working her way into Tayla's inner circle, listening to their secrets and making up stories of her own to share. Ivy was a little disappointed that Trace wasn't there because his lunch hour was at a different time, but she was up to the challenge.

As Ivy followed Tayla through her school days, she noted that Tayla had a class with the students who had special needs. The next day, Ivy and Eli showed up at the special needs class with a plate of cookies. Eli followed Ivy to the teacher's desk while Tayla paused from her task of helping a clumsy student sort books by size to glance at Ivy, who widened her eyes in mock surprise. "Tayla?" Ivy asked. Then she nodded. "Of course you'd be here. You're such a good person."

"So are you," Tayla said, glancing at the plate in Ivy's hands.

"Oh, this is nothing," Ivy said, "but you're sweet to say so. Hey, do you know my friend Eli Cole? You've probably seen him around."

"Oh, yes, you're in my English class, right?"

Eli nodded, his eyes darting to Tayla and then away.

"I see you at the games, too. Great shirt by the way, I love the color."

Eli plucked at his shirt and mumbled, "Thanks."

Ivy turned to the teacher. "I thought your class might like a little treat."

The teacher thanked her.

"I'll let you get back to work." Ivy headed toward the door.

"Ivy?" Tayla said.

Ivy turned her head. "Yes?"

"I hope you're going to the talent assembly."

"Well, of course, if you're going, I'd love to."

Tayla turned to smile at her student. "Danny's going to sing."

"Then I'll clap extra loud," Ivy promised with a warm smile

CHAPTER 11

Over the next few months, Tayla and Ivy's friendship flourished. On Tayla's birthday, Ivy gave her an Alex and Ani charm bracelet with charms to match her personality.

"Oh my gosh, Ivy, it's so pretty," Tayla said, holding it up to the light. "I hope you didn't spend too much."

"No, I got a great deal on it." Ivy hadn't paid anything for it, a simple touch and tuck into her purse, which she'd done plenty of times with other items, and no one was the wiser.

"It looks a little like the one you found before. Did you ever find its owner?"

"Yes, I did," Ivy answered, not wanting Tayla to guess that she'd stolen it. "I asked her where she got it, so I knew where to get this one. See, it has different charms."

"Hey, beautiful," Trace came up behind Tayla and put his hands on her shoulders, his Yankees hat with the brim forward for a change. Ivy's shoulders warmed as if his hands were on her instead. "Happy birthday!" Trace bent forward and gave Tayla a lingering kiss on her jaw. Ivy's mouth opened slightly, her pulse rising.

Tayla reached up and slid her fingers over Trace's hair. "Thanks."

"Wow," Trace said, his eyes on the bracelet, "that's pretty."

Tayla lifted her wrist, the charms swinging cheerfully. "Ivy gave it to me."

When Trace glanced at Ivy, she gave him a captivating sideways glance and her most impish smile. She'd practiced in the mirror, deciding that it made her look shy and sweet while showing off her sexy long eyelashes.

"Well, I was going to take you out to dinner, but maybe I need to get you something else." Trace sounded adorably uncertain.

"Time spent with you is better than any gift," Ivy assured him before Tayla could reply.

"She's right," Tayla said. "It's as if you read my mind, Ivy."

Tayla's increasing appreciation for Ivy's compliments, gifts, and understanding drew Ivy solidly inside her circle of popularity. Ivy obtained Tayla's friends by default and relished all her new "toys" to play with.

CHAPTER 12

At the end of the day, Trace stood up from his last class and pulled on his letter jacket, ready to take the shortcut through the nippy autumn air to football practice. With playoffs looming, Coach insisted on keeping the team's skills sharp.

Trace pulled the Yankees cap his dad had given him out of his backpack pocket and pulled it on. As it settled behind his ears, he recalled how his dad used to play catch with him, and they'd sit side by side on the couch with sodas and popcorn in easy reach while watching Yankees games on TV. He remembered his father's words the first time he'd slipped the cap on his son's head. "There you go, champ. With a fan like you, they're sure to take the pennant this year."

Things had changed since his mom and dad's divorce. His mother became depressed, and Trace didn't see much of his dad. It was as if he wasn't good enough for his dad anymore, which left a dull ache in Trace's heart.

As Trace passed through the outside door, he stuck his hands in his pockets.

What was this? He took hold of a palm-sized cellophane package and pulled out a small bag of trail mix with nuts, chocolate, and coconut flakes visible through the packaging.

Uneasy, Trace looked around. None of the other students stared at him or gave him an acknowledging chin lift or eyebrow raise. Then his glance passed over that new friend of Tayla's, Ivy. She was pretty in a pale, blonde way, but she wore too much makeup. She gave him a little wave. Trace waved back with the hand holding the trail mix.

That was stupid. He shoved the bag back in his pocket. Who was messing with his jacket? *Did she? Why?*

Maybe it was Tayla. They had college prep together, but she was a forthright kind of girl who was more likely to simply hand him something than slip it in his pocket. That was one thing he loved about her. He didn't have to guess what she thought or how she felt. She told him before it could become an issue.

He thought that maybe he'd like to marry her someday.

Not knowing where it came from, Trace tossed the bag of trail mix into the trash. His mind skipped off the topic of marriage like a stone skipping over frigid water. Trace didn't open up easily. It took him time to trust a person, because most people he'd once trusted had abandoned him at the first sign of trouble.

Ethan was a solid friend, and Tayla had been in his life long enough that he trusted her. She'd stayed with him through his fear of losing relationships, his bouts of paranoia, and his sometimes-clingy nature. She told him he was a bit too possessive, so he'd backed off while watching her from afar. If she could see what he saw, she wouldn't blame him for wanting to be with her. She was so kind and good-hearted, he felt like a better man in her presence.

With her gentle honesty, Tayla broke down his fortified walls and got past his secret self-defenses. The one thing she couldn't bear was dishonesty. She'd be more likely to stay with him if he confessed to robbing a bank than if he tried to hide it from her and she found out on her own. Keeping things from her had more power to kill their relationship than anything else.

But Trace couldn't imagine their relationship ever dying. Last week, she told him that she loved him.

One other person Trace could rely on was his great, great Uncle Warren. His door was always open with a warm welcome any time Trace got tired of being home. Uncle Warren was a World War II veteran who always made time to listen to Trace talk through any problems he cared to bring up. Keeping up with his Uncle's bursts of energy rendered a playful challenge.

During their visits, Uncle Warren gave Trace the best gift a teenage boy could ask for by teaching him how to drive a stick shift in his own blue 1950 Chevy 3100 series truck. Trace had never experienced such patient attention, or trust to handle such a treasured item. He was in auto heaven. The truck's rust spots didn't matter to him a bit. It even had its original wooden bed, mended in places. They spent many hours looking through parts catalogs and working on restoring the old beast to its former beauty.

Every Wednesday, Uncle Warren eagerly took Trace target shooting. He showed Trace how to load ammo into a magazine, push it into the gun, turn off the safety catch, take careful hold of the gun with both hands, aim, and squeeze the trigger.

Since today was Wednesday, as soon as practice was over, Trace grabbed his backpack, rushed out the school doors, and jumped into his uncle's waiting blue beast. "Let's go," Trace said. "I've been watching some shooting videos."

"You think they'll teach you more than I can?"

"Not more," Trace said. "Just a refresher."

Uncle Warren grunted. "Want to drive?"

"Sure do."

Trace drove steadily to the shooting range, proud that he no longer ground the gears. He readied himself in front of the target and fired his first round from his revolver. "The dang thing jumps in your hand." Trace complained.

"Yes, they do that, but you're getting the hang of it."

Trace fired again. "What a rush! I think I've got it. I'll do it again." Feet firm, arms extended, he fired, the hole in the target a little closer to the center than last time. Soon Trace had fired the whole magazine and was reloading the weapon. Shooting at targets at the range with Uncle Warren was a fine way to spend the afternoon.

It was even better when Grandma visited Uncle Warren and went along with them to the range. Grandma sure could handle a gun, and she had been a rock for Trace when he struggled to get through the pain of his parents' separation. Although he was a high school senior nearly ready to launch into the adult world, he still felt safe and loved in his grandmother's embrace.

CHAPTER 13

Several months later, in early May, Trace was walking toward the school parking lot when a soft hand slipped inside his. He turned to smile at Tayla. "Hey, beautiful."

"Hey yourself," she answered hiking her backpack higher on her shoulder and sliding her hand up his arm so she could walk closer to him. "Are you still thinking you're going to enlist?"

"Yup," he replied. "Doesn't every girl love a guy in uniform?"

"I can't deny that it's noble," Tayla said uncertainly, "but it could be dangerous."

Trace felt a little thrill at her concern for him. "And it could lead to great things for the future," he said.

"But how long in the future?" Tayla sounded wistful.

"Well, there's Navy Boot Camp."

"That sounds so harsh."

"You could call it Basic Training."

"Whatever it is, it's clear out by Chicago!"

"It's not much different than leaving for college," Trace assured her. He held up his index finger. "But it's better, because they'll pay for my education."

Tayla rubbed her warm hand an inch up his arm. "But I won't be able to see you."

"We'll stay in touch," Trace promised. "Just think, you'll know a highly skilled, technically proficient, disciplined, and motivated sailor from the renowned historic institution of the Great Lakes Naval Station." He glanced at her fondly. "Not everyone can say that."

"You sound like a recruiting poster," Tayla said.

"I've been recruited," Trace reminded her, "and I'm depending on you to help me get through Basic so I can become a medic. Your messages will be like gold."

Tayla nudged him. "And I'm told my chocolate chip cookies are worth more than gold."

"That's sweet of you, my sweet, but don't bother mailing them to Basic. They'll just get thrown away."

Tayla lurched to a stop next to Trace's car, her eyes wide with surprise as she pulled free of him. "What? You'd throw them away?"

Trace put both hands up, palms out. "No! I heard of a guy whose aunt sent him some treats for his birthday in Basic, and his drill sergeant took them from him and threw them in the garbage right in front of everybody."

"That's mean."

"Hey," Trace said, spreading his hands, "they've gotta break us down to build us back up into lean, mean, fighting machines."

Tayla slid her arms around Trace. "You'll never be mean."

Trace hugged her in return. He tried not to squeeze her too hard as he imagined being away from her for months. "You'll never know what you mean to me, Tayla. I love you."

"Love you more," she murmured against his shirt.

The school year raced to the finish. Graduation was a memorable event for everyone as Trace, Tayla, Ivy, and Eli received their diplomas with the rest of their class.

Right after the ceremony, Trace sought Tayla out and wrapped her in his arms. "Congratulations," he whispered into her ear.

"Thanks," she said, her voice bubbling with excitement.

She pulled out of their embrace too soon and called, "Hey, Ivy." That's when Trace noticed Ivy standing nearby in her cap and gown, watching them. "Take a picture of us, will you?"

"Sure." Using Tayla's phone, Ivy snapped a photo of the two of them.

Tayla glanced at the picture and laughed. "You had your eyes closed!"

"I did?" Trace looked at the picture and saw that his eyes appeared as slits. "That's my sly face," he said with a one-armed hug around Tayla's shoulders.

Tayla handed him her phone. "Now take one of us." She got into position beside Ivy. Trace took the picture, then watched the two girls exclaim over it. A shred of unease prickled his senses as he watched Ivy's blonde head linger so close to Tayla's dark hair. For some reason he couldn't define, he wanted to get between them. *Why?* He wasn't sure.

Then the Dean family swooped in to hug their daughter. Tayla's brother and sister clustered for a photo with Tayla, too. Ivy backed away until she stood so close to Trace that her gown brushed his pants. He eased a half step away. "Your parents here?" he asked.

She looked up at him with her intense blue eyes, her diamond teardrop earrings catching the sun's rays to throw sparkles onto his face. "My mom and I don't get along too well, and I haven't got a dad. I haven't seen my mom yet, but I'm sure she's here somewhere."

Uncomfortable, Trace said, "Oh."

Ivy touched his arm and said softly, "It's not your fault. You didn't know."

"Yeah."

Her hand lingered, and Trace reached his arm up out of her reach to brush his hand over his hair.

"I'm actually moving out of my house," Ivy said, watching Tayla with her family. Even Tayla's grandparents were there with hugs and a big envelope that Ivy was sure contained graduation money. Ivy deserved money for her graduation more than Tayla did.

"Where are you moving?" Trace asked just to make conversation. He didn't really care.

"I'm moving in with Eli's family."

"Oh." Trace was a little surprised. He thought Ivy would move to an apartment, or at least live with some other girls.

"I've been spending most of my time there anyway. I'm so glad to get away from my mother's influence. She's so controlling."

"Sorry to hear it," Trace murmured.

"You know how it is," Ivy said, leaning closer to Trace as if sharing a secret. "Being on your own and doing whatever you want is so freeing."

"Yeah."

"Tayla's going to Oregon State University, you know."

"Yeah, I know," Trace replied.

"She's lucky she gets to go 350 miles away from here."

"Maybe."

"Yo!" Ethan Harris strode up to Trace and gave him a hearty man hug with a couple of back slaps.

Trace's heart lifted. "Hey, o ld man!"

Ethan's eyebrows rose. "You're one of us alumnus now, old friend."

Then Trace's family converged on him, pushing Ivy out of his sight and mind.

Trace stopped by Tayla's house later that night for some warm goodbyes before he headed east to Basic and she went west to college. "Don't forget me," he begged as he held her close.

"Never," she replied, a catch in her voice. "I'll keep busy. So will you. Time will fly."

"Not fast enough," he said, and kissed her as if she were the only oasis in the desert.

CHAPTER 14

The Recruit Training Center was a crazy hotbed of activity as they processed all the new recruits. Bright and early the next morning, a loud whistle rudely awakened the trainees for their first day of normal duties beginning at 0600 (6 a.m.) and finishing with lights out at precisely 2200 (10 p.m.)

Trace was assigned to a division consisting of 80 men and women. All the divisions were housed in gigantic 1,000 person dormitories, called "ships," which were really nothing more than stacked apartments - government housing at its best.

After eight weeks of intensive, difficult training that nevertheless gave him a sense of purpose, Trace passed all his requirements. His mother, grandparents, Uncle Warren, and Tayla sat together to watch as he stood at attention on the parade field for graduation. His father didn't make it to graduation, which wasn't a surprise to Trace, but the hurt and frustration from Dad's absence was real.

Once the ceremony was over, his family and Tayla spent his weekend of liberty touring Chicago, the home of the pizza pie, with plenty of samples to test its famous claim. Uncle Warren made a point of saying how proud he was that Trace had joined the military family. "We'll be veterans together," Uncle Warren, joked. As he clapped his hand on Trace's shoulder in a spirit of camaraderie, his engraved watch glinted in the sunlight.

The weekend was too short for Trace to have much time alone with Tayla, but she managed to pull him aside long enough to whisper, "I'm so proud of you. Do you know how much I miss you?"

"I know," he said, pulling her closer. "I miss you, too." Trace kissed her, then whispered, "I love you Tayla, I really love you."

"I love you, too."

Trace finally said all of his goodbyes before returning to the naval base. From there, he moved on to a technical school in San Antonio, Texas, and immersed himself in studying a wide variety of medical procedures in order to fill his role as a Navy Hospital Corpsman. He also prepared to treat medical emergencies outside of combat situations.

Trace proved to be very proficient in many fields, including marksmanship. Most training in the U.S. Navy is done for combat missions, protection of naval assets, armed patrols, and self-defense. Aside from the required training, Trace simply enjoyed shooting. Focusing on rifle and pistol training, he qualified at the expert level and proudly wore his Marksmanship Medal.

After returning to San Antonio for additional education, Trace graduated with high honors. His family again gathered in San Antonio to celebrate his new accomplishment. They spent the weekend exploring the Riverwalk, enjoying great food, entertainment, quaint clusters of art exhibits, and unique shops. Mom, Grandma, and Tayla were in their element, spending most of their time in the shops and loving the souvenirs they found.

In December, Trace was excited to move on to his new station at the United States Marine Corps Camp Pendleton, San Diego County, California. He'd chosen a great career. He loved his medical training, and loved being by the ocean. He thought about raising a family in California as he picked up the exhilarating skill of surfing. While he enjoyed occasional weekend visits from Tayla and his family, it wasn't often enough. He missed them.

When she wasn't there in person, Tayla sent Trace plenty of upbeat messages full of her college activities, funny quips about what was going on in their hometown, and occasional references to her parents' warnings about the inevitable failure of long distance romances. *But I won't stop writing*, Tayla reassured Trace. *You might fall in love with a mermaid, but I'll still be here for you after she swims away.*

Trace wasn't satisfied with simply writing. He called Tayla whenever he could, and they talked as if no time had passed between them. "Remember the old high school Spring Dance?" Trace asked on a warm, breezy day.

"Yep, and I'm going."

"What?" Trace felt a catch in his heart. "You're not going to sit home and think of me?"

"No way," Tayla teased.

Trace gripped the phone a little tighter. "Who are you going with?"

"Danny."

"Danny Tripp?"

"Yes. I'm driving back to Meridian to take him to the dance. He's already ordered my corsage."

Trace loved the lilt in her voice, as if she were suppressing a giggle. She must be imagining his expression at finding out she was escorting one of the students with special needs to the formal dance.

"Tell him I'm jealous," Trace said warmly.

"He'll just laugh," Tayla teased.

"At least one of us will be having a good time."

CHAPTER 15

Six months before he was to return home, Trace got a call on his way to breakfast. Grandma's calls were always welcome. "Hi, Grandma."

"Trace," she replied, her voice curiously thick.

A sick feeling of dread stiffened his spine, and his steps slowed. "What's wrong, Grandma? Are you sick?"

"No." Grandma sniffed. "Uncle Warren."

Trace's dread turned cold. He shivered and leaned against the wall. "What's wrong with him?"

"Oh, Trace," Grandma's voice broke. "He passed away last night."

"What?" The floor fell out from under him and Trace sat down fast. "No!" Hot tears flowed from his eyes. "How? Why?"

"Oh, honey, he was just old. Not many men live to be 91. You know how much he enjoyed every minute he spent with you. It was simply his time to go."

"But I wanted to be there." Trace wiped at his nose with the back of his hand.

"He knows," Grandma assured him. "He was so proud of you. He was thrilled that you're his only relative that followed in his footsteps and went into the military."

A couple of soldiers passed Trace in the hall, looking down at him with concern.

Embarrassed, Trace jumped to his feet, told Grandma goodbye, and then headed back to his bunk. He had no secluded place to go, but he could lie on his bed and pull the covers over his head.

By the next morning, Trace had soldiered up. It was what Uncle Warren would have wanted. Now that his beloved uncle was gone, Trace was determined to live his life as Uncle Warren would have. He could have no better example to follow.

Trace obtained a 2-day bereavement leave to attend his uncle's funeral where, dressed in his formal white naval uniform, he was honored to participate in the final salute by playing the traditional somber military "Taps" he'd learned at boot camp. Then Trace bowed his head and said his tearful "goodbye" with a moment of silence.

After the service, Grandma hugged Trace and placed an envelope and something hard in his hand. Trace looked down to see that he was holding Uncle Warren's watch. Then he opened the envelope. Tears rose in his eyes as he gazed at his name on the title to the 1950 Chevy pickup truck.

He glanced at Grandma, eyes round with disbelief, but before he could say anything, she gently took hold of his shoulders. "He wanted you to have it." Then Grandma gave him a kiss on the cheek, her love fortifying him.

With the old watch fastened to his wrist so that Uncle Warren's initials pressed against his skin, Trace put his heart and soul into the rest of his training. The watch strengthened his determination, reminding him of his family's love.

When Trace returned home a year later, he joined the ranks of thousands of reserve military personnel who continued their duties in once-a-month training sessions for the duration of their enlistment, ready to be called into active duty on a moment's notice if needed. Otherwise, they were free to live their chosen civilian lifestyle. His specific assignment was to provide medical assistance, such as giving physicals and vaccinations, to other military personnel.

Trace's prize possession, his 1950 Chevy truck, had been stored in his grandparents' garage so Trace could restore it just the way Uncle Warren and he had planned.

Trace's heart tripped over itself at the sight of Tayla standing beneath a "Welcome Home" sign on his front porch. It looked as if the special needs class had been busy with markers on poster board to help make it. It was no surprise that Tayla would go back to the high school to enlist the help of the students she cared about with a project to help them feel needed.

The only problem was that Tayla wasn't alone. Her friend Ivy stood next to her, competing with Tayla for the biggest smile aimed at Trace.

Tayla ran down the porch steps and into Trace's arms. Ivy watched their embrace and kiss. When they finally turned around and headed back to the house, Ivy held up a plate. "I made you some of my famous brownies to welcome you home," she announced. "I hope you like chocolate, but even if you don't, you're going to love these." She gave Trace a playful smile.

"They're really good," Tayla affirmed. "They taste like the ones from Kneaders."

Ivy's smile never wavered. Tayla believed everything Ivy told her, even the lie that Ivy had made the brownies herself when she had, in fact, gotten them from Kneaders. She'd taken them home, cut them into smaller pieces, arranged them on a paper plate, and dusted them with powdered sugar to make them look different.

Trace didn't care about the brownies. He planned on spending all his free time with Tayla. Yet every time they had a date, it seemed that Ivy was somewhere in the vicinity. He didn't like her showing up as much as she did, but it seemed Tayla had forged a firm friendship with the blue-eyed blonde who never seemed to stop smiling. *Was that even normal?* Ivy came across as a happy person who was born with classically beautiful facial features, but she wasn't his type. Could anyone be that genuinely happy all the time?

Trace did his best to ignore Ivy. To his surprise, his love for Tayla had deepened over time. When he was called back to duty for a brief deployment to the Middle East, they kept up their stream of communication. At the end of two months, Trace was happy to return to Tayla.

While deciding which medical career to apply his scholarship toward, Trace and his school friend Zack Becker agreed to share expenses by renting a 2 bedroom, 1½ bath apartment together. They scraped up odds and ends to make their man cave comfortable, decorating with sports memorabilia, video game systems, oversized televisions, and a generous supply of beer and other adult-level amenities, making a popular hangout spot for their friends.

CHAPTER 16

Tayla had the summer off, but would head back to Oregon in the fall. Trace considered moving to Oregon, but he'd landed a great security job at Grammar Biotech in Meridian. The pay was better than anything else available, so he decided to work through the summer, save his money, and see how his plans to use his military scholarship went after that.

For the next couple of months, Trace saw Tayla every day. Ivy managed to show up just about every place they went, often in Eli's company, but Tayla didn't mind. She drew Ivy into their activities, laughing and chatting as if they were long lost sisters.

Trace's feelings were just about the opposite, but he kept his thoughts to himself. He couldn't figure out why Ivy was always around. Didn't she have any other friends to hang out with?

Trace introduced Tayla to the shooting range, and she took to it like a fish to water. He surprised her with one of two matching Beretta pistols.

With Trace's newly acquired expert instruction, Tayla soon learned to love the thrill of shooting at targets. Absorbing Trace's advice from his military training, she quickly became proficient with a gun.

Trace introduced other handguns, intriguing Tayla with all the options. She was perfectly at home trying nearly a dozen different guns rented from the shooting range, including semi-automatics to revolvers in calibers ranging from .22 to .45. The two of them went to the gun range often. Trace especially liked the fact that Ivy didn't show up there, so he had Tayla all to himself. What Trace didn't know was that Ivy had already placed a target on his back.

CHAPTER 17

Tayla surprised Trace at his apartment one evening before he left for his graveyard shift. "Hey," she said, nearly jumping up and down with excitement. "My parents are taking me to Cancun, Mexico, and I'm inviting some of my best friends to go along."

Trace grinned. "So am I invited?"

"You'd better believe it." Tayla moved in for a kiss. "A week from Friday. I know its last minute but mom got a super deal on the condos."

The week went by fast. Trace and Tayla arrived early at the airport to see Becca, Gwen, Ivy, and Eli among the partygoers.

Of course, Eli and Ivy would be there. Trace thought to himself.

Once they landed in Mexico and settled in at the hotel, they all headed for the beach. "Dinner's at six o'clock at the Cabana buffet," Tayla's mother announced.

Tayla grabbed Trace's hand and pulled him to the bar. "Buy me a drink, sir."

With a look of surprise, he let go of her hand. "Why, ma'am, do I know you?"

"I think you're gonna want to get to know me." Tayla giggled and ordered a couple of pina coladas. "Take these and go find us a table for dinner and I'll save us a place in line," Tayla whispered.

Trace nonchalantly passed behind Ivy and Eli in the buffet line just in time to hear her say, "Eli, I'm going to sit with Trace and Tayla."

"I'd like to sit by you guys too."

"I'll hang out with you later." Ivy insisted.

"So why did I even come if you're gonna ignore me. "

"You wanted to, that's why. I want to hang out with these guys now."

"Okay." Eli shuffled away, glancing back at Ivy with longing plain on his face.

Trace couldn't understand why Eli still wanted to be friends with Ivy after she dismissed him so heartlessly, but it was none of his business. He pushed Ivy out of his mind and carried the drinks to a table in the far corner. Then he joined Tayla in the buffet line.

"Now, I've got to go to the restroom," she said, bouncing from foot to foot. "I'll hurry, you go ahead. Just be sure to save my place."

"Sure thing." Trace filled his plate and sat at the cabana table beside Tayla's empty chair.

"Hi," Ivy said, strolling up to Trace and sitting in Tayla's place. She put her plate on the table.

"Hi," Trace said. "Uh, I'm sorry, but that's saved for Tayla."

Ivy giggled. "I didn't see her name on it."

"It's for Tayla."

"Of course," Ivy said. "I'll just help you save it for her."

"She should be here any minute."

Ivy leaned in close to him with a mischievous grin. "Then I'll move in a minute." She stuck her fork in a juicy piece of pineapple. "Have you ever noticed that as nice as Tayla is, she doesn't get what it's like?"

Trace shrugged. "What what's like?"

Ivy sighed. "You know, coming from a broken home. I mean, look at them." Ivy pointed her fork with the pineapple speared on the tines toward Tayla's parents, their heads close together, smiling as they surveyed all the young people enjoying themselves. "What I wouldn't have given if I could have grown up with a mom and dad who got along and showed that they loved me."

"What makes you think I come from a broken home?"

"Tayla told me. She said your parents are divorced and that's why you wanted to join the Navy, to get out of the house."

Trace felt a stirring of old memories and long buried fears creeping to the surface. The pineapple slid off Ivy's fork. Trace recoiled as it fell to the ground with a plop.

"Oops!" Ivy said, giggling. "We've got to find fun in whatever happens to us, don't we, Trace? Otherwise, we'd have no fun at all."

Trace swallowed. It was getting hard to breathe. "I don't know what you're talking about."

Ivy's blue eyes widened, her soft voice hypnotic. "Yes, you do. You know what it's like." She put her hand on his arm. "I know you do. I understand you, Trace. We've had the same kind of life with parents who either weren't around or didn't care much about us. That makes a difference."

When he didn't say anything, Ivy circled the face of Uncle Warren's watch with a gentle finger. Trace swallowed, his emotions tied to the watch rising to the surface, breaking through his cautious nature. Ivy leaned closer and grasped his arm with such force that he sat up straight.

"Am I interrupting?" asked a puzzled voice from behind them.

Trace whirled, feeling guilty for reasons he couldn't define. Tayla looked down at them uncertainly, a plate of food balanced in her hand. Trace got to his feet, pulling his arm free of Ivy's grasp. "I saved you a place," he blurted.

Tayla's eyebrows went up. "Where? I don't see one."

"Ivy took it."

Ivy looked up at Tayla, her face full of mischief. "I was just keeping your boyfriend company," she drawled, seeming in no hurry to get up. "It seems we have a lot in common."

Tayla's brow creased. "You do?"

"Not that much," Trace assured her.

Ivy turned in her seat and glanced around. Trace grew increasingly uneasy. *Why wasn't Ivy making any effort to get up and move? How am I supposed to kick Ivy out of Tayla's seat without making a scene?*

"There's an extra chair," Ivy said, pointing. "You could bring it over so we could all eat together."

Tayla gave Ivy a long look.

"I'll get it," Trace offered, dragging a third chair close to the table and pushing it toward the small space between his and Ivy's chairs. Ivy gave him a meaningful look, then scooted her chair incrementally away from his, leaving a space too narrow for Tayla's chair to fit.

"Move over more," Tayla said, her voice tight.

Ivy complied, then Trace moved his chair too making space for Tayla to squeeze in between them.

"This is amazing," Ivy gushed to Tayla. "You and your parents are the best. I've never had a chance to go to Mexico on a vacation, let alone one as wonderful as this. I'm having such a great time, and it's all because of you."

Tayla smiled. "You're welcome, Ivy. I'm glad you're having fun."

Ivy grinned down at her plate, proud of the seeds of conflict she'd sewn. It was exciting to see what happened whenever she stirred the pot of human emotion.

CHAPTER 18

Tayla and Trace enjoyed every minute together. They chased the crashing waves, listened to the whispering palm leaves sway as they lay in the sun, and enjoyed refreshing cold drinks along the white sandy shore. The sun shone so brightly, it hit the water and broke into thousands of shining crystals scattered across the surface.

Ivy watched their antics, her eyes focused on their clasped hands as they walked along the beach, Tayla's sheer cover-up swaying becomingly over her swimsuit.

Ivy's eyes narrowed. *What did Trace see in Tayla anyway?* Ivy could offer everything Tayla had, and more. Ivy understood him, but Tayla couldn't know how he really felt deep down inside. How could she? Besides, Tayla didn't care about Trace, not really, or she wouldn't be going so far away to college while he was in Meridian. Ivy would never abandon Trace like that.

Ivy's gaze fell on Trace's clothing piled on a chaise lounge. His things were next to Tayla's, of course.

Ivy sat on the edge of the chair and extended her arms overhead, idly stretching in a lazy twist from side to side to see who was watching her.

No one.

Pushing the Yankees hat aside, she slid her hand into Trace's shorts pocket until her fingers touched metal. Keys, these will work. Curling her fingers around the key ring, she pulled them free. Without a single twinge of guilt, she stood with the keys hidden in her hand

and carried them to her purse. Trace could easily believe they'd fallen out of his pocket and gotten lost in the sand or picked up by a vagrant. It didn't matter what he thought.

After Trace and Tayla returned from the ocean, laughing, he pulled on his pants and discovered the loss. He wasn't laughing now.

"This is terrible," Tayla commiserated.

"I'll help you look for them," Ivy offered. Trace's friends joined in the search, stretching from the patio to the ocean, kicking sand and looking under every object they passed. No one found the keys. Even though the week continued with water sports and fun, Trace was slightly on edge.

On the last day, after building silly sand castles and watching crazy teenagers rolling on the sand like snakes, Trace and Tayla retired to the shade of a cabana. "Hey, I've been wanting to ask you why you told Ivy I came from a broken home and joined the Navy to get away from my family," he asked.

"I don't know," Tayla said. "It must have just come out in conversation. I don't even remember telling her. Why?"

"Because Ivy made sure I knew she had the scoop on me," Trace said, his voice clipped, "but who I am and what I do is none of her business, so let's just keep it to ourselves."

Surprised at Trace's harsh tone, Tayla said, "Fine by me, but like I said, I don't remember telling her anything." Then Tayla softened as she imagined the stress of losing her keys somewhere in acres of sand. "I'm sorry, Trace." She took his hand.

"It just came as a surprise, that's all," Trace winked and lifted her hand for a kiss. "I still love you to the moon and back."

They talked until the Cancun stars lit the sky, not noticing Ivy in her secluded place under the bar patio where she'd been keeping a close eye on the lovebirds.

When Ivy finally stood, stretched, and sauntered over to Tayla's chair. Trace's grip tightened on Tayla's hand. "What's up?" Ivy asked. "I haven't seen much of you two all day."

"We've just been hanging out, enjoying the sun," Tayla said. "Where have you been? I haven't seen you around much, either." She looked past Ivy. "And where's Eli?"

Ivy gestured to the farthest end of the bar where Eli sat in a dim corner with his head down.

"He looks like he could use some company," Tayla said.

Ivy tipped her head and gave Tayla a look of adoration. "You're an angel. I'm sure he'd be quite cheered up by your visit."

Tayla gave Ivy a steely look, which was rather out of character for her, then stood and strode over to Eli.

"So," Ivy said, taking Tayla's seat. "It's just you and me."

Trace stood to follow Tayla.

Ivy tipped her chin. "You haven't been avoiding me, have you?"

Tayla said something to Eli, who nodded and stood to follow her. Tayla strode toward the ping-pong table, expertly snagging her friend Becca's arm. "Trace," Becca called, "We need you to play doubles!"

"Excuse me," Trace murmured before sprinting toward Tayla.

Ivy narrowed her eyes at the foursome as they positioned themselves around the table. Eli was the only one who noticed the calculating look on Ivy's face when he snuck a glance at her. He gripped his paddle, ready to do her bidding, whatever it might be.

CHAPTER 19

When the group returned from Cancun, Trace was grudgingly forced to recall the stress of wasted vacation hours searching for his lost keys as he spent even more time replacing them.

As the summer slipped away, he and Tayla spent as much time together as they could. Ivy still managed to show up on their dates, seeming genuinely surprised to meet up with them. After a brief exchange of polite greetings, Tayla found reasons to excuse themselves from Ivy's company.

Trace planned a surprise weekend escape with Tayla before she returned to college. They'd never been to Cascade. Knowing that Tayla had always wanted to go there for the fresh air and great hiking trails, he booked them a room at the Ashley Inn, situated in the center of an old valley so beautiful that the drive to get there would be a vacation in itself. Tayla would love the quaint vintage atmosphere and popular themed rooms.

Trace swung by Tayla's house, only to find Ivy and Tayla sitting on the porch. He didn't want to share his surprise with Ivy listening. "Hey, ladies, what are you up to?"

"Just hanging out in the shade, talking about you, of course," Tayla giggled.

"Yeah, want to get in on the gossip?' Ivy added.

Trace shrugged. "Thanks anyway, but I think I'm good in the gossip department for now. What I need is to steal my girlfriend."

Trace focused his gaze on Tayla. "I have something I really want to show you. Okay?"

Ivy speared Tayla with a gaze that demanded to be invited along, but Tayla quickly hopped out of her chair without a backward glance. "I'll call you later, Ivy."

"I guess I'll just sit here by myself, then," Ivy moped.

Tayla and Trace drove away, leaving Ivy to figure out her own entertainment.

Trace put an arm around Tayla. "How about we take off and go to Cascade? I've booked a night at the Ashley Inn."

Tayla's eyes lit up. "Oh, Trace, I've always wanted to go there! Have you heard how amazing it is? Do you know how much I love vintage? What room did you get?"

"Whoa, Tayla, I can only answer one question at a time." Trace laughed. "I picked the Blue Federal Rose room because I know your favorite color is blue and you love roses. I hope it's as nice as the pictures."

They got a quick bite to eat, then stopped at Tayla's house long enough for her to pack an overnight bag and tell her mother where they were going. Then they were on their way, enjoying a drive more beautiful than they'd imagined.

"There it is!" Tayla squealed, pointing through the windshield. "Trace, I just love it."

Trace stopped in the parking lot and was gratified when Tayla gave him the biggest hug he'd ever gotten from her. His surprise was going over better than he expected.

The Ashley Inn was unlike any hotel either had ever been to. Just walking into the lobby was like stepping back in time. "Hey, Trace," Tayla whispered. "Let's pretend this is our friend's estate, and we're his esteemed guests."

"Sure," Trace agreed. "Little weird but O.K."

Trace registered and got their keys. Tayla handed Trace her bag, took the key, and skipped up the stairs ahead of him. "Come on!"

"Just a minute, I have to lug all your stuff up the stairs," Trace replied. "I did tell you it was just for one night, right? I think you brought enough for a month."

"I packed everything I need," Tayla called back, "and I wouldn't mind staying for a month."

"They have a great breakfast buffet, too, and hot, fresh baked cookies for us tonight."

"No way, with milk?"

"With anything you want, babe."

Trace finally reached door number 14, which stood wide-open, showing Tayla standing mesmerized in the middle of the room. "I love it!" she exclaimed, turning and hurrying into his arms. Trace had to drop the luggage to catch her. "This is the best day ever," Tayla whispered into his ear.

"Just wait until tonight," Trace promised. "Look at that soaker tub right in the room. How romantic," He raised his eyebrows. "They even left us bubble bath."

Tayla flopped on the bed, relishing the beauty of the vintage elegant white four-poster. "Trace," she called in a low, seductive voice. "Why don't you come over here?"

Trace closed the bedroom door and locked it, then slowly unbuttoned his shirt as he walked toward the bed. "You look so perfect lying right there. Don't move a muscle."

Trace crawled up from the end of the mattress and lay down beside Tayla. Then they slowly removed each other's clothes. Tayla's soft body never felt so good against Trace's skin as he ran gentle fingers through her long black hair. "You smell so good."

Tayla wrapped her legs around Trace's firm torso, pulling him in tight. With a quick flip, Trace took control and softly fondled Tayla's body in an afternoon of passion that lasted until the sunset was just an afterthought, and the cookies were forgotten.

Morning was filled with new adventures, and one more surprise for Tayla. After a day of hiking and daydreaming, Trace sat on a bench with Tayla beside him and pulled a promise ring out of his pocket.

"I'm a little old fashioned, but I want you to know how much I love you," Trace confessed. Tayla held out a shaking hand and Trace slipped the slender gold ring on her finger. "Now that I'm back home, while you're at college, I want you to know that I'll be here for you when you're done," Trace pledged.

"I don't know what I did to deserve you," Tayla said, running her finger down his chest alongside his shirt buttons. "So when are you going to college?"

"The medical program I want to get into is taking applications next year," Trace replied. "I have to wait just a little longer, but it will be worth it."

With tears in her eyes, Tayla threw her arms around Trace with the words, "I really hate to leave you."

"We'll be together before you know it," Trace whispered, "and we won't have to say goodbye."

Tayla pulled back with a smile and wiped her eyes. "This is the best time I've ever had! I love you, I love my ring, and will never take it off. I can't wait to show everyone."

Trace and Tayla headed for home in a cloud of bliss, unaware of how the bling on Tayla's finger would trigger Ivy into action they'd both regret.

CHAPTER 20

Ivy showed up at Tayla's, pretending excitement to hear all about her trip. Tayla left out the intimate details, but was quick to show Ivy the newly acquired bling on her finger.

Ivy stared at the ring in silence. "It's beautiful." Then she asked with a cold smile, "Is it real?"

"Whether it is or not, it's the thought that counts," Tayla declared, fingering her ring.

With a little shrug of feigned disinterest, Ivy suggested a shopping spree to celebrate. As they walked in and out of the mall shops, Ivy carefully inserted questions about Trace's work schedule. Tayla blindly offered the information without wondering why Ivy wanted to know, and continued raving about her exciting weekend, leaving Ivy irritated and spiteful.

Ivy called Eli to express her frustration about Tayla having a promise ring that should be on her finger. "You need to find out when Trace's roommate will be away from home," Ivy told Eli. She may not have Trace's ring yet, but she had his keys.

"Who's his roommate?"

Ivy sighed. "Pay attention, Eli. It's Zack Becker."

"Yeah, okay, but why?"

"You don't need to know. Just be quick about it."

Ivy's obsession with Trace grew to the point that she often sat in her car in Trace's parking lot, sometimes for hours, waiting for him to come or go. Every time she saw, Tayla enter his apartment, her stomach twisted with jealousy. She documented every move she saw him make, and often followed when he drove away.

When she was with Tayla, Ivy made sure to add subtle digs about Trace. "Are you sure Trace will wait for you while you're at college?"

"Yes." Tayla held up her hand with the promise ring.

"I don't know. He's a good-looking guy. What if he finds someone else while you're gone?"

"He won't."

Ivy gave Tayla a bright smile and spread her hands. "Maybe you'll find someone great at college. You never know."

"We love each other," Tayla reassured her, "we'll be okay."

CHAPTER 21

Ivy waited impatiently for Eli's report. It seemed that Trace's apartment was a popular meeting spot for the guys to hang out, so it was rarely empty.

It was almost Thanksgiving when Ivy's phone rang. When she answered, a male voice said, "Hey, how ya been, Ivy?"

"Great. Who is this?"

"Reese, Reese Blake from high school." He gave a little laugh. "Remember the tall dark and handsome guy?"

"Yeah, what's up, Reese?" Ivy didn't really care.

"High school was some fun, wasn't it? Doesn't seem so long ago, and I just got to wondering what you've been up to."

"I've moved on," Ivy stated.

"Yeah, me too. I was just remembering some of the good parts of high school and thought about you. So how would you like to go to dinner with me and we can talk over old times?"

Although his compliment inflated her ego, Ivy couldn't see any advantage for her by going out with Reese. "Sorry, Reese, I'm really busy."

"Sure, some other time maybe. Can I call you next week?"

"My calendar is pretty full, so I don't know."

After a slight pause, not liking the brush off Reese said, "So...all right then, I'll try another time. See ya."

Ivy hung up without saying goodbye, her mind racing a mile a minute through her next move to get Trace. He was working that night, and Eli reported that Zack would be gone too. She could hardly wait for the cover of darkness to work her plan with his stolen keys.

Giddy with excitement, Ivy dressed all in black and parked a block away from Trace's apartment. She strode along the walk as if she belonged there. Sure enough, the place was dark. No one was home. With Trace's keys in hand, she let herself into his apartment, closed the door, and moved through the dark hallway like a sleek panther, opening doors until she found his bedroom. She knew it was his by the Yankees cap hanging on a bedpost. It was the only thing that seemed out of place. All the rest of his belongings were put away, no clothes or books on the floor, and his bed made with military precision.

Drunk with the thrill of being alone with Trace's things, Ivy used the streetlight shining in through the window blinds to open the drawers of his mismatched bedside stands. She used his chap stick, then lay on his bed and dripped his eye drops into her eyes. She imagined Trace lying naked beside her on the black and gray striped spread, running his fingers through her hair, then down her neck to her breasts. She wriggled with pleasure.

When she finally got up, she nearly tipped over the lamp beside his bed, and nearly tripped over his big brown chair to the right of it. Opening his dresser drawers, she lifted out his neatly folded clothing, touching everything, smelling it, even trying on a couple of his shirts. Spotting an envelope tucked up against the side of his drawer, she grabbed it, hoping to discover some secrets. When she found the title to a 1950 Chevy pickup truck inside, she shoved it back in place with disgust and continued invading his privacy.

She fastened Uncle Warren's watch on her wrist with delight, and then counted out the $2,400.00 cash hidden in the back of Trace's underwear drawer. She studied a picture of him in his high school graduation cap and gown with his arms around a woman on either side of him. She didn't remember them being there, but they were both old, so were probably some boring relatives.

Digging through Trace's T-shirts, Ivy felt something hard. When she pulled out his revolver, she gleefully aimed it at the picture of Tayla on his beside stand and whispered, "Pow, pow, pow!" She wanted to pull the trigger so badly that her finger trembled.

Then she froze in her awkward shooter's stance at the unexpected hum of the garage door opening. She should have posted Eli as a lookout. Now what?

Make it look like a robbery.

With the swiftness of excited panic, she stuck the gun in her pocket and grabbed Trace's laptop, wallet, and all the money from his drawer. Letting the big watch slide around on her slender wrist, she then ran down the hall and smashed the pane of glass beside the front door with the butt of the gun. She flung the door open and ran out into the cold cover of darkness.

Ivy raced back to her car, opened her car door and threw Trace's things on the front passenger seat. She buckled her seat belt and slowly drove past his apartment, hoping to get a glimpse of any action. She was disappointed.

When she got to Eli's house, she pulled into the third car parking space, slipped the watch off her wrist, and put it and the $2400 dollars in her purse. She gathered up all Trace's other things and dropped them into her trunk.

Ivy strolled into the house. "Hello, Ivy," Eli's mom greeted her. "You look like you've had a long day."

"You guessed it."

"Do you want a Coke or something? I sure could use one, on the rocks...it's been one of those days, if you know what I mean. It's inventory time for us at work, and that's always stressful. Go ahead and sit and I'll get one for us."

Trying not to smile too much about her new achievement as a cat burglar, Ivy thanked Claire.

"Have you seen much of Eli today?" Claire asked.

"Nope, I haven't, not since this morning." Ivy pulled one leg up on the couch and tucked it in under the other. "I called him earlier, but he didn't have much to say."

"Well, I thought he'd be home by now, but I guess he'll be here soon." She glanced at Ivy's dark clothing. "By the way, what's up with the all black tonight?"

Thinking quickly, Ivy answered, "It's the new thing, all black. Not sure I like it, though. Is it too much?"

"Can't go wrong with black."

"Thanks for the soda," Ivy said. "Tell Eli to come say good night when he gets home."

When Claire left the living room, Ivy went to her car trunk, gathered up Trace's stuff, and marched up to her room.

CHAPTER 22

Zack shuffled in through the kitchen door, tipped slightly sideways to balance the weight of the duffle bag clutched in one hand. As he headed toward his room, a cold draft blew against his face. *What's that? Did Trace turn the air-conditioning on?*

Stopping in the front room doorway, Zack noticed sharp points of glass glittering in the light of the street lamp shining through the broken window. Heart racing, Zack dropped his duffel bag and pulled out his phone. He dialed Trace as he cautiously looked around their place, not knowing if the vandals were still there. "Hey, man," he whispered when Trace answered. "Someone broke our window."

After a stunned silence, Trace asked, "They take anything?"

"Don't know I just got here. I'm looking around."

"Call the cops," Trace said. "I'm coming home right now."

By the time Trace drove up to the house, Officer Ted Holden was on the scene. "This window was broken from the inside," Holden said, crouching down to study the glass on the front room carpet and comparing it to the pieces outside on the walkway.

Officer Holden stood. "You guys have insurance?"

"No."

"Have you noticed anything missing?"

"I haven't checked yet," Trace replied.

"Go have a look-see while I talk to your friend here."

The moment Trace stepped inside his room, he saw that his laptop was missing. He went through his drawers and closet, the sickness of despair growing deeper as he discovered his other missing things. He hurried out to the living room. "Damn thieves," he shouted.

"What was taken?" Officer Holden listed each item in detail on his report. "Do you have any photos of these items?"

Trace provided a picture of him wearing Uncle Warren's watch, but could only report the amount of missing money and detailed descriptions of his wallet, Beretta, and laptop. Oddly enough, none of Zack's things was missing, leaving Officer Holden a little mystified

When the police left, Zack and Trace swept up the glass and taped a piece of cardboard over the broken window. Although he desperately wanted to talk to Tayla, Trace decided it was too late to call.

When Trace finally settled down enough to try to sleep, he discovered his eye drops in the wrong bedside stand. His chap stick was tinged with pink. *What the hell?* He shivered, and decided he'd better wait until morning to report the oddities to Officer Holden. Someone had been in his room, used his stuff, and stole things that mattered to him. His room was no longer safe, and even after he managed to doze, ordinary household sounds like the hum of the refrigerator motor snapped him awake.

By the time an exhausted Trace forced himself out of bed, Zack had left for work. Trace sat at the kitchen table, scrubbed his head with his hands, and called his landlord about the broken window. Then he called Tayla. "Hey, we were robbed last night."

"Oh, no!" Tayla cried. "Are you all right?"

"Yeah. We weren't here when it happened, but the bastard stole my stuff."

"That's terrible! Why would someone break into your apartment?" Tayla's indignation soothed Trace's soul.

"You know what's weird?" he said, "Whoever broke in didn't take any of Zack's stuff, but used my eye drops and my chap stick. Who does that?"

"That is so weird," Tayla agreed. "I wish I could come home a week early for Thanksgiving to help you through this."

"It's alright," Trace said, pleased by her desire to help.

"Even seeing you for a minute would be worth it."

"It's okay," Trace reassured her.

"Next week, then," Tayla said. "I have to see for myself that you're alright."

"Yeah, that's good. I'll see you then."

"I love you, Trace."

"Love you, too."

Trace avoided his bedroom until he had to get ready for work. Everything felt sinister now. Should he move? He didn't really want to. This location was ideal, and splitting the rent with Zack made it so Trace could save more money for his future, a future he planned to share with Tayla.

Trace walked outside and pulled out his key to lock the door when someone called, "Hey!"

Trace turned to see Ivy on the sidewalk, her arms wrapped around herself against the cold, her brow creased in concern. "What happened?" She indicated the cardboard window.

"We were robbed last night."

Ivy's mouth dropped open. "No! Who would do such an awful thing?"

Trace locked the door, not that it would do much good until the cardboard was replaced. The glaziers were scheduled to arrive after Zack got home. Even then, the window had proved easy enough to break. "They're investigating."

"Do they have any clues?"

Trace shrugged. He didn't want to talk about it. "What are you doing here, anyway?"

"I was just around the corner and thought I'd stop by and say hi." Ivy stepped closer. "Can I do anything? Help you clean up?"

"It's already done. I have to go or I'll be late for work."

"So late?"

"You know I work nights."

"Oh. That's tough. Well, I'm sure sorry about your apartment."

Trace walked to his car without responding.

"See you later, Trace." Annoyed by his lack of attention, Ivy stood and watched Trace get into his car and drive away.

CHAPTER 23

A week later, Trace picked Tayla up for dinner at Mi Casa restaurant, glad that her family was willing to share her during her brief holiday visit. As they drove, he said, "Ivy showed up at my place the other night."

"What for?"

Trace shrugged. "I don't know. I found her waiting outside my apartment. She's been texting me, too."

"What's she saying?"

"Just that she wants to help me get through the trauma of the break in."

"Hmm," Tayla grunted, not sounding the least bit happy. "That's what I'm for."

"That's for sure." Trace pulled into the restaurant parking lot.

"How did she even find out about it?"

"Don't know." He turned off the car, and leaned in to give Tayla a reassuring kiss, but it didn't last as long as he wanted.

"I didn't want to tell you before," Tayla said, "but Gwen told me that Ivy called her to ask where you worked."

"That's weird."

Tayla gave him a sidelong glance. "Don't you think she's pretty?"

"Sure."

Tayla's suddenly cold stare made Trace backpedal.

"There are lots of pretty girls in the world, but she's definitely not my type."

"So you aren't interested in her?"

"What? No! I'm with you, Tayla, all the way."

Tayla took hold of his hand. "I had to ask. I don't know why she seems to, I don't know, be stalking you or something."

"It's not because I want it!" Trace declared. "She freaks me out." Quickly changing the subject he said, "Let's go eat." He got out of the car and opened Tayla's door for her. Sliding his arm around her, he led her toward the restaurant, stopping to let a car drive past them. Trace stared in disbelief at Ivy's face smiling out at him from the driver's window.

Tayla tightened her hold on Trace, letting him know that she'd seen Ivy, too. "What's her deal, anyway? I'm tired of this. I'm going to tell her to back off."

"Be careful." Trace didn't know why he said that, but the sight of Ivy at the same place he'd taken Tayla for a date made him feel a bit queasy. She'd crashed their dates before, but that was usually at casual group functions. This felt different. Could it be a simple coincidence? Or was she following him? Or Tayla? Something wasn't right.

As they walked through the restaurant door, he looked over his shoulder and thought he saw Ivy's white Honda Accord parked at the end of a row, but it was too dark to be sure.

He and Tayla relaxed as they slid into a booth under subdued light. They ordered their food and were talking about Trace visiting Tayla at college, laughing at the silly methods he proposed to get there, when Tayla's phone buzzed in her purse. She ignored it. It wasn't until they were done eating and Trace was paying for the meal that Tayla checked her phone. Her easy manner disappeared as she tensed.

"What's wrong?" Trace asked.

Tayla turned the phone screen toward him so he could see the message from Gwen, which read, *Ivy told Ashley that she's going to break you and Trace apart.*

CHAPTER 24

When Tayla went back to college, Trace felt her absence keenly. He thought again about moving to Oregon to be near her, but his savings were growing to admirable proportions. In spite of his scholarship, he'd need money to start his pre med college classes next year. There would possibly be enough for Tayla and him to set up house after she graduated. Still, there wasn't any harm in checking on job possibilities during his visits to Oregon.

In January, Zack said, "Hey, Trace, there's a party tonight. Why don't you come with me, man?"

"I can't."

Zack laughed. "You don't have to hang out with any girls, just your buddies." Zack threw his hands up. "What else you gonna do?"

Trace sighed. "Text Tayla, or maybe give her a call."

"You do that all the time. Come on, man, have some fun. Don't ya think she's going out with her college friends while you're sitting home?"

Trace had to admit that made sense. It was also true that he was bored. Zack made a good point. How could hanging out with his friends hurt his relationship with Tayla?

"Okay," Trace said. "I'll go."

When they arrived, Trace couldn't help noticing Ivy and Eli standing across the room. "Hey, Trace," Ivy said, her bright smile sparking memories of Tayla and Ivy together in high school when Tayla was still within hugging distance.

"Hey," he said before remembering that Tayla had told him not to have anything more to do with Ivy. He turned away.

"Hey!" Ivy called, moving up beside him. "How's Tayla?"

It would be rude not to answer. Besides, she was talking about Tayla, not herself, so Trace didn't feel guilty when he answered, "Fine."

"Has it been awhile since you heard from her?" The sympathy in Ivy's voice was unsettling, especially since Trace wanted to talk about Tayla, too. More than that, he wanted to see her, to hold her in his arms, but that wouldn't happen for another week. No, eight days, more than a week.

Trace shrugged. "We text and talk on the phone every day." Then he said to Zack, "Hey, let's see about getting a drink."

Ivy followed them. "It must be hard to be so far away from Tayla. I wish she'd gone to Idaho State. I really miss her."

From the tone of her voice, Trace could almost believe it. Had he somehow misjudged Ivy? Did she recognize that she'd stepped over the line between Tayla and him? Was she truly sorry? He risked a glance at her. She appeared honestly subdued.

"Yeah," Trace sighed. He got a drink and looked around for someplace to sit.

"Yo, I gotta talk to Gwen," Zack said, and disappeared into the crowd. Trace watched him go, then sank into a chair. Without pause, Ivy crossed her legs and sat down on the floor next to him. Eli plopped down beside her.

"Hey, Eli, do you remember that assembly where Tayla did that funny monologue about Cinderella, with all kinds of other fairy tales mixed in?" Ivy laughed, and Eli joined her. Trace couldn't help smiling at the memory. "It was so great, she got such wild applause. She is one talented girl."

Tayla was talented, and so beautiful that she was bound to attract the attention of men on campus. The sudden thought of her flirting with other guys made Trace bristle. Why hadn't she gone to ISU? Did she really want to go to a more prestigious college than Idaho State University, or did she secretly want to get away from him?

CHAPTER 25

Tayla greeted Trace at his next visit with her usual enthusiasm. He held her hand as they crossed campus. After a few minutes, she reclaimed her hand to get a water bottle from her backpack. After taking a drink, she carried the bottle in her hand closest to Trace. *Did she do it on purpose?*

As they approached a co-ed group of three guys and two girls, Tayla made an abrupt turn off the walk. "I forgot I have to go check out a library book." Trace followed her to the library where she briefly searched the shelves until a tall young man brushed passed them, whispering, "How you doin', Tay?" accompanied by a warm smile.

"Good, Nate," she whispered back, smiling. Then she pulled a book off the shelf and carried it to the checkout desk.

"Don't you have electronic books these days?" Trace asked on their way out.

"Yes, but they haven't gotten all of them scanned in yet," Tayla said, clutching the book to her chest. "Besides, sometimes it's just more satisfying to turn actual pages, don't you think?"

Trace agreed.

They crossed the street to grab a bite for lunch at a popular sandwich shop where Trace told Tayla about seeing Ivy at the party. Tayla's eyebrows rose. "Did you talk to her?"

"Only after she asked how you were."

"She asked about me?"

"Yeah."

"What did you say?"

"I only said you were doing fine. She said she missed you."

"Well, I don't miss her," Tayla declared. "I'm glad I got away from Meridian."

Trace almost asked if she was glad she got away from him, too, but Tayla started talking about an entertaining concert that the music department presented, combined with a humorous performance by the dance club. Her laughter was so refreshing, that Trace didn't want to bring up any potential problems.

On their way out, a muscular young man with a ridiculous moustache held the door for Tayla. "What's up, Tayla?" he asked, eyeing Trace. "Who's your friend?"

"This is Trace," Tayla said. "We went to high school together. Trace, this is Brad."

Trace tipped his chin up. "What's up?"

"Not much," Brad replied. "See ya, Tayla."

"Yup," she replied with a little wave.

Frustrated, Trace asked, "We went to high school together?"

Tayla looked up at Trace, surprise plain in her eyes. "Well, we did."

"What about, 'He's my boyfriend?'" Trace asked. "That's messed up, Tayla."

Tayla set her mouth in a firm line, then said, "He doesn't need to know our business, Trace." She raised her eyebrows. "Don't tell me you're jealous." She held up her hand where the promise ring sparkled mischievously. "You don't expect me to be a nun and sit in my room, do you? It's possible to have friends of both sexes. We're just friends."

Trace reached for her hand. "I guess so. Sorry." As they walked, he couldn't help wondering, *who were these guys?* Was it all as innocent as Tayla said? He wanted to believe it.

When it was time for him to leave, Tayla gave Trace a warm, lingering kiss that felt like the old days. "I'm so glad you came," she said with her gaze fastened on his. "I'll be in Meridian in a couple of weeks. Can't wait to see you then."

Trace left for home, his emotions swinging from one pole to the other, wanting to believe that they were in as much love as ever, but wondering where he and Tayla really stood.

Over the next couple of months, days apart and the expense of travel wore on both of them. In between Tayla's visits, Trace spent more time going out with his friends. Ivy became a more familiar face, since she showed up at a lot of the same places.

When Trace got together with Tayla, she seemed more immersed in her college world. "I'm in the thick of it," she explained. "I'm more than halfway through earning my degree." She squeezed his hand. "I really appreciate your support. I'm not sure I could make it without you."

Did she really mean it?

CHAPTER 26

In March, Ivy texted Trace asking if she could bring him some lunch from a new restaurant. *They've got the best cheesecake in the world,* she promised.

Trace considered the request. He hadn't told Tayla how often Ivy was texting him. Trace didn't often respond to Ivy's messages, but tonight he was tired of his own cooking. Cooking! Hah. He'd slapped together a peanut butter sandwich. A hot meal followed by cheesecake sounded like heaven. *Yeah, sure,* he texted back before he could talk himself out of it.

Almost immediately, Ivy showed up at Trace's work with a restaurant carryout bag. It was clear that she'd already ordered the food before asking if he wanted it. Trace had to wonder if she'd been parked outside while texting him. It made him uneasy, but the delightful smell of hot food soothed his worries. "Thanks," he told her.

"Anything for you," she replied, matching his smile with one of her own.

Ivy began sending Trace more texts than ever before. Trace wasn't sure if he should tell Tayla, but it turned out he didn't have to. When Tayla called him, Trace answered, "Hey, Tayla."

Tayla's voice was uncharacteristically cold. "I hear you're hanging out with Ivy."

"Who told you that?"

"I got a text from Eli."

Trace scoffed, although his heart gave a little lurch. "He'd tell you anything Ivy told him to say."

"Is it true?"

"No!"

"Would Zack agree with you?"

"You could ask him."

"That's not an answer."

"Yes," Trace said, unsure if Zack really would agree. He'd better talk to Zack before Tayla got to him.

"If you don't want to keep our relationship going, just say so."

"I do!" Trace declared. "I went to a couple of parties where Ivy happened to be. I promise you, I'm not doing anything with her." *Except letting her bring me food.* In defense mode, Trace asked, "What's really going on with all those guys on campus?"

"All what guys?"

"Every time I visit, guys are coming onto you."

"They're just friends."

"They act like more than friends."

"You need to grow up, Trace."

"Maybe we both do."

There was a cold silence before Tayla replied, "Maybe we need to do more than that. Maybe we're growing apart."

Trace's voice softened. "Come on, Tayla. I still really love you." He realized as he said it that in spite of their distant relationship, it was true.

There was another pause, this one shorter. "I love you, too," Tayla admitted. She sighed. "There's just so much going on in my life right now, I don't want to have to worry about where we stand every time we talk."

"I understand," Trace said, comforted by her declaration of love. "Okay, so we're exclusively dating, but you can talk to other guys, and I can talk to other girls."

Silence.

"Okay? Just talk, right?"

Tayla sighed. "Yeah, okay, Trace, but be careful of Ivy, please stay away from her. There's something about her that's just, I don't know, sneaky, maybe. She makes me uneasy."

"I feel that, too."

"You really do?"

"Absolutely, and I can't ever imagine not caring about you."

"We never know what's going to happen, Trace. I love you more than any other guy in my life, but we just don't know what the future holds."

Trace had to reluctantly agree. He hung up, exuberant at the reassurance of Tayla's love.

Ivy's half dozen messages popped up when he checked the message notifications that had come in during his phone call.

Feeling lonely?

I've got a sure cure for whatever ails you.

Hungry for more cheesecake or something even better?

Did you see my last FB post? I was thinking of you the whole time I recorded it. Check it out.

There's a great new movie we could see to help you de-stress. My treat! I'll even buy the popcorn.

Do you want me to come over?"

Overwhelmed, Trace hit "reply" and typed, *STOP. I'm dating Tayla so you need to STOP TEXTING AND CALLING ME.*

CHAPTER 27

As Ivy read Trace's text, she filled with rage. *He doesn't get to do this to me.*

Trace's abandonment sent Ivy into a tailspin of fury. How dare he try to cut her out of his life? No way! Ivy grabbed her phone and scrolled through her contacts, found Reese Blake, and dialed. When he answered on the first ring, she said sweetly, "Hi, Reese, it's Ivy. You never called me back."

"Yeah, well, I thought you weren't interested."

"Of course I'm interested in you." Ivy's voice had turned to silk. "What girl wouldn't be? I was just really busy last time we talked."

"Really? It didn't sound like that. You just blew me off."

"I'm sorry if that's what you thought. My life is kinda crazy at times."

Ivy's thoughts were of Eli's most recent Trace report. He was headed to the movies with Zack and Ethan. "I was thinking...maybe we could catch a movie tonight." Her voice grew husky. "I'd really love to spend some time with you.

"Sure," Reese replied. "I'm free."

Reese picked Ivy up and drove to the theater while Ivy scanned the parking lot for Trace's car. When she didn't see it, she hung out in the lobby, asking Reese for popcorn and a drink, watching the front doors until Trace finally walked in. With an awkward shift of her shoulder, she made sure to catch his eye before sidling up close to Reese. When

Trace turned away, she was certain it was because he hated seeing her with another man, all the worse that it was one of his friends.

Ivy went out with Reese a few more times, always with a plan to intercept Trace, who would surely want her after he saw how desirable she was to his friend. She let Reese kiss her, then make out with her, exhilarated at being the center of his attention.

Ivy kept texting Trace, calling him, and waiting for him at his work. After his shift one Wednesday night, she was waiting for him not a minute past midnight. When he walked out of his building engaged in conversation with a coworker, he saw Ivy and quickly turned away.

"I'm going out with Reese," Ivy boasted to his back.

"Good for you." Trace replied, and then continued his conversation.

"Do you even care?"

Trace sighed and looked over his shoulder. "Not really." Then Trace turned to his coworker, "She's so wack...sorry."

"Man, I'd be a little worried if I were you. She seems like a crazy woman."

"Tell me about it," Trace sighed. "I can't get rid of her. Talk to you tomorrow." Trace got in his car and drove away without even looking at Ivy standing alone in the parking lot.

CHAPTER 28

Tayla's lakeside family cabin was a popular summer hangout. The family's boat and kayaks lined their long plank dock. The pink and orange sunsets and laid-back fishing were what Tayla's parents craved, but their daughter and her friends liked to add more adventure to their playful lake days.

Tayla's call to Trace was filled with the excitement of her summer news. "Trace, are you coming to the cabin this summer?"

"When?"

"The last weekend in June. I've invited all the gang to the annual summer party."

"Who?"

"Not Ivy," Tayla assured him.

"Good. Who else is coming?"

"Ethan, of course, Carrie, Mia, Becca, Gwen, Eli…"

"Wait. Eli?"

"Yes. I told him he could come only if he wanted to come without Ivy."

"And he agreed?"

"He did."

"Good for him! I can't believe it, but good for him."

"Yeah, can you come? It's the 24th through 28th of June."

Trace groaned. "No, I've got to work, and that's the weekend I'm moving…did you forget?"

Tayla sounded bereft. "Yeah, I did. My parents have already made the arrangements. Are you sure, you have to work the whole time? Maybe you could come for just one day. Will you just check, please?"

Trace went out of his way to try to get a day off, but it just didn't happen. His boss wasn't accepting any rationalization.

Trace gave up and called Tayla. "I'm sorry I can't go, but I'll make it up to you."

Tayla laughed in spite of her disappointment.

When ISU let out for the summer, a landlord anxious to fill vacancies left by college renters gave Trace and Zack a good rate on a townhouse. Even though the place was further west of town, it had more room and the rent was cheaper. With his new lease on life, Trace carefully evaluated his savings and decided he could afford new bedroom furniture at a clearance sale.

In spite of Trace's absence at the cabin, the summer bash was a big hit with boating, swimming, and evenings roasting marshmallows over the fire.

Eli didn't try hiding his surprise when Trace wasn't anywhere to be seen in the light of the campfire flames flickering over familiar faces. "Why didn't Trace come?" Eli asked, turning his stick over to brown the white side of his marshmallow.

"He has to work," Tayla said, twisting a lock of her smoky hair around her finger. "It sucks."

"Yeah, that's too bad," Eli said as his marshmallow caught fire. He lifted his stick and waved it in the air, which only made it burn brighter. Everyone chuckled at his marshmallow antics. Eli finally shook the marshmallow off to land on the sand in a smoldering ruin. "I've had enough anyway," Eli announced. "See you guys tomorrow." Then he left the group, pulled out his phone, and called Ivy.

"This is great," she said when Eli gave her the news. "You did good, Eli. Now find out where Trace's new apartment is for me."

Later that night, Eli found Zack and asked how he liked his new place. Eventually he got the address, and forwarded it to Ivy.

CHAPTER 29

I have him all to myself! Ivy put on her favorite white shorts and buttoned up her blue flowered blouse just enough to tie the tails high in the front to show off her flat midriff. She drove to Trace's new place and began texting him at 10:30 pm.

I heard you had to work and couldn't go with Tayla to her parents' cabin for the summer party. So sorry, that must suck for you. When Trace didn't answer, Ivy added. *I know what it's like to be left behind I couldn't go either.*

Was she kidding? Did she think Trace didn't already know the real reason she didn't go?

Do you want to hang out? She typed. *I'll come over and hang out with you.*

Trace vigorously type back. *It's not a good idea. My girlfriend is actually, one of your friends, remember? Besides, I moved.*

I know where your new house is. We would just be hanging out as friends. Ivy replied.

When Trace finally reached home in the early morning hours of the 27th, exhausted from a full night's work, Ivy texted, *I'm in your parking lot...can I come up?*

Trace rubbed his face, dizzy for want of sleep, then texted back, *No, I told you it's not a good idea.*

As tired as he was, Trace was also wound up. Perhaps if he watched a bit of television, he could relax. As he turned on the set in his bedroom, another text came in from Ivy. For the next half hour, he lay against the pillows by his headboard and watched a comedy while texting Ivy.

Her messages seemed less threatening now. She was just a person, after all. Even though she'd done some unsettling things in the past, perhaps it was just because she was lonely. He knew what loneliness felt like, especially now. He'd wanted to stay with Tayla, but he was here alone while she was still having fun with all her friends. He and Tayla had agreed they could talk to other people. He was a big boy. What would it hurt to talk to Ivy for a few minutes?

Are you ready for a friend? Ivy's next text read.

OK, Trace replied, regret settling in the moment he hit "send." Deep inside, he knew this was not a good idea, but on the surface, he was lonely. She'd worn him down by assuring him she knew exactly how he felt.

In spite of the late hour, as soon as he opened the door, his tired mind soaked up the adoration in her clear blue eyes and filed it away in his subconscious.

"Hi!" she said, giving him an awkward little wave with one hand, the other weighed down with bottles. "I brought us some wine coolers."

"Hi." Now that they were face to face, he couldn't think of anything else to say.

"What you watching?" Ivy followed him into his room where the dim light of the television was the only illumination. Closing the door behind her, she pushed his Yankees hat aside and sat on his bed.

"Not much of anything." Trace lifted the remote, his finger on the power button.

"No, leave it on," Ivy said. "I like this show." Glancing around his room, she said, "Wow, this place is a mess."

Trace shrugged and put the remote down. "What do you expect? We just moved in. I haven't had a chance to put anything away."

"I'll help you get settled." Ivy grabbed a tall box and dumped it out on Trace's bed.

"Careful," Trace called.

"What are these?" Ivy fingered several rolled cylinders.

"My vintage Star Wars posters, be careful with them."

"Awesome," Ivy gushed. "Let's put them up."

Once the posters were in place, Ivy grabbed another box as the canned laugh track rumbled through the room, so unnatural that Trace had a flash of gratitude that there was another living human being in the room, no matter who it was. They went through two more boxes before Trace's eyes started burning from fatigue. How long was Ivy planning to stay? On one hand, it was nice to have some help, but on the other hand, he really needed some sleep, so he hoped she'd leave.

He leaned against the wall as the main characters on the TV screen moved their faces closer together, until at last their lips met. The kiss didn't last long, because the guy's best friend spilled a bowl of popcorn over their heads.

Over the fresh sound of the laugh track, Ivy stopped sorting through a box and patted the mattress beside her. "Sit."

Trace took two steps, and then sank down onto the bed, dizzy with exhaustion.

She turned toward him. "I've had feelings for you for a long time, Trace."

A little catch thumped in his heart.

"I've always wondered why you haven't broken up with Tayla." Ivy's voice was gentle and caring, softening the impact of her words. "She's so far away, and she's so pretty, she can't help but meet other guys who are interested in her."

Hadn't he seen that for himself?

Ivy opened the wine coolers and handed Trace one. "I don't want to see you suffer when she cheats on you. She might not mind making you look like an idiot, but I don't want that for you."

Trace's sleep-deprived brain half-believed Ivy's words, but he said, "We've talked about this. She and I have. We have our rules. We're a team."

"Love, what rules?" Ivy shook her head sadly. "What kind of love is that? Real love has no rules." She slid her hand over his and leaned in to kiss him.

The sudden feel of her soft lips against his made Trace react physically. He returned her kiss rather passionately, then suddenly pulled back. Rubbing his eyes with the heels of his hands, he said, "This is not a good idea."

"You let me come over," Ivy whispered, tracing the skin of his arm with her fingertips. "Why would you do that if you didn't like me?"

"I wasn't thinking, I guess." Trace stood and walked across the room. He aimlessly picked up his hoodie.

"Why just sit here and wait for Tayla to come home on the weekends? That doesn't make any sense. Now you're making me feel stupid for even coming over here."

Trace folded his hoodie, then shook it out again. "You were just coming over as a friend, remember? I didn't invite you over. You asked if you could come."

"I know," Ivy agreed, her voice soft and shy, "but I really like you, and I thought if we could just be alone together for a bit, you'd let your guard down a little, because I know you like me, right?"

"As a friend," Trace admitted, thinking of the food she'd brought him, "but I don't want to hurt Tayla."

Ivy gave him a seductive smile. "Then let's just see where this goes tonight. What can that hurt? In fact, I don't think it would hurt at all." Ivy stood up to the sound of a fresh laugh track and slowly walked over to Trace, her hips swaying. She took the hoodie from his hands, dropped it on the floor, and began unbuttoning his shirt.

Desire exploded within Trace, taking over his body, moving his hands to copy Ivy's actions, unbuttoning her blue shirt, untying the knot at her waist. He was in a fog of passion, his tired mind surrendering control to his body's automatic reactions to sexual stimulation.

Ivy pulled his half-naked body down beside her on the bed. With her lips against his neck, she murmured, "Are you sure you want to do this?" She nibbled his earlobe, then circled it with her moist tongue. "You have a girlfriend, you know." Ivy carefully paved the way toward building on Trace's guilt with her seemingly caring words.

"Uh, yeah," Trace gasped, caught up in the moment, all logic gone from his mind about what this might do to his relationship with Tayla.

Ivy moved her hand to his pants, pulling down the zipper as she said, "Are you going to tell Tayla we did this?"

"No, let's keep it between us," he grunted, his reasoning mind elsewhere as his hands sought to touch every inch of naked skin on her body.

After his passion was spent, Trace lay exhausted on his bed, drifting off to sleep as Ivy slid her fingers through his dark curls. "I'm really glad you ended up wanting to hang out tonight." She snuggled up next to him, and they slept.

In the predawn darkness, Ivy left Trace's house full of confidence. She'd won. She'd pushed Tayla out of the picture. Trace loved her, and now he was hers to do with as she wished.

CHAPTER 30

Trace wasn't fully awake until a couple of hours after Ivy left. He sat up and put his head in his hands, sick with regret. *What had he done?*

Before he even hit the shower, he saw that he had eight texts from Ivy. He stared at them as if his phone was poisoned. He ignored them. By the time he got out of the shower, not feeling clean enough even though he'd washed three times, there were five more texts from Ivy. When he didn't reply, his phone rang. Ivy.

He was hungry, but too upset to eat. Ivy kept sending texts and trying to call until it was time for Trace to leave for work. He would have turned his phone off, but he didn't want to miss a call from Tayla.

Tayla. What was he going to do about Tayla? Somewhere in the back of his mind, he thought that Tayla would find out. Why was that? Was it something he'd said? Something Ivy said? He couldn't remember. All he knew for sure was that he didn't want to lose Tayla. Ivy had just been a warm body. Tayla was the real thing, the whole package of heart, mind, and spirit. As a bonus, she was good looking, too, but that wasn't the main attraction.

When Tayla finally called, Trace didn't tell her about Ivy. He listened to her exploits with friends and her declarations of affection for him. He told her he loved her with even more fervor than before. She laughed and said she loved him, too.

Trace hoped she meant it.

Trace drove to work and got out of his car, horrified to see Ivy hurrying toward him. "Is your phone broken?" she demanded.

"No," he said. "I told you it wasn't a good idea."

Ivy gave him a sly smile. "It's not what you said, it's what you did. You showed me you loved me."

"No," Trace insisted. "It was just...a human reaction."

"I know you love me," Ivy persisted. "We're in a relationship."

"We're not!" Trace shouted. "I've got to get to work." He hurried to the door, Ivy following him every step of the way, insisting that he loved her.

He stopped at the door and turned to face her. "I'm not breaking up with Tayla just because we had sex. I love Tayla, not you." Then he shut the door in her face.

All during his shift, Ivy continued texting him. *Did she never sleep?*

Trace dreaded leaving work to go home. It turned out his dread was for a good reason, because as he walked across the parking lot, Ivy intercepted him. "Why are you ignoring me?" she demanded.

"Stop texting me," Trace demanded. "I'm sorry about what happened, but you need to stop calling and texting me. I told you it wasn't a good idea. I feel really guilty and so should you. You're really being a bitch about this, and I don't want to see you again. "

Ivy looked at him sideways, her cunning smile chilling the night air. "I'm going to tell Tayla about us."

"Go ahead then." Trace feigned nonchalance even while it felt like a rock was sinking in his chest. "She's gonna find out anyway."

CHAPTER 31

Tayla met Trace at his apartment late in the morning, just after he woke up. "It's so good to see you." Trace gave her a light kiss. "Come on in." When Tayla was seated on the couch, Trace said, "Hey, I'm just going to shower and freshen up. Give me a minute, okay?"

Tayla smiled. "Sure."

Trace hurried into the bathroom. With the water running, he didn't hear his phone ring, but Tayla did. Picking it up, she saw Ivy's number on the screen. *What was going on?* Suspicious, Tayla opened Trace's texts and scrolled through the most recent ones from Ivy, anger building as she read their exchanges. Hadn't she warned Trace to stay away from Ivy? On impulse, she called Ivy from Trace's phone.

"Hey, boyfriend!" Ivy answered.

"He's not your boyfriend." Tayla's voice was cold.

After a second of silence, Ivy asked playfully, "Did he tell you?"

"No! Just stop it!" Tayla hung up.

When Trace walked into the room, smelling great, his wet hair in sexy curls around his collar, his bright smile full of love for her, Tayla took in a breath. She loved this guy. She bit her lips together and turned his phone toward him. Then she asked, "Hey, what's up with all the texts from Ivy?"

"I know it's so annoying." Trace sighed and sank down on the couch next to Tayla, his heart beating painfully. *How far had she read? Did she know?* "She thought she could come over the other night, and I told her to kick rocks, but ever since then, she just keeps calling and texting me."

"Well, you need to tell her to stop, and I mean now," Tayla said. "I already called her and told her to stop calling you. She knows I'm pissed off."

"Believe me, I am, too," Trace assured her.

Tayla gave him a sympathetic look, then leaned in to kiss him.

She didn't know!

Little did he know that Ivy wasn't about to keep this a secret for long.

CHAPTER 32

When Ivy's attempts to contact Tayla weren't welcomed or received, she continued to blow up Tayla's phone with messages until Ivy decided she had no recourse but to find Tayla and tell her the news in person. *She can't hide from me forever!*

Ivy drove over to Tayla's and found her backing out of her driveway. Ivy waited down the street, then followed Tayla to Walgreens, her heart speeding up like a predator sighting prey as she watched Tayla get out of her car. Hurrying across the parking lot, Ivy called, "Hey, Tayla."

Tayla glanced at Ivy, then away, and picked up her pace.

"I have something you'll want to hear," Ivy said.

"I already heard it." Tayla unlocked her car door.

"Not this."

Tayla slowly turned, her key fob aimed at Ivy like a weapon.

"Do you know how Trace said he couldn't go to the cabin last weekend?

Tayla's reply was a cold stare.

"I bet he told you he had to work."

"So?"

"He really stayed home because of me. That's when Trace told me he really loved me and we had sex at his place." Ivy was delighted to see Tayla's shoulders stiffen. *Were those tears rising in her eyes?* "I'm really sorry, but Trace doesn't want to be with you anymore, he just didn't know how to tell you."

"You need to leave." The quaver in Tayla's voice betrayed her attempt to appear strong and unmoved, giving Ivy the best entertainment she'd had in a long time.

Shaking her head in mock regret, Ivy announced with pride, "I just thought you should know."

Tayla got in her car and drove away faster than was safe in a parking lot. She managed to avoid crashing into another car, but her heart was broken. She lost her fight with the tears, and let them flow down her face in hot streaks. Her throat was so tight it was hard to breathe.

She wanted to believe Trace. She'd thought hard about what he said. She even planned to go to his place to talk face to face as he'd suggested to see if she could read the truth in his eyes. She would hear him out, but she already knew from their long, intimate relationship that he hadn't told her everything going on between him and Ivy. There was a slight sideways glance in his eyes that tried to hide a shadowed secret in their soft brown depths. She needed openness and honesty. She couldn't live with anything else. If Trace told her that he'd had sex with Ivy and that he was sorry, Tayla could have worked with it. She understood how guys could give in to passion for a woman's flesh, and she also knew that she was more than that to Trace, if he'd only be honest.

Her heart caught with a fresh stab of pain. She loved him, but she couldn't live with a liar. He wasn't the Trace she'd fallen in love with.

She sat in her car after getting home, tears of hurt running down her face. *Could Ivy be lying? She's been sneaky and trying to cause trouble.* She wiped her tears, reached into her purse, pulled out her phone and dialed Trace. When he answered, she spoke. "Ivy just cornered me in the parking lot at Walgreens, do you know what she had to tell me? Don't even think about lying to me. Just tell me the truth."

"I don't know. What?" Trace trembled with the lie he had just told.

"You and she having sex the weekend you stayed home from the cabin. Is it true?"

"Tayla, no, she's just trying to break us up. Don't let her do this to us. I love you, you know that."

After a brief silence, Tayla said, "We'll see." Then she hung up.

Trace held the silent phone to his ear for a moment before slowly lowering it to his lap. He had to at least try to talk to Tayla again. He'd call her tomorrow.

Certain that Tayla was out of the picture, Ivy approached Trace again with a surety that she could slide right into Tayla's place. When Trace wouldn't let her in, Ivy was so stung by his rejection that she decided if she couldn't have Trace, no one would.

With manufactured tears, Ivy told her friends and acquaintances that after he'd promised to leave Tayla, he'd had sex with Ivy, and then tossed her aside like garbage. Ivy spread her self-absorbed lies like poison. "Tell everyone he's dangerous." Wiping her wet blue eyes, she added, "Girls need to know that Trace Aragon is nothing but a debauchee. It's all a sick, twisted game to him."

CHAPTER 33

As Ivy and Eli stalked Trace's Facebook and Instagram pages to see what he was up to, they discovered that he'd made his "Friends" list private. The social disconnects sent Ivy into an intense rage.

"Eli," Ivy said over the phone, "You've got to do something! I have to get him back!"

She heard Eli chewing something. After swallowing, he said, "You never really had him."

Ivy was shocked into momentary silence before exploding. "What did you say? How dare you? You wouldn't have any friends if it wasn't for me, and you know it. Maybe we weren't meant to be friends after all. You owe me, Eli. Now help me do something about this." Ivy hung up and let Eli stew about her stony silence.

After suffering through a few days of no contact, Eli quickly discovered his attempt at taking control of his own thoughts and putting them into words had backfired. He couldn't take isolation from Ivy for fear she'd desert him. Acting under the familiar umbrella of her spell, Eli suggested planning a surprise party for Ethan Harrison's 21st birthday, a milestone in anyone's life that was worthy of celebration.

Ivy fell in with planning an extravagant Las Vegas birthday party for Ethan. Eli booked a double suite at the Venetian Hotel and ordered lots of food and beer with his generous credit card allowance. He hired a DJ and invited all of Ethan's friends, including Trace.

"Hey Zack, are you going to Ethan's party?" Trace asked.

"Wouldn't miss it, you?"

"Yeah. I'm not scheduled to work, so I'm good to go."

"It's gonna be the bomb," Zack said with a grin. He liked plenty of beer, which seemed to ramp up his Attention Deficit Disorder (ADD.) He could be rather amusing when he was drunk.

"Don't you know it?" Trace replied with no clue to the party's sponsor.

"Are you bringing Tayla?" Zack asked.

"I don't think so," Trace replied slowly. "I'll ask Tayla to go with me, of course, but I mean…she's probably busy. I don't think she'll leave her schoolwork."

Zack raised his eyebrows. "What if poison Ivy's there?"

"Ha!" Trace barked out a mirthless laugh. "That's a good one! I'm not letting Ivy decide where I go and who I hang out with. Ethan's my friend, so if she's there, I'll just keep my distance. You can help me - run interference, block, and tackle, whatever it takes."

"Yeah, right," Zack said dryly.

Tayla said she couldn't come, but asked Trace to tell Ethan "Happy Birthday" from her.

Trace and Zack traveled to Las Vegas where many of their friends had already arrived. Some were swimming in the pool, and those who were old enough to hit the casinos were spending time there. When everyone gathered back in the suite for food and birthday cake, Ivy shouted, "Let's get this party started!"

Cheers greeted her announcement. The birthday song was sung, the cake cut, plates loaded with food, and beer poured. Trace kept a wary eye on Ivy, but she miraculously stayed away from him as he ate. Eventually he relaxed and laughed with his friends.

A few beers later, Trace felt pretty good. After using the bathroom, he wandered out onto the balcony to take in the breathtaking view of glittering colored lights dancing in the dark desert valley.

"Want another beer?"

Trace turned to see Ivy holding a frothing party cup toward him. The slight buzz in his brain made him blink a couple of times.

"Give me another chance," Ivy begged, glancing over her shoulder to see if Eli was in position with his phone camera pointed their way. He was. The trap was set.

Trace lifted a warning palm toward Ivy. "I told you…"

Ivy dropped the beer. It splashed on the floor, spraying both of them. Trace stepped back and glanced down. That's when Ivy grabbed him around the neck and forced a kiss on his lips.

Trace shoved her backward, her feet splashing in spilled beer, a smile of triumph on her face.

"What are you doing?" Trace demanded.

"Why are you denying it?" Ivy shouted. "You promised you'd leave her."

The chatter stopped as the partygoers focused on the disturbance.

"You crazy bitch!" Trace pushed past Ivy and stormed back into the hotel room.

Eli made a circuit of the room, showing anyone who'd missed it, a still photo from the video he'd recorded of the passionate kiss, casting wide spread doubt of Trace's loyalty to Tayla.

What had he done?

Trace left the party and locked himself in his room.

Tayla would for sure leave him if she ever saw that photo.

Afraid there was no going back, Trace curled up on his bed like a chastised child and fell into a troubled sleep.

The next morning he woke up to banging on his door. "Trace, open up, it's Ethan. Come on, open the door."

Trace sat up, rubbed his swollen eyes, then slowly walked to the door. "Ethan, I'm really sorry about messing up your party last night. I didn't know Ivy was going to get crazy."

"Yeah, what was that all about?"

"Dude, I really screwed up. Come in."

Ethan walked into the room and took a chair while Trace sank down on the bed. "You know the summer party at Tayla's cabin?"

Ethan nodded.

"I couldn't go. Then Ivy showed up at my apartment after work. I was really tired, not thinking straight, you know. And we wound up having sex."

Ethan's expression said it all.

"I know, stupid," Trace agreed. "Now I'm afraid it will cost me Tayla." Trace dropped his head and rubbed his hair with nervous fingers. His voice shook. "I need to explain things to Tayla so she'll understand that it didn't mean anything, but I can't get rid of Ivy. She won't stop calling and texting. Look, you gotta see all the texts." Trace raised his head, swiped at his eyes with the back of his hand, and opened his phone. "She keeps showing up at my work, and she comes out of nowhere to be at my place." Trace handed his phone to Ethan with Ivy's text window opened. "You can scroll forever. There are hundreds, if not thousands of them."

"Wow, bro," Ethan said, glancing through Ivy's texts. "You need to tell someone she's stalking you." Ethan read a few more, then added, "And she might get even crazier than she was last night."

"I know," Trace sighed. "That's what my mother said when I showed her. I feel so stupid because I thought she was okay at first, but now she's gone psycho on me. I don't know what to do. If I report her for stalking me, then maybe this sex thing would come out. I've been thinking I should just move to get away from her. Maybe it's time to go to Oregon. A big paycheck isn't everything."

"Hey," Ethan said, handing Trace's phone back. "I'll move with you."

"Yeah?"

"I don't know about Oregon, though. I've been thinking about maybe transferring my job to Salt Lake City. I'm just ready for a change."

Trace looked up at Ethan with a spark of hope in his red-rimmed eyes. "Are you serious?"

Ethan leaned forward and clapped a hand on Trace's knee. "Yes! I'm twenty one and ready to see more of the world."

"Let me check with Tayla."

"Okay. Let me know soon if we're headed west or south."

Trace nodded slowly. "Will do."

Ethan stood and pulled Trace up into a brief man hug. Then he stepped back. "You might want to shower and change."

Trace gave him a wry smile. "Yeah, I'm a mess. But I think I can really get cleaned up now."

After his shower, Trace took a couple of Tylenol and let them work while he dressed. He called Tayla and was disappointed when she didn't answer. He didn't leave a message. After joining Ethan for breakfast, Trace went to his room to pack and called Tayla again. "Hi, there," he said when she finally answered.

"I only answered to tell you to stop calling me." Her voice was so cold, Trace shivered.

"What?" he asked, "Why?" But he knew.

"I got a text from Eli, along with a very interesting picture."

"It's not what it looked like," Trace said, desperate for Tayla to understand what really happened.

"I was at the welcome-back-to-school rally," Tayla said, her voice near breaking. "A big cheer went up just as I opened Eli's message. Can you imagine how ironic that was? People all around me cheering for the Ducks, all that cheering, *cheering*, Trace, while I read the heartbreaking message and saw that horrible photo. It made me sick. You've been lying to me all this time. Ivy and you together? When you'd denied it for months?" Tayla's voice went flat. "And I believed you."

Trace's head pounded with pain. "Please, Tayla, it's not what you think. Just listen," he begged.

She sniffled, then went silent. To her credit, she listened to what he had to say, then replied, "I don't know. I'm sorry, but after seeing the evidence and hearing something different from so many other people, I have a hard time believing you."

And why should she? He hadn't told her the part about having sex with Ivy.

"It appears to have been going on for quite some time, and Ivy told me that you had sex with her."

"Nothing's going on!" Trace insisted.

"I want to believe you, Trace, but I just can't. I was so upset I had to leave my real friends wondering why I left the rally when I'm a school ambassador. I've had enough. I'm going home."

"I'll drive out and see you," Trace offered. "I can be there tonight so we can talk this out face to face. I'll take you out to eat, or see a movie, whatever you want."

"I'm not going to my dorm room. I'm going to my family in Idaho. You lied to me. I don't think I ever want to see you again."

The hot topic in Meridian was Tayla's break up with Trace, and that she'd gone home for a long weekend to shore up her heart so she wouldn't have a nervous breakdown at college. Ivy devoured all the details she could find on Facebook and Instagram before going on the prowl.

CHAPTER 34

Trace moped around his apartment as if he were the last man on Earth. Constant pain in the pit of his stomach caused by his own failure to be honest with Tayla seemed like more than any human could bear.

Seeking relief, Trace confided a short version of the truth about Tayla to Zack. "Brother," Zack said, "you need to get over Tayla."

"I tried telling her what happened, but she doesn't understand."

Zack took another bite of his peanut butter sandwich. "That's rough."

"I told her Ivy was the one who came on to me at the party, but she saw the picture and said that other people told her I was the one who kissed Ivy." Trace threw his hands up. "They swore I'd been after Ivy for a long time!"

"What people?"

Trace shook his head. "I don't know. Ivy of course and Eli the snake. He told Tayla I was the one chasing Ivy, and that Ivy finally fell into my trap. You and I both know it was completely the other way around."

"That's thin." Zack gulped his milk. "But if Tayla won't believe you, then why not, you know, just move on?"

Trace rubbed his eyes. "Because Tayla's the one for me, I know it. It would have been easier to end it when she was off at school, but there's something about her that gets to me. I want her, Zack."

Zack pushed the rest of the sandwich into his mouth, then talked around it. "Well, sorry, bro, but it sounds like she doesn't want you."

"You're right," Trace said, his jaw tight. "Especially since Ivy told her we had sex."

"Whoa."

"Yeah, she told her we had sex." Trace repeated.

Zack squinted one eye. "Did you?"

Zack was too unpredictable to trust with the whole truth. No way was Trace going to open up as he had with Ethan. "No, I didn't have sex with her. Do you think I'm crazy? I just need to think of something to get Tayla back."

"Don't see that happening."

Trace ignored Zack and tried to think of any possible way to make Tayla understand the truth, at least as much truth as he was willing to tell her. Would talking to Tayla's parents help? Could he get them on his side?

It turned out that he couldn't make them see his point of view. They remained squarely in Tayla's camp.

Trace couldn't remember feeling so empty in his life. It was as if his soul was starving. Without Tayla, the world was a morose, barren landscape. Even the early autumn sun was too cold. In brief moments, the pain was so intense that he wished he'd never met Tayla, had never fallen in love with her. Then his thoughts snapped back to searching for a way, any way, that he might possibly win her back to his side.

Deep in thought, he finally decided that he was sick of his own company and drove to the mall to try to lose himself in the crowd. Soon after he entered the double glass doors, he saw Reese and gave him a nod. "Hey."

Reese only glared at him.

"What's up?" Trace asked with a puzzled frown.

"You dirt bag, you're really a piece of shit."

Trace was shocked. He'd gone to the mall to try to feel better about himself not worse. He could have stayed home and called himself every name in the book, plus a few that weren't. "What'd I do?"

"Taking advantage of Ivy like you did."

Trace put his hands up. "Hey, I don't know what you're talking about, man."

"Yeah? Forcing her to have sex with you, explain that."

"What?" Trace's face grew hot. This was getting out of hand. It was bad enough that Ivy had told Tayla. Trace had denied it, desperate to make Tayla understand that Ivy meant nothing to him. That sexual encounter held no more emotion for Trace than a sneeze, so in his mind, it may as well not have happened at all. "I didn't force her to do anything."

"That's not what I heard."

"Well, you heard wrong."

"Or maybe you remember wrong," Reese said with clear disdain. "Ivy's telling everyone what you did, that you forced her into it. You raped her, man."

"Never," Trace declared. "Believe me I didn't force Ivy into anything. She means nothing to me. I love Tayla."

Reese's mouth quirked up in a sardonic smile, "But does Tayla love you? I heard her family won't even let you in the house. They cut you off, just like I'm doing." He pointed a stern finger at Trace. "You shouldn't treat someone as vulnerable as Ivy like that, man. It's not worthy of you."

Trace left the mall disheartened and called Ethan. "Have you applied for a transfer yet?"

"It's ready to send as soon as I know where we're going. Is it Oregon, or Salt Lake?"

"Salt Lake City." Trace swallowed, trying to control his voice. "Looks like it's no more Tayla. So there's nothing for me here."

"Oh, man, sorry about that."

"Looks like I'm just a dirt bag around here. Ivy's lies have backed me to the wall."

"The transfer should go through in a couple of weeks at most, probably sooner."

"Sooner the better." Trace quietly turned in his two weeks' notice and started to make plans for the move.

CHAPTER 35

Rejected by Tayla's family and wide circle of friends, Ivy was running out of options. She had Eli, and Trace, or so she thought. Even though she'd accused him of being cruel, Ivy called Trace several times a day, texting him between calls far into the night. *Talk to me. I need a friend. I understand you. We can fix this. I don't like fighting all the time.*

In desperation, Trace replied, *Stop...please, for the love of God, admit you were just trying to ruin Tayla's and my life together.*

For relief, Trace turned his phone off at night, but when he turned it back on in the morning Ivy's texts pinged onto the screen like machine gun bullets. His only defense was to try ignoring her. He quit answering her calls or replying to her texts altogether, but he couldn't stop her from following him around. When she showed up at the grocery store just seconds after Trace went inside, he left and drove away without the groceries he needed.

Ivy sent him another ominous text. *I am at your apartment, and if you don't talk to me I am going to ruin your life. This is your last chance.*

Trace ignored her and called Ethan. "Two more days, I'm ready to go. How about you, are you ready to get outta here?"

"All set."

"I'm changing my phone number."

"Trouble?"

"Yeah."

"A three letter word?"

"Yeah, I don't think she's crazy enough to drive clear from Meridian to run into me at a grocery store in Salt Lake City, but I don't want her to know where I am. You haven't told anyone, have you?"

"Relax. Only people from my work and my family know where I'm going, and as far as they know, it's just me leaving. I haven't told anyone we're going together."

"Good. I'm ready to cut all my ties here and start a new life."

"I'm with you, man."

Salt Lake City opened a whole new world of possibilities. Trace saw the changing colors of leaves on the trees as predicting a bright future. Trace soon found a new job in sales that was flexible enough to work well with his reserve military duties, and the University of Utah offered great medical training that he was confident he could fit in around his job. With high hopes, he applied for his medical program.

To his surprise, he discovered that not only did he like sales, but he was really good at it. His new manager, Christian Phillips, was a decent guy who had some of the same interests as Trace, and they soon developed a friendship. They both like watching sports on TV, so occasionally got together after work to cheer their team through the big screen TV at Trace and Ethan's new apartment.

Trace's new phone number was blessedly silent. Even sales calls were tiny annoyances after what he'd put up with from Ivy. The loss of Tayla still hurt, but he didn't think of her all day every day anymore. Things were going so well that Trace didn't suspect the worst trouble he could imagine was headed his way. Because he'd dared to leave Ivy, she would have her revenge.

CHAPTER 36

Ivy waited for everyone to leave the house on Thursday, September 15 before calling the Ada County Sheriff's Department at 10:32 am. "Hello?" she said to the voice that answered the phone, making her words sound small and scared. "I want to report…I was raped."

After giving her address, Ivy hung up with a satisfied smile. This should get Trace's attention. He'd be sorry he dared move away, as if that would keep her out of his life. She'd found the perfect political window to cry "rape" with all the #metoo claims around. *Why not, me too?* Why should she care that for every false accusation like hers, many police hours would be wasted and a real rape victim will have to wait for justice.

Officer Ted Holden had been promoted to head of the sex crime unit. When he and female officer Kate Redden were dispatched to Ivy's address to take her statement, Holden's stomach clenched. His daughter Chloe hadn't spoken to him since that terrible night with Ivy. He never wanted to see Ivy Greene again, but couldn't think of a way to excuse himself from the case without giving himself away. He let Redden lead the way up the steps to the home on Whisper Cove Drive. When Ivy pulled the door open, dread seeped into Holden's soul, warning him that this encounter couldn't lead to anything good.

Ivy's eyes went wide at the sight of her visitors, then narrowed as she smiled.

"Good morning, Ms. Greene, I'm Detective Holden and this is Officer Redden," Holden said, trying to moderate the contempt in his voice.

"Hello." Ivy held out her hand. Redden shook it while Holden brushed past. Ivy showed them a cozy room just off the kitchen where a wall of uncovered windows allowed warm sunlight in. Holden made his way to a comfortable overstuffed couch while Redden walked across the room to sit in a chair next to an end table.

Redden shuffled a couple of forms to the top of her clipboard, then carefully asked, "You called because you were raped, is that correct?"

Ivy lowered her gaze. "Yes."

"Can we call someone for you?"

"No, that's ok," Ivy shyly answered.

"Do you need any medical attention?" Redden's voice was soft and comforting. "I can ride to the hospital with you if you'd like me to."

"No, I'm alright. I don't want to go to the hospital."

"Ivy, after we take your statement you'll need to have a rape kit done," Redden insisted. "It's very important to get all the physical evidence we can."

Ivy sighed. "Uh...it happened in June, so it won't do any good at this point."

"Why did you wait so long to report it, Ivy?"

"I was so embarrassed and ashamed. I didn't want anyone to know. He made me feel so dirty, and I was afraid he'd hurt me if I said anything."

"Tell me the date and the time the rape occurred, Ivy."

"It was June 26th, 2016, and it was, I think around 2:30 in the morning."

"Let me clarify," Redden said, leaning forward. "Was it the early morning of June 26th, or the early morning of June 27th?"

"Well, I went to his apartment around 12:30, so I guess it would have been the early morning of the 27th," Ivy recalled. Redden proceeded to take Ivy's statement of the alleged rape. Holden didn't believe a word of it.

Redden asked, "Can you identify who raped you, Ivy?"

"Yes, he...was a friend, at least I thought he was. Trace Aragon raped me."

"So you know him, correct?"

"Yes. We've known each other for a long time."

Recognizing the name, Holden jumped in with a question. "Did the rape happen here at your place?"

"No, we were at his apartment."

"We'll need the address." Redden stated.

Redden took the information and moved on. Trying not to upset Ivy, she carefully asked, "Can you describe where it happened in Trace's apartment?"

"His bedroom." She sniffled and continued. "He'd just moved into his new apartment, and I was helping him unpack some of his things."

"Can you describe his bedroom for me?" Redden inquired.

She recalled. "I remember his bed was black, and he had a couple of black night stands that didn't match, and a big ugly brown chair with a floor lamp next to it."

Redden scooted to the edge of her chair to ask the next question. "Can you remember anything else about the room?"

"Well, there were some photos on his night stands and...oh, we hung some Star Wars posters on his wall."

Holden asked the next question. "What were you wearing at the time?"

Ivy swiveled toward him and snapped, "What does that matter? He raped me!"

Holden leaned back, weary of her playacting, with which he was all too familiar from his previous encounters with her.

Redden intervened. "We need all the evidence possible. The more details you can give us, the better, that's all."

Ivy sighed and rolled her eyes at Redden. "Okay, okay... I was wearing a blue flowered cotton blouse that buttoned up the front with white shorts and white sandals."

Holden made a note, then asked, "Did you save the clothes you were wearing?"

Ivy innocently replied, "No. Should I have?"

"Absolutely," Holden said. "Your clothes might have had his DNA, which would be evidence."

"What about Trace, what was he wearing?" Redden asked.

Ivy's eyes bounced around the room then answered, "Jeans with a T-shirt. His belt was brown, I noticed it because of the New York Yankees buckle, and he had on the stupid baseball hat he always wears."

Redden continued writing and stated, "Let's start from the beginning. Tell us what happened."

"Well...he invited me over to his apartment when he got off work. It was late. When I got to his apartment, we went to his bedroom and watched TV, put up posters, and unpacked boxes for a while. We talked about his girlfriend and things we had in common. We joked around, and then started kissing a little bit. That led to Trace making sexual advances toward me. I thought he was kidding at first, but when he kept pushing, I told him to stop. Then he threw me on the bed, grabbed my wrist, and held it over my head with his right hand, unbelted his pants with his left hand, then pulled my shorts to my knees and raped me. I tried to push him off but he was too strong."

Redden looked at Ivy with concern, "Ivy this next question might be uncomfortable for you, but I have to ask."

Holden stood. "I need to run out to the patrol car for a second. I'll be right back."

Redden knew that Holden was politely excusing himself so she could ask a personal question. "We need to know, did he penetrate you?"

Ivy looked surprised and answered innocently. "What do you mean?"

Redden asked, "Did Trace force you to have sexual intercourse with him?"

Ivy put her hands over her eyes and began to cry. "Yes. I told him to stop over and over. I was so scared because he was hurting me."

"Did you have any physical injuries from the attack?"

"My wrists hurt afterwards and I had bruises on my right arm and my thighs."

"You're safe now," Redden stated. "We'll get you the help you need."

Holden tapped on the door, and then let himself in. When he walked past Ivy, his face turned away from Redden, he glanced at Ivy with repulsion.

Ivy stared back at him with loathing, but she had a mission and needed Holden to help her accomplish it.

Holden resumed his seat and asked, "Was there anyone else in the apartment besides the two of you?"

"Maybe," Ivy replied. "I think his roommate Zack was there, but I didn't want to scream because I was embarrassed and afraid."

Although Ivy's performance of a young woman suffering shame, embarrassment, and fear was good, Holden knew how deceitful she was. Yet, if he challenged her story, it could open up the past and bring a world of hurt down on his head. Even if no one truly believed her story about him, doubt would follow him wherever he went.

Then there was Chloe. He got reports from his sister-in-law, but desperately missed seeing his daughter. He'd give up anything if he could undo the pain he'd caused his little girl. But he had no way of going back in time to right that terrible wrong, and no way of knowing if she would continue keeping her silence about what happened that terrible night.

Holden shifted in his seat. "You need to come down to the Sheriff's Department where we can take a formal statement."

"Why? I just told you what happened!"

Officer Redden gently touched Ivy's wrist. "I know, but we need a formal statement. So would it be okay if we drive you to the station?"

"I guess so. Let me get my things."

As Holden and Redden left with Ivy, Holden couldn't help wondering what Ivy was up to.

CHAPTER 37

Ivy helped to compile a list of proposed witnesses against Trace. Then Holden unearthed Trace's Salt Lake City address and phone number and called for an interview.

Not knowing that he wasn't obligated to talk to the police, Trace agreed to speak with Holden without even knowing what it was about. Trace learned too late that if law enforcement asks to talk to an individual, they're most likely gathering evidence for a case, which could be against the person they wish to interview, and anything said may be used as evidence. The police are permitted to use lying, trickery, and other types of coercive methods to obtain a confession from a suspect.

Holden's first call to Trace was answered with a magnanimous, "Hello?"

"Hello, is this Trace Aragon from Meridian, Idaho?"

After a brief pause, Trace responded, "Yes…who's this?"

"Detective Holden from the Ada County Sheriff's Department, do you remember me from your break-in a while ago?"

Relieved that it might be good news about recovering his stolen property, Trace quickly responded, "Yes, I remember. Did you find out who broke into our apartment?"

"We're still working on that, but I have a few questions I'd like to ask you if that's okay?"

"Sure. What?"

"When did you move away from Meridian?"

"A couple of weeks ago, why?"

"Just following up on some information I need, that's all. Why did you leave Meridian?

"Personal reasons."

Holden's voice grew stern. "What were the personal reasons, Trace?"

Irritated by the question, Trace answered, "I don't think it's any of your business why I moved. Did you find my stuff?"

Shocked at the abrupt answer, Holden's voice pitched the next question without pause. "Do you know Ivy Greene?"

Trace's heart fell into his stomach. He spit out the word, "Yes."

"Do you know her very well?"

Trace swallowed. "We hung out. Why?"

"Have you seen or talked to her lately?'

"No. I moved, remember?"

"Did you ever date her?"

"No, we just hung out sometimes."

"Did you ever hang out alone with her at your apartment?" Holden pressed.

"No. I had a girlfriend, so we always hung out with friends, never alone. Where's this going, Detective?"

"Ivy Greene has come forth and accused you of raping her on June 27, 2016."

Trace went silent with shock. He'd never expected this. What should he say? How much trouble would he bring down if he admitted that he and Ivy had sex? The lie he'd told his friends was at the front of his mind, so he blurted, "We've never even been together that way."

Holden cleared his throat. "Where were you at 2:30 am on June 27, 2016?"

Trace thought desperately. "I don't remember, that was a few months ago. I probably worked late that night, came home and went to bed. I was on graves, and usually didn't get home until after midnight."

"Can anyone verify you were home asleep?"

Trace's voice rose. "My roommate, maybe, but he might have been working, too. He worked crazy shifts. You can call him, but like I said, it was a long time ago. How are we supposed to remember that?"

"What's your roommate's name?"

Trace wasn't sure if he should give out that information, but didn't dare refuse to answer. "Zack Becker."

"Do you have a phone number for him, Trace?"

"Nope. After I moved we didn't keep in touch anymore so I deleted it from my contacts."

Holden wasn't getting much information, and frankly, he didn't believe this kid raped Ivy anyway. Holden didn't tell Trace that he wasn't buying Ivy's story, or that she was trouble, through and through. Holden wanted to be done with her once and for all, so he politely ended the call with, "I'll be in touch if I need any more information from you." Holden hung up.

Trace was furious at the lies Ivy told to cause him this trouble. He had no idea she'd go to such lengths for revenge.

Holden called Ivy. "After investigating the accused, we won't be pressing charges of rape. For lack of evidence, we don't plan on pursuing your case any further."

"Oh, no?" Ivy shouted. "Do you remember the night Chloe found us in bed? You're a pedophile, and you're on the police force. You made me have sex with you. I didn't want to, but you were so…well, you know how this will go, right? Oh, and remember Mia? She's a witness. So is Chloe." Ivy's voice turned persuasive. "So I know you'll do the right thing. You'd better believe I won't hesitate telling on you, Ted. Now go and arrest Trace for raping me."

Shaken by her threat, Holden had no doubt that Ivy would follow through. Disgusted at the way she twisted the situation to her advantage and sick with fear at the hold she had over him, he sat back in his chair and picked up the police report. Even if he arrested Trace, it didn't mean a court would convict the young man. Holden could go ahead with the arrest and the boy could still get off, but Holden had to have some reason for the arrest, even if it was too thin to hold up in court.

Holden re-read the list of friends to interview. Perhaps one of them would offer some small thing for which to apprehend Trace. Hopefully that would get Ivy off his back. As he read through more information, stalling to put off the distasteful duty Ivy had dumped on him, he realized that he hadn't checked Trace's employment records at Grammar Biotech. He should at least verify Trace's work schedule.

When he called the company, he discovered that Trace was, in fact, in town working on the 26 of June until 12:00 am as he'd told Holden. *So far so good, nothing dubious here.*

Next, Holden got a warrant to have both Ivy and Trace's cell phones pinged, and their historical phone data retrieved, which proved that both Trace and Ivy's cell phones were at the same location in the early morning hours of the 27th.

Holden sat up. This changed the picture. Maybe Trace hadn't been truthful about Ivy being at his apartment after all. His and Ivy's cell phones were together, which made it extremely likely that the two of them had been together, too. This was sufficient circumstantial evidence to make a case and an arrest. After that, it would be up to the prosecutor.

CHAPTER 38

Following up on a list of Trace's friends, Holden began calling. "Hello, Zack. This is Detective Holden with the Ada County Sheriff's Department. How are you today?"

Zack's cautious reply was, "Fine."

"I'm calling because I think you may have some information on a case I'm investigating. I'd like to visit with you. When are you available?"

"I'm working today until 4:00."

"Where do you work?"

"Umm...at Ridley's over on Meridian Road."

"Great. I can meet you in the parking lot around 4:15, if that works."

"Yeah," Zack replied, then hung up as if his phone were on fire.

Holden arrived at Ridley's and found Zack pacing in the parking lot. When Holden invited Zack to join him in his patrol car, Zack glanced around, rubbing his palms against his pant legs.

"This shouldn't take long," Holden assured him.

Zack climbed in the passenger seat, closed the door, and tried to roll down the window.

"The windows are locked," Holden explained.

Zack rubbed his hands over his knees. "What do you want to talk to me about?"

Holden explained about Ivy's accusation, then asked, "Were you home at 2:30 am, June 27, 2016?"

Zack rubbed his forehead. "I don't know. Geez that was a long time ago."

"Do you remember Ivy coming over?"

"No, I was probably asleep at that time, like most people."

"Did you see her car at the apartment earlier that night?"

Zack shrugged and picked at his fingernails. "I don't know what car she drives."

"Alright, then, did you see a white Honda Accord in the parking lot?"

Zack put a finger to his mouth, worrying at a cuticle with his teeth. Looking miserable, he moved his finger to say, "Well, maybe, I'm not sure. It might have been there."

His voice full of patience, Holden urged, "Think back. Maybe it was parked close to Trace's car."

Zack gave up on the ragged cuticle and pushed his hand through his hair, his knee bouncing. "I think I did see a white car. Maybe it was a Honda."

"Did you hear Ivy scream or shout at any time that night?"

"No." Zack stared out the windshield, then out his side window before adding in a softer voice, "Not really."

"Not really?" Holden asked, lifting an eyebrow. "So you aren't sure? Do you think you might have heard her trying to scream?"

Zack looked around the car as if seeking an escape hatch. "I'm not sure." He shrugged. "If she was there I might have heard her."

Holden made a note, then turned toward Zack and asked, "Zack, has Trace ever lied to you?"

Zack snorted. "He's always lying about shit."

"So Trace lies?"

Zack shrugged. "Who doesn't?"

"Are you aware, Zack, that 95% of all rape victims are raped by people they know?"

"Huh," Zack grunted, "no." Zack shrugged again. This kid was so edgy that Holden could almost read his mind. *Whatever you say, officer.*

"So, then Trace could have raped Ivy, maybe?" Holden asked, not liking his indecisive tone. Zack's nervousness was affecting him.

Zack glanced up at the headliner, then back down, avoiding Holden's gaze. "Well…I don't think he would, but I guess he could have."

Holden straightened in his seat, wishing he was at an interrogation table so he could put his elbows on a firm surface and lean toward Zack to force eye contact. "Did you two get along?"

"Sure."

"Was Trace ever aggressive toward you?"

"No, nothing like that," Zack answered, glancing sideways at Holden for the first time. Then his eyes slid away. "I mean, we argued some, but we got along for the most part. Then he moved out and went to live with some other friend."

Holden took a stern approach with his next question. "Have you been truthful with me today?"

"Yes," Zack said, fingering the door handle.

Holden leaned forward, studying Zack's profile. "If I find out you've lied to me about anything, I'll be coming back to arrest you."

Zack's fingers tightened on the handle. "I swear, I haven't lied, I swear!"

"Thank you, Zack," Holden said. He made another note. "Those are all my questions for now."

Zack jumped out of the car and hurried away without looking back.

CHAPTER 39

The next person on Holden's interview list was Tayla Dean. Holden grabbed a cup of yesterday's coffee and sat at his desk. He took a sip, shivered at the taste, and shuffled through his paper work on the Greene rape looking for Tayla Dean's phone number. When he found it, he picked up the phone and dialed.

When Tayla answered, he said, "Good morning, Tayla. My name is Ted Holden, I'm a detective from the Ada County Sheriff's Department. Do you have a few minutes I can talk with you?"

"I'm really very busy," Tayla said. "I've got to get to a class shortly, but I have a minute."

Do you know Ivy Greene and Trace Aragon?"

Bewildered Tyala answered, "Yes. Ivy used to be my friend, and Trace used to be my boyfriend."

"You went to school with both of them, is that correct?"

"Yes."

"How long were you and Trace together?"

Tayla softly replied, "All of high school, a little over three years, and a couple of years after."

"Have you heard anything about Ivy's rape accusation against Trace?"

"Yes. Everyone's talking about it. They want to know what I think, but I'm not sure of the details."

"What have you heard?"

"Just that Ivy says Trace raped her. That's all."

"Do you think Trace is capable of rape?"

Tayla's answer was quick and firm. "No way! If you want to know the truth, that doesn't sound like Trace at all. Ivy told me that she and Trace had sex at his apartment, and after that, someone took a photo of them kissing at a party. Why would she kiss him after it happened if he'd really raped her? That doesn't make sense. Anyway, Trace and I fought over him cheating on me with Ivy, and I broke up with him and I no longer consider Ivy a friend."

"Who texted you the photo of them kissing?"

"My friend Eli Cole."

"I'd like to get a copy of that photo if possible." Holden insisted.

"I can forward it to you."

"Thanks, that would be great" Holden replied. "Do you remember what weekend Ivy said they had sex?"

"Um...it would have been, let me think, the last weekend in June; because she said it was the weekend Trace couldn't come to my parents' cabin for our summer party, because he had to work."

"So, June 27, 2016, he would have been home or working and possibly with Ivy, right?"

"Well, all I can say is that he wasn't with me."

"Tayla, were you and Trace intimate?"

Tayla shyly replied, "Yes."

"Was he ever rough with you or made you do things you didn't want to do?"

Tayla's reply was adamant. "Never!"

"Did Trace drink a lot?"

"He drank at some of the parties we went to, but we all did. Why?"

"I'm just wondering if he had a drinking problem. Sometimes when people drink, they get a little out of control. Do you think that may have been the case with Ivy and Trace?"

"I don't know. He never drank that much when I was around him."

Holden pitched his next question. "You never thought he would cheat on you, either, right?"

"No," Tayla admitted. "I didn't."

"Did Trace ever lie to you?"

"What do you mean?"

"Did he lie to you about seeing other girls?"

"Well, he didn't tell me about Ivy."

"So he does lie?"

"I guess so."

"I have just one more question," Holden said. "When was the last time you talked to Trace?"

"I haven't talked to him for quite awhile."

"Can you give me an estimate?"

Tayla sat silent in thought, "It's been months, I'd have to check my planner to be more precise."

"Please call and let me know if you can think of anything else that could be helpful. Thanks for your time, Tayla." Holden gave her his number and concluded the interview.

CHAPTER 40

Not wanting any trouble with the law, Trace agreed to talk to Holden again. He was too embarrassed to ask for help, from his family or anyone else, and didn't realize the importance of having personal legal representation from the very beginning of any legal questioning.

He was scared. Should he change his story and admit to having sex with Ivy? If he did that now, would his earlier denial spiral out of control and land him in jail? He'd heard jail stories that terrified him to the point that he could scarcely eat. So he decided to stick to his lie, justifying it because he hadn't raped Ivy and the sex meant nothing to him anyway. He pinned his hopes on the naive belief that the justice system would prevail. *It will all work out. I'll be found innocent, because I am.*

"I've done some investigating," Holden told Trace over the phone. "I've verified with your previous employer at Grammar Biotech that on the night of the 26th of June, you were at work like you said you were. Things were looking good until I 'pinged' both your and Ivy's cell phones, and they were at the same location that night at 2:30 am. So my conclusion is that you're lying to me about Ivy being at your apartment."

Trace paced the floor as his gut twisted in knots.

Holden's voice grew stern. "You need to tell me the truth. I have witnesses, and I can have you arrested for obstruction of justice for lying to me."

Trace's chest was nearly exploding from his pounding heart. "Ivy was always coming over, sitting in my parking area," he explained. "Sometimes she'd be there when I came home from work. That's probably why the phones showed up at the same place."

"So you're telling me Ivy was not inside your apartment?"

In misguided self-protection mode, Trace declared, "No! I worked the late shift until 12:00 am."

"She claims you raped her at 2:30 am in your bedroom."

"She's lying!" Trace insisted. His knees trembled so badly that he sank down onto a chair. "I moved to Salt Lake because she's been stalking me. I had to get away from her. You can ask my friends. You can read her texts to me if you want."

Holden wouldn't admit that he could sympathize with Trace. Ivy was a piece of work. But from the inconsistencies uncovered in his investigation and interview information, things weren't adding up to equal Trace's innocence. "I'll ask them, believe me, and if you're lying, I'll arrest you for obstruction of justice and you'll go to jail for that, too."

Suddenly faint, Trace dropped his head to his knees. If he admitted the truth now, he was sure to find himself behind bars. Even if he insisted it was all Ivy's idea to come over and we had sex, Holden probably wouldn't believe him now anyways. Trace let out an involuntary moan of despair.

"You okay?" Holden asked.

"Yeah." Trace lifted his head and wiped his brow with the back of his hand. *I just lied again. I'm not okay. I'm having a heart attack or something.*

Holden used his interrogation tactics training to continue drilling Trace over and over about his answers. Although intimidated, the threat of being thrown in jail and abused by inmates made Trace stick to his original story. "I'm telling you that Ivy has never been in my apartment and I did not rape her."

As Holden continued hammering questions at Trace in an effort to get him to confess, he couldn't help thinking of the burglary call he got a while back at Trace's apartment. Something wasn't right with all of this. Knowing Ivy as he did, he had plenty of reservations about her ability to tell the truth. Maybe both of them were lying to him.

The tension was plain in Trace's voice when he finally said, "If I'm not under arrest, stop calling me." He hung up the phone and hoped the whole mess would go away. *Was that even possible?* He'd lied to Holden about Ivy ever being in his apartment, as well as the fact that they had sex that night. He gripped his head with his hands, wishing he'd never met Ivy Greene.

Holden felt the same way, particularly when he called Ivy to update her on his investigation and she said, "If you don't arrest Trace soon, I'll go straight to the police and tell them that their sex crimes detective raped a high school girl, and you'd better believe that my story will be better than yours."

Sick with regret, Holden hung up. He believed her.

CHAPTER 41

Trace answered his phone on the morning of February 1, 2017, to hear the dreaded voice of Detective Holden say, "Trace Aragon, you need to turn yourself in to the Ada County Sheriff's Department by Friday the 3rd of February, no later than 2:00 pm, or a warrant will be issued for your arrest."

Trace's heart dropped so fast he felt dizzy. "What are you talking about?"

"Trace, are you listening to me? You need to turn yourself in for charges of rape or a warrant for your arrest will be issued, do you understand?" Holden sternly stated.

Trace hung up, his shocked mind paralyzed. Frozen with fear, he stared at the wall as if it were the last day of his life. *Why couldn't Holden see he was innocent?* If he had to turn himself in for a false rape accusation, it was possible that he could be mistakenly found guilty and sent to jail for a crime he didn't commit. He might never get out again. He'd rather be dead. What would this do to his mom, to Grandma?

He took in a painful breath and closed his watery eyes. *This is all going to work out. They'll find the truth about my innocence, and this will all be behind me. If only I hadn't lied to the cop.*

When he opened his eyes, fear and panic still ruled his heart and mind. It took a couple of hours before Trace was able to make himself tell Christian that he had to leave work for a few days to face a false accusation.

Christian's eyes went wide. "Whoa, buddy, what'd you do?"

"Nothing! This girl says I raped her, but I didn't. She's just out for revenge."

"Some revenge," Christian muttered.

"Yeah, tell me about it."

When Trace told Ethan about the phone call from Holden, Ethan gazed at him somberly. "I wish you hadn't lied to that cop."

Full of despair, Trace said, "I know! But it's too late now."

Two days passed faster than Trace thought possible. He got in his car and headed to Meridian, the drive taking no time at all, because all too soon, he was parked in front of the Sheriff's Department. He managed to get out of his car, but his feet were suddenly paralyzed. Shaking uncontrollably and fighting back tears, he stared at the building. What would happen to him in there? Trace's inner little boy needed his mother or grandma to console him, but they didn't even know where he was. He had to do this himself. Taking in a shuddering breath, he reminded himself that he was innocent, so everything would surely turn out okay. Clinging to this thought, he was able to move to the glass doors. Wiping his tears away, he stood tall, opened the door, and walked inside. He turned himself in and was booked for rape based on circumstantial evidence. When asked if he wanted an attorney, he still believed he'd be found innocent, so said he didn't need one.

Once in custody, Trace was escorted to a small soundproof room with three chairs and a rectangular metal table, isolating Trace in cold, unfamiliar surroundings. He'd never been in trouble with the law before. As he waited two hours for fingerprinting and a mug shot, anger at the circumstances that brought him here warred with confusion and fear. When he finally stood before the unforgiving camera lens, it captured an anguished face so drained of color that it scarcely resembled the confident young man everyone once knew.

He was given an orange jumpsuit to wear. As he pulled it over his shaking legs, the smell of chemical laundry soap made him sick. After he was put into a cell, the sound of the door locking behind him triggered a pulse of claustrophobia. He slammed his eyes shut and breathed deeply, then gagged. Unable to hold back the tears, he collapsed onto the thin mattress on his bunk. Some of the jailhouse guards he'd gone to school with passed his cell, looked at him with disgust, and made scornful comments as if he'd already been convicted.

This wasn't supposed to happen. It wasn't what he expected. He thought his innocence would be recognized by now, that he'd be told it was all a mistake and he could go home. *Is my life over?*

Trace was broken, alone, and ashamed for a crime he hadn't committed.

He wasn't offered anything to eat until the next morning. In retrospect, the 30 hours spent in jail was nothing compared to what he was about to endure over the course of the next several months, a trial that would affect the rest of his life.

Trace hated dragging his family into the horror of this false accusation, but he finally called his dad for help. Dad arrived at the jail with raised eyebrows, his mouth slightly open in disbelief. "What happened?"

"It's all a mistake, Dad."

His father rubbed his face with a weary hand. "Well, son, I don't know how I'm supposed to manage to scrape together $20,000 for bail or even $2000 for a bail bondsman. You'll just have to wait until they arraign you on Tuesday."

In despair, Trace protested, "Dad, please, I can't stay in here that long."

"The only thing I can do is call your grandparents and see if they can come up with the money."

Trace knew his grandparents wouldn't let him sit in jail. He didn't want them to know he was there, but he saw no other way to escape.

Once bail was posted, Trace dragged himself outside, glad to be free but saddened that his grandparents were the ones waiting for him to come through the jailhouse doors. As soon as he caught sight of them, he hurried to explain. "I'm so sorry, it's not what…" he stopped, choking back tears, his throat so thick he couldn't speak.

"It's alright," they said, wrapping him in a warm hug, Grandpa on one side, Grandma on the other. "We'll make it through this."

"I'm sorry you had to pay so much money."

Grandma tightened her hug. "Don't worry Trace, it's alright."

Infused with hope from their love, Trace hugged them back, the need for tears gone in the warmth of their embrace.

When he pulled his phone out of his returned belongings and powered it up, notifications flowed in from Twitter, Facebook, and Instagram. Text messages and missed calls let him know that a social media campaign had been launched against him. Trace stared in despair at his arrest posted all over the Internet, including an image of his mug shot with the message, "Trace Aragon is a RAPIST…women, look out for this man. You are all in danger of Trace Aragon." Ivy's fifteen minutes of fame cost Trace dearly in the social media-crazed age, where people are quick to pass judgment and slow to research facts.

Not all the avalanche of comments was bad. In fact, most of the posts defended Trace's good character and expressed belief of his innocence. Yet there were many negative posts from strangers, as well as people Trace had thought were friends, making him out to be a monster who'd repeatedly raped women.

Trace tried to defend himself, but no matter what he said, his circle of friends shrank, leaving him shunned and secluded.

CHAPTER 42

Ivy was assigned a trained victim's advocate named Sharon to help her healing process and possible trial. Giddy with the new attention focused on her, Ivy was enjoying her contrived rape victim status as she latched onto mild mannered Sharon, who wore modest clothing, sensible heels, and kept her brown hair short.

Sharon confided to Ivy that she'd become an advocate because she'd been married for 23 years to a controlling, violent man. After they divorced, he came to her home one night and raped her. When Sharon began talking about the resulting trauma of that terrible night, Ivy interrupted, "This isn't about you, it's about me. I was the one raped here. What's going to happen to Trace?"

Sharon stared at Ivy for a moment, then said, "I don't know. That's up to the attorneys, and the court, and depends on..."

"You should know!" Ivy yelled. "Why won't you tell me? You're supposed to help me. That's your job." Well-practiced tears sprang from Ivy's eyes. "I don't have anyone. I haven't any support from my mother, I haven't talked to her for a long time, and now I'm afraid of what Trace might do to me now that I told about him."

"It's okay," Sharon said, awkwardly patting Ivy's shoulder. "I'll help find the resources you need, and I'll help you fill out any needed paperwork. I'll be by your side the whole way."

CHAPTER 43

Trace realized the mistake he'd made, of not hiring an attorney at the first call from Detective Holden. Trace hadn't known that citizens have the right in any circumstances to decline to speak to law enforcement without an attorney. He was sick with regret that he hadn't just hung up the phone on Detective Holden and called an attorney.

Trace finally realized with stark, frightening clarity that his innocence may not be proven naturally through the course of the investigation. He'd trusted the justice system, which is usually a good thing, but discovered that it's safer to recognize its faults. The system's job of putting guilty people in jail and protecting the innocent wasn't failsafe. Especially in rape cases, the saying, "innocent until proven guilty" didn't seem to apply. Even months after the alleged event, a simple statement by the "victim," even without hard evidence to back it up, could be accepted and result in a harsh conviction.

Being wrongly accused of a rape meant the real possibility of serving serious time. Without a good defense attorney, Trace faced the real likelihood of being found guilty.

To his detriment, he'd lied to a detective and hadn't hired a lawyer before questioning. His best chance, now, was to find a good defense attorney.

Trace's family searched online and asked everyone they knew for referrals until they finally found Elizabeth Gowen, a highly respected defense attorney. She had more than 20 years of legal experience and is one of the state's premier trial lawyers. She has defended thousands of clients against criminal charges including false rape allegations. She is highly regarded in the legal community for her tenacious defense of clients and her numerous charge dismissals and acquittals she has obtained for her clients.

Gowen understands the sensitive nature of sex crimes cases and she understands that self-purported "rape victims" are not always victims. Using her experience and knowledge of the law, she assured Trace and his family that she will aggressively defend Trace and make every effort to protect his freedom, his record, and his rights.

CHAPTER 44

Gowen hired a 32-year veteran FBI agent turned private detective, Jay McIntosh. With Trace's help, they compiled a list of Trace's peers as character witnesses.

McIntosh moved quickly to schedule interviews. He called Ivy's friend, Sara Summers, who'd known Trace for a long time, and asked for an interview. Without knowing what it was about, she replied, "I guess that would be fine."

"I can come to you."

"That would be helpful. I leave for school at 10:00 and have to work right after, so if you could come before then?"

"Great, text me your address and I'll see you in the morning."

McIntosh's demeanor was pleasant as he sat down with Summers and turned on his recorder. "For the record, I'm Jay McIntosh, working with attorney Elizabeth Gowen. Would it be okay if I record this conversation?"

Summers raised one shoulder, and then let it drop. "I guess."

"This might be a bit hard for you, but I need your truthful insight about a few things." McIntosh nudged the recorder closer to her. "Do you know Ivy Greene?"

"Yes."

"How about Trace Aragon?"

"Yes, I know them both."

"Are you aware of the rape accusation Ivy has made against Trace?"

"No! Ivy claims she was raped by Trace?" Summers shook her head. "I don't believe that for a minute. Ivy's always had a crush on him and wanted to make Tayla and him break up. Ivy told me all about her plan, about how she seduced him into having sex with her. She didn't say anything about him raping her." Summers suddenly stopped talking and glanced anxiously at McIntosh.

"Go on," he urged with a warm smile. "You're doing fine."

"Ivy told me on several occasions that she was going to get Trace at any cost. I don't know why Ivy's doing this to Trace now. Sometimes she gets crazy and does stupid things. One time she started a fight with a friend and later admitted the whole incident was 'for show' and asked me what I thought of her acting skills. But this is the worst thing she's ever done." Summers shook her head. "This is not cool."

McIntosh found the hour-long interview full of promising information, and moved onto Zack Becker with renewed optimism. "Is this Zack Becker?"

"Yes," Zack mumbled into his phone. "Who's this?"

"Jay McIntosh, private investigator. I'm working on a case that involves Trace Aragon. Do you have a minute?"

"Trace's gone now, so why bother?"

"It's an ongoing case," McIntosh explained. "I'm working with the defense, gathering evidence."

"I already told my story to that policeman."

"I'd like you to tell it to me."

Zack sighed. "Well, if you really want to talk to me, I guess I can make time."

When they met, McIntosh's first impression of Zack was that he was rather laid back, perhaps even lazy. He could imagine the young man partying, then sleeping a lot to nurse his hangovers until he absolutely had to go to work in order to buy more beer.

"Would it be okay if I record this conversation?" McIntosh asked. "My notes aren't as good as a recording, and I can go back and refer to it if I need to."

"No problem," Zack replied, lifting his ankle up onto his knee and tugging at his pants hem.

"Let's begin. Do you know Trace Aragon?"

"Yeah, I've known him since junior high."

"Were you friends?"

"Maybe," Zack shrugged. "If you want to know the truth, I always thought he was kind of a pussy."

"How so?"

"I used to push him around pretty good." Zack snorted a laugh. "I tried to get him to fight me in seventh grade and he ran like a little girl."

"So how did you guys wind up being roommates?"

"In high school we started hanging out more and he was, like, more mature. He didn't hold a grudge, I guess. Besides, it saved me some rent money to share the place, you know?"

McIntosh made a note. "Do you know Ivy Greene?"

"Not very well, she was at some of the parties I went to. She used to stop by our place and ask for Trace all the time. Sometimes she wanted to wait for him to get home from work."

"Was Trace glad to see her?"

Zack plopped his foot back down on the floor and laced his fingers. "Sometimes, he liked her, I guess, but he was put off by her just dropping in like that. One night she threw a tantrum when Trace got home from work and he told her she had to leave."

"Were the two of them ever alone in your apartment that you know of?"

"Don't know." Zack said. "I worked weird schedules."

"Do you remember Ivy coming over on the early morning of June 27th around 12:30 am?"

"Like I told the cop, last summer? Really? How am I supposed to remember that? I was probably asleep or maybe at work."

"You don't know?"

Zack looked up, then away. "I didn't write it down, okay?"

"I guess you know Ivy's making a claim against Trace for rape."

Zack sat forward in surprise. "They've really charged him? I thought it was just another one of her stunts to get attention. That sucks for him."

"Can you find out what shift you worked on June 26 and the 27th, 2016?"

"Nope. I'm working at a different job now."

"We'll maybe I can check with your former employer. Would you've been able to hear noises if you were home?"

"Like what noises?"

"Screams for help or a struggle."

"Yeah, of course. The walls are paper thin."

Jay rubbed his chin. "Where were your bedrooms located?"

"Next to each other."

"So you think you might have heard something if Trace was raping Ivy?"

"Probably," Zack replied. "I yelled at Trace to turn his freaking music down often enough." Zack snorted. "Trace didn't rape Ivy. She's just making it all up because she's mad Trace didn't break up with Tayla for her. You know Ivy had a crush on Trace, right?"

"I've been told that. Do you suppose she might have been a little jealous?"

"More than jealous, she was obsessed."

"So do you don't think Trace raped Ivy?"

"I can't see Trace doing anything like that," Zack replied. "He's a little hard to get along with sometimes, but he wouldn't do that."

"One last question, would you consider Trace a trusted friend?"

Zack spread his hands. "If I didn't trust him, I wouldn't have roomed with him, would I?"

"Good answer." McIntosh gathered his things. "Thanks for your time, Zack."

McIntosh's next interview was with Ethan Harrison. McIntosh found valuable unspoken information from reactions to questions and body language during interviews, so after a six-hour drive, he arrived at the Sprint store Ethan managed. Glad to get out and stretch his limbs, he walked in the store, introduced himself as the man who'd called to set up this interview, and shook hands with Ethan. "Is there somewhere we can talk for a few minutes?"

"Come into the back office."

McIntosh followed Ethan and got permission to record the conversation. "I'm here to ask a few questions about your friend Trace."

"Sure." Ethan leaned back in his chair. "What can I tell you, besides that he's a great guy?"

"How long have you known him?"

"We've been friends since junior high."

"Have you ever known him to be aggressive or violent?"

"No." Ethan shook his head. "As a matter of fact, he was the one who got bullied in school. He always just walked away." Ethan waved his hand through the air. "It used to make me so mad that he let them bullies get away with it."

McIntosh made a note. "Did he have many girlfriends?"

"A few, but he was with Tayla the longest."

"Do you know Ivy Greene?"

"Yes, from school. I didn't care for her much. She's a drama queen, if you know what I mean, always looking for attention. She used to come along to Tayla's family cabin with the rest of us. Ivy had the worst crush on Trace, so when she tried to break Tayla and him up, Tayla stopped inviting her. Trace always tried to avoid Ivy because Tayla would get mad at him." Ethan shook his head. "Trace and I caught Ivy just sitting and waiting at his apartment one night. I have no idea how long she'd been there. Weird, huh?"

"I'd say so. Do you know about her accusation that Trace raped her?"

"Yeah, I do. I feel so bad for him. I know he didn't do it, because it's not in his character at all."

"You've never seen him mistreat a girlfriend?"

"Are you kidding me? He even opens the car door for his grandma."

McIntosh made another note. "I had to ask. That's why I'm here. I need to get as much information about Trace and Ivy as I can."

Ethan stood. "Trace wouldn't rape anyone!"

"So noted," McIntosh replied. "So you'd say that Ivy Greene was obsessed with Trace?"

"Absolutely," Ethan leaned against the wall. "I'd also say she's a little crazy, too. Trace showed me some of the texts she sent him, some making threats."

"You saw the texts personally?"

"Sure did. I told him he needed to report her, but he didn't want to."

"Why not?"

"He's just too nice. Like I said, he's always been that way. He thought she'd just stop and go away."

McIntosh stood. "Thank you for your time. I may need to talk to you again."

"Sure anytime."

McIntosh gathered his things, went to his car, and called Elizabeth. "It's my opinion; Trace's case is easily defendable."

"Good," Elizabeth Gowen replied.

"I'll make copies of my interviews and personally deliver them to Detective Holden when I get back."

"Alright, good work. Thanks, Jay"

CHAPTER 45

McIntosh was soon on his way to the Meridian Sheriff's Department, with the copied interview recordings. He pulled into the Front Street parking lot as close to the main entrance as he could get. Putting the memory stick in his pocket, he walked through the double glass doors and approached the sliding window of the dispatcher. "I'm here to see Detective Holden or Officer Redden."

The officer behind the window pointed down the hall toward a man and woman walking their way. "You're seeing them."

McIntosh nodded and headed toward the female officer, assuming it was Redden. "Hi, I'm Jay McIntosh."

Holden took McIntosh's offered hand while Redden stood straight with her hands behind her back. "Detective Holden, what can I do for you?"

"I'm a private investigator working for attorney Elizabeth Gowen who's representing Trace Aragon." Was it McIntosh's imagination, or did Holden flinch? "I've interviewed a few people who provided valuable information that would be helpful in your investigation." McIntosh pulled the memory stick from his pocket. "I've got an audio copy of their statements here for you and the prosecutor to review."

Holden put his flat palms out toward McIntosh like twin stop signs. "No thanks, we have all we need to prosecute Trace Aragon."

Redden interrupted. "Maybe we should..."

Holden stopped Redden mid-sentence, his voice raised. "Like I said, we have all we need to prosecute him."

McIntosh looked at the device in his hand. What was going on here? "This is valuable information that might change the decision to charge Trace." He pushed the stick closer to Holden.

Holden took a step back and dropped his hands. "Nope. Not interested in hearing anything you have at this time. We have to get back to work. Have a good day." Holden motioned to Redden, and they walked away without looking back.

In a quiet voice Redden asked, "Don't you think we should have taken the recordings? He said they could be useful."

Holden gave Redden a look of worried contempt. "No. Don't question my judgment on this."

McIntosh followed them for a few steps before calling, "Look Holden, I'm not just some rookie Private Investigator. I'm a retired FBI officer, and I've never known an officer of the law to refuse possible evidence on a criminal case. I think you should at least listen to it."

Holden held up a hand as they kept walking until they disappeared around a corner.

McIntosh stared after them, shocked that a police officer wouldn't take crucial evidence in a criminal case.

CHAPTER 46

Three days later, when Trace was formally charged with felony rape, Elizabeth Gowen met with him to discuss his options. "I need to be sure that you understand the severity of this charge," she said. "Rape is an unlawful sexual activity, usually sexual intercourse, or penetration, however slight, of oral, anal, or vaginal openings, carried out forcibly or under threat of injury against a person's will, or with a person beneath a certain age, or incapable of valid consent because of mental illness, mental deficiency, intoxication, unconsciousness, or deception.

"Sexual assault laws usually define it as a felony. Sentences can range from probation to a year to life in prison, depending on circumstances. Some states require a minimum sentence, or withhold probation or early parole. Other states allow judge's discretion on sentencing, including probation. Many states identify different degrees of the crime, determined by a victim's vulnerability, type of force used, and bodily injury.

"In your case, Idaho state law declares that rape is punishable by imprisonment for not less than one year, and may be extended to life at the discretion of the District Judge, who shall pass sentence. Do you understand?"

With an apprehensive glance, Trace answered, "I guess so."

During their lengthy discussion, Trace decided that his best chance was to give full disclosure, which changed the dynamics of the case. He admitted lying to Detective Holden. He explained the true circumstances behind the rape accusation, and his fear of getting in worse trouble if he admitted to having sex with Ivy.

Gowen stared at him with steely eyes. "You should have told me this right at the beginning," she told him sternly. "This information would have changed the way that we conducted our investigation. You may have seriously jeopardized your own defense by withholding this information."

Trace hung his head. "I'm so sorry."

"It's bad enough to lie to the police. How do you expect me to defend you if you're not completely honest with me? You have to tell me everything, is that understood?"

"Yes," Trace pled, "I'm sorry. I'll tell you everything, I promise."

Gowen sighed. "Well, there's nothing to do now but move forward."

Gowen took a new tack and filed for a court date to get all the discovery evidence, including Holden's recorded interviews and witness statements.

"Trace, I want screenshots of all Ivy's texts," Gowen said.

Trace ended up with hundreds of pages of text messages from Ivy.

Do you want to hang out?

I know we are supposed to be together.

I know you love me.

Let's not fight over this.

Why are you doing this? Admit you wanted it, too.

I'm sitting in your parking lot. Let me come up and we can talk.

Tayla doesn't want you anymore. Let's work on us, OK?

This is your last chance to talk to me.

Months and months of texts led up to the point of their consensual sexual encounter. If Trace hadn't cast a derogatory light on his character by lying to Holden, it would have been an easy win. That one fact might have a heavy impact on the jury, who'd take under consideration that this young man lacked honesty, which could sway them to think that despite his protests of innocence, he was capable of lying about rape.

Under serious defense consideration, Gowen could see right through the accusation for what is was. She explained to Trace that false rape accusations, not all, are made by women with narcissistic tendencies and are looking for attention and seeking revenge. She came to the conclusion that Ivy would most likely present her version of the story with dramatic narcissistic flair.

Gowen reassured Trace that she is well seasoned in handling narcissistic behavior disorders and that she understands the drama of high-risk cases that involve narcissists.

While Trace's defense team worked toward their best strategy, Ted Holden labored under pressure from Ivy to make Trace pay for what she claimed he did to her. Holden had hoped that Trace wouldn't have the money to hire a good attorney, which would make it more likely that he'd take a plea deal, which would simplify Holden's role. Ted's problem with Ivy would be temporarily solved, and Ivy would have her revenge.

CHAPTER 47

Letting his workplace know of his situation would be tough, but Trace knew there was no way around it. He sat at his desk, head in his hands, until he heard Christian ask, "Hey, Trace. What's up?"

Expecting support or at least understanding, Trace took Christian aside and unloaded the details of his plight.

"They really charged you with rape?" Christian blurted. "Dude, they don't just charge you with something like that without a reason. They must have something on you."

"No, they don't!"

"Come on, Trace, man up."

From that point on, Christian no longer associated with Trace because he wanted to keep his reputation untainted by the rape accusation. Proving that he wasn't such a good friend after all, he informed the entire workplace of Trace's rape charge.

At first, the Director of Human Resources made a decision to wait for the outcome before taking any action, which gave Trace hope that he wouldn't lose everything good in his life. Then Christian manipulated information to the point that Trace lost his job.

Even without a conviction, Trace's arrest ended his military career and his chance for a college education from military service. After Gowen wrote a letter to Trace's Commanding Officer, a general discharge with honorable circumstances was ordered. Trace's proud commitment to the military was suddenly over. Everything he'd worked so hard to achieve for his future and that of his country was lost to him forever.

Other people Trace thought of as friends were also lost along the way, leaving Trace very alone as he faced the prospect of being found guilty of a crime he didn't commit and sentenced to jail. Long nights led to empty mornings. With no job prospects, his unbearable life seemed best handled by crawling back into bed to lose himself in hours of sleep, the only thing that made the world's unfairness leave him alone for awhile.

Ethan used their years of close camaraderie to console and encourage Trace, but Ethan's work schedule left Trace alone for hours. When he wasn't asleep, Trace suffered in lonely solitude.

CHAPTER 48

Prosecutor Jillian Webb, wasn't interested in Trace's side of the story or his feelings, she'd hoped to clear her cluttered calendar with a quick win, so she offered a plea deal. The rape charge would be reduced to sexual battery with no contest, a Class A misdemeanor. The deal would include probation for up to 24 months with no sex offender registry and no time in jail.

After meeting with Webb, Elizabeth sat Trace down and explained the position Webb was taking. "Webb has her victim, her witnesses, and she feels pretty good about where this will end up if we go before a jury, so she's offering you a plea deal, Trace. You need to know that this plea deal will show on your record as if you had pled guilty to sexual battery."

"But I'm not guilty!"

"Let me finish explaining what sexual battery is. It is an unwanted form of contact with an intimate part of the body, made for purposes of sexual arousal, sexual gratification, or sexual abuse. It may occur whether the victim is clothed or not. The penalty may just be probation, but even the possible fine of up to $2,000.00 and/or jail time of up to a year would be a lot lighter penalty than if you're found guilty."

"I don't want to go to jail!"

"I'll be honest, Trace. I'm also concerned about you going to trial, because even though we have a strong case toward proving Ivy is lying, you also lied. Besides, after reading her statement and seeing her video interview, this girl really scares me. She's a very good liar. I want to keep you out of prison. My advice is that you consider this deal. It's a sure thing, and would likely keep you from a long prison sentence if you were found guilty.

"Still, a sexual battery charge on your record could make your life miserable for a long time." Elizabeth caught Trace's eye. "It's a tough decision, but if you plead not guilty and go to trial, you have a 50/50 chance of being found guilty."

Eyes wet with tears, Trace said in a small voice, "I don't know what to do."

"Talk it over with your family," Elizabeth advised.

After careful deliberation with his family, Trace decided that he was innocent and wanted it proven in court. In spite of what had happened, he still had faith in the system, and now he had an attorney to help him navigate it.

When he announced his decision to plead not guilty, a preliminary hearing was set.

CHAPTER 49

Trace and his mother pulled up to the Ada County Fourth District Courthouse for the preliminary hearing early on June 5, 2017, only to see Ivy and Eli walking up the courthouse steps. Although dressed in a new H&M suit, Eli paled beside Ivy, who looked young and naive in a simple blue dress that covered her knees. Hair clips pulled her shining blond hair back on either side of her head. She looked like an angel, but Trace knew what evil really lurked beneath that innocent disguise. His stomach lurched, and he shivered with a sudden chill.

"Trace?" his mother asked.

"That's Eli with Ivy," Trace explained. "He's the guy that posted all the crap about me on Facebook and Instagram."

"We'll just sit here for a minute," Trace's mother comforted him.

Trembling, Trace said, "I can't believe she's going through with this."

"Take a deep breath. It's going to be alright."

Once the pair was gone, Trace and his mother got out of the car, walked the long path to the broad span of stairs leading to the courthouse doors, he climbed the stairs and stepped inside. Then Trace stopped dead in his tracks.

"What's wrong?"

"I don't know where to go. How am I supposed to know where to go?"

"Easy," his mother said. "Come on. It's this way. Everything will be okay."

When Trace spotted Ethan and three other close friends waiting for him, he greeted them in a voice thick with emotion. "Hey, guys."

With slaps on the back, they walked with him through the security checkpoint. Then they gave him hugs before releasing him into the courtroom where Elizabeth Gowen waited. She escorted him to the defense table beyond the pony wall, which separated the defendant from the spectators. Trace was so relieved to see his grandma stoically seated behind the pony wall that he went to her and gave her a grateful hug. Encouraged by his family and friends, Trace sat down with a little more optimism than he'd had when he woke up that morning.

At trial, the prosecution was charged with proving each element of the alleged offense beyond a reasonable doubt, but the preliminary hearing only required probable cause, or enough evidence to justify a belief that the accused had committed the alleged crime.

Unofficially, each side used the preliminary hearing to check out the other's evidence, which tended to be only a portion of what they had, rather than showing the whole hand. Because it's not required, the defense often doesn't offer any evidence at all.

Trace and Gowen had settled in at the defense table when Trace turned to see Ivy and Eli enter the courtroom, Gowen leaned in to whisper, "Is that the only person coming with Ivy? Why isn't any of her family present?"

Trace shrugged. "Don't know."

Elizabeth straightened and wrote something on her notepad.

Ivy glanced around the courtroom. With tears of persuasion running down her face, she announced, "I don't know where to go. Where's my victim's advocate?"

When Webb tried to calm her, Ivy muttered in alarm, "I'm fearful for my life! He has to go to jail!"

The bailiff cautioned her to be quiet. When Ivy obeyed, he announced the Honorable Judge Donner, a balding man in his 50's with a comfortable paunch who entered the courtroom and sat on the bench with no jury present.

"Is everyone ready this morning?" Donner asked. Not waiting for an answer, he continued, "I've reviewed the evidence of this case, and have decided there is enough to support a reasonable belief that a crime of rape has occurred, and that Trace Aragon committed the crime of rape. Trace Aragon, you've been charged with one count of felony rape, and I am binding this over for trial."

Trace looked at Gowen, hopelessly confused. He was sorrier than he could say that he hadn't been truthful from the start. Trace wished with all his heart and soul that he could wake up from this living nightmare and it would all be over.

CHAPTER 50

Trace's grandmother was so distraught she pushed herself to her feet and wrung her hands, wishing she knew what to do. The judge was wrong. Trace would never rape anyone.

Heart racing with anxiety, Grandma glanced over at Ivy. *How could she do something as evil as this? Didn't she have a conscience? Didn't she know how her lies were destroying her grandson's life? What kind of upbringing had she had? And who was the boy with her?*

As she studied them, her gaze was captured by something on Eli's wrist, a watch, a very familiar watch. She moved a step closer just as Eli put his hand on Ivy's shoulder, bringing the watch into plain view.

It was Uncle Warren's watch. No doubt about it.

Grandma hurried to the defense table and pointed. "That boy is wearing my uncle's watch."

Gowen's gaze fixed Eli, "What?" Gowen asked.

"It was stolen from Trace's apartment awhile back."

"Are you sure it's the same one?"

"Positive! We need to go get it before he gets away."

"Bailiff," Elizabeth Gowen called. She pointed at Eli. "Stop that young man."

Eli's eyes went wide as the bailiff approached and took hold of his arm. "Come with me, sir."

Ivy watched the ruckus as Eli walk away in the bailiff's clutches, her eyes narrowed. What was going on? Had Eli done something he hadn't told her about? He'd better not have. What would he say about her? Ivy smirked. Nothing. Eli would never betray her.

When Gowen explained the accusation to the bailiff, he asked Eli, "Where did you get the watch you're wearing?"

Cheeks flushed, Eli replied, "It was a gift."

"From whom?"

Eli's gaze darted to Ivy, then back, "A friend."

"I need a name."

Eli stared at the bailiff for a moment, then dropped his gaze, remaining silent.

"Officer," Trace said. "The watch has the initials "WVJ" engraved on the back."

"Let me see the watch, young man."

Eli clearly didn't want to take it off, but the bailiff's presence was more than he could defy. Sure enough, the initials "WVJ" were etched on the back of the watch casing.

"Come with me," the bailiff demanded. "I have a few more questions for you."

Eli followed him, head bowed, refusing to glance at Ivy again.

When Trace's apartment burglary case file was opened, Eli's watch matched the stolen one perfectly. Refusing to divulge who gave him the watch, Eli was arrested for felony burglary and taken into custody.

Ivy had never told Eli where she got the watch. Now that he knew about the burglary, he could guess, but he wouldn't tell anyone, even if he knew for sure. The evidence was on his wrist, not hers, and he couldn't imagine going up against Ivy.

Still unsure of what had happened, Ivy tried to get hold of Eli. He wasn't home, so she went out looking for him. He didn't answer his phone or any of her texts. That wasn't like him at all. Finally, Ivy got a call from Eli. "Where are you?" she demanded.

"At home," he said. "My dad bailed me out after I was charged with felony burglary for stealing the watch you gave me."

"What have you done?" she screeched.

"Don't worry." Eli's voice was weary from Ivy's manipulative hold entrenched in his psyche. "I'm not telling anyone how I got the watch."

In spite of the top-notch attorney his parents hired, Eli couldn't get off totally free. He was sentenced to 90 days in jail and twelve months probation.

Ivy dutifully visited Eli. After all, she was his support, and expected the same from him, but to make sure he'd continue to do as she wished. She let him sit in jail for long periods of time with no contact from her, knowing he'd continue to be a dutiful ally for her.

CHAPTER 51

McIntosh acquired yearbooks from Mountain View High School and carefully thumbed the pages, looking for clues that might lead to more names and information about the people Trace and Ivy associated with. His search for new evidence turned up Carrie Paterson as possibly having information on Ivy and Chloe Holden.

Holden? It couldn't be, could it?

McIntosh met Carrie at Starbucks a week before Trace's court proceeding. After gaining permission to turn on his recorder, McIntosh asked, "Could I talk to you about Ivy Greene?"

"Sure."

"Do you know Ivy Greene?"

Carrie tipped her head. "Not well. We went to the same school." Rolling her eyes, Carrie added, "She was always causing a scene. I stayed away from her. She was trouble."

"Do you know Chloe Holden?"

"Yes. We were pretty good friends. We hung out all the time until she moved away."

"Do you know why she moved?"

"Yes." Carrie's expression went sour.

Intrigued, McIntosh asked, "Can you tell me?"

Carrie raised her eyebrows. "Well, I hate gossip, but," her voice took on a questioning tone, "maybe it isn't gossip if you're asking for legal reasons."

"I believe you're right," McIntosh encouraged.

Carrie spread both hands on the table. "Chloe came to me in tears one day. When I asked her what was wrong, she told me that she'd caught Ivy and her dad in bed together. She was so mad and embarrassed, I'm surprised she'd tell anyone. She said Ivy had been spending a lot of time at their house and they'd become pretty good friends." She gave McIntosh a sideways glance. "It's for sure that she was spending lots of time with her and less time with me or Mia. Well, anyways, one night when Ivy begged off a football game they were going to, Chloe invited Mia to go with her instead."

She looked at McIntosh and laced her fingers together.

"Then what?" McIntosh prompted.

"Chloe and Mia left the game early and went to Chloe's house where they found Ivy and Chloe's dad in bed together." Carrie's eyes widened. "Chloe was devastated. We can't figure out why he'd disgrace the memory of her mother like that." Carrie tipped her head. "Did you know that Chloe's mother had passed a couple of years before that, so it was just her and her dad?"

"No, I didn't," McIntosh said with an encouraging nod. "You're doing fine, Carrie."

Carrie's eyes widened. "I couldn't believe what Chloe told me. I said she should report Ivy to someone, but Chloe didn't want to make things worse. Besides, her father could lose his job. She was so embarrassed that she wouldn't stay there, and moved in with her aunt, Mrs. Holden's sister. I think her name's Diane or Denise...something with a 'D'...oh, it's 'Darla.'"

Carrie beamed, and McIntosh said, "Very good, Carrie."

"I haven't heard from Chloe since she moved." Carrie frowned. "It's weird because we were pretty good friends. I think she just wanted to cut off this part of her life, because it hurt so much, you know?"

"Do you know where her aunt lives?"

"No." Carrie dropped her gaze. "Like I said, I haven't heard from her, but her dad works for the Sheriff's Department, and I bet he knows where she is."

"Is Ted Holden her father?"

"Yes." Carrie leaned forward to stare at McIntosh. "Do you know him?"

"Not personally, but I know of him. Thank you for your time." McIntosh stood.

Carrie nodded. "I just hope Chloe's alright."

"We'll see." McIntosh picked up his tape recorder, jumped into his car, and took off, eager to report to Elizabeth. Verifying Carrie's story would give them a huge break.

Elizabeth agreed that finding Chloe Holden was a priority. The fact that Ivy hadn't lost her virginity to Trace would definitely help Trace's case by proving that Ivy had lied, but at this point, they needed to leave Ted Holden out of it.

It turned out that Chloe wasn't hard to find, but hesitated at McIntosh's request to speak with her. When he assured her that the reason was to try and save someone from Ivy Greene, Chloe finally agreed to meet him at her aunt's house.

The next day, McIntosh drove an hour and a half before pulling up in front of Mrs. Whipple's home. When he rang the doorbell, Chloe answered.

"Hello, Chloe, I'm Jay McIntosh. We talked on the phone yesterday."

"I remember," Chloe, said eyes down. "Come in."

When they were seated and McIntosh received permission to record, he said, "I'm working with defense attorney Elizabeth Gowen on a case of alleged rape."

Chloe spat out the girl's name, "I thought this was about Ivy."

"It is. How well do you know Ivy Greene?"

Chloe's face paled and her eyes narrowed. "Well enough to know she's a bitch from hell!"

McIntosh tried not to show his surprise at Chloe's vehemence. "She filed a rape charge against Trace Aragon."

"Trace would never do such a thing," Chloe declared. "He was a lady's type of guy, so mild mannered and polite. Everyone I knew liked him." She clenched her fists. "Ivy's gone too far again."

"What do you mean?"

Chloe's voice rose. "She just uses people and leaves a mess behind. She doesn't care how badly she hurts anyone else, hell, everyone else. All she cares about is herself."

"Can you give me more details?"

Chloe suddenly shut down. "I don't want to talk about it, about her. Even saying her name is like chewing on poison." Chloe stared at McIntosh with sudden suspicion. "Who told you I knew that bitch?"

"I can't reveal my sources."

"Was it Carrie Patterson or Mia Rowley?"

"I really can't say." McIntosh fixed Chloe with a sincere gaze. "But anything you tell me could go a long way toward stopping Ivy. I heard that you were once pretty good friends, then something happened to end it. Would you be willing to explain? It could significantly help our case."

Chloe stared at McIntosh for a long moment. "She's a liar and a cheat. Is that good enough?"

"Not really. We need proof of that."

Chloe wrapped her arms around herself in a pitiable hug and licked her lips. "Well, we used to spend almost all of our time together. I thought she was my friend, so we welcomed her into our home. My dad and I let her come over a lot because she didn't get along with her mother."

"What ended your friendship, Chloe?"

Tears rose in Chloe's eyes. "Well, it's still pretty painful."

"I know it might be hard, but could really help our case."

Chloe let out a breath and relaxed her arms. "Me and Ivy were going to a school football game, but at the last minute she called because she felt sick. So, my friend Mia and I drove to the game, but it wasn't very good, so we left early. We were going to Mia's house to watch a movie, but stopped by my house so I could change clothes.

I was surprised to see Ivy's car in the driveway and got this really weird feeling." Chloe shivered. "We hurried inside, but didn't see Ivy or my father anywhere, not until we went upstairs." Chloe grimaced. "We heard noises from my father's room, opened the door, and found Ivy and my father in bed together." Tears ran down Chloe's cheeks. "I thought I was going to be sick. Mia stood beside me as Ivy looked up at us with a smirk and said, "Ted called me to come over and keep him company."

Then my father yelled at her and told her to get out and go home.

That's when I took off down the stairs with Mia right behind me, yelling for me to stop, but I didn't." She shook her head in misery. "I had to get out of there.

"My father pulled on his pants and came running after me, too. 'I didn't call her,' he said. 'She came over on her own.'

"I believed him, but he shouldn't have done what he did." Her voice rose. "He should never have done what he did!" She stopped, dropped her head, and wiped her cheeks.

"It must have been awful," McIntosh sympathized. "Did you talk to you father about it afterwards?"

"No," Chloe said in a hopeless voice. "He apologized over and over, but what could he say to fix it? Right?" Her damp eyes searched McIntosh's face. "I can barely stand to look at him."

"I'm sure your dad is extremely sorry, and I'm certain that he loves you very much. I have a daughter myself, and I'd be devastated if I ever lost her, no matter what the circumstances."

Chloe sniffed and wiped her nose with a tissue. "Aunt Darla said I could move in."

"How are you doing here?"

"Better." Chloe's face darkened. "Except that Ivy called me a couple of times. I didn't answer."

"Chloe, do you believe that Ivy is capable of lying about Trace raping her?"

"Oh hell, yes!"

"Would you be willing to testify in court?"

Chloe's eyes widened, and then she broke down in tears. "I don't know. I thought I'd left all this behind. I try not to think about it, but I really miss my dad. He was all I had left after Mom died. I can't even imagine looking at him now without falling apart. He was a really great dad, and Ivy helped fill some of my emptiness until all this mess happened. I don't trust anyone anymore. I don't know what to do." She looked McIntosh in the eye. "I'd have to testify against my dad, too, right? Could he lose his job or maybe go to jail?"

McIntosh spoke as gently as he could. "You'd have to tell everything you saw, but I can't say what would happen to your father."

Chloe took a deep breath, studying her hands in her lap. Then she lifted her gaze. "Ivy shouldn't be allowed to hurt anyone else. I still can't believe my dad did this to me." She took in a breath. "Yes, I'll testify."

"Thank you, Chloe. I'll let you know when we need you again." McIntosh gathered his equipment, then called Elizabeth as soon as he got to his car to let her know that Chloe not only confirmed Carrie's story, but agreed to testify in court.

"Just the break we've been looking for. Our strategy just changed, Jay."

CHAPTER 52

The Aragon case came to trial on December 6, 2017, with the state prosecuting Trace Aragon for the felony rape of Ivy Greene. Despite the police investigation, there was no physical evidence: no blood typing, semen samples, or even photographs of scratches or bruises. The prosecutor believed that Ivy Greene alone would be far more convincing than any physical evidence. Both the prosecutor and defense teams strategized their cases before trial, trying to predict the order to call witnesses for best advantage.

Trace clung to the hope that the American justice system would ultimately right the wrong of his arrest and prove his innocence, but he put all his affairs in order just in case the unthinkable happened and he ended up in jail.

On the morning of December 6, Trace slowly put on his clean white shirt and gray suit. As he tied his blue and gray tie with trembling hands, he thought, *Today could be the beginning of events that might send me to prison for something I didn't do.* It was suddenly hard to breathe, as if the tie was a hangman's noose around his neck. Tears slipped down his cheeks as his faith in the justice system, pitted against Ivy Greene, wavered. Yet he had no choice but to go through the tortuous legal journey ahead of him.

Trace's family followed him through the cold metal doors of the courthouse and funneled through the security check. Directed to courtroom 3B, they crowded onto an elevator and rode in somber silence. As the door slid open on the third floor, Trace saw Elizabeth

Gowen motion him toward a room just off the hallway. Trace followed her, ready to go over everything one more time, while his family and friends waited in an alcove outside the courtroom.

The elevator doors opened and Ivy strode out in a flouncy dress that cascaded just above her knees. The simple pleated tucks accentuated the bottom ruffle. Her hair was pulled up into a youthful ponytail, and she carried a pink flowered journal. She turned to a girlfriend beside her, giggling, until she caught sight of Trace's supporters. Smile fading, she grabbed her friend's arm and pulled her into the restroom.

Elizabeth and Trace emerged to join Trace's friends and family just before the bailiff opened the courtroom doors. Everyone filed in, passing Officer Redden and Detective Holden seated in the back row.

Gowen and Trace were at the defendant's table, known as the 'well,' across the aisle from Ivy and the prosecutor. Sharon was beside Ivy's friend on the bench behind them. "All rise," the bailiff announced. "The Fourth District Court of Ada County is now in session, the Honorable Judge Donner presiding."

Everyone stood as the judge walked into the courtroom, his round face serious above his black robes as he seated himself. When the others in the courtroom sat down, Judge Donner asked the bailiff to call the day's calendar.

"Your Honor, the People vs. Trace Aragon. Case # B1755062"

Ivy opened her notebook and began writing with a pink pen as the door on the right side of the courtroom opened to admit the jurors. Five men ranging in age from early 30's to mid 60's, and seven women who appeared to be between their early 20's and mid 50's settled themselves in the jury box. As they listened to Judge Donner read the charges, the jurists glanced at the top of Ivy's bent head as she continued to write in her journal. "Are both attorneys ready to begin the trial?" Judge Donner asked.

Elizabeth Gowen and Jillian Webb said they were.

"Then let's proceed."

The prosecutor stood. "Good morning, your Honor, and members of the jury, my name is Jillian Webb and I represent the State of Idaho in this case of rape. This is my opportunity to outline the evidence and call witnesses that will show the defendant, Trace Aragon, lured Ivy Greene to his apartment in Meridian, Idaho, at 12:30 am, on June 27, 2016, and forcibly raped her against her will. Ms. Greene never imagined that after hanging out with her friend, she would later experience so much pain, grief, and humiliation.

"I will show evidence of Mr. Aragon engaging in communication with Ms. Greene that night, inviting Ms. Greene to his apartment. I will show evidence that they were, in fact, at Mr. Aragon's apartment that night. I will introduce evidence that Mr. Aragon lied to the police during the investigation. You're going to hear the defense's side of the story, and you're going to hear a sad story about how Ms. Greene falsely accused Mr. Aragon of rape, and how it has ruined his life. The defense wants you to hear his story and feel sorry for him, because the defense wants you to believe the rape of Ivy Greene never happened.

"The truth is justice doesn't care about his story. Justice only cares about the law and what we can be prove. I'm going to show you that Mr. Aragon broke the law when he brutally raped Ms. Greene. It doesn't matter why he did it, or how it came about.

As members of the jury, it's your job to make sure he pays for his crime."

Ivy kept writing as her attorney continued, "Ms. Greene is a victim of a brutal and degrading act of rape, which she will live with for the rest of her life. At the conclusion of the case, I will ask you to convict Trace Aragon of rape as charged. Thank you."

Gowen leaned over to Trace and whispered, "Look at the jury after I stand up, look them in the eyes." then stood and walked out from behind her table to stand before the jury. "Good morning, my name is Elizabeth Gowen. It is my privilege to represent Trace Aragon in this case before you today.

"You've heard the prosecutor explain what she hopes will be proven, but the prosecutor did not tell you all the facts. The prosecutor stated that my client was 'identified' as the rapist, but in fact, the supposed victim, Ms. Greene, is a woman who had consensual sex with my client on the night in question. As further explanation, it was at her request that she met him at his apartment late that night or early morning of June 27. The alleged rape is nothing more than an attempt to get revenge and attention. I will prove that there is no physical evidence, no eyewitnesses, and that the alleged rape was reported three months later.

"Trace Aragon did not rape Ivy Greene. He did have consensual sex with her. Both of them were sober and of legal age. When you look at the many cases of people who've been wrongfully convicted, we can all agree that mistakes can be made and we must renew our efforts to make sure that innocent people aren't charged in the first place. Once a prosecution has started, it's important that the criminal justice system keeps eyes and ears open for any sign of evidence that we may be on the wrong track. Therefore, I would ask you to keep an open mind and listen to all the evidence and then return a verdict of 'not guilty.' Thank you."

CHAPTER 53

"Prosecution," Judge Donner ordered, "You may call your first witness."

Webb stood. "Your Honor, the People call Officer Kate Redden to the stand."

Notebook in hand, Redden strode to the front of the room. The clerk asked, "Do you promise that the testimony you shall give in the case before this court shall be the truth, the whole truth, and nothing but the truth, so help you God?"

Without hesitation, Redden declared, "Yes, I do."

Webb clasped her hands behind her back. "Please state your name and how long you've been on the job at the Ada County Sheriff's Department."

"Kate Redden, badge number 2756. I've been on the police force for eleven years, and was promoted to the Sex Crime Unit eight years ago."

"Were you the officer who responded to Ms. Greene's 911 call?"

"Yes, along with Detective Ted Holden."

"What was the date and time of the call?"

"September 15, 2016, at 10:32 am. We were dispatched to the call and arrived at Ms. Greene's home at 10:47 am."

"When you arrived at Ms. Greene's home, what did you find?"

"She met us at her door seeming distraught, nervous, and very embarrassed. Our principal concern is to attend to any medical needs that the victim may have, so we asked if she was hurt and if we could call someone for her. We suggested that she go to the hospital to get checked out and have a rape kit done."

Judge Donner interrupted. "To whom do you refer?"

"Ms. Greene, the victim, your Honor," Redden clarified.

Webb continued, "Was she transported to the hospital for any injuries?"

Redden spread her hands. "No. At that time, she told us the rape had occurred three months earlier, on June 27, 2016."

Webb glanced around the room. "Was that surprising to you?"

"No." Redden shook her head. "Many rape victims delay reporting their attack due to fear, shame, and embarrassment."

"During your interview, did Ms. Greene seem confused or mixed up with the questions you were asking?"

"No, she did not."

"Did you later videotape Ms. Greene's statement at the Sheriff's Department?"

"Yes, I did."

"Was the victim's statement consistent with the oral statement you'd taken earlier?"

"Yes, it seemed to be."

"Who was in the interview room at the time?"

"Ms. Greene and myself."

"Why wasn't Detective Holden in the interview room?"

"Rape victims are more comfortable with female officers, and the fewer people they have to talk to...well, it's much easier for them to recall the event."

"I completely understand." Webb nodded and Ivy continued writing in her notebook as Webb took a step to one side, then faced Redden again. "Was Ms. Greene able to identify her attacker?"

"Yes, she clearly identified him as Trace Aragon."

"What evidence did you collect?"

"There was none other than her statement. As I said earlier, it occurred three months prior."

Webb nodded. "Did she give you details of the rape?"

"Yes, she described the physical attack in detail." Redden referred to her notes in order to tell the court what Ivy had reported to her and Holden.

"Was Ms. Greene able to give you a description of Mr. Aragon's bedroom where she said the rape occurred?"

"Yes, she described it in detail."

"What did she tell you about the bedroom?"

Redden looked at her notes again. "She described it as being a small room, the bed was black, flanked by two black nightstands. There was also an old brown chair, black dresser, and a floor lamp."

Webb leaned towards Redden, and then turned right, facing the jury. "Did you interview Mr. Aragon about the rape allegation?"

"Yes. He said he was in town working on the night in question. His employment time card proved this. He also told us Ivy had never been to his apartment. We retrieved historical cell phone data which proved both Ms. Greene and Mr. Aragon's phones were at the same time and location on the night in question."

Webb held up two plastic bags. "Your Honor, I offer the defendant's time card, marked as Plaintiff's Exhibit #1, and the cellular data record document as Exhibit #2 for identification into evidence."

After Gowen, had a chance to see them, Judge Donner admitted the exhibits and remanded them to the bailiff for marking.

"Do you believe Ms. Green was raped by Mr. Aragon?"

"Objection, your Honor," Gowen said. "Counsel is asking the witness to give an opinion."

"Sustained," Judge Donner ruled.

Webb turned away. "No further questions, your Honor."

CHAPTER 54

Hello." Gowen greeted Redden for cross-examination. "You must see a lot of horrible things in your line of work. I suppose rape is one of the worst."

Redden replied with a tip of her head.

"It's your job to investigate crimes, take all the available evidence, and pass it on through our criminal justice system, is that correct?"

"Yes."

"On December 28, 2016, were you and Detective Holden approached by Jay McIntosh, a retired FBI officer, now in business as a private detective employed by my firm in regards to this case?"

"I believe so," Redden replied cautiously.

"Did he offer you evidence for this case against Mr. Aragon?"

"Yes. He said he had statement recordings or something."

"Did you refuse to take the evidence?"

Redden hesitated before answering. "Detective Holden did."

"Why would Holden refuse to investigate any evidence given to you by anyone in a criminal case?" Rubbing her forehead, Gowen waited for Redden's response.

Redden's body tightened "We had enough circumstantial evidence to charge Mr. Aragon with the rape."

"Wow." Gowen appeared surprised by her answer. "Is it possible the evidence McIntosh had, could have been the missing piece to Mr. Aragon's case in which possibly no charges would have been made at all?"

Redden considered her answer before replying, "I suppose it's possible, but like I said…"

Gowen quickly cut her off. "Your Honor, at this time I would like to enter the recorded statements as Defense Exhibit #1 for identification and have it marked into evidence."

Judge Donner agreed.

"At this time, your Honor, I would like to play the recorded statements offered to Detective Holden and Officer Redden. The statements were made by Sara Summers, a friend of Ms. Green and Mr. Aragon, Zack Becker, and Ethan Harrison, long time friends of Mr. Aragon." Gowen walked over and pressed 'play.'

The jury sat in suspense while the recording played. Gowen stood in front of her table watching the jurors' expressions. Ivy looked up, trying to make eye contact with each juror while a few tears rolled down her otherwise expressionless face.

At the end of the statements, Gowen tapped the "off" button, walked back to the witness stand, and continued. "Do you think this information should have been turned over to the Prosecutor as evidence?"

"Objection," Webb overtly stated.

"Over ruled, answer the question."

Redden looked at Holden for direction. "I…suppose, it couldn't have hurt."

"Do you think it may have helped Mr. Aragon's case?" Gowen moved around the floor, looking at the jurors and then looking back at Redden.

"I guess it might have helped," Redden offered.

Gowen took a couple of steps towards her table and turned. "Let's go to the day you and your partner went to Ms. Greene's apartment. Was she alone when you arrived?"

"Yes."

Gowen tipped her head. "Did you find it odd that she was by herself? No family or close friend there to support her through the traumatic ordeal of being raped?"

Redden shrugged. "Sometimes rape victims are ashamed."

"I understand." Gowen paced a couple of steps as if deep in thought, then returned to stand before the witness. "Did you follow up on the description of Mr. Aragon's bedroom?"

"No, we did not."

"Why?"

"He'd moved to Salt Lake City, Utah, by the time we got the call."

"So you couldn't verify any of the crime scene evidence, like bedroom items she described. Is that correct?"

"No, we could not."

Gowen raised her eyebrows as if in disbelief. "So this case is being prosecuted from mere speculation and circumstantial evidence?"

"Objection, your Honor," Webb stated with disapproval.

"Sustained."

Gowen didn't flinch. "Did you and Detective Holden recover any physical evidence the day you took the call?"

"No."

"Let's be clear...you stated Ms. Greene didn't have any torn or soiled clothing from the rape at the time you and Detective Holden took Ms. Greene's statement, is that correct?"

"Correct, she didn't have any."

"Were there any pictures of the bruises she claimed she had gotten in the attack?"

"No."

Gowen walked over to the Exhibit table, picked up the Plaintiff's Exhibit #2, the cellular data document, and glanced at it. "Regarding the Plaintiff's Exhibit #2, is it possible Ms. Greene could have just been sitting in Mr. Aragon's apartment parking area and not in his apartment?"

"Yes, I suppose so."

Gowen's next questions came quickly. "Was a rape kit done for the alleged rape of Ms. Greene?'

"No."

"Were there any witnesses?"

"No."

"So, the historical cellular data for the phones and Ms. Greene's statement against Mr. Aragon were the only pieces of evidence you had to make this rape case and the cellular phone data is circumstantial evidence at best."

"Objection, your Honor," Webb interrupted.

"Sustained. Move on, Ms. Gowen."

"Back to Ms. Greene's alleged bruises. Do you suppose they could have come from something or someone other than Mr. Aragon?"

With hesitation, "Yes, I suppose."

"Have you ever had a victim self inflict bodily harm?"

Webb spoke up, "Objection, your Honor."

"Overruled," Judge Donner declared. "Answer the question."

"Yes, however, we have no evidence she did this to herself."

Gowen turned away. "No further questions at this time, your Honor."

CHAPTER 55

Webb stood and declared, "The People call Eli Cole."

Once the bailiff swore in the witness, Webb approached the stand. "What is your relationship to Ivy Greene?"

Eli looked at Ivy. "We've been friends since before grade school."

Webb took a step closer. "Are you still friends with Ms. Greene?"

"Yes."

"Can you tell us what kind of person Ms. Greene is?"

Eli cleared his throat. "Well, she's been my best friend for a long time. I have a lot of affection for her because we've been through so many things together. She's always been there for me." Eli brushed hair from his eyes. "She's an honest, trusting, caring person who would help anyone."

"Is Mr. Aragon a friend of yours?"

"Yes. We were friends in school."

Webb glanced at the jury, then back at Eli. "Does Ms. Greene confide in you about personal things?"

"Yes."

"Did she tell you she'd been raped by Mr. Aragon?"

Eli sat up straighter. "Yes, she did."

Gowen spoke up. "Objection, your Honor, hearsay."

Webb countered with, "Qualified with exception, your Honor."

"Overruled," the judge, declared. "I will allow it. Please answer the question."

Eli spoke as if choosing his words carefully. "She came to me all upset. When I asked her what was wrong, she told me Trace had raped her."

Webb's voice softened. "When did she tell about the rape?"

"I had just gotten home from a weekend trip with Trace's girlfriend and her family."

"What did she tell you?"

"Objection, hearsay," Gowen declared again.

"Overruled, Ms. Gowen. Answer the question."

"She told me that Trace wanted her to come over to his apartment Saturday night, on June 26. He'd stayed home from that same weekend trip I was on with his girlfriend, Tayla. I guess he had to work, at least that's what he said."

"Objection, your Honor, witness speculation.

"Sustained."

"He said he wanted Ivy to keep him company. After she got there, he wanted to do the deed."

"Explain the deed, Eli."

"He wanted to have sex with Ivy, but she didn't want to, but he went ahead anyway, and she wasn't strong enough to stop him."

Webb walked over to the jury box. "Did she have any bruises or scratches on her body?"

Eli rubbed a spot on his arm. "She had some bruises on her right arm."

"Did you believe Ivy?"

Eli gave an incredulous snort. "Why would she lie to me?"

"I need a yes or no answer Mr. Cole. Did you believe her?"

"Yes."

Webb concluded with, "I have no other questions at this time." She returned to her table where Ivy turned a page and wrote some more.

Gowen stood and turned toward Eli. "You stated that you've known Ms. Greene for a very long time. Did Ms. Greene ever tell you she liked Mr. Aragon?"

"Yes. She had a crush on him in high school."

"Did you and your friends spend a lot of time with them?"

"Yes."

Gowen turned the page of her legal pad and continued. "Did you and Ms. Greene put together a birthday party for Ethan Harrison in Las Vegas, Nevada, July 30, 2016?"

Eli hesitated, "No, just me."

"Why would you plan such an extravagant birthday party for Ethan in Las Vegas?"

"He's a good friend, so why not?"

"Did Ms. Green go to this party?"

"Yes, we drove down together."

"Did you see Mr. Aragon and Ms. Greene on the balcony at the Venetian Hotel?"

"Yes."

"Did you video record a conversation and take photos of an interaction between them on your cell phone?"

"I think so."

"What was the conversation you heard?"

"Trace was trying to kiss Ivy and she yelled at him. She asked him why he wouldn't admit it or something like that. I guess she wanted him to admit he'd raped her."

Gowen turned toward the bench. "Your Honor, I ask that this video recording be labeled as evidence for the Defense as Exhibit #2."

Judge Donner accepted the evidence and Gowen played the video recording, which clearly showed Ivy making the advance to kiss Mr. Aragon. When Ms. Greene yelled, her words were, "Why are you denying it? You promised you'd leave her."

Some of the jury members shuffled their feet, others shifted their positions, most of them frowning as they watched video evidence that didn't match the witness's testimony.

"I think you misunderstood the context of the video recording," Gowen said when the video ended. "Why were you videotaping them?"

Eli pinched his lips together, then said, "I record everything. When I heard them arguing, I just turned my phone toward them and pushed 'record.'"

"Did you send the photo or video to anyone?"

Eli fidgeted for a moment, looked at Ivy, and then at Webb. "I'm not sure if I did or not."

"May I treat this witness as a hostile witness, your Honor?"

Judge Donner indicated agreement.

"Didn't you forward the photo to Mr. Aragon's girlfriend minutes after you took it?"

Eli sat as far back in his chair as he could, putting as much distance as possible between himself and his questioner. "Oh, yes, I did. I'd forgotten that."

Gowen smiled. "Mr. Cole, why did you send it to Ms. Dean?"

"I thought she should know about Trace and Ivy."

Standing firmly in front of Eli, Gowen asked, "Did Ms. Greene ask you to video record or take pictures of them on the balcony and then send it to your friend Ms.Dean?"

"What?" Eli moved in his seat as if unable to find a comfortable spot. "No."

"Remember, you're under oath to tell the truth."

Eli's reply was sharp. "I said no!"

Gowen turned, walked back to her table, and picked some papers. After a quick glance, she turned around. "Were you incarcerated for felony burglary?"

Webb interrupted. "Objection, relevance?"

Gowen explained, "I'm laying a foundation to the character of this witness and his relationship to Mr. Aragon outside of school."

"Overruled," Judge Donner declared. "I will allow it."

Gowen repeated, "Were you incarcerated for felony burglary?" "Yes."

"Was one of the victims of the burglary Mr. Aragon?"

"Yes."

"Are you guilty of this crime?"

"I took a plea deal."

Gowen's voice grew firm. "Did you steal Mr. Aragon's watch, revolver, wallet and its contents, computer and twenty four hundred dollars?"

Eli glanced at Ivy, but her head was down as she continued writing in her book. Eli's breathing grew heavier as sweat beaded on his forehead.

"Non-responsive, your Honor," Gowen stated.

"You will answer the question," Judge Donner declared.

"I only had the watch, I don't know about any of the other stuff."

Gowen frowned at him. "Do you know where the wallet, revolver, computer, and twenty four hundred dollars are today?"

"No."

"Again, I remind you that you are still under oath and there is a harsh penalty for perjury."

"Objection," Webb said. "Badgering the witness, your Honor."

"Sustained," Judge Donner ruled.

Gowen switched tactics. "You told the bailiff, Officer Williams, that the watch was a gift. Who gave you the watch?"

"Objection," Webb declared. "Relevance, your Honor."

Judge Donner repeated, "Sustained."

Gowen's change in tone startled the courtroom as she boldly barked the question, "Has Ms. Greene ever asked you to lie for her?"

Eli shifted in his seat as if it had a fire under it. "Umm." He glanced at Ivy, who'd always had the answer, the ready, easy lie. *Why wasn't she looking at him? He went to jail for her, and she wouldn't even look at him. What did she expect him to do now?* "No," he finally choked out. "I don't know."

"Yes or no Eli, has she ever asked you to lie for her?"

In desperation...*Why won't she look at me?* He answered, "No."

"Was she involved in the break in?"

"Objection!" Webb all but shouted. "Relevance, your Honor."

"Sustained," Judge Donner said yet again. "Careful, Ms. Gowen."

"Withdrawn." Gowen clenched her jaw, knowing that Eli knew more than he was saying. Finally, she said, "No further questions at this time."

As Eli stepped down from the witness stand, Ivy looked up at him with contempt, her evil gaze burning his soul like poison.

CHAPTER 56

Webb shuffled through her papers before announcing, "The People call Reese Blake."

As soon as Reese was sworn in, Webb asked," What is your relationship to Ms. Greene?"

"I dated her back in," Reese squinted at the ceiling, "2016."

"How long did you date her?"

"About two months off and on."

Webb took a step closer to Reese. "Did she tell you that Mr. Aragon raped her?"

Gowen spoke up. "Objection, your Honor, hearsay."

Judge Donner folded his hands. "Sustained."

"Can you tell us what kind of person Ms. Greene is?" Webb asked.

Reese grinned. "Ivy's the kinda happy girl that enjoys being with others, you know? She was always part of the school activities."

"Did you and she become intimate?"

"Nah," Reese leaned back. "We didn't date for long. Even though she seemed sincere about wanting to go out with me, she didn't seem interested in that way."

Webb nodded. "Did you know Mr. Aragon well?"

Reese bobbed his head back and forth. "Well enough. Sometimes he was an annoying showoff, but mostly we were pretty good friends, I guess."

"Was Mr. Aragon interested in Ms. Greene as a girlfriend?"

"He seemed to be with her a lot, which made me mad, 'cause Trace knew I liked her. He was the type of guy that went from one girl to the next with hardly a breath in between." Reese leaned forward as if sharing a secret. "That's a little shady if you ask me."

"Objection, your Honor," Gowen said. "The question called for inadmissible speculation on the part of the witness. I move that the testimony be stricken from the record."

"Sustained," Judge Donner ruled. "The jury will disregard the last statement."

Webb let a half smile escape. They could disregard the question all they liked, but it was still stuck in the jury's minds.

"But once he started dating Tayla, he was more of a one girl kind of guy," Reese added.

Webb stopped smiling. "No more questions," she snapped.

Judge Donner turned his attention to the defense table, "Your witness, Ms. Gowen."

Gowen stood and walked toward Reese. "Did you ever know Trace to be untrustworthy?"

"Well, if flirting with a girl I liked doesn't count, then, no."

"No more questions for this witness, your Honor."

"Let's recess for the lunch hour and reconvene at 1:00 this afternoon. Court is dismissed." Judge Donner stood and retired to his chambers.

The bistro across the street seemed perfect for a quick lunch, but it was always packed midday, so Trace and Ethan ordered "to go." Everyone gathered in the north lobby of the courthouse to eat. Appetites were sparse, but Trace drew strength from spending time with his support group before returning to the courtroom.

CHAPTER 57

Court reconvened promptly at 1:00 p.m. Tension ran high as Webb called Ms. Greene as her final witness. Ivy finally put her pen down beside her pink notebook and followed the bailiff with downcast eyes. When she reached the witness box, her shoulders slumped as if carrying the weight of the world before swearing in a barely audible voice to tell the truth. She sat down as if fearing the chair would bite her. Her round blue eyes darted around the courtroom as if searching for danger.

"Hello, Ms. Greene," Webb said. "I know this is hard for you. You probably wish you didn't have to be here, but you've come today to identify your attacker and to get justice for the crime that was committed against you."

Ivy glanced at Trace. Before her eyes darted away, tears began rolling down her cheeks.

"Can you tell us what happened on the early morning of the 27th?" Webb asked.

Ivy wiped a tear away. "Well…Trace stayed home from a trip with his girlfriend, Tayla Dean. It was late Sunday, June 26th, 2016. We started texting back and forth, around…I'd say about 10:30. Eventually Trace asked me to come over to his apartment at about 12:30 in the morning because he'd been working late and just got off. I didn't think it was a good idea, but I was bored. He was, too.

"His friend Zack and he had just moved into the apartment. When I arrived, he took me to his bedroom. We unpacked some of his things, moved some furniture around, and hung some posters. We sat on his bed looking at some CD's and watching TV. It was fun until he tried kissing me." She slid a finger across her bottom lip. "I told him I didn't think it was a good idea because we were just friends and he was dating my girlfriend, Tayla, at the time. I really thought he was just kidding around. He's kinda like that.

"Then he suggested we have sex. He tried kissing me again. I'd already told him no, and was so uncomfortable that I turned my head away. When I started toward the door, he told me to come back. I should have just left, but I didn't. This was Trace. I knew this guy, or at least thought I did.

"When I finally realized how serious he was about having sex with me, I got scared. I didn't know what to do, except tell him to stop messing around."

Ivy pinched her lips together, her chin quivering for an instant. "That's when he grabbed my breasts, pushed me onto the bed, and pinned my arms. I asked what he wanted. He said, 'You know what I want' and proceeded to pull down my underwear and shorts. When he started to unbuckle his belt, I realized that I was going to be raped.

"He pulled his pants down and put his... his..." Ivy put her fingertips on her lips, and then glanced at her attorney. Curling her fingers into a fist under her chin, she lowered her gaze and whispered, "...his penis inside me and forced me to have sexual intercourse. I was so frightened. I couldn't stop crying." Tears ran down Ivy's face. "It hurt so bad. I told him to stop."

"How long did the sexual intercourse last?"

"About five minutes, I guess."

"Did you have any physical injuries from the attack?"

"The inside of my thighs felt like they were bruised. My arms hurt and I did have some bruises on my right arm. My...vaginal area was bleeding because I'd never had sex before. I was raised in a strict Christian house and I wanted to save myself for marriage. I wanted to be a virgin for my husband. I've never been so scared in my life, so scared I felt sick. I was so embarrassed and felt so...guilty."

Her eyes made a pleading cry for approval and empathy, hoping the jurors would completely believe and understand her silent suffering.

"Why didn't you resist Trace's advances in the beginning and just leave?" Webb asked.

"I should have," Ivy replied. "By the time he got aggressive with me, it was too late. He was too strong and I couldn't get away. I begged him many times to stop, but he wouldn't. He just kept going until he completely violated me. I was a virgin and now, well, I can't say that anymore. When it was finally over, he told me to go home, like I was nothing.

"I grabbed my things and got dressed as well as I could. It was hard because I was trembling. I was still so scared, and hurt, and I wanted a shower so bad. I drove myself home and barely made it before I threw up. I showered for what seemed like hours, just to get rid of every bit of him. I was far too ashamed to tell anyone, and I especially didn't want to go to the hospital. I heard they have to get all kinds of samples for evidence." Ivy shuddered. "I couldn't stand being touched anymore. It would have been too degrading."

"Do you need a minute, Ms. Greene?' Webb offered.

Ivy sniffed and dabbed at her eyes. "No. I'm sorry, this is just so hard for me." She offered a tremulous smile while looking at the jury. "I'm fine." Her display of innocent fear was very convincing.

"Please describe Mr. Aragon's bedroom as you remember it the night of the rape," Webb said.

Ivy sighed and her eyes wandered around the courtroom. "Well, I remember the bed was black and he had two night stands, but they didn't match. I think they were black, too. There was a big brown chair. It was really old and ugly, and there was a floor lamp by it. He had a black dresser, too."

"Is there anything else about the bedroom that you can remember?"

"Yes, he had a photograph of him and his mother or grandma, someone hugging him, on his dresser. I remember staring at it, wondering who they were, and did they really know who Trace was?"

"When you confided in Eli the following Tuesday, did you tell him all of the details of the rape?"

With a mask of despair on her face, Ivy forced an expression of concentration. "Eli was the only one I trusted at the time. I was so afraid that Trace might try to use force to stop me from telling anyone."

Webb walked closer to Ms. Greene. "Did you show Eli some bruises on your right arm?"

Ivy made her eyes round and innocent. "No. Eli noticed them and asked if the bruises were from Trace."

"Did you receive the bruises from Mr. Aragon during the attack?"

Ivy's eyes teared up again. "Yes, I did."

"Why didn't you take a picture of the bruises?"

Ivy spread her hands in a helpless gesture. "I didn't know what to do about any of it. I was too traumatized."

Webb softened her tone. "Why did it take you so long to report the rape?"

All the jury members' eyes were trained on her when Ivy answered, "I was ashamed and embarrassed. I was hurt, both body and soul. I thought I'd be able to work through it myself.

"It helped that Trace moved away. I tried to move on with my life, but depression and thoughts of suicide became a real problem for me. I've been diagnosed with PTSD from this experience, and I'm suffering from flashbacks, like it's happening again and again. I couldn't take it anymore. That's why I reported it. I know it was three months too late, but I needed help." She looked through her wet eyelashes at the jury.

"Thank you, Ivy," Webb said. "No further questions."

CHAPTER 58

Gowen drew in a deep breath, stood tall, and strode to the middle of the courtroom. "Hello, Ivy. I have some questions I hope you can answer for us today. Will that be O.K?"

"Yes." Ivy agreed.

"Did you like high school?" Gowen ask softly.

"Yes," Ivy replied with a small smile and a bob of her head. "I loved it."

"What were your favorite classes?"

Ivy clasped her hands in timid delight. "Journalism and I also loved my drama class."

"How many years did you take drama?"

"All three years of high school."

Gowen walked back to her table and picked up a couple of pamphlets. "Ms. Greene, did you perform on stage at any time during your three years in drama?"

Ivy's face brightened. "Yes, I did a lot of stage performances."

"I have a couple of play bills here." Gowen raised the papers in her hand. "I see that you performed in both of these plays, and headlined in one of them, 'Oklahoma,' one of my favorites, by the way." Gowen nodded toward Ivy. "Good for you. You must be very talented. Did you have to audition for these plays?"

Ivy fingered her ponytail. "Yes, of course. You don't just get picked out of the student body. You've got to have some acting talent."

"I see." Gowen lowered the playbills. "Will you please tell us how you prepare for a particular role when performing in front of an audience."

Webb quickly spoke up. "Objection, your Honor. This testimony is not relevant to the facts of this case."

Gowen turned toward the judge. "I want to set a foundation for character skills, your Honor."

"Overruled," Judge Donner stated. "Answer the question."

Ivy rolled her eyes at Gowen. "Once I know the script and imagine myself in the role, it's really quite easy," Ivy boasted. "I can role play just from one script reading."

"Performing in front of an audience doesn't frighten you, like the audience we have here today?" She pointed to the jury.

"Objection."

"Sustained," Judge Donner's stern reply, accompanied by a raised eyebrow, indicated a bit of agitation at Gowen's tactics.

Gowen turned away, then turned back to face Ivy. Almost as an afterthought, she asked, "Ms. Greene, do you have social media accounts such as Facebook or Instagram?"

"Yes, I do."

"Your Honor," Gowen said. "At this time I would like to offer the Defense's Exhibit #3 for Identification into evidence, social media posts by Ms. Greene for the years 2015-2016."

"Objection, your Honor," Webb said. "Relevance?"

"Relative to her acting skills," Gowen explained.

"Overruled, you may continue."

As Gowen submitted the stack of pages for consideration, a message Ivy posted on a Monday morning sat on top, accompanied by a seductive image of her in a towel that barely covered her crotch. The top of her rounded breasts protruded from the loosely held terry cloth. The message read: *Just got out of the shower, Look at my reflection.*

Below it was Tuesday's message that read: *What do I have to do to get some attention?* The image showed her leaning forward with plenty of cleavage visible, and a seductive pout on her lips.

Wednesday's message was, *Why is no one giving me love and attention??? I deserve some.* The accompanying picture was of Ivy sprawled on mussed bed sheets in a shortie nightgown that was sheer enough to show the dark shadows of her nipples and pubic hair.

Judge Donner accepted the evidence, which Gowen also presented to Webb and the jury. Then Gowen produced a poster board containing a collage of just a few of the Instagram posts and photos Ms. Greene had posted. Gowen turned to Ms. Greene with the question, "Why do you post such provocative images and verbiage?"

Ivy shrugged. "Everyone does. It doesn't mean anything."

As Ivy spoke, Webb stared at the images that hadn't been in any of the police reports or evidence that had appeared on her desk to date. Recognizing the problems this new evidence presented to her case, Webb interrupted. "Irrelevant, your Honor."

Judge Donner frowned in disbelief, as if wondering how sexually provocative messages accompanied by nearly nude photos were irrelevant. "Overruled."

Gowen faced Ms. Greene and asked a different question. "How long have you known Mr. Aragon?"

"Since our sophomore year."

Gowen jumped on the answer. "That's a long time. Were you ever afraid of him during those school years?"

"No," Ivy wrinkled her brow. "We were never alone. There were always other people around."

"The early morning of June 27, 2016, did you willingly go to Mr. Aragon's apartment?"

"Yes."

"Did you wish he were your boyfriend?"

"He was Tayla's boyfriend."

"Was it your idea to go to his apartment?"

Ivy licked her lips, then said, "I don't understand the question."

"Did you text Mr. Aragon and invite yourself to his apartment?"

Ivy held up her palms. "He was the one who texted me and said he wanted me to come over."

Gowen turned toward the judge. "Your Honor, at this time I'd like to offer Defense's 'Exhibit #4' for identification into evidence." Producing a few sheets of paper, she explained, "These are the texts between Ivy and Trace on the night of June 26, 2016."

Ivy: *What are you doing? I heard you didn't go on the trip with Tayla. Do you want to hang out?*

Trace: *It probably isn't a good idea because I have a girlfriend and she's actually one of your friends ya know.*

Ivy: *We would just be hanging out as friends. I'm already in your parking lot...can I come up?*

Trace: *No, I told you it's not a good idea.*

Ivy: *Tayla will never know.*

Trace: *Just go home.*

Ivy: *I'm already here, just let me come up for a few minutes.*

Trace: *OK, but you can't stay long.*

Webb was stunned at Gowen's evidence. She leaned over and asks Ivy, "Why didn't you show me these text messages?"

"I did you must have not read them all." Ivy smirked.

Of all the texts messages Ivy provided to Webb as evidence, she had never seen these before leaving her in a state of bewilderment.

Judge Donner accepted the evidence, and Gowen handed a copy of the texts to Webb and the jury. Then Gowen placed a collage of the posts on an easel. Turning to Ivy, she asked, "Ms. Greene, after you went into Trace's apartment, did you in any way try to seduce Mr. Aragon?"

Ivy glanced at the jury. "No. We were just talking and watching T.V."

"Did you at any time tell Mr. Aragon you had feelings for him and wanted him to break up with his girlfriend, Tayla Dean?"

"No! Tayla was my friend, and I wouldn't hurt her that way." Ivy stopped and glanced around the room. "I only told him he should break up with her if he wasn't happy. After all, she was going to school 300 miles away. "

Gowen picked up her note tablet, wrote something, and tore off the page, keenly aware of Ivy's intense gaze on her. Gowen handed the paper over the banister to McIntosh. He read; *leave the courtroom for a small distraction.* McIntosh got up and left.

Ivy stared at him as he disappeared through the double doors. *What was that about? What was in the note? Where was he going? I'm sure it was about me. What did that lawyer write about me?*

"Ms. Greene? Excuse me, Ms. Greene?" When Ivy finally refocused on Gowen, the attorney asked, "Did you and Mr. Aragon have consensual sex the early morning of June 27, 2016?"

"I didn't have sex with him," Ivy snapped. "He raped me. That isn't that the same thing."

As Gowen's cross-examination proceeded, a different Ivy emerged, one that left the box of tissues on the witness stand undisturbed.

"Why didn't you stop texting Mr. Aragon after he told you to stop?"

Ivy rebutted with rage. "He kept texting me!"

"Your Honor, permission to treat the witness as hostile?"

"Yes. You will answer the question Ms. Greene." Judge Donner stated.

Gowen again ask the question. "You continued to text and call Mr. Aragon after he clearly told you to stop, isn't that true?"

Slouching back into the chair, Ivy looked at Webb for direction before responding, "I just wanted to hang out. I was bored, that's all."

Gowen turned toward the judge. "Your Honor?"

"Answer the question, Ms. Greene."

Ivy sniffed. "What was the question?"

"Why didn't you stop texting Mr. Aragon after he told you to stop?" Gowen repeated.

Ivy stared Gowen down. "I wanted to hang out, like I told you."

"Ms. Greene, you stated that you were a virgin prior to your alleged rape, is that correct?"

"Yes."

"The vaginal bleeding from first time sex can be scary. You must have been terrified. You stated you put your clothes back on the best you could and left. Were your underwear and shorts bloody, Ms. Greene?"

Mystified by the question, Ivy replied with some embarrassment, "Yes."

"Did blood get on your car seat while you drove home?"

Ivy's face paled, a look of puzzlement stealing over her face.

"Of course there was blood on my car seat." *Stupid bitch and your stupid wretched questions.*

"You never mentioned cleaning your bloody car to the police or to the court. Why is that?"

"I did mention it to the police. They must have forgotten to write it down. I remember it, the blood in my car."

"Yet you didn't save or photograph any of the bloody evidence."

"Objection!"

"Sustained."

Gowen patiently walked back to her table, then turned. "Had you ever been in Mr. Aragon's bedroom prior to the alleged rape?"

"No, just in his apartment."

"Can you remember anything else about his bedroom that will help us here today? Take your time, we just you to be sure you haven't forgotten anything."

Ivy's eyes roamed the courtroom. "Like I said earlier, pictures…oh, I remember putting some of his things in his dresser, and I came across an envelope with his name on it. It had a document in it, a truck title, I think."

Gowen looked at the jury, and then rolled her glance around the courtroom, only to see panic in Trace's eyes.

"Your Honor, may I have a moment with my client?"

Judge Donner nodded. "Let's take a 20 minute recess."

Gowen sat by Trace, leaned in close, and asked, "What's wrong?"

"She couldn't have seen that envelope. It wasn't there. When I moved into my new apartment with Zack, I gave the title to my grandma for safekeeping and that furniture she keeps talking about was in my old place. When she came over to my new apartment, I'd bought all new furniture."

"Interesting," Gowen said. "Come on." She led Trace into the hall, where they gathered with McIntosh and Trace's family.

"The only way she could have seen that truck title is if she was the one who broke into my apartment," Trace told them. "That would explain the pink color on my chap stick, and why Eli had my watch. She gave it to him! Now we can get her."

"Slow down, Trace, unfortunately, she's not on trial for breaking and entering."

"But why's she describing my old furniture and not the new stuff?"

"I'm not sure. It could be that her illegal visit to your room was more memorable, so is stuck in her memory. When she visited your new place, she had other things in mind." Gowen turned to Trace's grandmother. "Did Trace give you the title to his truck after he moved?"

"Yes, he gave it to me the day he was moving. Why is that important? What's going on?"

Gowen looked at McIntosh and smiled.

"But shouldn't you…" Trace began.

Gowen stopped him. "Trust me, I'll handle this."

They returned to the courtroom where Gowen continued her cross-examination of Ivy. "Let's go back to the bedroom furniture. Was there a matching footboard?"

"No."

"What about any other furniture in the room?"

"There was a black bed, his dresser, a brown chair and a lamp." Ivy gestured to Gowen's notebook. "Write that down, so you won't need to ask me anymore."

"I'm sorry, Ms. Greene, I'm just trying to help you remember anything you may have missed. Every little detail is important."

Webb frowned from her place at the prosecutor's table and shook her head. Gowen didn't bother trying to hide her satisfied smile from Ivy, who quickly searched her memory, wondering if she'd said something wrong, but she couldn't think of anything. *This stupid attorney thinks she's smarter than me, but she's wrong, oh, so wrong.*

"Ms. Greene, you stated you've been diagnosed with Post Traumatic Stress Disorder and depression, it that correct?"

"Yes." Ivy nodded.

"How long were you treated for PTSD?"

"I only went a couple of times. It was too expensive."

"What medical doctor diagnosed you?"

Ivy squirmed from side to side in the chair. "I'm not sure. I can't remember, it was at a clinic."

"Do you remember the name of the clinic where you saw the doctor?"

"No, but my victim's advocate also said I had PTSD."

"So you can't remember the clinic or the doctor's name?" Gowen asked again.

"My victim's advocate, Sharon McBride, works at the Crisis Center for Women."

"Your Honor?" Gowen insisted.

"Answer the question, Ms. Greene."

"Which doctor diagnosed your PTSD?" Gowen asked.

"I don't know, I told you I can't remember."

"Is Sharon McBride a psychologist, a licensed therapist, or is she just a volunteer at the Crisis Center for Women?"

Irritated by the question, Ivy replied, "I don't know. You'll have to ask her."

"Just for the record, your Honor, Sharon McBride is a volunteer at the Crisis Center for Women. She is not licensed to counsel or diagnose anyone."

Looking Ivy straight in her blue eyes, Gowen rolled out her question. "Ms. Greene, did Trace Aragon rape you, June 27, 2016?"

When Ivy narrowed her eyes, her gaze's innocent veneer stripped away. With a look of disgust, she replied. "Yes, if he hadn't, we wouldn't be here now, would we?"

Pleased that Ivy's haughty answer gave a glimpse of her true personality, Gowen said, "No further questions, your Honor."

Judge Donner concluded the day. "We will resume at nine o'clock tomorrow morning."

After the Judge retired, Gowen approached Webb and suggested that she reconsider the strength of her case.

"I believe Ivy's story," Webb declared, gathering her things. "Ivy, can we have a word?" Gowen watched them walk around the corner, mystified. Surely, Webb was intelligent enough to see through Ivy's lies and manipulation.

Neither Ivy nor Webb had any idea that the story Ivy just told was about to fall apart.

CHAPTER 59

The next morning, Trace and his mother drove around the courthouse, desperately looking for a parking spot. "There's one," Trace announced, pointing. "Grab it, I can't be late!"

They met family and friends at the security point and hurried up to the courtroom, where Gowen patiently waited. She gave Trace a reassuring hug before they walked confidently to their table.

"Is the defense ready to proceed?" Judge Donner asked.

"Yes, your Honor."

Gowen called Ethan Harrison to the stand. "Good morning Ethan. Do you know Trace Aragon?"

"Yes, I do."

"When did you first meet him?"

"Ninth grade, we went to Mountain View High School together."

"Would you consider yourself friends with him?"

"Yes. We've been best friends since ninth grade."

"Did Trace ever confide in you about Ivy Greene?"

"Yes. Ivy was always texting or calling him. Sometimes we'd be hanging out at his place and she'd just show up without being invited. It bothered Trace."

Gowen tipped her head. "Did you personally see any of the texts?"

Ethan's eyes widened. "Yes, and some of them were threatening."

Gowen's eyebrows rose. "Your Honor, at this time I'd like to offer Defense's Exhibit #5 for identification into evidence." Gowen handed Webb a copy of the texts.

Ivy: *Why are you ignoring me?*

Trace: *Stop! I'm sorry about what happened, but you need to stop calling and texting me. I told you it wasn't a good idea.*

Ivy: *If you don't tell Tayla about us, I will!*

Trace: *Go ahead. She's gonna find out anyways.*

Ivy: *I'm at your apartment, and if you don't talk to me, I'm going to ruin your life. This is your last chance to talk to me.*

Trace: *Please stop! For the love of God, just stop trying to ruin mine and Tayla's lives.*

Once the texts were marked as evidence for the defense, Gowen shared them with the jury, then asked, "Do you and Trace now live in Salt Lake City, Utah?"

"Yes. We moved there in September 2016."

"Why did you and Trace move?"

"He wanted to get away from Ivy. He thought putting some distance between them would stop her from harassing him and I was wanting to transfer to another store. So, we decided to move together."

Gowen tapped her chin. "Did it help?"

"To my knowledge, yes, but he changed his phone number, too, and I didn't hear of her calling or texting anymore."

"Ethan, do you trust Trace?"

"Yes I do. He's a really good guy."

"No further questions."

Webb stood and began her cross-examination. "Hello, Ethan. Did you see all the texts between Ivy and Trace?"

"I suppose not all of them."

"So maybe Trace just showed you the ones he wanted you to see."

"Objection, your Honor, leading the witness."

"Sustained, let's move on." Judge Donner ordered.

"No more questions for this witness, your Honor."

CHAPTER 60

Gowen patted Trace on the shoulder before she stood and called Tayla Dean to the stand. "Can you tell us how you know Ivy Greene?" Gowen asked.

Tayla hesitated, glanced around the room, then replied, "I went to high school with her."

"Were you friends with MS. Greene?"

Tayla adjusted herself in her seat. "A long time ago."

"Are you still friends with her?"

"No, not at all!"

"Please tell us why you're no longer friends with her."

"She broke Trace and me up."

"Would you please give the court more details on how this was accomplished?"

"I used to invite her with other friends to my family's cabin. Since Trace was my boyfriend then, he usually went with me. Ivy knew he was my boyfriend, but kept snuggling up to him and talking trash about me. She became so annoying I had to tell her to stop talking to him."

"Objection, your Honor."

"Sustained."

Gowen asked, "You moved to Oregon to go to college, is that correct?"

"Yes. I'm going to the University of Oregon."

"To your knowledge, did Ms. Greene and Mr. Aragon continue communicating with each other while you were in Oregon?"

"Yes, I saw texts and people told me about them being together at parties."

Tapping her pen on her tablet, Gowen asked, "Would you say their relationship had become more than just friends?"

Tayla's face grew uneasy "I guess so... they did end up having sex."

"How did you find out about Mr. Aragon and Ms. Greene having sex?"

"Ivy cornered me in a shopping parking lot and told me that Trace and she had sex the weekend he stayed home from my summer party."

"Did Ivy tell you Trace had raped her?"

"No. She said they had sex, and seemed very pleased about it."

"Objection."

"Sustained."

"Do you remember which weekend it was?"

"We went to the cabin on the June 24th, and we stayed until the 28th."

"Do you know why Mr. Aragon didn't go with you?"

"He told me he had to work."

"Did you and Mr. Aragon talk about Ivy and him having sex?"

"Yes. He denied it."

"Did Mr. Aragon lie to you about other things during your relationship?"

Tayla glanced at the ceiling, then back at the attorney. "Nothing I know of."

"Did you trust Mr. Aragon during your time together as girlfriend and boyfriend?"

Tayla nodded and sighed. "Yes."

"Are you and Mr. Aragon still friendly?"

Tayla's glance flicked to Trace, then away. "No, not really."

"Have you talked with him about this alleged rape?"

"No."

"Do you know Eli Cole?"

"Yes."

"Did Eli Cole text you a video or photo of Ms. Greene and Mr. Aragon kissing?"

"Yes, he sent me a picture of them kissing and a video of them arguing, too."

"Did you hear Mr. Aragon apologize to Ivy for raping her?"

Tayla frowned. "Not specifically. I heard him say that he was sorry for what happened, but he didn't say why he was sorry. Something about him promising, he would leave me for her. I don't know...I stopped listening to it, I was so mad at the time."

"Were you and Mr. Aragon intimate as a couple?"

Tayla looked down. "Yes, we were."

"Did he ever make you do anything you were uncomfortable with?"

Tayla looked up. "Never."

"Was he ever aggressive with you?"

"No, never."

"So until he cheated on you, did you and Mr. Aragon have a good relationship?"

Through suddenly teary eyes, Tayla glanced at Trace. "Yes. He was a great guy until then."

"Do you think Trace Aragon is capable of rape?"

"No." Tayla's voice was firm. "I don't."

"No further questions."

Webb slowly stood and walked around the table toward the witness. "Ms. Dean, did Mr. Aragon flirt with other girls?"

Tayla shrugged. "Some people thought so, but he was just being a nice guy."

"Did he flirt with Ms. Greene?"

"Some people might call it that." The corner of her mouth quirked up. "He was a little insecure, so sometimes he complimented other girls just to see if I'd get mad, to make sure I still loved him. We knew each other so well that it was just a game we played."

"Did you ever see any texts from Mr. Aragon to Ms. Greene?"

"Yes. They went back and forth more times than I like to remember."

"Did you tell Mr. Aragon to stop texting her?"

"Yes."

"Did he?"

Tayla's expression hardened. "Yes, for the most part. She sent him so many texts, that I saw a few replies he sent her after I told him to stop. Trace and I argued over it."

Webb gave a slight nod. "Do you think they liked each other?"

Tayla's answer was strained. "Apparently, after all, they had sex."

"You say Trace was a good guy until he had sex with Ivy. Do you suppose maybe you don't know him like you thought you did, and maybe, just maybe, he's capable of other bad things too?"

"Objection," Gowen said, "Leading the witness."

"Sustained," Judge Donner said. "Rephrase the question."

Webb put up a hand, satisfied that she'd already planted the thought in the juror's minds. "No more questions."

CHAPTER 61

Spectators filled the courtroom seats before Judge Donner asked, "Counsel, are we ready this morning?"

Both attorneys nodded and Gowen called her first witness, Detective Ted Holden.

Holden almost stopped breathing. The late night service of a subpoena had Holden in a panic. *The defense is calling me as their witness. Why?* Holden stood, straightened his tie, and walked to the witness stand.

"Detective Holden, how long have you been with the Ada County Sheriff's Department?"

"Eighteen years. Two years ago I was promoted to Lead Detective in the Sex Crime Unit."

"In the two years as Lead Detective, have you investigated other rape cases?"

"Yes, several."

"How many would you say?"

"I'd say, maybe eight to ten over the last two years."

"Gowen moved in for the next question. " Prior to this case, did you know either party, Ms. Greene or Mr. Aragon?"

Holden replied, "Yes, I was called out to a reported burglary at Mr. Aragon and his roommate's apartment awhile back."

"Did you know Ms. Green before this case?"

Holden readjusted himself in his chair before replying, "Yes, she went to school with my daughter."

Gowen leaned in closer to Holden, "Has Ms. Greene ever been to your home?"

Holden looked at Ivy and then back at Gowen. "She occasionally spent time there with my daughter."

"Would you say your daughter and Ms. Greene were close friends?"

"Yes, I would say so."

"Detective Holden, would you say that the relationship between Ms. Greene and your daughter affected the way you handled this case?"

"No, absolutely not," Holden sharply stated.

"Can you explain to the court why you refused to consider evidence gathered by our private investigator containing statements from individuals with information pertinent to this case?"

"I felt we had all the evidence we needed to turn this case over to the prosecution."

"No further questions for this witness at this time."

Judge Donner looked at Webb, who shook her head. "No questions for this witness."

Holden stepped down from the witness stand and returned to his seat, relieved to have gotten through his testimony unscathed.

He had no way of knowing that his relief would be short-lived.

CHAPTER 62

"Your Honor, the defense calls Chloe Holden to the stand." The courtroom stilled as Chloe walked through the double doors of the courtroom. Holden suddenly knew why he'd been called to the stand for the defense.

Detective Ted Holden sat on the edge of his seat and watched with wide eyes as his daughter trudged to the witness stand as if facing her own execution. He stared at his beloved daughter's face, desperate for her to look at him. He wasn't sure what he'd do if she met his eyes. He wanted to mouth the words, "I'm sorry. Love you. Miss you," but she studiously avoided his gaze.

Holden's body grew cold with regret. Would Chloe tell what she'd seen on that hellish night in his bedroom? He shivered with apprehension. He didn't want to hear it, especially not from her mouth. But if she told, would she finally be able to forgive him?

Chloe was sworn in and sat down stiffly. Shifting her weight in the chair, she did her best to avoid not only her father's eyes, but Ivy's as well, which was easier, since Ivy's head was bent over her notebook again.

"Good morning, Chloe," Gowen said. "I'm going to ask you about a few people today. Do you know Ivy Greene?"

Chloe's answer was faint. "Yes."

"Are you friends with her?"

Chloe's eyes blazed with sudden passion. "No!"

Gowen took an involuntary step back, and the judge frowned at Chloe, clutching his gavel handle.

Gowen turned her step into a swivel, turning sideways as if intending to move that way all along. She glanced at her notes, then asked, "Do you know Detective Ted Holden?"

"Yes." Chloe's voice was tight, as if there wasn't enough room in her throat for the words to fit through.

"What is your relationship with him?"

Chloe hesitated, then said barely loud enough to be heard, "He's my father."

"Do you live with your father?"

Chloe's vehement answer wasn't quite as loud as before. "No!"

"Can you tell us why?' Gowen asked.

"We don't get along anymore." Chloe reached for a tissue.

"Were you ever friends with Ms. Greene?"

As if tasting something foul, Chloe answered, "We used to be best friends. We became friends, my father and I let her come to our house because she said she didn't get along with her mother."

"Why aren't you friends anymore?"

Chloe's gaze wandered to her father, who leaned forward in his seat, gazing at her with such longing that Chloe was momentarily confused. His lips moved. Had he really whispered that he loved her?

Hot tears fell from Chloe's eyes as she turned her gaze away from him. She had to do the right thing, no matter how much it hurt. "I found Ivy and my dad in bed together."

A collective gasp was followed by heads turning in Holden's direction, but he ignored the looks of disgust, his gaze steadfast on his daughter.

"What were the circumstances?"

For the first time, Chloe glanced at Ivy, then away, blinking as if her eyes hurt. Then she took in a ragged breath and spoke rapidly. "Ivy and I were supposed to go to a football game, but she said she was sick, so I went with my friend Mia. The game was boring, so we left early to watch a movie at Mia's." Chloe grabbed a tissue and pressed it to her face. "We stopped at my house so I could change clothes. We were surprised to see Ivy's car in my driveway. We didn't see her or my dad when we went inside, then we heard voices in Dad's bedroom. I opened the bedroom door, and couldn't believe my eyes. Ivy's clothes were on the floor, and she was sitting naked on top of my dad." Chloe glanced down and twisted her tissue so hard it broke into two shredded pieces. "They were having sex." Chloe took another tissue. "Ivy looked at us like she was pleased with herself."

"Objection."

Judge Donner looked at Gowen and nodded his head to move on. "Sustained."

Chloe wiped away more tears. "When my dad realized we were there, he pushed her off, told her to get dressed and go home. I ran downstairs and my friend followed me out to my car. Ivy told me that my dad had called her and told her to come over because he was alone and he wanted her, but I didn't believe her. She's a liar."

"Objection."

"Sustained, the jury will disregard the last statement." Chloe lowered her head and sobbed into her tissues. Deep down, she believed her father was still a good man who was deeply ashamed of what he'd done.

Nevertheless, the truth was that no matter how Ivy had talked him into it, he'd had sex with her. Chloe was only here because she didn't believe for a minute that Trace had raped Ivy, and he didn't deserve punishment for something he didn't do.

"I know how hard this must be for you." The sympathy in Gowen's voice seemed real. "Did your father apologize to you?"

"Yes," Chloe replied, her voice clogged with tears. He'd apologized to her repeatedly, in word, texts, and letters. Now her testimony had devastated his career. He'd likely be fired. "He said he was sorry over and over, but I didn't want to hear it."

"So your father admitted to having sex with Ms. Greene?"

Chloe choked on her words. "He didn't have to! I saw it with my own eyes. He tried to explain, but I couldn't stand to be around him, so I moved out and haven't spoken to him since."

"How old was Ivy at the time?"

Chloe shrugged. She didn't want to make things any worse for her father. Let someone else do the math. "I don't know when her birthday is. We were both seniors, so she might have been 18."

"Why are you testifying today, Chloe?"

Chloe sighed as if drawing breath from the bottom of a deep well. "Ivy's no virgin, as she said she was and she lies. What I saw proves she lied."

"Objection, your Honor!"

"Sustained, Ms. Holden, just answer the questions, please."

"Chloe," Gowen asked, "are you testifying today to get even with Ivy?"

"Maybe," Chloe sniffed, then blew her nose in a fresh tissue. "I don't know. But I'm mainly here to tell the truth that Ivy will go to great lengths to ruin anyone if she wants something badly enough."

"Thank you, Chloe."

Webb breathed deeply as she shuffled the papers on her table without really looking at them. Then she set the papers down, cleared her throat, and approached Chloe for cross-examination.

"You've been estranged from your father for how long?"

Chloe sighed with a little hitch in her voice. "Since the night I found them together."

"So you never really heard his side of the story."

"No. I haven't talked to him."

"Isn't it possible that you could you have misunderstood the situation?"

"No! They were clearly having sex."

"No further questions."

As Chloe left the stand, Gowen turned to Judge Donner. "Your Honor, I would like to recall Detective Holden to the stand."

Judge Donner allowed the redirect, and Holden approached the stand as if dragging his feet through tangled grass. When he was seated, Gowen reminded Holden he was still under oath and then asked, "Detective Holden, earlier I asked you if you had ever met Trace Aragon or Ivy Greene. Do you remember?"

Lifting his chin, Holden replied, "Yes."

"Why didn't you tell the court at that time that you knew Ms. Greene as more than just your daughter's classmate?"

Holden looked at his daughter seated in the courtroom, her head bowed. With tears rising in his eyes, he answered, "It's clear why I did not."

"Did you have sex with Ms. Greene?"

Holden's chin lowered. "Yes, I did."

"Was she a minor at the time?"

Holden sighed from the bottom of his soul. "I'm not sure. Chloe was 18, and they were both seniors, but I don't know." His voice lowered. "Regardless, I knew better."

"So when you and your partner arrived at Ms. Greene's apartment to take her statement about being raped, you recognized her, yet you still took the case?"

"Yes, in spite of my better judgment. Ivy made it plainly understood that if I didn't arrest Mr. Aragon for rape, she'd tell about us."

"Did you believe her story about being raped by Mr. Aragon?"

"No."

"Objection, your Honor."

"Sustained."

Gowen asked, "Was Ms. Greene a virgin before the alleged rape by Mr. Aragon?"

Holden appeared to age ten years before he replied, "No, she was not."

Gowen pointed her pen at Holden. "I have one more question for this witness." Gowen's candid face stared directly at Holden. "If Ms.

Greene had not threatened you, would you have arrested Mr. Aragon for rape with the evidence you had?"

Holden's somber tone answered. "No."

Ivy shook her head "no" at the jurors, letting her tears loose. "He's lying! They all are," she shouted.

Judge Donner demanded, "Restrain your client, Ms. Webb."

Webb took Ivy's arm. Her whispers calmed Ivy down and she melted back into her chair.

"I have no more questions for Detective Holden."

Holden stepped down, barely keeping himself upright. Although the prospect of facing legal action shredded his nerves, he was strangely relieved at having the truth come to light. It would no longer hang over his head like a suffocating cloud that could descend at any moment.

He glanced at Chloe, who was looking at him with what seemed like compassion. Could it be true? Could this crossroads possibly mend his relationship with Chloe? If so, any amount of public humiliation was worth it.

CHAPTER 63

Trace was about to testify in a case that could irreparably damage his life, so Gowen spent hours preparing for him to take the witness stand, asking him extensive questions followed by a mock deposition where she posed related questions, both in tone and content, that were likely to be asked by the prosecution. When Trace was able to answer concisely and clearly, they walked away from their meeting, confident that he was prepared for the next day.

Trace couldn't keep daylight from invading his room the next morning. *Everything hinges on what I say today, and once said, it can never be unsaid,* Trace dressed and gathered his things. *Why can't I think straight this morning?* He panicked when he couldn't find his keys, only to discover them in the wrong pocket. He found small comfort in the warmth of his mug and small sips of coffee, which was all he could force down. He didn't want to go, but wanted it to be over with, anxiety and restlessness playing tug of war with his emotions until he nearly fell apart. When he heard the double tap from his mother's horn, he abandoned his coffee, grabbed his jacket, and ran out the door.

The steps that led up to the wide plaza in front of the courthouse building were the same as yesterday, but now seemed insurmountable. He stopped dead when he saw the flag waving in the breeze. "I used to salute the flag every morning, Mom. What's happened to my life?"

"Come on, let's go inside. You'll get through this."

Gowen greeted Trace with a confident smile, and hurried him into a conference room for one last talk before taking their seats. The courtroom was silent as Ivy was the last to walk in, deliberately looking at Trace as if trying to catch his glance. Then she quickly took her seat beside Webb and opened her notebook.

An annoying facial twitch beat at the corner of Trace's right eye, barely there, but enough to elevate his anxiety. Arms folded tightly across his chest, his foot tapped frantically as he stared out the hard water stained courthouse windows. The brisk sunny morning could either open the door to his freedom or snap his dreams in two.

The bailiff announced the judge, and the jury was seated for the final day of testimony.

After Gowen called Trace to the stand and he swore to tell the truth, she said, "Hello, Trace. You're here today because Ms. Greene has accused you of rape. Do you understand this charge?"

Trace nodded, swallowed, and said, "Yes."

"Have you ever been in trouble with the law before?"

"No, never."

"Not even a speeding ticket?"

"No."

Gowen gave Trace a stern glance before turning her attention to the jury. "Detective Holden testified that you lied to him. I'd like to ask you about that." Her gaze went back to Trace. "Did you lie to him when he asked if Ms. Green had ever been in your apartment?"

"Yes."

"Why did you lie?"

"I don't know. The way Detective Holden asked made me think I was in trouble for something, but I didn't know what. He kept asking the same questions over and over. He was so intimidating. I was really scared I might get in big trouble if I said she'd been in my apartment. I know it was stupid to lie."

"Did you feel threatened by Detective Holden's questioning?"

"Yes."

"How so, can you explain?"

"Well, he kept saying I was guilty, that he knew it and could prove it. I asked him guilty of what? Then he'd change the subject back to Ivy being in my apartment. He brought up my friends and parties, dates that were over a year ago, and he threatened jail and unpleasant dealings with inmates. He was messing with my head, if you know what I mean."

"If you were so scared, why didn't you call an attorney at that time?"

"I didn't think I needed one, because I hadn't done anything wrong. Then Detective Holden told me he had witnesses and proof that I'd raped Ivy." Trace put a fist on his chest. "I knew he didn't, because I didn't rape her but I was scared. I couldn't even process what he asked me after that. I just wanted him to stop badgering me, so finally I told him I wasn't going to talk to him anymore."

"Trace, did Ms. Greene text you on a regular basis?"

"Yes."

"Did she bring you lunch while you were at work more than once?"

"Yes."

"Why did you accept food from her and respond to her texts and phone calls?"

"I don't know. She was friendly, and she was a friend of mine and Tayla's."

Gowen walked over to the jury box and softly tapped the railing with her fingertips. "Did you like Ms. Greene, Trace?"

Trace felt sick at his answer. "Yes, I did, at first. I thought she was kind of cute."

Ivy looked up, straightened, and tugged at her new dress that the store assistant swore looked so flattering on her. *I knew he liked me. It just took this for him to admit it!*

"When Ms. Greene was in your apartment, did she help you put your things away?"

"Yes," he admitted.

Her gaze fixed on Trace, Ivy hadn't written anything in her notebook for several minutes. Gowen watched the jury's body language, the shifting in the seats, raised eyebrows, slight nods, confusion on some faces, other expressions that seemed to want more convincing. Some seemed to be listening and making mental notes. Some appeared studious while others looked overly concerned. Was Gowen's attempt to expose Ivy by planting road signs of narcissistic behaviors working?

"Ms. Greene stated she hung out with you and your friends. Is that true?"

"Yes, she was one of the regulars, almost always with us."

"Did that bother you?"

"Sometimes Tayla and I wanted to be alone, but Ivy seemed to always show up."

Maddened by Trace's last statement, Ivy leaned back in her chair and looked at the jury with disbelief. *What the hell? Tayla wanted me there, and so did you.* Her demeanor shifted, and she fingered her ponytail with restless agitation.

Gowen mirrored Ivy's gesture by fingering her own hair before asking her next question. "Did she help you move any furniture that night?"

"Yes, we moved my dresser to the opposite wall."

"Could she have gotten her bruises by moving your dresser?"

"Yes. She could have gotten them from moving my boxes, too."

"Did you put the bruises on Ms. Greene's arm?"

"No, I did not."

"Why did you lie to your girlfriend about Ms. Greene?"

"I didn't want to lose her. I was stupid."

Gowen offered a moment of silence before asking. "Trace, did you and Ms. Greene have consensual sex on June 27th, 2016 at approximately 2:30 am?"

"Yes."

"I have one last and very important question. Trace, did you rape Ivy Greene?"

Trace leaned forward and clearly stated, "No, I did not."

"No more questions." Gowen winked at Trace and returned to her table.

Webb approached Trace with slow, deliberate steps. "Did you ever hang out with Ms. Greene alone prior to the night in question?" Webb asked.

"No, not that I remember."

"What about at parties? You seemed to be at a lot of them."

"Objection."

"Sustained."

"Evidence shows you responded to Ms. Greene's texts and calls on a regular basis, and even accepted her bringing you lunch while you were at work. Why would you do that if you weren't interested in her?"

Trace shrugged. "Like I said earlier, we were friends. I thought those were things friends did."

Webb said firmly, "Come on, Trace, wasn't it your intention to have sex with Ms. Greene on the night of June 27, 2016?"

"Objection, Your Honor."

"Sustained," Judge Donner tipped his head at Webb, noting his disapproval.

Webb walked to the witness stand. With one hand on the railing, she blurted, "When you raped Ms. Greene, did you still want to be her friend?"

"Objection!" Gowen demanded.

"Sustained."

"No further questions," Webb stated.

CHAPTER 64

Jillian Webb was first to present her summation, reviewing evidence for the jury in a manner designed to persuade them to vote in favor of Ivy's accusation.

"Ivy Greene leads a simple but promising life," Webb began. "She attends college and works to pay her way. She was on track to a bright future until the early morning of June 27th, 2016, when she was invited to a friend's apartment. Ivy had no idea that Trace Aragon was about to brutally change her life forever. Mr. Aragon lured her into his bedroom where he insisted on having sex. When Ms. Greene told him, 'No,' he became aggressive and raped her.

"You might ask why she went to his apartment so late at night. At the time, she trusted him and never thought he'd be a threat to her in any way. Mr. Aragon led her to believe he liked her. He accepted her lunches, her phone calls, and texts. He lured Ms. Greene to his apartment by letting her think it was a friendly meeting. Most regrettably, in this case, hindsight is 20/20. Giving in to his lust, Trace Aragon raped Ivy Greene. He lied to the police about Ms. Greene ever being at his apartment. Witnesses stated under oath that they, too, have witnessed Mr. Aragon lying. He even lied to his girlfriend.

"Ms. Greene's friend Eli testified that he saw bruises on Ms. Green's right arm from the attack. He also testified that she confided details of the rape to him. She explained why she didn't report the rape until three months later. Detective Redden told us many rape victims delay reports of sexual violation due to trauma, embarrassment, and fear. Ivy was not only ashamed, but afraid for her life. She's developed Post Traumatic Stress Disorder, and as a result she suffers from depression, anger, disrupted relationships, and even thoughts of suicide.

"Does Ms. Greene remember everything about her rape? Maybe not. Would you under such traumatic circumstances? Many women, young and old, report sexual assaults years after the incident. They share the same fear of public humiliation as Ms. Greene. Women need to be supported in the fight against rape, empowered by knowing that their fears are taken seriously.

"If Mr. Aragon is found 'not guilty' of this horrible crime, please keep in mind that his next victim could very well be your wife daughter, mother, granddaughter, or friend. Keep innocent women safe from cruel, unfeeling men. Find Trace Aragon guilty of felony rape. Thank you."

Webb turned and walked back to her table.

Gowen stood silently for a few seconds before speaking. "Sexual assault accusations draw a fine line, because we want to provide justice and protection for anyone who's a real rape victim. On the other hand, we also need justice for those who are falsely accused of these crimes. Mr. Aragon voluntarily chose to give up nearly two years of his life in a military capacity to protect and serve his country. Now it's time for us, the justice system, to protect him from the malicious intent of Ivy Greene.

"Is Ms. Greene using her accusation of rape as a weapon of power and revenge? Is she craving attention at unprecedented levels? Is becoming a victim fulfilling that desire? Ms. Greene herself told us how she can act any part at any given time. Is she acting the part of a rape victim? Is there any evidence to prove the accusation that Trace Aragon raped Ivy Greene? Exhibit 1, the texts on June 26, 2016, clearly shows that Ms. Greene invited herself to his apartment, instigating her own presence in Mr. Aragon's room at 12:30 am that night. He admits they had consensual sex.

"Ms. Greene claims she told Mr. Aragon 'no,' but Zack Becker, Mr. Aragon's roommate, didn't hear her yell, scream or even shout 'no!' There were no signs of a struggle. We can assume a two-bedroom apartment would be small enough to hear almost anything coming from a connecting room.

"She didn't report this alleged assault until three months later. There is no physical evidence of an alleged rape, there is no rape kit, torn clothing, or pictures of scratches or bruises. The only evidence presented here today is what Ms. Greene claims happened and the circumstantial evidence of the cell phones being in the same place at the same time. Witnesses have stated that Ms. Greene seemed fixated on Mr. Aragon, even to the point of stalking him. Witnesses also stated that Ms. Greene told others of the sexual encounter she had with Mr. Aragon without ever mentioning that he raped her. Would anyone who was truly ashamed or afraid even mention the experience? She bragged to Mr. Aragon's girlfriend, Tayla Dean, about having sex with him without mentioning a single word about rape."

Gowen walked over to the jury box and grabbed the railing with both hands. Looking squarely at each one of them, she continued. "Detective Holden confessed under oath he was a past sexual partner of Ms. Greene's, proving that she, under oath, lied about being a virgin. From everything, you've seen and heard, you can believe she also lied about Trace Aragon raping her.

"The bottom line is that there's no evidence to support her accusations. It boils down to his word against hers. Trace has been truthful in every question asked him in this courtroom. Ms. Greene has lied to multiple people, and lied on this witness stand. It's been proven in this courtroom that she can't tell the truth.

"To add dimension to the question the prosecution put to you in her summation, consider that the next false accusation of rape could be made against your husband, son, grandson, father, or friend. I urge you to carefully consider the evidence with your eyes wide open and find Trace Aragon not guilty. Thank you."

Gowen returned to the defense table and took Trace's trembling hand. Seeing the beads of sweat on his upper lip, she leaned close to his ear and whispered, "Take it easy. It's almost over."

"What if they come back with a guilty verdict?" Trace murmured.

"Then we'll appeal," Elizabeth assured him.

CHAPTER 65

After the emotional closing arguments from both sides, Judge Donner addressed the jury. "All the evidence from both sides has been presented. Ladies and gentlemen of the jury, it is now time for me to instruct you on the law of this case, after which you will be asked to deliberate and determine if the State has proven its case against Trace Aragon beyond a reasonable degree of doubt.

"It's my responsibility to instruct you concerning the legal principles you must consider during your deliberations. It's your responsibility to access the event that gave rise to the charge against Trace Aragon and decide what happened that night in June.

"There is a fundamental principle you must understand and always recall during your deliberations. When a person is accused of criminal wrongdoing, he or she does not have to prove innocence. It is the task of the prosecutor to prove guilt beyond reasonable doubt. If the evidence before you does not go that far, Mr. Aragon is entitled to be found not guilty.

"The evidence in this case was, at times, conflicting, and possibly confusing. It is your task to sort through all the testimony. You may accept all or most of the testimony given by some witnesses and reject all or most given by others.

"It's important for you to decide how the event between Ms. Greene and Mr. Aragon occurred. If you decide that both Greene and Aragon consented to having sex, then you must consider and apply different legal principles and find Mr. Aragon not guilty of rape.

"If you are satisfied that Mr. Aragon's actions were unlawful, but cannot be sure beyond a reasonable doubt that Mr. Aragon intended to rape Ms. Greene and cause grievous harm to her, then you will find him not guilty of rape.

"If you find that Mr. Aragon's actions were unlawful and caused grievous bodily harm to Ms. Greene, then you will find him guilty of the crime of rape.

"Ladies and gentlemen, you may now retire to the jury room and begin your deliberations. The clerk will give you a copy of the indictment. You may also take the exhibits with you into the jury room if you wish."

The twelve jurors left the courtroom single file and entered the deliberation room where twelve chairs were spaced around a rectangular wooden table. The table was set with twelve pens and twelve notebooks. The additional chairs were filled with purses and coats. Besides two restrooms, a service counter sat at the far end of the room, equipped with a coffee maker, under counter refrigerator, and microwave oven so the jurors wouldn't need to leave the deliberation room for any reason other than emergencies.

The jurors had a difficult job. The life of a young woman and the life of a young man dangled in front of them. They carefully went through the case, pointing out holes in testimony, inconsistencies, the overall lack of evidence, and the lies. While deliberating, each one of the jurors agreed the prosecutor simply had not proved her case, and relied too much on Ivy's disjointed testimony. They understood that, as frustrating as it might be, it was better to let a guilty man go free than put an innocent man behind bars and ruin his life forever.

When the jury finally sent word that they'd reached a verdict, Trace's family and friends clung to the hope he'd be found not guilty.

In case he might hear the dreaded word, "Guilty," and be taken into custody, Trace had arranged for Ethan to take his personal effects and drive his car back home. Trace felt faint as the bailiff announced for the last time, "The Honorable Judge Donner presiding."

Everyone's eyes were on the jury members as they entered the courtroom and took their seats. Even Ivy looked up from her notebook to straighten her dress and toss her hair.

Trace wondered if it would be easier not to look when the decision was read. He glanced at his hands twisted together in a nervous knot in his lap.

The jury was guided back into the courtroom and they each settled into their seats. "Madame Foreperson, have you reached a verdict?" Judge Donner asked.

A female juror of about 35 stood. "Yes, we have, your Honor." The written verdict was handed to the bailiff, who handed it to the judge. Judge Donner read it and returned it to the bailiff, who put it back in Madam Foreperson's hand.

Judge Donner's voice filled the courtroom "Will the defendant please rise."

Trace stood. Although afraid of what he might hear, he couldn't look away.

"Please read the verdict," Judge Donner said.

"We, the jury, find Trace Aragon not guilty of felony rape."

Trace's body nearly collapsed with relief. He could scarcely breathe as tears flowed down his face.

"Trace Aragon," Judge Donner said in a kindly voice, "you are free to go."

Trace's family and friends crowded around him, offering hugs and joining him in tears of joy.

Ivy slouched in her chair in disbelief. She didn't say a word, just stared straight ahead. When Sharon leaned in to offer a consoling hug, Ivy shoved her away. All of a sudden her eyebrows crashed together and her eyes widened. "Have you all lost your minds?" she screamed, her sharp voice full of rage. "This wasn't supposed to happen. Where's my justice?"

The bailiff strode toward her, but before he could reach her, Ivy grabbed her notebook and pen, slung her purse over her shoulder, and stormed out of the courtroom.

"Wait up," Ivy's friend yelled.

Ivy dashed down the courthouse stairs, her friend trailing behind. Ivy's rage carried her through the parking lot to her car, where she smacked the hood with her purse. *Where's my keys, the damn keys?* Struggling to find them, she finally yanked them free, unlocked the door, and sat fuming in front of the steering wheel. *He doesn't get to do this to me! He'll pay for what he's done. They all lied. It's not my fault.*

Just as Ivy's friend opened the passenger door, Ivy flung her notebook against the rearview mirror with such hostile force that the mirror flew across the dash and smacked into the windshield.

"I...think I'll just walk home," her friend said before slamming the door and jogging away.

Immersed in her emotional meltdown, Ivy scarcely noticed. When her wrath finally receded, she started her car and drove out of the parking lot. Her vindictive plan for Trace's attention had failed, but she vowed that Trace wasn't just going to walk away from her and out of her life.

She drove to Eli's house and found him sitting in his car with the engine running. She parked, flung open her door and grabbed her purse. Slamming the door shut, she stormed toward Eli's car. Her keys gripped in her hand, she pressed them into the side of Eli's car, gouging a trail in the paint as she walked up to the driver's door.

"What the hell, Ivy?" Eli shouted, jumping out of his car. "You're a crazy bitch, just like they say!"

"Don't you ever call me crazy, you snitch. You just left me there, and you said all the wrong things, you stupid idiot."

Eli stared at the face of his friend and suddenly saw a stranger. His incarceration had not been pleasant, in fact, he was back in counseling for some of the things he'd had to endure, but he'd done it all for her. He glanced at his damaged car and felt a sudden kinship with it. He was damaged, too, by the same hand.

"Ivy?" Eli's mother walked down the front walk toward them. "Is everything okay?"

Ivy's face transformed into her angelic demeanor. "Yes, Claire."

"How did court go today? It must have been a rough day for you guys. I sure wish I could have made it, you know, for support and all. I know your mom and you well...I wish I could have been there."

With rage in her voice, Ivy replied, "Don't you know it yet? They found him not guilty. I have no justice, and your son, yes, Eli, botched his testimony. I'm sure that's why they declared Trace not guilty."

"Well, I don't know if Eli's testimony would have had that much impact on a jury."

"Of course you'd side with your son." Ivy's pretty face was marred by deep lines of anger. "His stupid testimony certainly didn't help. He's part of them and they all lied."

When Claire turned her head away from the raging girl, she noticed Eli's damaged car. "What happened here?"

"Ivy's sorry ass, that's what happened." Eli gave Ivy a scornful glance. "She didn't get her way this time and took it out on my car." Eli felt as if he were standing on the edge of a precipice. It was scary, but he felt powerful, too.

"Ivy?" Claire's voice was full of shock. "Why? Our family has been nothing but nice to you." Her brow creased. "I think now would be a good time for you to leave. Has Eli told you we're moving?"

"No, he didn't mention it. I'll look for another place."

"No," Claire said. "I mean you need to leave right now. Get your things and leave."

Ivy's eyebrows shot up. "Where am I supposed to go?"

Claire gave her a crooked smile. "Not our problem, Ivy. Call your mom, I guess."

Ivy whirled on Eli, her face a mask of rage. "Why didn't you tell me?" she hissed.

"Well, let's see, maybe because I was in jail," Eli replied, his voice harder than Ivy had ever heard it before. "But I'm telling you now. Pack your shit and leave, now."

"No problem, you little fag." Ivy shoved past Eli so hard that he stumbled. She strode inside to pack her things. By the time she climbed back into her car, loaded down with her possessions, she was emotionally dead except for a tiny little spark, a spark that left her cold, very cruel, and damn the consequences.

CHAPTER 66

Although immensely grateful for his not guilty verdict, Trace had a rude awakening when he realized that his life would never go back to normal. He was caught in a ruthless undertow from his legal proceedings that came with a disturbing ripple effect, making his life harder than it had ever been before.

He had no way of earning income since his arrest, which meant his bank account was drained, but at least his slate was now clean. The fastest way he knew to get back to work was his former job. In spite of Christian's big mouth, Trace had enjoyed the sales company, knew the ropes, and made good money. Deciding he'd work with a different manager, he re-applied to his former employer with confidence.

When Christian replied that there were no current openings, Trace was disappointed. *But, hey, nothing stays the same.* Then Christian offered him an unexpected olive branch. "We'll be sure to let you know if something comes up, Trace. I've got your number."

Then he'd just have to find some other work. Hardening his emotional armor, Trace applied for several jobs that were well suited to his skills but was repeatedly turned down. In a travesty of justice, every background check always brought up the charge of rape against him. Even though he'd been found not guilty, the charge was still attached to his background check like a malevolent leech sucking his employment opportunities away.

Doesn't anyone care that it was a false accusation? I was found innocent! As hard as he tried, his applications never crossed the finish line. It was as if he were living under a curse.

He hung onto the hope that something would soon open up at his old company. If he could just hang on until then, he'd be alright. He clung to this bit of optimism until he found his old sales position advertised on the job boards with four openings. He stared at the words, reading them again and again, each one chipping away at his confidence and leaving behind dry dust.

They'd lied to him. *Why? Because he was arrested? Didn't they know he'd been found innocent?*

When he felt he could speak clearly, he called and asked for Christian. "I want one of the job openings you've listed."

After waiting through five seconds of silence, Trace heard, "Sorry. We're not going to hire you back."

"But I'm innocent! The jury said I'm innocent! So why not?"

"We have a reputation to maintain. This is goodbye, Trace."

Trace hung up, wondering if he was caught in an alternate reality, a hostile plane he didn't know how to maneuver. Although it was only late afternoon, Trace shut down his computer, turned off the lights, and crawled into bed.

Why can't I move on? What's wrong with me? This dull ache in my heart won't go away. Will I be like this forever? My chest feels like it's crushed under a hundred-pound weight. I'm so desperately unhappy, I could erupt into tears at any minute.

Why'd Ivy do this to me? I didn't mean to hurt her. She didn't have to do me dirt like this. She lied and messed with my head. Why didn't she just leave me alone?

I hate the nighttime. I'm so miserable. What I wouldn't do just to lose myself in sleep!

The next morning, Ethan knocked on Trace's door. "Hey!" Ethan twisted the knob and inched the door open. "Where were you last night?"

Trace rolled over in bed and pulled the covers up to his chin. "Here," he grunted.

"What? I didn't see you when I got home." After a moment's pause, Ethan said, "So you went to bed early?"

"Yeah."

"Enough with the beauty sleep," Ethan said. "When are you going to get a job and pay your share of the rent?"

Trace sat up, hair wild, hands stabbing the air. "No one will hire me! My old company said there were no openings that they'd tell me when there were, and then I found an ad for four people to hire for my old job. Four, Ethan. They wouldn't even interview me."

"You don't want to work for those scuzzbuckets anyway. Find someone who appreciates you."

"Do you know what, Ethan? Even though I'm innocent in the eyes of the law, every time I get a background check, my arrest shows up. It's still there, and it doesn't bother mentioning that the jury declared me not guilty. How messed up is that?"

"Pretty messed up," Ethan agreed, pushing the door open and leaning against the jamb. "So what are you going to do about it?"

Trace shrugged. "There's nothing I can do about it."

"Wrong. You can get your ass out of bed and go find yourself a job."

Trace stared up at Ethan through bleary eyes.

"I'm serious. You sitting there in your sorry-ass bed isn't going to make your life any better." He pointed a finger at Trace. "You've got bills to pay and I'm telling you right now, I don't have any money to spare."

Ethan was barely quick enough to catch the pillow Trace threw at him. He threw it right back. "Come on," he said, wiggling his fingers in an invitation for Trace to come closer. "Show me what you got."

Trace leapt from the bed and barreled into Ethan, forcing him to step backwards to keep from falling over. "Get out of my way," Trace shouted. "I've got a job to find."

Ethan straightened his clothes and headed for the door. "Word of advice. Brush your teeth before your interviews."

Motivated by his friend's challenge and his seriously overdrawn bank account, Trace shored himself up for another job hunt. Although the world seemed against him, his family was willing to help him get some prepaid credit cards to pay his bills. "You'll get through this," Trace's mother encouraged him. "You're still young, and you have a lot to offer the world."

One day while searching for work, he headed for the elevator at a possible job location just as the doors started closing. He hurried to catch it until a woman in her mid 30's stuck her hand out from the elevator to stop the doors closing. She smiled at him.

Trace stopped dead still, unable to force himself to get in that elevator with a woman. No way. If he was alone with her even for a minute, she could say that he did something to her, and he'd have to go through court hell all over again. Not happening. He'd climb 50 flights of stairs first.

She stared at him with an encouraging smile, but he waved the back of his trembling hand toward her. "It's okay, I'm going the other direction." As she let the doors slide shut, Trace sucked in a big breath, trying to fend off what felt like a heart attack. He suddenly realized that he was afraid of women.

He thought back to how he'd subconsciously avoided looking at or walking near them since his trial. He wouldn't speak beyond what was required for social acceptance. He didn't strike up conversations with anyone, and shrank from other peoples' glances, wondering if they'd seen his mug shot online. Were they scrutinizing his features before telling the people around them that there was a rapist standing right there?

When Trace was alone, he often suffered severe bouts of regret that crawled up his spine with serrated feet and lodged in his head, ripping his memories open to torment him. *Why had he been so stupid? Why was he so weak that he let his defenses down and had sex with Ivy? It wouldn't have happened if he'd moved to Oregon. Damn the money. If he'd only known what a crap mess he'd make of his life for just a couple more dollars an hour, he never would have stayed. He thought he was strong and in control, but he was a spineless wimp and why'd he lie to a cop? He'd lost a great opportunity to go to college for a single sexual encounter that didn't mean a damn thing. Even worse, he'd lost the chance to carry on Uncle Warren's honorable legacy in serving in the military. He'd made his own life hell. He was a poor excuse for a man. He was worth nothing at all.*

Trace's grandmother kept close tabs on Trace, making sure he was okay and cheering him up. On one of her regular calls, she invited him to lunch. A burger and fries were usually good cures for whatever ailed a man.

Sitting across the table from Trace, his grandmother seemed surprised at what she saw. "Why, Trace, you've lost weight. Aren't you eating?"

"I'm not hungry, Grandma. I can't eat."

"You're always hungry."

"My stomach's twisted up in knots all the time. I've got stomach aches and panic attacks." Trace started to tear up. "Grandma, I don't have the strength to face any more disappointments. That's part of the reason I haven't got a job. I don't want a background check run and just hear "no" again. It's too embarrassing."

Holding back her tears, Grandma said, "You look like you haven't slept, either."

Trace shrugged. "I can't sleep. I hate nights! I have too many nightmares."

Grandma put down her fork, leaned across the table, and took her grandson's hand. "Okay Trace, what happened to you wasn't fair, not fair at all, but in case you haven't noticed, everyone gets garbage dumped on them now and then, some more than others." Grandma tapped the table. "It's just different kinds of garbage. Are you hearing me, Trace?"

"Yes," he replied, shoulders slumped, head down.

"Look at me Trace."

He obediently lifted his gaze.

"The hell you've been through, well, I can't even imagine it, and what you still are going through. Be mad, get angry, then go out and be happy and successful. That will be the best revenge on Ivy. You can't change what happened. You can only change what you're doing right now. I know you, and I wouldn't want to be in your way when you come back swinging. Your family loves you, and we will support you however we can. You know that. So eat your burger. It's your favorite."

Trace held his grandma's intense gaze, then exhaled a deep breath as if a pressure valve had been opened. He reached out and picked up a fry.

When Grandma dropped Trace off at his apartment, all Trace wanted to do was reset his life.

"Hey, man," Ethan greeted him, "let's go do something."

A distraction sounded perfect. "What should we do?"

"Let's hike up Timpanogos Mountain."

That was the last thing Trace expected to hear. "What? Why?"

Ethan shrugged. "It'll be fun, and you'll burn up some of your stress. How about it?"

"Yeah," Trace said, warming to the idea. "Yeah, maybe I'll go with you."

"Let's go next weekend."

"Sounds good."

Borrowing heavily on his family's and Ethan's beliefs that he still had something good to offer humanity, Trace renewed his commitment to find a job, and submitted applications. The day before he and Ethan planned to hike Timpanogos, he got a phone call. "Trace Aragon?"

"Yes."

"This is Bob Weaver, Human Resources director at Mountain Man Pharmaceutical Supply. How are you?"

"Fine." A mild sense of panic descended as Trace tried to figure out why the HR director was calling him the day after his application went in. No one had responded this soon before. Would the director chew him out for daring to ask for work when he'd been arrested for rape? That was worse than being ignored.

"I like your resume," Weaver said. "Could you come in on Monday for an interview?"

Trace was stunned. Hadn't this Weaver guy run a background check? Didn't he know the situation? Trace would have to tell him or else he'd look bad if it came out later. But what if bringing up his past cost him the only job offer he'd seen so far? Weaver might never find out about the arrest.

Trace didn't know what to say. He couldn't think straight. But he could talk to Ethan about it over the weekend. Maybe he'd even call Grandma. She'd helped him so much already, maybe she'd know what to do. "Yes, I can come in."

"Great. How about 10:00. Is that okay?"

"Sure."

On one hand, Trace was excited for the interview but as he lay in bed that night, he prepared himself for another disappointment.

CHAPTER 67

After Ivy's altercation with Eli, she moved into a small studio apartment, which was nothing she was proud of. She seethed over her burned bridges, blaming the citizens of Meridian for the situation. Her mother had been unapproachable for years, and since Ivy also lacked any compassion for her mother, there was no love lost there. Eli was out of her life. His parents were moving away, and he was going with them. Rather than regretting his lost friendship, she saw it as a mere inconvenience. People were merely her instruments to manipulate in order to fuel her narcissistic needs.

In Ivy's twisted mind, she'd accused Trace of rape in order to focus his attention on her, to make him realize how powerful she was, to make him appreciate her. She was at the very edge of sanity. The Joker, played by Heath Ledger, said it best, "As you know, madness is a lot like gravity. All it takes is a little push."

After Ivy chased Zack down at Ridley's Market, he swore that he didn't know Trace's address.

How could Trace think he could just leave and change his phone number? Why hadn't he simply admitted that he wanted her more than Tayla? Why abandon her? Ivy searched his friend's social media accounts for hours, but couldn't find him in Salt Lake City, Utah. *Why there? It was a stupid place to live, but Ethan would know where he was. They were best friends. He certainly wouldn't want to talk to her, but she was clever. She knew how to manipulate people. She could get him to slip up and say something.*

Ivy called the Sprint store on Meridian Road, but the phone just rang and rang. *Just answer the damn phone.* She called again and again. *What business doesn't even answer their phone?*

Ivy's instant gratification reflex was short. She grabbed her keys and flew out the door, storming to her stupid covered parking space, a little piece of pavement that was a joke, because it wasn't even close to her so-called apartment. Once she reached her car, she jumped in and sped away. She hopped on the freeway right in the middle of lunchtime traffic and shifted impatiently from lane to lane. *Get outta my way, bitch!*

She called the Sprint store again, hoping to get an answer, but there was still none. With one hand on the wheel and her phone in the other, she called again. Failing to check her blind spot before switching lanes, she cut off a white Mercedes. The female blonde haired driver honked profusely, then made violent hand gestures. *Don't look at me, fool. You're the one who can't drive.*

Ivy screeched to a halt in front of the store. Before hopping out, she pulled the visor mirror down, touched up her lipstick, and smoothed her eye shadow. With her purse in hand, she swept inside the store.

"Hello, can I help you?" a tall, handsome associate asked.

"I'd like to speak to Ethan Harrison."

"Actually, I took his place." The Ethan imposter smiled. "How can I help you?"

"By telling me where Ethan is."

"He transferred to a Salt Lake store."

"Really?" Ivy purred. "He didn't tell me he was moving. Of course, I moved, too, and we haven't talked since." Ivy leaned on the counter and pressed her shoulders in slightly to show her cleavage to best advantage. "Do you know which store he went to?"

The manager's eyes flicked back up to Ivy's face, and he blinked. "Let me find that for you. I'll be right back." He cast another quick glance at her neckline before turning and walking to a desk to consult a fellow associate. He came back and reported, "He went to manage the store just off 2100 south." He smiled hopefully. "Is there anything else I can help you with?"

You wish. "Nope." With a smirk, Ivy went back to her car and called the Reign Day Spa and Salon for an appointment with Carlos. This was not her regular salon or stylist. She didn't want anyone she knew to see her new look. She'd unveil her deceitful new plan on her own timetable.

CHAPTER 68

Rich patrons could afford the high-class salon's rare and unique designs anytime they wanted, but everyone else had to budget their resources in order to enjoy the ministrations of Reign Salon's skilled stylists and ambiance. Each hair station was finished in a retro design, with floating mirrors for a circular view of every hair creation. Each clip and every comb through was in plain sight for the customer's inspection.

When Ivy pulled up to the salon, she was pleased to find a sign with "Welcome Ivy" posted in front of a convenient parking space. *Wow. This certainly was the best salon in town, to recognize her importance.*

The specialized attention boosted Ivy's ego. She strutted up the paved walkway and opened the door to face a slender woman who smiled and said, "Welcome to Reign Salon."

"Hi, I have an appointment with Porsche."

Just then, a confident woman with boundless energy dressed all in black masculine clothes headed straight toward Ivy. "Hi, I'm Porsche. Need a change, do we? Come with me." Hips swaying back and forth like a yacht on the sea, Porsche led the way to her station. "What type of music do you prefer, Ivy?"

"Anything will do, actually, how about some hip hop?"

"Perfect. I have just the thing." With a flick of a switch, the music was playing. "Would you like cucumber water before we get started?"

"Yes." Ivy took a seat in the well-padded chair. "Wow, this place is great."

Porsche smiled and handed Ivy a chilled glass of cucumber water. "You'll like it even better when you're done. So, what can I do for you?"

"I'm thinking of going brunette, and maybe, I don't know, a layered bob, just below my chin? What do you think?"

Porsche stepped back and surveyed Ivy with a critical eye. "Yes, your face is the perfect shape for a bob." Porsche picked up pieces of Ivy's hair as she made suggestions. "You simply would kill it as a brunette."

"I need a change."

"Well, then, I suggest a lighter shade of brown with some subtle highlights, then thicker highlights on the sides to frame your face. What do you think?"

"I love the idea. I'm a little nervous though. I haven't had short hair in a long time."

"You're going to love it. I promise."

After her cut, colorweave and style, Ivy had to admit that she looked like something out of a magazine photo shoot. Porsche suggested a pair of Kate Spade glasses to set off her new look, maybe in navy or even bold red. "No one would ever suspect it's you," Porsche said with a wink.

CHAPTER 69

Trace got up a couple of hours before he needed to get ready for his job interview. He showered, shaved, and dressed carefully. He couldn't make himself eat much, but forced down a piece of toast and drank some sugared coffee. Then he brushed his teeth, bared them in the mirror to check for food, took a deep breath, and headed for his interview.

Weaver was a big man with a firm handshake. While Trace was by no means relaxed when Weaver invited him to take a seat, Trace was more comfortable in this man's presence than most other people he met

Weaver took a seat beside his desk, rather than behind it, leaving nothing between the two of them. "Trace," he said, leaning forward with his elbows on his knees, "as I said on the phone, I like your resume. Now tell me a little about yourself."

Trace gave Weaver some general background information, and Weaver countered with encouraging smiles, nods, and a few appropriate comments. "I like you," Weaver said. "You're a great fit for the Mountain Man Medical Pharmaceutical sales team. We'd like to hire you."

Trace's heart soared while his stomach plummeted. He had a job! As long as he kept his mouth shut, he'd be back at work, earning a paycheck like a regular citizen. It would feel so good, all except the worry that one day Bob Weaver would see Trace's arrest record and yank the job out from under him. As much as he wanted to shake

Weaver's hand and accept the job on the spot, Trace would live in fear every day. It would be better not to start work at all than to be fired after he was settled in.

Trace rubbed his palms on his pant legs. He wasn't sure he could say the words right, but he had to say something. Steeling himself for yet another rejection, Trace said, "Mr. Weaver, I'd…"

"Please. Call me Bob."

Trace gave him a weak smile. "Bob. I'd like nothing more than to work for you. I just would like to know if, uh, if you ran all the background checks on my application."

"Of course," Bob replied, leaning back in his chair with a warm smile. "We saw your legal records. You were arrested for rape, but you're not in jail, so I figured you were cleared." He spread his hands. "Am I wrong?"

"No," Trace said, a spark of hope lighting inside him. "I was found not guilty by a jury."

Weaver nodded in understanding. "I was falsely accused of a crime."

Trace opened his mouth, but no sound came out.

Weaver kept on speaking as if Trace hadn't just done a fish imitation. "I was in the vicinity of the crime when it was committed. I was a teenage boy with the wrong hairstyle, the wrong kind of clothes, smelled like tobacco, and came from a broken home." He held up his forefinger. "I also knew the victim. So it had to be me, right?" His smile disappeared. "Even though my innocence was proved at trial, my life was hamburger for a long time." He raised one eyebrow. "I know what you're going through."

Trace fought back sudden tears. "Thanks for understanding, Mr. Weaver; you don't know how much I appreciate it."

Weaver nodded and sat up straight. "I'm glad you brought up the background check. It speaks volumes about your character. I don't see any problem with hiring you. Like I said, you have an impressive resume, and a great personality. I'm confident that you'll be a great asset to our company. So, are you ready to get to work?"

Not trusting his voice, Trace nodded. As Weaver gave him the job details, Trace could scarcely believe his luck. The pay was good, there were great benefits, and while he'd be out on sales calls from time to time, Trace would have his own office downtown to use as his base of operations. *Was this real? Could his life really be getting back on track?*

Ethan rejoiced with his friend, and a few phone calls to other friends and family were welcomed with, "We told you so!"

The new job was a great fit, and the dignity of employment helped Trace gradually warm up to his coworkers. He grew more comfortable around women in general, but still couldn't be alone with one. If he had to speak with a woman, he'd make sure someone else was in sight, a witness who could verify the truth of any alleged offense against him.

Trace enjoyed the downtown location. He appreciated the freedom of venturing out for lunch and finding new places to eat. He was grateful for the simple fact that he had enough money to buy lunch.

One day as he headed out at noon, one of his coworkers asked, "Have you tried the taco truck around the corner?"

"No," Trace said. "Should I?"

"It's better than you might think," the man said, "and it's affordable."

"Thanks." Trace found the truck, got in line, and studied the colorful painting on the truck's side featuring their best selling items.

"Have you eaten here before?" The unfamiliar female voice behind him made Trace freeze. Was she talking to him? He stood still, like a deer camouflaging itself with stillness. A touch on his arm made him flinch. "Is this your first time?" the same female voice asked. "Do you need help to choose?"

Trace swallowed hard. He thought about skipping lunch, but this woman sounded sincere. There were people in line in front of him, and two food truck employees who'd vouch for him if necessary.

Deciding he could safely answer, he turned to see a young woman smiling up at him, her curly brown hair surrounding a face that he'd describe as country cute, if he had any interest in describing a woman. She didn't wear any foundation to cover the light dusting of freckles across her nose, just a modest coat of mascara on lashes framing friendly brown eyes. If she had any other makeup on, it looked so natural he couldn't tell. Offering a cautious smile, he had to admit to himself that he liked the look of her open, friendly face. It didn't appear to be hiding anything. He gave her his standard short answer. "No." Then he surprised himself by expanding the conversation. "Is it any good?"

Her eyes sparkled with genuine delight. "Oh, my gosh, these are the best street tacos you'll ever have."

Without thinking, Trace blurted, "Good to know! In thanks for your review, how about I buy your lunch today?"

The young woman laughed. "You're sweet." She touched her chest with slender fingers tipped by soft pink nail polish. "I'm Olivia Owens." She pointed across the street. "I work in the building over there, at the Law Offices of Dawson & Lorrette."

At the mention of lawyers, Trace could barely speak around a sudden tightening of his throat. "Oh."

She tipped her head, a wordless question. "Oh," Trace said again. "I'm Trace Aragon. I work around the corner at a company called Mountain Man Pharmaceutical." He pointed.

"You know," Olivia said, "it's funny that as close as we work, we haven't seen each other before."

"I haven't been there long." It was like a miracle that Trace could speak more than one sentence to Olivia. He'd likely never see her again. A pang of unexpected disappointment pricked his chest.

Over the next week, his disappointment turned to hope when he and Olivia met three more times for lunch. As they got ready to go back to their workplaces, Trace couldn't believe the words that came out of his mouth. "Would you like to see a movie with me?" He clamped his mouth shut. *I shouldn't have asked. Please say no!*

"I'd love to," Olivia said, "but no chick flicks, okay?"

His fear easing a bit, Trace reminded himself that there would be other people in the theater. "Okay by me. What do you like to watch?"

Olivia tipped her adorable head. "How about some action and adventure?"

"Sure, my favorite. How about tomorrow night? I can pick you up after work in front of your building, if that's OK."

Olivia was on board. "Great. We can leave from here."

The next day, Trace was a mess while waiting for five o'clock to roll around. *Five straight up, and I'm outta here.* He hustled to the men's room, did a quick mirror check, brushed his teeth, then rushed out to catch the elevator.

Trace drove around the corner in time to see Olivia walking out of her building dressed in casual jeans that fit her curves nicely, a wide necked sweater, and cute brown boots. Her face wore traces of subtle makeup and her curly brown hair was pulled back with a white headband, letting little curls escape around her face.

As Trace spent more time with Olivia, his fears diminished. He knew mentally that not all women were like Ivy, but now his soul believed it, too. As his fondness for Olivia grew, he no longer feared that she'd stab him in the back with a false accusation, but what would she do after his Big Reveal? When he told her, would she refuse to see him? What would her family think? What parent on earth was okay with their daughter dating an accused rapist?

Trace had to tell her the truth. No more lying.

He invited Olivia over on Saturday night for dinner. *At least she'll be impressed that I know how to cook.*

She arrived to find the table set with candles and the food ready. Trace lit the candles and they sat down to eat. Olivia tried making conversation, but Trace's answers were uncharacteristically brief, and most of his food was still on his plate when hers was half gone.

Olivia put down her fork. "What's wrong?"

Trace sighed. "I have to tell you something, but it's really hard to for me to discuss."

Her gaze softened. "You can tell me anything, Trace."

"Okay. Well, then. Here goes." He took a breath, then blurted, "I was arrested for a crime I didn't commit." *That came out easier than I thought it would.*

Olivia couldn't hide her surprise. "What happened?"

Trace told Olivia everything, including the lies he'd used to try to cover up his actions. By the time he finished, the food was cold, but Olivia's hands were warm in his grasp. "I can't believe you've had to go through all that," she said, her eyes full of compassion. "What kind of girl would do that to another human being, especially one as nice as you?"

Trace couldn't keep the tears from running down his face. Olivia handed him her napkin. "If you thought that would scare me off, you're wrong. I'm not going anywhere."

Trace wiped his face, her reassuring words stopping his tears. "Thanks for understanding, Olivia. You're the best person I know."

Olivia gave him a heart-stopping grin. "And don't you forget it."

They laughed as they ate. Cold food had never tasted so good.

CHAPTER 70

Ivy packed her car and drove south, every passing mile reinforcing her belief that she and Trace belonged together. A dreamy smile curved her lips as she told herself that he wanted her so much that his thoughts had sent for her to come to him.

No one knew where Ivy Greene was, and no one cared. Even if anyone took the trouble to look, they wouldn't find the old Meridian Ivy in her current state of mind. The jury verdict had triggered in her a mental slide far from reality.

Ivy reached Salt Lake City late Sunday night and checked into a hotel close to the Sprint store where Ethan worked.

On Monday morning she showered, dressed, and put on a ball cap. A little before 9:30, she drove to a parking lot across from the Sprint store and parked. She waited until, sure enough, Ethan pulled up in his blue Jeep, not one minute late. He tucked his iPad under his arm, walked to the store, and unlocked the doors.

Ivy's wait for the next phase of her plan gave her time to fill out the forms she'd downloaded to change her name. *Heather McCall? How about Daniele Holston, or maybe Samantha Stout? Yes, I like Samantha Stout.* Petitioning the courts by filing a few forms and answering a few questions seemed pretty straightforward. She had to include her old name, new name, Social Security number, and reason for her name change. She was raped, that surely was a good enough reason. She also had to promise that she wasn't changing her name to escape debt or criminal liability. Simple.

Once her forms were filled out, she sat in the parking lot, keeping watch until the afternoon heat became unbearable. Then Ivy drove to the Salt Lake City courthouse to turn in her paperwork. Finding parking here was a frustrating experience compared to Meridian there were parking meters everywhere. By the time she found a place to pull in, she had twelve minutes left. *Surely that would be enough.* She hustled around to the front doors of the huge court building, the grandeur of the architecture slowing her down. *Wow. And she'd thought the court buildings in Meridian were big.* She pulled open the large glass door and headed for the directory board. *Geez, that was lucky, the office is right here on the first floor.* Behind the counter stood a middle aged woman with glasses. "May I help you?" she asked.

"Yes, I have my paperwork to legally change my name," Ivy said, handing the papers across the desk. "I hope I filled them out right."

"Well, let me just look it over. Umm...page one looks good." The woman stopped on page two and glared at the reason for the name change. Her voice softened when she looked at Ivy. "I know it's none of my business, but the reason you're changing your name...you poor girl, are you okay?"

"Yes...I guess so," Ivy answered timidly. "I just don't want him to find me. He took a plea deal."

"How awful for you," the woman sympathized. "Well, sweetie, it looks like you have everything in order, so I'll file this for you today and you'll get a notice in the mail when you can legally change your driver's license and Social Security number. I wish you the best. Is there anything else I can do for you?"

"Do you know of any job openings?"

"Not off hand. Have you tried Workforce Services? They always have jobs posted."

"No," Ivy sighed, letting her facade slip and her arrogant personality show through. "It's not my kind of place, if you know what I mean. That's for homeless people, or people who've been fired." Catching the shocked expression on the woman's face, Ivy quickly said, "I mean, I would prefer not to go there."

"I see...well, good luck and have a nice day." The woman shook her head and turned away.

Figuring Ethan would work an eight-hour day, Ivy drove back to the parking lot across the street from the Sprint store just in time to see Ethan wave good-bye to some co-workers. He pulled the sunshades from his windshield, started his jeep, backed out, and drove toward the street. Ivy pulled out right behind him, following not too close, but close enough not to lose him.

He made a quick left turn and pulled into the supermarket. Ivy missed the turn but was able to make a U-turn as Ethan parked, jumped out of his car and walked briskly into the store. Ivy parked one space over from Ethan. She waited until he came out of the store and walked right behind her car without noticing her. She watched him throw the grocery bag into his passenger seat and climb in. He opened a bottle of sweet tea and a bag of chips before backing out and driving away. Distracted by one chip at a time, Ethan didn't notice Ivy tailing him.

A left hand turn and then a right led to Kensington Avenue where Ethan pulled up to an apartment with a two-car garage. It was in a fairly busy cul-de-sac in an upscale apartment complex with a public park across the street. From a parking space by the park, Ivy had a direct line-of-sight to both the front door and the garage of his apartment. There was enough traffic coming and going in the parking lot that she was nearly invisible sitting in her car.

As the garage door lifted, Ivy's heart stopped. There in the garage was Trace's black truck. She had found him.

CHAPTER 71

Salt Lake City was now Ivy's "Home Sweet Home." She pulled out her notebook from habit and wrote *I will show Trace and everyone else…. I'll show them how brilliant I am.* She looked over her list.

1. Change hair color and cut it short. *Check.*
3. Move to Salt Lake City. *Check.*
4. P.O. Box. *Check*
5. Find Ethan and Trace. *Double-check and highlighted.*
6. Get a job.
7. Find an apartment.
8. Get new car.
9. Get new credit card.

Ivy's funds were limited to what she'd saved while living with Eli and a credit card. That would have to support her until she got a job in Salt Lake.

After waiting a long two weeks, the court notice approving her new name, Samantha Stout, finally showed up at her P.O. Box. She made another entry in her notebook.

10. DMV. *Check.*
11. Social Security office. *Check.*

On Tuesday, she was going to get a job, not just any job, but a job close to Ethan's, because if she could keep track of Ethan, she wouldn't lose Trace. She'd noticed that a bookstore just around the corner from the Sprint Store had a "help wanted" sign in the window.

That would do nicely. Ivy got up early, dressed in sweats, and hustled down to the hotel's breakfast room for a quick bite to eat. After a relaxing shower, she unpacked her favorite denim skirt and ironed her collared white blouse. Her heels weren't too high, and a matching handbag completed her job-hunting attire.

The short drive up 2100 south revealed some exciting new places to eat and live. She stopped and inquired about a few apartments along the way. After making herself familiar with a few places around town, she pulled into the nearly full bookstore parking lot at 10:30 am. *Busy bookstore.*

Ivy replaced her sunglasses with her new pair of navy-rimmed glasses with plain clear lenses, hopped out of her car, and walked into the bookstore. She glanced around to see a skinny male clerk wearing a bookstore apron hurrying toward a door in the back wall.

"Excuse me," Ivy said.

The young man pulled to a stop and looked her over, an appreciative smile stealing over his face.

"Hi...I'm Samantha Stout. I noticed the sign in your window. I'm here about the job." *Wow, the name Samantha just rolls off my tongue. I love it! Samantha Stout.*

"Awesome," the clerk said eagerly. "If you want to sit over there, I'll get the manager."

He left, and in a minute, a middle-aged woman with shaggy brown hair that needed a trim approached Ivy. "Hello, I'm Megan, the manager. Todd said you were interested in applying for a job at our bookstore."

"Yes," Samantha replied with a practiced smile. "I just moved here from Wyoming. I have my resume if you'd like to look at it." She reached into her purse.

"Great. Do you have time to chat a little bit today, Samantha?"

"Sure."

Megan led the way to a table near the window and sat down. Glancing over the resume, Megan asked about Ivy's journalism courses and what her future plans were. Samantha answered the questions, but her cunning final response closed the deal. "I'm writing a book, 'Life's Abundant Attractions,' as my first release, but I've got lots of story ideas."

"Wow," Megan replied, impressed. "A bookstore is definitely a place for writing inspiration. Can you come in tomorrow to fill out some paperwork so we can get you on the schedule?"

"Sure," Ivy replied. *The job is mine!* "What time would you like me to come in?"

"First thing, we open at 10:00."

Samantha thanked Megan and headed to her car. On the way back to the hotel, she couldn't stop herself from going in the Sprint store to test her new look on Ethan. Would he recognize her?

She walked in slowly, drawing the attention of several employees, including a chubby guy whose nameplate read, "Travis." He jumped to his feet and asked, "Can I help you?"

"I hope so," Samantha said. "My phone broke, and I'm looking for a new one. I'm thinking of switching to Sprint while I'm at it."

"Are you under contract on your other phone?"

"Nope," Samantha smiled at Travis. "Do you have any good deals?"

Ethan came out from the back carrying a box. When he noticed Samantha, he froze in shock. Samantha's gaze strayed to him, then without a flicker of recognition, slipped away to study the phones Travis pointed out to her.

Ethan pivoted, hurried into the stock room, and called Trace. "Hey man, you're not going to believe this, but a dead ringer for Ivy just walked in the store."

With panic in his voice, Trace asked, "Are you sure it's not her?"

"Pretty sure. This one wears glasses, has shorter hair, and it's a different color, too, but, man, I just about lost my lunch. She didn't seem to recognize me, either. Man, that crazy bitch really has me rattled."

"Me too. See if you can get her name and call me right back."

Ethan left the stock room and walked to the counter where Travis was writing up Samantha's new contract. Ethan looked over Travis's shoulder and read, "Samantha Stout, Salt Lake City."

Samantha was busy studying phone cases, showing no interest in Ethan or his antics.

Ethan returned to the stock room and redialed Trace. "It's not her."

"Are you sure?"

"Yeah, after I got a good look at her, I could see that her clothes and makeup are totally different. Her name is Samantha Stout, and she lives here in Salt Lake. Like I said, she's a dead ringer, could be her twin. Crazy, right?"

"Go see what she's driving. Make sure it's not a white Accord."

Ethan walked into the showroom, but Samantha Stout was nowhere in sight. When Travis said she'd left, Ethan ran outside, but Samantha had already driven away, and no one had noticed her vehicle.

Ethan dialed Trace again. "Too late, man, she already left. Sorry. It wasn't her. It was just really weird."

In spite of Ethan's assurances, Trace's day went sour. Whether it was Ivy or not, his heart skipped a hundred beats at the mere thought Ivy might find him one day.

CHAPTER 72

The apartment manager on Derby Avenue accepted Samantha's application, and she moved right in. The neighbors seemed nice enough but a little nosy. As they helped move the few boxes she had and chatted over pizza and beer outside on her apartment stairs, they asked where she'd moved from, if she was married, or if she had a boyfriend. Of course she lied. She wasn't going to tell them anything about herself, because they didn't need to know her business. As far as they knew, Samantha was a sweet, charming young lady from Wyoming.

It didn't take long before Samantha had her apartment nicely furnished. With her new job as the assistant manager at the bookstore, it was pretty easy. Even getting a new car wasn't hard. "No credit needed" helped for sure.

Samantha had her eye on a black Camry over on 4500 South. She pulled into the car dealership and dropped the visor mirror to double-check her makeup and hair as a well-dressed salesman approached her window. The tap of his knuckle on the glass got her attention.

"Hi," Samantha said, climbing out of her car with a wiggle of her hips. "That was fast. How did I get the best looking guy on the lot to help me?" She batted her baby blue eyes. "I'm interested in the black Camry over there."

"It's a beauty for sure. I'm Caden."

"Samantha."

After an awkward handshake, Caden asked. "Want to take it for a test drive?"

"I sure do, but can you get me a bottle of chilled water first? I'm so thirsty. I just moved here from Wyoming, and the heat is killing me."

"Sure, be right back. I'll open the car up for you and you can get comfortable." He handed her the keys and snapped on a dealer plate.

Samantha hopped in the driver's seat and put both hands, ten o'clock, two o'clock, on the steering wheel, adjusted the rear view mirror, and relished the smell of her soon-to-be new car.

"Here you go." Caden climbed in beside her and put a bottle of water in the cup holder beside her seat. The car purred as she pulled into traffic. "Take a right at the next light." Caden spilled his sales pitch as Samantha drove, offering many compliments during the ride.

"Turn right here?" Samantha asked.

"Yes, it will circle us back to the dealership," Caden said, turning toward her. "What do ya think? Do ya like the sleek look it has? Kinda like you, sleek and sophisticated."

"You're so sweet." Samantha gave Caden an alluring smile. "Yes, I love it. You don't think black is too bold for a girl, do you?"

"Not at all, you look like you can handle this car just fine."

"Now if I could just figure out my way around this town, I'd be in great shape."

"Maybe I can show around sometime?" Caden offered with a hopeful raise of his eyebrows.

"Yeah, maybe…" *Not on your life. I'm not here for a date.*

His attention and compliments had won her signature on the dotted line, better yet, her flirtation had won her a great deal on her dream car. *I've got my shiny new black Camry, leather interior and custom rims, all the finer things in life!*

Pleased with her new address, new car and new life, Samantha was certain no one would discover her true identity, except for Trace, when she was ready to reveal it to him.

CHAPTER 73

On her second day of work, while Samantha was talking with a middle-aged customer named Opal, a young man with dark, curly brown hair wearing a military uniform walked into the bookstore. He looked so much like Trace that Samantha swiveled her head to stare at him, barely noticing the black and tan German shepherd heeled obediently at his side.

Trace? Here in her bookstore? Samantha stared at the guy as he wandered to a shelf and picked up a book. Samantha sashayed across the room. "Hey!"

The young man turned, his eyes lighting up in appreciation at the sight of her. "Hi," he said, smiling.

"I'm sorry," Samantha said. "I thought you were someone else."

The man nearly saluted. "Murdock Swindon." He pointed to the nametag sewn on his camouflage uniform. "My family calls me Murdy. How y'all doin' this morning?"

Samantha studied Murdy's face. "I'm fine." She put on a smile. "And where is this family that calls you Murdy?"

"West Virginia, ma'am," he answered with his handsome southern drawl.

Ma'am? Samantha laughed, thinking of all the entertaining possibilities this situation offered. "Samantha will do. How did you get from West Virginia to here?"

"I joined the military."

A military man, just like Trace! This guy was definitely worth getting closer to.

With fiction on the tip of her tongue, she stated. "My brother, Trace, actually he's my stepbrother, was in the Middle East, but he was killed."

"I'm so sorry." Murdy's lip twitched. "I was over there, too."

"But you made it home." Samantha moved in beside him and wrapped his arm in a hug, pressing her breasts against him. Murdy went suddenly still. Satisfied with his reaction, Samantha stepped back. "What does your father do?"

"Farms," Murdy cleared his throat. "He's a farmer."

"Oh, that explains why you're so good with animals." Samantha glanced at the dog, noticing for the first time that he wore a red service vest. Her voice raised a notch as she bent over to pet him. "He's a good boy. Aren't you, boy?"

The dog wagged his tail.

"He is." Murdy looked at his dog with obvious pride. "Digger helps me so much, I don't go anywhere without him."

Samantha looked at him in a question without words.

"I came back with PTSD," Murdy explained.

"Oh, that's tough," Samantha sympathized. She glanced at the shelves. "Can I help you? Are you looking for something in particular?" She moved in closer to Murdy, enjoying the feel of his slight shudder at her intimate touch.

"Uh, well, I..." Murdy bent over to pet Digger before saying, "I was looking for a book that might help me with my PTSD. I'm doing the counseling thing, but a book might help, too. It took me a long time to even admit that I had a problem."

Samantha glanced over the shelves while moving to the self-help section of the store, her eyes scanning the spines until she saw a book with "PTSD" in the title. She pulled it down and handed it to Murdy. "Here you go."

"Is this a good one?"

"The best," she said, not knowing anything about the book. "My brother had problems with the same thing and this helped him a lot. Come on." Samantha led the way to the sales counter and rang up the purchase. While putting the book in a bag, Samantha slid her gaze up to Murdy's face. Although it was 45 minutes before she was scheduled for lunch, she said, "I have to take my lunch break now. Have you eaten lunch yet?"

"No, not yet." Murdy rubbed an ear while giving Digger's leash a tug.

Samantha gave Murdy a seductive smile, already maneuvering herself into his life. Through her eyes, this guy looked enough like Trace to fill the void and be a surrogate for him while she worked to get the real thing back. "There's a place close by where we can grab something to eat."

They talked easily over lunch and by the time they were done, they'd made a date.

"It's pretty cool ya still go out with me, knowing bout' my PTSD and all." Murdy gave her a shy smile. "Not every girl is so understanding."

"I understand a lot," Samantha assured him. Not wanting her neighbors to see him, she added, "I'll meet you at the restaurant."

"I really look forward to getting to know you better," Murdy confessed, without a clue of what he would have to go through by falling for the pretty bookstore clerk.

CHAPTER 74

After work, Samantha drove straight to the park across from Trace's apartment complex. She parked her car, got out, and walked around to get her bearings and find the best place to watch for Trace. Figuring he'd park in the garage, she walked back to her car and moved it to a better vantage point. Before she turned off the engine, she was delighted to see Trace pull in. She kept her eyes focused on him as he slipped out of his car and strode into his apartment with a jaunty air. He looked good, so good, and happy. She knew he'd be even happier when he found out that she was there.

Samantha pulled down her visor and anxiously studied her face, making sure her eyeliner was even, her hair perfectly in place, and her teeth were clean. *Lip gloss, I need lip-gloss. Trace will surely want to kiss me.* She dug in her bag, searching, and then spilled it on the seat. Things went rolling everywhere. *Damn it!* She felt around under the seat for her lipstick tube, but couldn't find it. This was intolerable! Maybe it had fallen down beside the passenger door.

She got out, walked around her car, and opened the door. There it was! She grabbed it, slipped into the passenger seat, and pulled down the visor. She applied the color carefully, pursed her lips, and capped the lipstick. Then she lifted the visor in time to see Trace pulling out of his garage.

Where was he going? Starting her car, she drove out the same exit Trace had, but his car was nowhere in sight.

She sat there, fuming, until a stupid black sedan pulled up behind her. *Idiot.* She pulled out onto the street and drove frantically, looking for Trace.

After several attempts to find him, her calm was reclaimed. *Oh well.* Samantha slowed back down to the speed limit. She knew where he lived and that was good enough for now. The game was back on.

CHAPTER 75

Samantha dressed for attention in a low cut blouse tied high to expose her bare midriff over tight hip-hugger jeans. Murdy wouldn't be able to keep his eyes off her.

When she pulled into a parking space at Comer Mejor, Salt Lake City's most popular Mexican restaurant, she noticed with delight that Murdy already stood at the door, scanning every incoming car. The fact that he wasn't a minute late and was looking for her let her know he was nicely wrapped around her finger.

As she swayed her hips in a seductive walk toward him, Murdy's eyes roved down her body and back up again. He pulled the restaurant door open for her with a big smile.

"Where's Digger?"

"In the car."

Feigning concern, Samantha looked over her shoulder toward the parking lot. "Will he be alright?"

"He's used to it," Murdy said. "The window's down. He's fine."

As they waited to be seated, Samantha flirted with Murdy. Keenly aware of the other customers staring at her, she basked in their attention.

When they were finally seated, Samantha ordered an extravagant meal. She giggled at Murdy's jokes. Murdy was mesmerized by her charm and good looks. Samantha kept Murdy entertained with false stories about her fake brother Trace. Murdy either laughed or shook his head in sympathy, stating that he could relate to everything she said. Samantha soaked up his attention.

When they walked out of the restaurant, she gave him a quick kiss on the cheek before turning and swaying her hips as she walked toward her car, confident that Murdy's eyes were focused on her.

Although Samantha was unshakably connected to Trace, Murdy was a fascinating new toy to play with. Thriving on the attention of her new conquest, she went out with Murdy again, setting her hook.

On her first day off, she got up early and drove to Trace's, hoping to discover where he worked. As she waited in the parking lot, she noticed a light gray Range Rover pull up to the front of his place. Peering idly at the driver's side, she identified a woman behind the wheel. Samantha had little interest in this other woman until she saw Trace hurry down his walk and climb in beside the driver.

Samantha sat forward. *Who was this? What was she doing with Trace?*

She anxiously followed the car until it stopped in front of a downtown building. She focused on Trace as he got out. Then the young woman stuck her head out the driver's side window as Trace walked around the car. To Samantha's horror, he gave the girl a kiss before hurrying through the door of some office building.

Samantha gritted her teeth, put her sunglasses on, and followed the Range Rover as it rounded the corner.

Olivia entered the parking garage below some professional offices without looking back. Samantha descended into the gloom of the underground parking space right behind Olivia. She pulled into an empty slot within sight of the parked Range Rover as Olivia strode toward the elevators. Samantha jumped out of her car and followed Olivia into the building.

Reaching the elevators at the end of the hall before Samantha, Olivia pushed the button. The elevator doors slid open; Olivia walked on and turned to see Samantha signaling for her to hold the doors. With a smile, Olivia kept the doors open. "Thanks," Samantha said, breathless.

"No problem." Olivia pushed the 7th floor button.

When the doors closed, Samantha turned toward Olivia. "I'm Samantha."

"Olivia."

What a horrendously ugly name. Olivia? Really! "You smell so good."

"Thanks."

"What perfume are you wearing?"

"It's called 'I Love Love' by Moschino."

"I'll have to give it a try," Samantha said.

The elevator doors opened and Olivia left with a friendly wave. Samantha kept pressing the button to keep the door open as Olivia walked down the hall and entered the law office of Dawson & Lorrette.

An irate Samantha let the doors close. She rode back down the elevator, fuming about the girl who was trying to steal Trace from her. She couldn't possibly work in an attorney's office. She must be a client.

Samantha sat in her car waiting for Olivia to come out. The day passed, and it wasn't until 5:12 p.m. that Olivia walked through the parking garage and got into her car. Samantha had used her waiting hours to tell herself plenty of evil stories about this girl, but now she had to believe that she must be working at the law office. Samantha grudgingly admitted to herself that it was a prestigious job, better than hers.

Samantha followed as Olivia drove back to the building where she'd dropped Trace off, and there he was, waiting for her, breaking into a huge smile at the sight of her car. *That must be where he works.*

Eyes narrowed, Samantha watched Trace get in Olivia's car. Then she followed them to the dry cleaners, her hands so tight on the wheel that her fingers hurt. The hurt felt good. As she watched Trace go inside the dry cleaners, she thought of crashing into the bitch's car, but some part of her brain registered that since it was bigger than hers, it probably wouldn't get her the results she wanted.

She studied Trace walking out with his arms full of shirts wrapped in plastic. Samantha imagined pulling one of those plastic bags over Olivia's head and holding it closed until she quit kicking.

Olivia surprised Trace with an extra stop on the way home.

With a look of confusion, Trace looked out the window at The Puppy Shop and asked, "Why are we stopping here?"

"Just for fun, you'll see. You've got to see the cutest little thing ever. A couple of girlfriends from work came over with me on our lunch break, and OMG, Trace, baby Beagle puppies." She jumped out. "Come on Trace, they're so cute!"

Trace climbed out and followed Olivia into the shop. She headed straight to a kennel full of puppies, then looked up at Trace with her own "puppy dog eyes." "I'm in love with them!" She pointed, then turned to the shop clerk who appeared at the cage. "Can I hold this one?"

"Sure." He reached into the cage. "I remember you from earlier." He placed the squirming puppy in her arms. "I think he likes you."

Olivia cuddled the puppy for a moment, then held him out to Trace. "Here," she said, "you hold him."

Trace lifted the puppy up to his nose and made some ridiculous noises.

"He likes you, too!" Olivia exclaimed.

Realizing what a geek he was being, falling for a puppy, Trace handed the puppy back to Olivia.

After a few more minutes, Olivia reluctantly put the puppy back in its kennel. They walked back to the car, teasing each other about what it would be like if they had a puppy. They hopped into the Rover and drove to Trace's apartment. Olivia, laughing, took half of his shirts and followed him toward his apartment.

Samantha couldn't stand it anymore. Someone had to save Trace from making the biggest mistake of his life. Samantha started her car and drove toward them, pushing on the accelerator, but they reached the alcove to Trace's apartment just before she got there, just in time for Samantha to see Trace's arm around Olivia, his head bent to deliver a gentle kiss to her willing mouth.

Seeing Trace so happy with Olivia delivered a truly devastating blow. All the emotional walls Samantha had set up to defend herself counted for nothing now, allowing a battalion of feelings and twisted thoughts to break her psyche down even further. Sliding into madness, she took on the role of a true sociopath, making all of her former cruelty look like playtime. Frustrated, Samantha stepped on the gas and sped out of the lot.

Trace turned toward the revving engine in time to see a black car exiting the lot too fast, with a woman at the wheel. Even though she was passed before, he could see who she was, a chill of foreboding slid down his back.

Ridiculous. He was conquering his social fears. He was dating Olivia, and she was the best thing that ever happened to him.

Trace turned back to his door and led Olivia into the warmth and safety of his apartment.

CHAPTER 76

Samantha's mood toward her work changed drastically, but it wasn't her fault. It was never her fault. She cherished the hurt inside. Instead of unbearable pain, its bitter warmth kinda tickled. Her boss wasn't giving her the credit she deserved. She always got the crap hours. Knowing she was better than this stupid job fanned her anger and frustration into hot and destructive aggression, as she grew more envious of Olivia's clothes, car, and job.

Completely dissatisfied with the degrading bookstore job, Samantha determined to find a better job that she deserved. She applied to debt collection agencies, hoping it might give her access to some of Trace's or Olivia's personal information, but no jobs were available.

One day, Samantha's favorite customer, Opal, approached her. "Do you know of anyone with good people skills that might be looking for a job?"

Samantha brightened. "I am."

"I kind of hoped you'd say that."

"What kind of work?"

"We're looking for an intake clerk over at Clarkston Rehabilitation Center."

"Yes," Samantha said eagerly. "I'm definitely interested."

"When can you come in?" Opal asked.

"How about coming in tomorrow morning?"

"Great. See you then. Just ask for me." Opal handed over a business card. "Oh, and email your resume to me before you come in."

"Yes, of course."

First thing in the morning, Samantha got ready and drove to the rehabilitation center. "Hi, Samantha," Opal said. "I'm glad you could come in today."

Samantha followed Opal down the hall, saying, "I'm so excited. You seem really busy. Thanks for making time for me today."

"No problem."

"I really appreciate it, and I just love your dress. That color looks great on you."

"Thank you." Opal gave Samantha an appreciative smile. "I bought this in New York last year. I don't have much time for shopping, but I scheduled a day for it while I was there. Have you ever been to New York?"

"A couple of years ago, my mom and I went to New York for a Broadway show," Samantha lied. "It was so much fun. I picked up a couple of blouses. As a matter of fact, this is one of them."

"Great selection," Opal said, nodding. "We've been looking for someone with good grooming skills and a pleasing personality. Hopefully your work history will match."

"I sent my resume."

Opal beamed. "Perfect. Preparation is important to this job." She studied Samantha's resume and asked a few questions, then sat back with a satisfied smile. "When can you start?"

"Anytime."

"Tomorrow? I know its short notice but I really need to fill this position."

"Yes," Samantha said. "I'm available."

Opal extended her hand. "You're hired."

As soon as she left, Samantha called Megan at the bookstore. "I won't be in for my next shift."

"Don't you feel well?"

"I'm quitting."

After a brief silence, Megan's question came out cold. "Short notice, don't you think?"

"I have a better job, and I have to start right away." With no concern for leaving Megan shorthanded, Samantha hung up.

Her next phone call was to Murdy. "I got a new job at the Clarkston Rehab Center! Can you believe it? I start tomorrow. You just don't know how excited I am to be out of that bookstore."

"Fantastic!" Murdy said. "How 'bout I take you out to dinner tonight to celebrate?"

"Sounds like fun."

Samantha carefully plotted her next move with Murdy. If she played her cards right, this night would lead to Murdy doing anything she wanted.

CHAPTER 77

When Murdy called to say he was ready to pick her up, Samantha replied, "Wait 20 minutes, then I'll meet you at the 7-11."

Since she was considering allowing Murdy into her apartment for the first time tonight, she dressed in her chosen man bait, a revealing blouse over a short, tight skirt and spiked heels that gave her a wiggle guaranteed to reel in any red-blooded man.

Murdy pulled into the 7-11 parking lot just as Samantha strolled in off the sidewalk, keenly aware of stares from passersby. Disappointed that she hadn't had a chance to go inside the store yet for even more admiration, she called out, "Just a minute. I have to use the restroom," and pranced into the 7-11. Minutes later, she finally emerged and climbed in Murdy's car.

They drove to one of the most popular places in town where they were seated in a back booth. As they ate, Samantha flirted and laughed. Then she set her hook even deeper. "I'm so comfortable with you, Murdy. You're so much like my brother, Trace." Lowering her mascara-laden lashes, she confessed, "I miss him so much. I could tell him anything."

Murdy reached out, took her hand and with his relaxed southern charm, he spoke. "You can tell me anything, too, Samantha." When she didn't answer, he continued, "I wish we could have met sooner. It would have made coming home so much easier. I had family and all, but we seem to just 'get' one another, you know?"

Samantha raised her eyelashes until she was peering at Murdy beneath a seductive fringe of black. "I know. When Trace didn't come home, it was so hard for my mom and me." She offered Murdy a cautious smile. "We don't get along too well, and I hadn't been living at home, so when we got the news…well, you know, it was like I had to deal with it on my own."

Murdy gave her hand a gentle squeeze. "You got me now." His voice grew even more intense.

Samantha sighed and dabbed at her eye with a manicured finger. "I've been abandoned so many times that I have a hard time trusting anyone."

"You can trust me, Samantha," Murdy insisted.

Samantha excused herself and headed for the ladies room. As she was leaving the bathroom, she straightened her shirt, then picked up her purse. She headed out the door and rounded the corner. She stopped cold when she saw Olivia sitting at a table. Backing up into the shadows, she waited. Sure enough, Trace sat down right beside Olivia.

Samantha took a deep breath and strolled right by their table, purposely bumping into the table next to theirs. When Trace looked up and saw Samantha, he froze, chills of despair running down his back.

"Are you okay?" Olivia asked.

"That girl…she looks just like Ivy, the one I told you about in Meridian, but with short hair, and it's a different color. Ethan said he saw a girl that looked like Ivy in his store the other day, too. It's just weird, it gives me the creeps."

"Umm…she was at my office building," Olivia said nervously. "She got into the elevator with me last week."

Trace watched the girl hurry back to her table where Murdy sat. After seeing, she was with a guy of her own helped convince him that she wasn't really Ivy. She didn't even look at Trace, not once.

Inside, Ivy congratulated herself. *What a performance!* Her attention was on Murdy, just Murdy, not giving into any distractions.

She snuggled up to Murdy, tucked her arm under his, and laid her head on his shoulder. *Well played!*

"This has been really nice," she said, fairly sure that her display of affection was being watched.

"Yes, I think so too." Murdy paid for the meal, then as proud as a man can be with Samantha as his eye candy, he took her hand and walked her to the parking lot. Just as they reached the car, she looked up at Murdy with a wide-eyed innocent gaze. "Do you want to come over to my apartment?"

"Are you sure?" Murdy asked. "You haven't been too keen on me coming over before."

Samantha sighed and gripped his hand harder. *It was late enough none of her neighbors should be around to see him.* "I feel like it's time for me to let my guard down and see where this might go for us."

"Great!"

They arrived at her apartment a couple of blocks from the 7-11. Samantha was fumbling with her keys when a neighbor walked by with a two bags of groceries swinging from her hands. "Samantha!" she cried, a smile spreading across her nosy face. "Is this your hot date?"

Irritated, Samantha jammed her key in the lock and twisted it. "Maybe," she mumbled, ducking inside and pulling Murdy in with her.

"What was that?" Murdy asked as Samantha shut the door. "Does she know about me?"

"I may have said something in passing," Samantha said. "She always wants to know my business. That's why I like it better at your place."

Samantha would deal with her stupid neighbor later. *My life isn't available for inspection. I need to get away from these nosy neighbors.*

Murdy wondered across the room, noticing a picture of Trace setting on the mantel, and asked. "Who's this?"

"That's Trace." Samantha snapped the picture away from him, pulled Murdy to the couch, and made him sit down beside her.

"Are you okay?" he asked cautiously.

Samantha let out a breath. "It's that dumb nosy neighbor." Then her voice softened and she ran her fingers alongside Murdy's neck. "But she's out there and we're in here."

Murdy put his arm around her waist and pulled her close to him. She pressed her palms to his chest and purred, "I'm not sure about this," with a shy glance at his face.

"Not sure of what?" Murdy asked his husky voice low. "We can go slowly. Hey, we don't have to do anything tonight if y'all don't want to." His eyes looked hungry. "But ya sure are sweet."

"Let's see how it goes." Samantha lowered one hand onto his thigh and leaned in to kiss him. Then her hand slid up to unbuckle his belt. Murdy groaned and lost himself in a night of passion with Samantha.

CHAPTER 78

Olivia has to go!

Samantha drove to the law office of Dawson & Lorette and rode the elevator up to the 7th floor, rubbing her cheeks until they were pink while conjuring tears. As the elevator doors opened, she straightened her shirt and crumpled a couple of tissues in her hand.

When she burst inside the law office, a startled receptionist with a nameplate that read "Marsha" glanced up through red-framed glasses and closed a folder on her cluttered desk.

Samantha sobbed, "I need to see an attorney! Would it be possible…" then dabbed her nose with the tissues.

Marsha's eyes went wide behind her magnified lenses. "What's it regarding?"

Samantha bit back another sob and wiped her cheeks. "It's…it's a personal issue. Oh, please, can't one of your attorneys help me?"

"Do you have an appointment?"

"No. Do I need one? Can't someone see me today?"

"It's best to have an appointment." Marsha indicated the mess on her desk. "We've been having some technical problems with our computers, and everyone's busy trying to cope."

"Please," Samantha whispered, squeezing out more tears. "I don't know what else to do."

Marsha adjusted her glasses. "I'll go check and see if anyone is available. You'll have to excuse me for a minute."

"Oh, thank you, with all my heart, thank you!"

As soon as Marsha was out of sight, Samantha checked to see if anyone was looking before leaning over the counter, phone camera ready, and flipping open the folder. She quickly snapped photos of all the information she could get, stopping only when she heard Marsha's footfalls drawing closer. She slapped the folder shut and twisted her face into an expression of utter sorrow.

"I'm sorry," Marsha said. "They're all too busy right now, but I can make an appointment for you."

"I'm not sure of my schedule," Samantha said with a sniffle. "I was hoping to see one today."

"Do you have our phone number?"

Samantha shook her head.

"Here's a business card." Marsha plucked one from a plastic holder and handed it to Samantha. "You can make an appointment with any one of our attorneys." She adjusted her glasses.

"Thank you again," Samantha said with a pitiable smile. "You've been very helpful."

"Good luck," Marsha called as Samantha shuffled out the door.

At home, Samantha opened her photos and studied the information on the stolen documents, then checked employee photos online. When she had all her ammunition, she masterfully crafted a well-written letter to the law office of Dawson & Lorette to include lies and misinformation.

Dear Sirs,

I've pondered this for a week or so before deciding it's in the best interest of all concerned to inform you of my observation.

My husband and I often visit your beautiful city, and were having dinner at a Salt Lake restaurant last weekend.

We were seated next to a table of four young ladies, and during the course of our meal, we overheard the one with curly brown hair and brown eyes tell the others about a case covered by the law office of Dawson & Lorette. We thought it was a bit unethical and unprofessional as she mentioned your clients, Donald and Janet Rhodes. I'm sure they'd be outraged that their personal information and the legal issues against them were a topic of public dinner conversation. She mentioned the Rhodes' address in the Avenues in Salt Lake City, and even commented on the good looks of the attorney, Nathan Shaw, working their case. The Rhodes' personal tragedy being aired in public was very upsetting to me and my husband.

The girls were giggling and not bothering to keep their voices low as they discussed various issues of the case. I finally figured out the brown-haired girl responding to the name, "Olivia," was indeed the one that works at your firm. She was dressed so professionally, I believe she may have met her friends' right after work.

I don't know if this information is of any concern to your firm, but as a business owner, I pride my company with professionalism and client privacy.

I will leave this information in your firm's hands to do with as you see fit.

Regards,

Samantha sealed the envelope, addressed it to the senior partner, Richard Dawson, and placed a stamp on the corner. Of course she didn't add a name or return address. Her heart was light as she mailed the letter that would destroy Olivia.

The letter arrived in the following day's mail. Richard Dawson called in his partner, Lewis Lorette, to discuss the contents. Then they brought in Olivia Owens to answer for herself.

Olivia found Mr. Lorette sitting in a chair facing the desk, with Mr. Dawson seated behind the wide polished expanse of mahogany. "Please sit down, Olivia. We received a most disturbing letter from an outside source verifying names, address, and attorney specifics about one of our cases that you purportedly shared in public with a group of friends."

In shock, Olivia's eyes widened. "I don't know what you're talking about, Mr. Dawson. I'd never do such a thing."

"We didn't think you would. The letter wasn't signed, which makes its origin suspicious. Yet, the compromising information is so accurate, it could only have come from this office, and you have access to it. Your name and description were included in the letter."

"I didn't do it!" Olivia declared. "May I at least see the letter?"

Dawson handed it over. Olivia's shock and disbelief as she read the damning words was heartbreaking. *Who would do this?* "I haven't been out to dinner with any girlfriends for a long time, and I certainly wouldn't talk about any of our clients. You know me, Mr. Dawson." She turned in her chair. "You too, Mr. Lorette. Please believe me."

Dawson took the letter back. "Your record so far has been spotless. I'm inclined to believe you, Olivia."

"Your work here is exemplary," Mr. Lorette agreed, "but I'm afraid we must terminate your employment."

"But I didn't do it," Olivia whispered as tears rose in her eyes.

"Regardless of your guilt or innocence, we have a strict protocol for this type of situation," Dawson said. "Due to liability, we have no other recourse than to let you go. I'm sorry, Olivia."

Olivia was silent with shock. She'd worked so hard to get this job, then worked her way up to an impressive salary, with even more opportunity ahead of her. Being fired would ruin any kind of positive referral she might hope to get for a similar job.

"What if you find out who really did it?" she asked, not doing a very good job of keeping her wretched emotions out of her voice.

"Then we will revisit the situation," Dawson said kindly.

"We would love to have you back if it was under other circumstances," Lorette added.

"Again, Olivia, I'm sorry." Dawson rose from his chair. When Lorette stood, Olivia got to her feet and stumbled from the office.

She stood in the hall trembling. *I didn't do this!* With a shaking hand, she called Trace. "I just got fired for something I didn't do."

"What?" Trace knew all too well how innocent people could suffer. He just didn't want that for Olivia.

"Someone wrote an anonymous letter telling lies about."

"Anyone can say anything nowadays." Trace went suddenly cold at the ominously familiar situation. "How can they fire you without proof?" His words sounded hollow to his own ears. He knew how it could happen. This was all too familiar for comfort.

"The letter said I divulged personal client information to friends, but I didn't, Trace! I didn't do it!"

"Of course you didn't. Did you explain it to them?"

"Yes." Olivia's voice broke. "They believed me, I think."

"I'm almost done with work," Trace reassured her. "Where are you?"

"At work, I have to get my things."

"I'll come over as soon as I get off and we can talk."

"What am I going to do?" Olivia sobbed.

"We'll figure it out," Trace assured her, knowing how hard it was to mount an effective defense against a liar. "I know you're innocent." *Just as I was.*

As soon as Trace reached Olivia, he wrapped his arms around her and let her cry on his shoulder. The heartbreak was so real to him that he couldn't keep from crying, too, as he tried to fight back memories of his own terrifying experience. He had a bad feeling about all of this. Something wasn't right. Not right at all.

CHAPTER 79

Samantha continued to go out with Murdy as she refined her plot. Murdy's heart was definitely committed to the relationship. He thought he'd found the real deal. It wasn't just that she had a sexy body. In his eyes, she was everything.

However, for Samantha, the novelty of the perfect loving couple was beginning to wear off. She was seeing Murdy in a more realistic light, noticing things about him that didn't fit her fantasies of perfect love she had with Trace. She was getting bored with her repertoire of romantic gestures, imaginary daydream scenarios she played out in her head to entertain, distract, frighten, or, in the case of her sexual fantasies, arouse. No matter what tactics she used, Murdy wasn't Trace.

Nevertheless, the cool chill of October set in motion a night of passion for Murdy and Samantha. In her bright-dyed denim jeans, she struggled away from Murdy's white Jeep with the weight of two pumpkins they'd picked out.

"Wait," Murdy insisted. "Let me get those."

"No, I got them, just hurry up and open the door, its cold out here."

Murdy held the door, then hustled in behind her, grabbing the pumpkins out of her arms and placing them on the counter. Murdy sat down as Samantha picked up the smallest pumpkin and set it on his lap. "This one's yours, so start carving," she told him. "Mine's the big one, and it will look better than yours." She gave him a challenging smile. "Watch and see."

Late into the night, Samantha and Murdy gutted and carved their pumpkins with paring knives and spoons over newspaper. Murdy pulled out his Swiss Army knife and finished shaping his pumpkin's ferocious teeth, eyes, and nostrils in jagged slashes. Samantha's pumpkin registered surprise, the face drawn with inexpert distortions of triangles for a nose and eyes. The mouth was just a turned up wedge shape.

By one in the morning, they were finished. Murdy, who'd bent his long torso forward to work, sat back in his chair and looked sleepily at the lights out across the street.

"You were right, your pumpkin is much better than mine," Murdy graciously lied.

"Damn right!" Samantha said. "Just kidding, wait 'til we get the candles in them."

"Look at me," Murdy said. Samantha stopped bundling squishy newspapers with pumpkin guts and glanced up into his eyes. "Do you know how much I like you?"

"Sure do!" She set some yellow candles inside the pumpkin shells and lit each one before fixing the pumpkin lids over the little flames. "See?" she said.

"Did you hear me?"

"Yes, I like you too."

They sat together for a moment and looked at the eerie orange faces glowing in the night.

"I'm exhausted." Samantha said. "Do you want me to stay over tonight?"

"Yes, ma'am, what a great night, right?" He proclaimed in a soft passionate voice.

"Don't blow out the candles. Let's watch them 'til they go out. I'll put new ones in tomorrow." Samantha winked at Murdy.

Murdy pulled Samantha close and slipped his hand under her shirt, carefully lifting it over her head. His rugged hand fingered her bra clasp as she unbuckled his belt and lowered his pants. They slowly crossed the room to the couch, with her on top, his hard military body giving way to her soft, caressing touch. Her mind drifted with the slow rocking movement, soothing and gentle, she slipped into the past, when she and Trace had made love.

Later, they drifted off to sleep in each other's arms in the light of the flickering jack-o-lanterns, Murdy none the wiser that Samantha's fantasies were leading toward his devastation.

CHAPTER 80

It was Samantha's day off, a lazy day of wearing sloppy sweats and no makeup. She wasn't finished with Olivia, not by a long shot. She slipped on a hoodie and drove over to the office of Dawson & Lorette. When she canvassed all three levels of the parking complex, she didn't see Olivia's car anywhere. Samantha waited for a couple of hours but there was still no sign of her. *They must have fired her because of the letter...I knew it would work. She had it coming.*

Bored, Samantha headed home. While entertaining herself with frequent mirror checks and changing the radio dials, Samantha's phone rang. She answered, shocked to hear a voice from her past. "Ivy, its Mom."

Time stood still for a moment before Ivy snapped, "Why are you calling me?"

"Well, honey, I really miss you and would like to come see you. You left without telling me you were going, or even letting me know where you went. I've been so worried about you."

"You have? Then why did it take so long to call?" Ivy didn't bother hiding the contempt in her voice. "You don't care about me, you never have. I had to rebuild my life away from you and everyone else in Meridian."

"That's not true," Laura protested. "Maybe we didn't get along all the time, but I do love you, you know that."

"No, Mom, I don't. It's your fault that things didn't work out for me there. You made me feel unloved, and you were so embarrassing, that I had to move and change my name. I'm Samantha Stout now, not Ivy Greene, so get it right."

"Samantha Stout?" Laura sounded as if she was holding back a laugh.

"You never supported me, you always put me down. It's your fault I left without telling you."

"Can I come see you?"

"I live in Salt Lake City now. I have my own apartment and a great job. I'm doing just fine without you."

"Please, Ivy, I mean Samantha, maybe we could work on our relationship. What do you think?" Laura begged, casually flicking through her phone contacts. "I was thinking about moving, too. I can transfer my job to Salt Lake. Maybe we could share expenses and live together for a while."

"I don't know...*I could use the extra money.* You'd have to live by my rules this time. It's my apartment." *Maybe she can clean up the place...hmmm...I could use her for other things, too...*Ivy changed her tone. "Sure Mom, I'll text you my address, but call me first before just showing up."

"I can be there in a couple of weeks," Laura said, and then hung up without another word.

Her request for a transfer was welcomed by her peers, and she was soon on her way to Salt Lake City, leaving the cruel, uncaring citizens of Meridian far behind.

Arriving late afternoon the following Tuesday, Laura drove to Ivy's apartment. She knocked on the door, but when there was no answer, she returned to her car and waited for a while with the motor running. Then she decided to get a hot cup of coffee at the Starbucks just around the corner. *How convenient, a Starbucks on every corner.*

Just as Laura stopped at Ivy's apartment with her drink, Ivy pulled up behind her and jumped out of her car. "Mom! I told you to call first!"

"Sorry...I wanted to surprise you." Laura wrapped her scarf around her neck, walked to the back of her Enclave, opened the hatch, and began pulling out her things.

"I have a life, and I don't want you just showing up!"

"Help me with my stuff," Laura said. "It's cold out here."

"Mom, stop! This is my place, my rules, remember?"

"Yes, I know. We can go over all that after we get inside. Come on, it's cold."

The nerve...just coming over without calling. "So, what's your plan, Mom?" Ivy took hold of the smallest case.

"I start my job next Monday, so until then, I guess we can do whatever you want. Do you have any friends? A boyfriend? Maybe we can hang out or something." Laura followed Ivy to her apartment, lugging a couple of suitcases, her purse slung over her shoulder.

"You can make your own friends," Ivy said, opening her door. "I have to work, so you'll have to entertain yourself."

Laura wandered through the apartment, which plainly wasn't good enough for her as she commented on the small rooms in a neighborhood on the wrong side of town. Then she picked up the photo of Trace. "Isn't this the boy you had a crush on in Meridian?"

Ivy grabbed the picture. "No! It's none of your business. It's someone I'm dating, if you really need to know." Ivy shoved the picture into a drawer.

"He's handsome. I'd like to meet him."

"Don't think so, Mom."

"Why not? Sooner or later, I will. Come on; let's go get something for dinner. I'll buy."

Laura and Ivy had to find new ways to play together in Salt Lake, but by whose rules?

Let the games begin.

CHAPTER 81

Monday rolled around and Laura made claim to the bathroom first thing. Before 6 a.m., she had already applied seven products to her face, spent a lot of time and effort on her beauty routine of makeup, hair, clothing, and nails. The first impression she made on her first day on the job would be amazing, and nothing less.

Ivy knocked on the bathroom door. "Mom…I need to get ready for work, too, you know."

"I know, but I have to leave earlier than you, so give me a few minutes. I'm almost done."

When Laura came home from her first day at work, she was bewildered, because there was no place to park, again. *Where am I supposed to put my car?* Driving around the lot, she thought, *I'm not walking clear across the parking lot. Here I go...this will do, someone else will just have to walk.* She turned left into a parking stall, marked "reserved," jumped out and ran into the apartment.

"Ivy, where the hell am I supposed to park? This parking lot is ridiculous. I want my own spot."

"Well, you're not having mine." Ivy's voice rang from the bathroom.

Laura walked towards the crack in the bathroom door and peered in to see Ivy primping in the mirror.

"Where are you going?" Laura asked.

"Out with my boyfriend, Murdy," Samantha bragged, intentionally trying to annoy Laura. "He's so good looking. I kid you not, he's so handsome."

"I saw his picture," Laura said. "I'd love to meet him. I'll just touch up a bit before he gets here."

"Nope, I'm going to his place to watch a movie."

"Why don't you have him come over here and we can all watch the movie?"

"Are you so old that you've gone deaf? I said I'm going to his place."

"But what am I supposed to do all night?"

"Find your own boyfriend. You never had a problem with that before." Samantha smirked.

I'm not staying home all by myself, Laura thought.

She went to her bedroom, closed the door, stood in front of her closet, then grabbed her blue pencil skirt and white linen blouse from the rack and tossed them on the bed. She puckered up her lips and pulled her face tight, staring into her dresser mirror. *Hmmm.* Turning her head side to side, she thought, *There's nothing unreasonable about a little Botox here and here.*

Laura touched up her makeup, pulled on her skirt and tuck in her blouse, then opened her bedroom door then announced that she wouldn't be home until late.

"You look nice, Mom." Laura seemed surprised at Ivy's comment. "I won't wait up for you," Ivy said. "I might even just stay over at Murdy's."

"Then lock the doors behind you when you go," Laura called as she waltzed out the door.

Laura was a flirt. Samantha wasn't about to turn Murdy loose when her mother was waiting in the wings with her man claws out.

Samantha drove over to Murdy's and was greeted with the biggest smile yet. "Look at you!" Murdy couldn't wipe the smile from his face.

Samantha spun around like a sultry leaf caught in a dust devil.

"Is this all for me? Murdy asked.

Samantha tipped her head and gave him a cute little nod. "Do you want it all?"

"You'd better believe I do." Murdy and Samantha laughed.

As Murdy helped Samantha with her coat, she blurted, "Did I tell you my mom is here?"

"No. I thought y'all didn't get along."

"Well, she just showed up at my place the other day, literally, I came home and there she was. She wanted to surprise me."

"Wow...I can't wait to meet her."

"She turned my apartment into a battleground."

He raised his brows. "Do I want to meet her?"

"She not all that bad, I guess, but she's sort of controlling. She's grudgingly agreed to assigned chores, of a sort."

"How 'bout we all go out for dinner tomorrow night?" Murdy suggested. "What do you think?"

"I don't know. I guess we could. I'll ask her when I get home."

Samantha's late night turned into morning, and she had to hustle home to get ready for work. Laura was in the kitchen working on breakfast when Samantha came in.

"Guess, you'd better hurry up if you don't want to be late," Laura said as she buttered her toast.

"Murdy wanted me to ask if you want to go to dinner with us tonight."

"Really?" Surprised and a little confused, Laura quickly agreed. "Of course, it'll be fun. Where are we going?"

Samantha shrugged. "Don't know. Just be ready at 6:30. I'll swing by and pick you up." Samantha jumped into the shower.

Laura came home a little earlier than usual and carefully prepared for dinner. When she saw Samantha pull up outside, she ran out the door. Laura shimmied into the passenger seat and buckled her seat belt. "Right on time, I'm so excited to meet your guy."

"Who'd you get so dressed up for, Mom?"

"I just wanted to look nice, that's all, no big deal, Ivy."

"Samantha, remember, and you're from Wyoming, I told him we were from Wyoming, so don't forget!"

"Why Wyoming?"

"I don't know. Just don't screw this up for me!"

"I won't. Let's just go have a good time."

Samantha, Laura, and Murdy playfully talked and joked as they ate. When they finished, Laura gave Murdy a hug that lingered longer than Samantha liked. "Thanks so much for dinner and the good time, Murdy," she murmured.

Samantha pulled Murdy back while Laura walked ahead of them to the car. "So what do you think of my mom?"

"I think she's great! She certainly doesn't look old enough to be your mother. Y'all could be sisters." Murdy pulled Samantha close. "She's not so bad."

Samantha gave Murdy a dirty look.

Murdy stepped back. "What's that for?"

"Sisters? Really? She's over 40."

Murdy chuckled. "Calm down. I'm just sayin' she looks good for her age. You'll probably inherit it, and look like a babe your whole life." Murdy walked Samantha to her car. "See you tomorrow, babe.

Ivy's interest in Murdy is rekindled because she sees her mother as competition.

Nice meeting you, Laura." Murdy turned and headed toward his jeep.

"I really like him, Ivy. I think he liked me, too, and I didn't spoil anything for you."

"Yes, Mom, you did fine."

The volcanic eruption simmered as Laura and Ivy's days slowly intertwined with deception and lies.

CHAPTER 82

Samantha was used to jumping out of bed, grabbing a cup of coffee, and heading off to work but something had changed. With complaints of vomiting, nausea, and exhaustion, she could barely make it through the day without desperately needing a nap. She had been up off and on all night tossing and turning. She woke up slowly, her stomach so squeamish that she wished she'd stayed asleep. Had she eaten something bad? She pulled a pillow over her head and curled up on her side until she couldn't stay in bed any longer.

Laura had already left for work, leaving the coffee pot on, with a note, "Wake up sleepy head. Samantha. See, I remembered! I left you some hot coffee brewing. See you later."

It wasn't too bad having Mom around again, at least for now. So far, she helped around the apartment, and paid her share of the bills.

Staring into the bathroom mirror at her disheveled brown hair, a thought that had been creeping up on her clicked into place. Samantha was a few days late for her period, but the shock of her mother's phone call and then her unannounced arrival had pushed the possible meaning to the back of her mind. *Could I be pregnant?* Being single and casually dating Murdy, but with intimate benefits, made a missed period a potentially life changing event. Samantha filled the bathtub and soaked in warm, fragrant water, eyes closed, imagining she was in a lounge chair on a tropical island with a cold drink, Trace beside her, smiling, holding her hand, and stroking her arm.

Eventually she got out of the tub, dressed, and wandered into the kitchen to make herself some tea. She stood staring out of the window their life together. She tipped her cup for the last few drops of tea, grabbed her coat, and headed for the store to pick up a pregnancy test.

When Samantha returned home and saw Murdy parked in front of her apartment, she twisted her purchase up in its plastic bag and stalked over to his car. Meeting his smile with a scowl, she demanded, "What are you doing here? I didn't tell you to come over!"

Murdy's smile faded. "I know, but I knew it was your day off and wanted to surprise you by taking you to lunch."

Samantha's expression soured. "Don't ever come over here unless I tell you to."

Bewildered, Murdy raised his palms. "I'm sorry, okay, just calm down." His voice lowered to a caressing tone. "Is something going on, Samantha? Maybe it would help if we talk about it."

Samantha snapped. "You just don't get to coming over here without permission."

Just then, Laura walked across the parking area toward them. "What's going on?"

'Nothing," Ivy insisted. "Go away."

"Don't be so crabby, I just came home for lunch."

"It's none of your business. Just go inside, Mom," Ivy scolded. "I'll be there in a minute."

"Okay."

"Don't talk to your mother like that." Murdy blurted, watching Laura glance back over her shoulder as she walked away, raising her eyebrows, and giving him a coy smile, pleased at his attempt to protect her honor against Samantha's harsh words.

"Don't tell me how to talk to my mom," Samantha snapped. Then she took a deep breath and lowered her voice. "Look, I don't feel good today. I just came from the pharmacy." She lifted her bag. "I want to be left alone."

"Oh, babe, I'm sorry."

"Just go home, and don't call me," Samantha demanded. "If I want to talk, I'll call you."

"I'm always here," Murdy said, still wondering what was so awful about him just showing up. *Was she having PMS, or what? What was up with her mom, too?*

Samantha dashed into her apartment and locked the door.

"What was that all about?" Laura asked as Ivy ran for the bathroom.

"Mom! It's not your business."

Laura watched out the window as Ivy engaged the lock on the bathroom door. Ivy's handsome boyfriend was just sitting in his car. Laura took the shawl from the couch, wrapped it around her, and sashayed outside. When Murdy saw her, he rolled down the window. "Hi Laura. It sure is nice to see you again."

"I moved in with Ivy a couple of weeks ago, so you'll be seeing a lot more of me, I hope. My job transferred me here."

"Oh really?" His brows drew together. "Sorry about the scene with Samantha. I don't know why she got so put out."

"She gets that way all the time." Laura leaned on the open window. "I'm surprised you haven't had it thrown at you already. She's kinda spoiled." Laura giggled. "My fault, I suppose."

"Well, I better get outta here," Murdy said. He rolled up the window and started the engine.

Laura stood in the cold, watching Murdy drive away, anticipating her next meeting with the handsome young man.

Samantha opened the pregnancy test and carefully read the instructions. She sat on the edge of the bathtub waiting for a good three minutes, as the second pink line on the plastic test stick got darker and darker. The joy of that little pink plus sign showing she was pregnant was worth more to her than any crazy symptoms or stories of painful childbirth. Grabbing her stomach, she stumbled to her bedroom and fell onto her bed with tears of joy. Trace would be so happy. *I have to find a way to tell him. I could go to his work and surprise him, or maybe I should stop by his house.* Telling her mom wasn't an option. She couldn't keep a secret if her life depended on it. This was Samantha's secret for now, hers and Trace's.

The next morning, Samantha called Murdy, her soft voice appealing for forgiveness. "Hey, I'm sorry for yesterday."

"Yeah, you were a bit over the top, Samantha. I had good intentions, and you just blew up like a crazy woman."

Samantha paused, slowly replied with dangerous calm, "Don't ever call me crazy."

"You know what I mean?" Murdy said reasonably. "I didn't mean really crazy, just that you weren't yourself."

After another longer pause, Samantha asked, "Can I come over after work tonight so we can make up?"

"You have my permission to come over," Murdy joked.

Silence.

"Just kidding, babe, my door is always open. Hey, want me to come and get you?"

"No." Samantha had to get herself settled back into the role she intended to play. "I'm going to do a couple of errands on my way over."

Feeling a little relief Murdy said, "Great. I'll be here waiting."

The winter night had started closing in, making it not quite dark yet, but it was coming quickly. Samantha perched her glasses on her head, grabbed her purse and coat and headed over to Trace's. She drove around his place a couple of times until she saw him pull out of his garage. She slowed and waited until he drove out of the complex.

When Trace drove out onto the street, he noticed the same type of black car following him again. *Who would do that?* To test if he was really being followed, he repeatedly sped up, hit the brakes, and even turned right from a left hand lane.

The black car was like his shadow.

He frantically pulled into the Power Fitness parking lot, opened his door, jumped out, and searched the darkness behind him, looking for his tormentor.

When Trace turned back to his truck and reached into the back seat, Samantha pulled to a slow stop at the curb and watched Trace looking for her. She nearly opened her door, until she noticed Olivia standing at the gym entrance doors. *Can't he go anywhere without that stupid bitch?*

Samantha pulled into the parking lot, backed her car into a corner parking space, and pulled down the visor.

Trace lifted his gym bag out of his truck, then noticed a black car parked in a corner space. He stared at it for a few seconds, then walked to the gym doors where he gave Olivia a one armed hug and kissed her forehead. "Look at that black car over there in the corner," Trace said, giving Olivia a nudge. "It's freaking me out."

Olivia squinted into the dim parking lot. "Why?"

"It just followed me here, I'm sure of it. I've seen that car drive by my apartment, too, and even my work."

"Maybe we should go see who's in it."

"Yeah, let's do it."

Hand in hand, they started toward the black car.

Just then, Samantha's phone lit up with a text from Murdy. 'Hey, you're still coming over, right? It's getting late."

"Yes, be there in a bit.'

"There's someone in the car," Olivia said. "There was a light inside. Did you see it?"

"Yeah," Trace replied. "Let's see who it is."

Samantha lifted her head and saw them coming. She tossed her phone onto the seat, put her car in drive, and headed straight for them. Trace pushed Olivia out of the way onto the ground as the car sped past and out of the parking lot. Then Trace helped Olivia up.

"Are you okay?"

"Yes," Olivia replied, trembling, her lips tight. "I'm just so freaked out."

"It's worse than I thought," Trace said. "We could have been killed."

"We should call the police."

"And tell them what?" Trace's faith in the police was nil. "What are they going to do? We don't have a license plate number or anything. Did you even see the person in the car?"

"No."

"I didn't either."

"I don't know what to do, but we need to do something." Olivia sounded so lost and scared that Trace relented.

"I'll call them, but I know what they'll say." He dialed 911 and reported the incident. Trace and Olivia waited inside the gym for the police to arrive. The officers took their statements and left them a contact number in case they remembered anything else.

"Told you...big help, right?" The police visit only served to ramp up Trace's anger about the situation.

"Trace, I'm scared."

Olivia's fear triggered Trace's combat defense. He put an arm around her in a reassuring hug. "I won't let anything happen to you."

Furious that Trace was with that tramp, Samantha headed for Murdy's, vowing that no one would stand in her way. She would get everything she wanted.

CHAPTER 83

Murdy tidied up his place for Samantha, fed Digger, and put him in the spare room so he wouldn't bother them. Murdy didn't want anything to set Samantha off.

Hearing her car pull up, he anxiously opened the door and greeted her with a big hug. To his relief, she returned the embrace. She even joked with him about the previous day as they sat together on the couch. Then she grew quiet. Murdy studied her beautiful face. "What?"

"About yesterday...I didn't want to see you because I have something to tell you and didn't know how."

"It can't be all that bad, can it?" Murdy asked, although he couldn't fight the feeling that he was sliding on the deck of a sinking ship. "You can tell me anything, you know that, right?"

Samantha looked up at him for reassurance. "You might not think so after this. I've been having morning sickness, and missed my period. Yesterday, I did a pregnancy test and it showed positive."

Murdy's eyes grew big. "Wow...that would be a good reason to blow up for sure."

Samantha lowered her gaze. "I'm pretty sure it's yours."

Stunned, Murdy demanded, "What do you mean...you're pretty sure it's mine? I thought we were seriously together." His voice hardened. "Who else have you been with?"

Samantha raised her voice to match his. "I never told you I wouldn't see anyone else."

Murdy jumped up and paced the floor. "What the hell! Maybe that's the real reason you didn't want me just showing up at your apartment. Maybe I'd find someone else there."

"Maybe," she said easily. "You don't own me. It's my apartment and it's my business who I have there. Like I said, you had no right showing up uninvited."

Blood boiling, Murdy turned to Samantha and said through clenched teeth, "You better leave."

Samantha stood. "It's fine with me if you don't want to accept responsibility for this baby."

Totally amazed, Murdy replied, "Me? You just said it might not be mine." He scrubbed his fingers through his hair. "I think you need to just go home."

"Well, if it is yours, you'll take responsibility for it, I'll make sure of that." Samantha walked to the door and yanked it open. Just before slamming it shut behind her, she called, "No one makes a fool out of me!"

After a long, sleepless night, Murdy trudged to the kitchen for a cup of morning coffee. Then he took a quick shower, deciding he had to see Samantha before she left for work. He walked out into a thick snowstorm. *Damn.* The weather and traffic made his drive longer than he'd planned. When he parked and headed for Samantha's door, he could just make out Laura heading his way through the falling snow. "Laura." He bellowed.

Laura looked up, shielding her eyes against the swirling flakes. "Samantha's not here."

"Do you have a minute to talk? I need some advice."

Pulling her scarf up over her face, Laura said, "Sure. I left early so I could go to Starbucks for my morning cup before work. Want to join me?"

"Sure would. I'll follow you over." Murdy walked Laura to her car and opened the door with a gentleman's gesture. Once she started the engine, he hurried to his Jeep and followed her.

They sprinted into Starbucks and shook off the snow. They ordered their drinks, and then sat at a corner table. "What's going on?" Laura asked. "You look like you could use a friend."

"Well, your daughter is truly a mystery," Murdy admitted. "I can't figure her out. I thought we were getting pretty serious, and then she tells me she's been seeing other people. I didn't see that coming."

"She's always had guys after her. She likes the attention, so she doesn't tend to be exclusive." Laura said with a smile. "You think she's cute, don't you?"

"She's gorgeous! Other guys must think so, too." Murdy spread his hands. "But I thought she was the real deal, and now you're saying she didn't mean any of it?"

"No, don't get me wrong, I'm sure she has feelings for you, and I can see why you'd mean something to her. I love her, I do, but she's a handful, if you know what I mean. She's high maintenance."

Murdy sighed and glanced at his watch. "I have more questions than you probably have time for. I don't want to make you late for work, with the bad roads and all, maybe you could stop by my place after work, and we can finish talking?"

Laura agreed wholeheartedly. "Text me your address and I'll be there shortly after six," she promised.

"Great." Murdy stood. "The roads might still be a bit hairy, so be careful. Thanks again for your time this morning."

Murdy sat at his kitchen table and scrolled through his computer, his mind consumed with Samantha's shocking news. Suddenly, Murdy decided to google Trace Aragon. What was it she thought Murdy had in common with him? If he could find out, it might help him understand her better.

Typing 'Trace Aragon' into the search engine brought up the heading, Idaho man charged with rape. Trace Aragon goes to trial. With growing dismay, Murdy read through all the accounts he could find, trying to compare Trace Aragon's online photos with the one he'd seen in the dimness of Samantha's apartment. He hadn't been paying much attention to family pictures when he'd been allowed inside Samantha's place, but he had no doubt this was her brother, a brother who looked eerily like Murdy himself. Murdy shivered, thinking of men who'd been jailed because of mistaken identity. *That could seriously happen here.*

Why hadn't Samantha told him that her brother was charged with rape? He thought they'd drawn close enough for that kind of trust, but he was obviously wrong.

With keen interest, Murdy continued trolling the Internet. He checked social media sites for more clues, from Facebook to Instagram and back to Facebook until he discovered Eli Cole's post about Trace Aragon attacking Ivy Greene, which led him to a picture of Ivy.

He froze, dread running through him like cold poison. "No," he whispered. How could it be? Except for the hair and glasses, Ivy Greene was a dead ringer for Samantha Stout.

His brain tried to make sense of it. *Well, don't I look like Trace Aragon?* Still, he knew that was just a resemblance. Deep inside, he had a sick certainty that Ivy Greene was Samantha Stout.

With a growing sense of deception, Murdy dug deeper, finding an Instagram post with a comment stating that Ivy Greene was the victim who filed rape charges against Trace Aragon.

Murdy sat back in his chair. *Who is Ivy Greene? Who is Samantha Stout, and who is Trace Aragon, really?* One click led to another, until Murdy discovered that Trace Aragon lived right here in Salt Lake City.

His head hurt. Murdy slouched back into his chair, glaring at the screen, his PTSD kicking up enough anger to cloud his mind. Anxiousness and depression threw themselves in the ring as he pushed himself to his feet and paced his apartment back and forth, one room to another, Digger at his heels, whining anxiously.

Finally, Murdy collapsed on the couch and Digger crawled into his lap. Murdy held his big dog, staring at the computer. The computer screen stared back, daring him to take action.

A soft knock at his door startled him. He looked at the time. Six o'clock. Then he remembered that Laura was coming over.

He reluctantly opened the door. "Hi." he stepped back. "Come in." He reached for her coat collar, and Laura let him help her slip her arms out of the sleeves.

"Thanks. I can't believe how cold it is outside."

Murdy draped her coat over a chair with a confused frown.

"You look like you've seen a ghost," Laura said. "What's wrong, Murdy?"

"Tell me about your son, Trace," Murdy said, heading for the couch and dropping onto it. "I guess it would be your stepson. And who is Ivy Greene?"

"I don't have a son or stepson." Laura sat on the other end of the couch, carefully calculating her answers. "Samantha is an only child, and I guess you'd have to ask Samantha about Ivy Greene."

"I don't understand your daughter at all. She's driving me crazy. So please, just tell me what you know."

"All I can tell you is that she's not who you think she is. I know! Let's go out and get a drink, and then maybe we can figure all this out."

"Okay." Murdy sighed. "I'm probably blowing things out of proportion. A drink and a friend is just what I need right now."

A friend indeed, thought Laura as they bundled up in their winter gear. The snowstorm was still wreaking havoc outside as they hopped into Murdy's Jeep and ended up at The Grill across town. Once they were seated, Murdy's phone lit up with a call from Samantha.

"Just ignore her." Laura suggested smoothly. "She can wait. After all she's put you through, she can definitely wait." Then Laura's phone showed an incoming call from Samantha. She dismissed it, and she and Murdy got their drinks.

"Who is Trace Aragon?" Murdy coyly demanded. "If he's not your stepson then who is he?"

Laura leaned forward, capturing Murdy's eyes with her gaze. "The only Trace Aragon I know was a boy Samantha had a crush on in high school, but he had a girlfriend and didn't pay much attention to her."

Murdy's tone stiffened. "He was arrested for rape, right?

"I don't think so. He was a good kid. Why would you think that?"

"I read a news article on the internet about him being arrested for rape. Ivy Greene was the victim."

Laura's eyes grew wide with surprise. Although she'd lived in Meridian during the court proceedings, she hadn't paid attention to anything outside of her own social circle, and Ivy definitely hadn't been in her social circle for a while. "Please don't say anything to Samantha until I can talk to her myself," Murdy pleaded. "Please?"

Laura touched his hand with reassurance. "Where did you see the article? I'd like to read it."

Murdy shrugged his broad shoulders. "I just googled Trace Aragon and it popped right up. There's quite a bit about him on the internet."

"You're so clever," Laura said, her eyes soft. She stroked his hand with her fingertips.

He glanced down at her touch. "I'm glad you're here, I don't know what to do about your daughter."

"I'm sure she can explain everything," she murmured, "You're a good man."

"I don't know if your daughter thinks so."

Laura shrugged and withdrew her hand. "Like I said, she's high maintenance." It was time to leave. Looking out the window, Laura said, "Oh, my goodness, look at all that snow," she laughed, "and I thought Idaho was bad!"

"Boy I guess it's getting bad." Murdy agreed slowly. "I reckon I should take you back to your car." Instead, he ordered them another drink, and they continued to talk about Samantha.

Laura was getting tired of talking about her daughter. She wanted to talk about her and Murdy. She knew the bar lighting was flattering to her complexion, so she slyly offered Murdy a few compliments that brightened his gaze and warmed the smile he gave her.

After another hour, Murdy finally stood to leave. "Look," he said, "here's my number, thanks for letting me vent. Let me know if you ever need anything."

Laura added his number to her contact list, and then took his phone from his hand, letting her touch linger before adding her number to his contacts under "Laura" and adding five stars. When she returned his phone, she gave him a warm hug. He responded, holding her tightly for a few seconds, her breasts pressing into his impressive chest muscles. She wouldn't have minded him holding on longer, but he let go, gave her a grateful smile, and helped her with her coat. They got in his jeep and he took her back to her car.

After carefully driving back to the apartment, Laura waltzed in with a big smile on her face. Samantha glowered at her from the couch. "Where have you been?" Samantha demanded. "I had plans tonight, and you screwed them up. I can't get hold of Murdy, and you were nowhere to be found. Have you been drinking? I smell alcohol, in this weather. Really, Mom!"

"A friend and I stopped by The Grill for a drink after work. Is that all right with you?"

"What friend?"

"Not your business, Samantha!" Laura relished the irony of her statement.

CHAPTER 84

The morning offered Murdy a headache, but no lasting solace, in spite of the comforting hours spent with Laura the night before.

Suddenly he grabbed his keys, told a reluctant Digger to stay, and got in his jeep. He headed over to Samantha's, or Ivy Greene's, whoever the hell she was. Traffic was backed up for morning rush hour, and he tapped his wheel as his anxiety rose. He should have brought the dog. By the time he maneuvered through the agitating traffic to Samantha's apartment, he was too late. She'd already left for work. Laura was gone, too.

Murdy couldn't wait. It was time to confront this person. The need to sort it all out so his mind could calm down was so great that he braved the irritating traffic to reach the Rehab Center. He knew Samantha was working, but all he needed was a minute. A couple of questions wouldn't take long.

He got out of his car and headed for the clinic doors, feeling suddenly vulnerable without Digger at his side. He wouldn't make that mistake again, but for now, he had to calm himself down.

Walking through the doors, he saw Samantha at her desk. *I just need answers to a couple of questions.* He'd even be content if she'd just promise to talk to him after work.

When she saw him headed toward her, she jumped up from her chair and shouted, "He's the one I told you about!"

Murdy stopped as if he'd suddenly found himself standing on cracked ice. What was Samantha talking about?

Backing behind a coworker, a large woman in a flowered dress too bright for her complexion, tears rose in Samantha's eyes. "I'm afraid he'll hurt me again. Call the police!"

The middle-aged coworker dialed 911 and paged resident security as she shielded Samantha.

Could Samantha somehow have mistaken him for the other guy she was seeing? Trace the rapist?

"A dangerous man just walked into the rehab center," Samantha's coworker said into the phone.

Realizing she meant him, Murdy tried to explain, "Now, wait a minute. I'd never hurt her. I didn't…"

"Sir, would you please step outside with me?" Murdy turned to see a man in a security uniform striding toward him.

"I'm going," Murdy said, putting his hands up and turning to hurry out of the building ahead of the guard. He jumped in his Jeep and peeled out of the parking lot before the police arrived.

Shutting himself in his apartment, Murdy held Digger on his lap, trembling at the frightening turn of events. Just when he got enough courage to confront her, how had Samantha so completely turned the tables on him?

When he heard a knock on his door, he sat still, willing whoever it was to go away. "Police," a voice called. "We need to talk to you."

Could he go on pretending he wasn't home? But his car was outside. The security guard undoubtedly had a good look at it as Murdy made his escape. Waiting would only bring more trouble.

Reluctantly, Murdy opened the door with Digger at his side. He needed a friend.

"Could we come in?" the taller officer asked.

Digger pressed against Murdy's leg. "I'd rather just talk here," Murdy said.

The officers glanced at each other, then the taller one said, "We'd like to come in and ask you a few questions about an incident that occurred at the Clarkston Rehab Center this morning."

"I can answer the questions from here," Murdy insisted, pushing his fingers into Digger's fur. The dog sat stoically in place.

The shorter officer said, "For your safety and ours, would you please either secure your dog or step outside?"

Murdy hesitated, "Just a minute." He reached for Digger's leash on a hook by the door, snapped it to his dog's collar, and commanded, "Sit." Then he took up the slack and faced the officers again.

The short officer took a step back and pulled out a notepad and pen. The tall officer gave Digger an uncertain glance, then asked, "Were you at the Clarkston Rehab Center this morning?"

"Yes, but when I was asked to leave, I left. No problem. I just left."

"Do you know Samantha Stout?"

"Yes, but I didn't talk to her, either. I don't know why she's making all this trouble."

"She claims you and her had a fight last night and your threatened her. Is that correct?"

"No!" Digger stood at the panic in Murdy's answer, his intense dark eyes focused on the police officer. "Sit!" Murdy commanded. Digger obeyed. Murdy lowered his voice. "I didn't threaten her. I never would, no way!"

"We think it would be a good idea for you to stay away from Ms. Stout," the taller officer said, glaring at Digger, then back at Murdy. "Do you understand what we're saying?"

"Yes," Murdy replied. "No problem."

As the officers returned to their patrol car and drove away, Murdy shut himself safely in his house and gave Digger a dog bone. "Good boy, good boy" he said, his mind strayed from his faithful companion.

Why had Samantha acted that way? It was like she was a different person. As Murdy thought through recent events, he decided that everything had been great between them until the day he showed up at her apartment uninvited. Then she told him she was pregnant. Now he had to wonder if that was even true. Maybe she made that up along with whatever else she was mixed up in but if she was pregnant, and he was the father, he had to know.

The officers told him it would be best to stay away from her, which wouldn't be hard in her current state of mind. Somehow, he had to ask her about Trace and he needed to know why she looked exactly like Ivy Greene from Meridian, Idaho.

When he figured she was off work, Murdy texted, *Hey, what was that all about this morning? I just wanted to talk about the baby. Call me, please?*

Samantha quickly replied. *We can talk later. I'll call you when I get home, but stay away from my work and my apartment.*

Relieved that the problems would soon be resolved, he replied, *Okay. Talk later.*

As soon as he was done texting Samantha, Laura called. "Murdy, I have some information I think you need to know."

"What is it?"

"I'd rather tell you in person. It's quite a blow. Can I come over right away?"

"Sure, come on over."

When Laura showed up, she put her car keys in her coat pocket, set her purse on the counter, and opened it. She pulled out a folded piece of paper and opened it as she walked toward Murdy and held it out. "Is this the article you read?"

Murdy glanced at the headline. "Looks like one of them." He sat on the couch and gestured for Laura to sit by him as he read further. Then he glanced up and waved the papers at Laura. "I still don't understand how anyone could do this to someone. Trace must be wiped out."

"Murdy...I have something important to tell you." Then Laura spilled out the truth about her daughter, and all the lies Samantha had told. "I never even knew about the rape," Laura said, her eyes filling with tears. "No wonder people were acting cold towards me. How could I not have known? Ivy...I mean Samantha, didn't tell me. No one told me anything, or maybe I could have helped." Tears spilled over her cheeks. "It's my fault. I should have seen this coming."

"You did the best you could, don't feel guilty about it, especially if she never told you," Murdy said, taking her shoulders in his big, warm hands. "How were you supposed to know if she didn't tell you?"

"I just should have been there for her, that's all." Laura leaned in toward Murdy, and he folded her into his arms as she cried. By the time Laura left, she was satisfied with Murdy's affection. She intentionally left her purse behind, ensuring that she would see Murdy again.

CHAPTER 85

In no hurry to call Murdy, Samantha took the long way home. Staring out the windshield, she thought of baby names, daydreaming about what the baby might look like. *Just like Trace. I miss him so much!*

Samantha's obsession led her to Trace's apartment again. She sat there for a few moments, nervously clutching her phone and eyeing his doorway. She reached into a bag on the floor of her car and pulled out a couple of bags of trail mix, which she had planned to leave on his doorstep, certain that he would remember her thoughtful gesture from school.

She discreetly walked up to his porch, then came to a stop as she heard his garage door opening.

She quickly turned and ran to her car. Jamming the trail mix beneath her seat, she slammed the car door and started the engine as she watched Trace drive off. She followed him across town. She was right behind Trace when he pulled up to The Puppy Shop. She drove slowly past the front door, circled around, and parked.

Trace hustled inside the store to find a new batch of Beagle puppies scrambling for his attention. Olivia was scared, and he was determined to do all he could to help her feel better. Thank goodness, her apartment allowed pets.

Trace chose the puppy that most closely resembled the one Olivia had held before, then had the clerk wrap a gift bow around the puppy's neck. Trace paid the cashier, including dog food, a leash, a dog bed and dishes, then gathered up his new little friend and carried him out to his truck. *She's going to love this little guy.* He couldn't wait to get to Olivia's house.

Where was he going with that cute little dog? I'd love to have that puppy. Samantha's palms started sweating. The sick feeling in the pit of her stomach let her know that something wasn't right, in her fantasy world, even if her mind didn't believe it. She followed Trace, carefully keeping her distance. Turning the corner confirmed her suspicions. Trace got out and headed for Olivia's door. *I knew he was cheating on me!*

Trace watched Olivia's eyes grow wide when she opened her door. Her arms extended, and he put the puppy into them. "What have you done, Trace?"

"I brought Bruno home."

"Bruno?"

"The name means 'armor' and 'protection,'" Trace explained, "so he's going to take care of you when I can't." He petted the puppy's soft ears. "It also means brown and he's that, too."

Olivia held up the puppy and rubbed noses with him. "I love Bruno!" She set him on the porch and he pounced around, making a great effort to keep his head above the bow. They giggled at Bruno's energy. Olivia reached down and slid the bow from his neck. Then she scooped the puppy up, kissed Trace just before they all went inside her apartment, and shut the door.

Trace's romantic gesture triggered a rage of contempt within Samantha's own reality, sending her fairytale delusion around a very, very dark corner. Her unbearable envy bubbled over. *That puppy is ours, damn it! Why is he giving it to that girl?*

Samantha dropped the visor and stared into the mirror. The mirror stared back with fixed eyes. *He will be mine and only mine!* She lifted the visor, licked her lips, and murmured, "I swear I will do something evil to that girl, she'll be sorry she ever laid eyes on Trace."

She sat fuming in her seat, disgruntled and distraught. *He couldn't really love that girl.* Thoughts of poisoning Olivia or stabbing her in the neck with a rusty fork seemed very real. Samantha opened her notebook and began to write, page after page. Finally, she put her book away and drove back to her apartment, oblivious of the traffic around her.

When she got home, she shuffled slowly to her bedroom, took a bath, got into her sweats, and fixed something to eat. By the time she put her dishes in the dishwasher, she had a text from Murdy. *Hey, are you home, yet? I thought you were going to call when you got home.*

Samantha clicked her tongue in annoyance. *Yes, I'm home, but needed to get something to eat first. Hold on.*

Can I just come over so we can talk? Murdy typed with an agitated emoji at the end.

Ivy insisted. *No, I'll come to your place, and I don't want a scene like the last time!*

Understood. When can you be here?

I'll leave now. See you in a few.

Worried that Murdy might do something stupid, Samantha went to her closet and pulled out Trace's stolen pistol. She palmed the gun and made sure it was loaded, and slipped it into her purse. She was ready.

When Murdy answered her knock, she walked right past him and set her purse on the kitchen table. Then she turned to see him staring at her as if afraid to speak. Good. She had him where she wanted him.

"I'm glad y'all came over," Murdy said, sliding his fingers over Digger's head. "The police told me to stay away but I reckon if you're the one coming to see me that should be alright."

Samantha smiled, liking the sound of the police officer's warning. She could use that.

"Want to sit down?" Murdy asked carefully while Digger stared at her, ears erect.

Samantha sat in the center of the couch. After a moment, Murdy took the chair opposite her and rubbed his forehead. "First of all, I just want to talk, okay? I'd just like some information."

Samantha stared at him.

Murdy, a little skittish, took in a breath, "There's a couple of things I'd like to discuss with you, but the first one is finding out if the baby's mine."

Samantha snorted. "That's not going to happen for about nine months."

Murdy rubbed his hands on his thighs, and Digger pushed at them with his nose. Murdy absently rubbed Digger's ears. "I have to admit that it's still rough to hear that you slept with someone else while we were together."

Samantha sighed. "How many times do we need to go over this? I don't see a ring on my finger. We didn't have any agreement about not seeing other people. That's on you if you thought that."

"Well, I thought we had something special, something that didn't need words." His fingers worked over Digger's fur.

Samantha rolled her eyes. "I think we ought to stop seeing see each other, because I don't like it when you accuse me of being a slut or something."

Murdy leaned back, surprise plain on his face. "I haven't said anything of the sort. Those are your words."

Samantha lowered her head and said in a sulky voice, "You're causing me to get upset. That's not good for the baby."

Just then, Samantha's gaze focused on her mother's purse sitting on the counter, and her sulky voice turned angry. "Why is my mother's purse here?"

"Ummm…she came over today, and she must have forgotten it."

"Why was she here?" Samantha stood, grabbed Laura's purse, yanked it open, and rifled through it.

"She told me some things about you and Trace Aragon," Murdy admitted. When Samantha glowered at him from beneath her eyebrows, he rubbed his chin and lowered his gaze. Maybe it would have been better to change the subject, because he didn't want to make things worse, but on the other hand, how could they get much worse than they already were? He hated this conversation. Hell, it wasn't a conversation; it was maneuvering around verbal land mines.

In sudden frustration, he blurted, "Tell me about Trace Aragon raping someone in Meridian, Idaho."

Samantha's face froze as if she just realized she was speeding toward a steep cliff without room to turn aside. She sank back down onto the couch, silent as a statue, her eyes showing no emotion as she dropped Laura's purse to the floor. Then something seemed to light a fire in her. Eyes blazing, she shrieked, "What are you even talking about?"

His self-defense mode kicking in, Murdy shouted back, "I found Trace Aragon's name on the internet connected to a mug shot, but it gets better, Samantha." His voice dripped sarcasm. "My search led to some guy named Eli Cole who posted that Trace was a rapist. Are you with me? Then I started checking his friends on Facebook and Instagram, and what do ya think I found? Samantha, what did I find?"

Samantha folded her arms. "I'm not going to answer you. I knew better than to come over here. You're just trying to start a fight. All you ever want to do is fight with me. This isn't about me , it's about you and your PTSD."

"Answer me!" Murdy commanded. "What did I find? Ya know exactly what I found. Ivy Greene, right, you look exactly like her. Exactly! I also found out that Trace Aragon isn't your stepbrother, and he lives twenty minutes from here. What the hell, Samantha?"

"I'm out of here." Samantha stood and so did Murdy.

With rage in his voice, Murdy blurted out. "Ya ruined Trace's life. Is it my turn next?"

"Maybe you raped me, too," Samantha retorted. "No one will believe you didn't if I say you did." She poked Murdy's chest with her finger, and Digger growled. "Shut up!" Samantha snarled at the dog. Fixing Murdy with a steely gaze, she said, "He raped me. I had to move away and change my name."

Murdy stared at Samantha in alarm. "You had to change your name...and then claim that Trace was your stepbrother? How sick is that, Samantha?" His features twisted, "or Ivy?"

Trace was found not guilty in court because you lied. What else have you lied about? I've heard some of it, but I believe in going straight to the source."

Just then, Laura knocked, opened the door, and slowly peeked around the doorjamb. "Hey, I forgot my purse. Sorry for the intrusion." Her eyes widened as she stepped inside. "Oh, sorry, I didn't know you were here, Ivy...I mean Samantha. I could have just called and asked you to bring it home."

"You stupid bitch! I knew you'd ruin everything."

Samantha reached for her purse and pulled out the gun. "Stay away from me, Murdy," she said, aiming the gun at him. "You've hurt me enough. Both of you have. I can't take your abuse anymore."

Digger let out an anxious bark while Murdy backed away as if Samantha were covered with leprosy. "What abuse?" His forehead creased, Murdy asked. "I've never touched ya in a hurtful way. You're one crazy bitch."

Through clenched teeth, Samantha warned, "I told you never to call me crazy."

Digger barked again.

Aiming the gun at Digger, Samantha shouted, "Shut up, or I'll shoot you first!"

Stepping in front of Digger, Murdy softened his voice. "I'm sorry, Samantha. I need to think before I speak. Now just give me the gun before something happens that none of us wants." He slowly held out his hand.

"Give him the gun," Laura yelled her voice high with panic. "You don't want to hurt anyone. We love you."

"I know you're under a lot of pressure," Murdy soothed. "I'm really sorry. I'm just worried about you, babe." Samantha flinched, and Murdy hurried on, desperately searching for the right words. "If you're really pregnant, and if the kid is mine, I want to raise it with you. You won't have to worry. I don't want you to worry."

"If...I'm pregnant?"

A chill slid down Murdy's back at her soulless expression.

"Of course I'm pregnant, you idiot, but it's not your baby. It's Trace's. We're getting married." Samantha gave Murdy a smug grin.

Murdy shook his head. Without thinking, he muttered, "You're out of your mind if you think he'd want anything to do with you."

Samantha tightened her grip on the gun that was still aimed at Murdy's chest. "What did you say?"

Murdy put his palms out. "Think about what you're doing." He tried to sound reasonable. "Does Trace even know you're here, in Salt Lake City? Think about it. After what I read about you charging him with rape, I'm pretty sure he doesn't want anything to do with you, so for sure he wouldn't have had a role in getting you pregnant."

"Stop saying that." Samantha's voice was dangerously shrill. "Of course he knows I'm here, he loves me." She waved the gun hysterically. "He wants this baby. He wants to raise it with me."

Digger whined, darting a look from Samantha to Murdy and back again.

"Give me the gun, Samantha," Murdy urged, trying to calm the tremor in his voice. "Come on just put it in my hand."

"No!" she declared, steadying her aim again. "Stay away. You've hurt me enough. Trace would never hurt me like this."

Samantha's story was going in circles. Nothing he said made any difference. If she was determined to shoot him, she would. His life was at stake no matter what, and Murdy didn't see any other option but to end the standoff.

Before he made his move, Laura suddenly lunged toward her daughter, her hand colliding with the gun. They grappled, struggling for control, until *BANG!* A bullet exploded from the barrel. Samantha's arms flew out as she arched backwards.

Horrified, Murdy lunged forward and caught her limp body on its way to the floor. Digger barked like a maniac as Murdy laid Samantha down, then pulled his bloody arm out from under her. *What happened to you, Samantha?*

Laura dropped to the floor, tears rolling down her cheeks as she clutched her daughter's limp hand. "I'm sorry, Ivy, I'm so sorry."

In a panic, Murdy dialed 911 and spoke as clearly as his racing heart and short breath would let him. "We need an ambulance. My girlfriend's been shot. Y'all need to hurry, she's bleeding real bad."

A caring, professional voice responded, "What's your name, sir?"

"Murdy, Murdy Swindon."

"And what is your location?"

Murdy told her the address just before Laura screamed, "Why did you let this happen, Murdy?"

Dispatch inquired. "Is there someone else in the house with you?"

"Yes, my girlfriend's mother."

"Help is on its way, Murdy. Are you in any danger right now?"

"No…it's my girlfriend, she's the one."

"What's your girlfriend's name?"

Laura's yelling and Digger's barking made it hard for Murdy to stay focused. "Ah…Samantha Stout."

"Murdy, is Samantha breathing?"

"Yes, but not very well." Murdy choked. His PTSD was on overload. A sense of uncontrollable fear swept over him. He had faced stressful events, danger, and uncertainty every day while in the Middle East, but he was overwhelmed with helplessness at seeing Samantha lying in a lake of blood.

"Murdy, tell me what happened." Dispatch was repeating the request for the third time.

"They were fighting over the gun and it went off," Murdy blurted.

"Who's 'they?'"

"Samantha and her mom."

"Where's the gun now, Murdy?"

"On the floor, she's bleeding a lot. They need to hurry," Murdy insisted.

Staring at her bloody hands, Laura murmured, "Please, God, don't let her die!"

Dispatch asked, "What's Samantha's mother's name?"

"Laura…I don't know, I can't remember her last name."

"That's okay. Is she hurt?"

"No, she's okay."

"Murdy, is Samantha still breathing?" asked the dispatcher.

"I think so, barely," Murdy replied.

Needing more information, the dispatcher asks, "Where is Samantha bleeding from?"

"I think her chest; I think...I don't know...it happened so fast...there's blood everywhere."

Hearing the horror in Murdy's voice, the dispatcher calmly said, "Help is right around the corner, Murdy. Just hold on."

Laura screamed, "Oh my God!"

"Murdy, I need you to tell me what's happening," the dispatcher urged.

"She's not doing so well, y'all need to hurry." He paused, then said with relief, "I hear the sirens. They're here."

"I'll stay on the line with you until the police are in your house."

Samantha's eyes were rolled back. Her breathing had nearly stopped. It seemed like a lifetime before the emergency team surrounded her with their medical equipment. Samantha's pulse was weak and her blood was everywhere.

A female responder radioed to the hospital emergency staff. "We have a young female, approximately 22 years of age, gunshot wound to the chest. Breathing is irregular, pulse is shallow, blood pressure 70/40. We are transporting now."

She was alive when they hooked up IV's and loaded her into an ambulance that screamed its way to the St. Mark's Riverton Hospital. The medical staff pulled the gurney from the ambulance as soon as it arrived. Samantha was wheeled into surgery, where doctors desperately tried to stop the bleeding and remove the bullet.

Police officers quickly took charge of Murdy's apartment, tagging it as a crime scene. After shutting Digger in the bedroom, Murdy and Laura were escorted outside and handcuffed. Evidence was bagged and the police ran the serial number of the Beretta pistol recovered from the crime scene through NCIC, National Crime Information Center, which revealed that the weapon was stolen.

After giving their statements, Laura and Murdy were released. They rushed to the hospital, ran through the ER doors, and headed to the nurse's station. "The woman with the gunshot wound, Samantha Stout, where is she?"

"Are you family?"

"Yes, I'm her mother," Laura said, sliding her hand around the back of her neck. "Is she okay?"

"She's in surgery. The doctors are doing everything they can for her. Please wait over there, and I'll let them know you're here."

"Thank you." Laura murmured.

Murdy wiped the back of his hand across his eyes.

"I can't believe she did this," Laura said as she sank down onto a vinyl couch. "Why did she have a gun? Where did she even get it?" She stared at Murdy in bewilderment.

Murdy shrugged. "I didn't know she had one."

They waited through hours of worry, confusion, and remorse until the heavy double doors finally opened and a tall man wearing blue scrubs approached them. Taking his sterile cap from his head, he asked. "Are you the family of Samantha Stout?"

"Yes." Murdy stood first, helping helped Laura to her feet. "Is she alright?"

"It was touch and go for a while, but we've stabilized her for now. We were able to remove the bullet but it destroyed the some of the bones of the spinal column and looks to have permanently damaged the spinal cord. Time will reveal the range of her paralysis, but with the extent of damage, I suspect she'll be paralyzed from the waist down and will probably be in a wheelchair the rest of her life. She'll still be able to fully use her upper body and will be able to breathe normally without assistance. However, this kind of damage at the T6-8 levels could also affect her sympathetic nervous system so problems with her blood pressure, heart rate, pooling of blood in the lower extremities and temperature regulation could likely be a result as well. She's actually lucky to be alive."

The doctor continued. "If it would've been a hollow point bullet…well, she probably wouldn't have survived, let me explain, hollow-point bullets expand upon hit to produce a bigger wound channel enhancing the probability of intersecting something vital like a main artery or an important organ. Usually, a personal protection handgun is loaded with hollow point bullets. I would suspect this gun was loaded for target shooting. So like I said, she's very lucky."

Laura began to cry in a way she never had before. Murdy put his arm around her, overwhelmed with grief himself.

"One more thing," the doctor said gently. "Did you know she was pregnant?"

Murdy managed to say, "Yes, we just found out yesterday."

"I'm sorry to say that the trauma of her injuries caused the fetus to abort. We did everything medically possible, but sometimes it's not in our hands. I'm sorry we couldn't do more."

CHAPTER 86

The investigation traced the M9 Beretta pistol back to the 2015 Zack Becker and Trace Aragon burglary in Meridian, Idaho, which had landed Eli Cole in jail. Further investigation convinced detectives that Eli Cole had lied for Ivy Greene, now Samantha Stout, who had actually been the one to break into Trace Aragon's apartment.

Laura and Murdy's testimony of the event that transpired that fateful night, the fingerprints on the gun, and legal information about the woman who'd once been Ivy Greene, cleared Murdy and Laura of any wrongdoing.

Laura was relieved that she'd moved away from Meridian. If this had happened there, everyone would have known about the shooting, and her life would have been destroyed. The gossip, rejection, and ostracism would have been even more horrible than when she'd left. Luckily, the shooting happened in Salt Lake City to Samantha Stout, not Ivy Greene. Surely, no one in Idaho would ever be able to put two and two together.

Laura stayed by Ivy's bedside for days as police walked in and out of the room, waiting for a chance to question Ivy.

When Ivy finally opened her eyes and took a slow look around the room, she asked with halting speech, "Mom, where am I? Where's Trace?"

Laura squeezed Ivy's hand. "I'm just going to get the nurse." She stepped out of the room and hurried to the nurse's station. "She's awake," she called, then returned to her seat beside Ivy's bed. "You're in the hospital."

In sudden cowed panic, Ivy's eyes widened. "I can't feel anything! Why aren't my legs moving? What's wrong, Mom? What's wrong?"

Tears rolled down Laura's face. "You were shot. Remember, you had a gun. Do you remember fighting with Murdy in his apartment?"

"Where is he? Where's Murdy? I don't see him or Trace. I need to talk to Trace. He needs to know what happened," Ivy said in a pail, panicked voice.

"I haven't seen Murdy since the night you were brought to the hospital. He was so upset about the fight. He blames himself. I tried to stop you, but the gun went off."

"Where's the doctor? Get the doctor; he needs to tell me why I can't feel my legs. He can fix them, right, Mom?"

The pained look in Laura's eyes said it all. She couldn't stop her tears as she said, "No, Ivy, there was too much damage to your spine. I'm so sorry." Laura held Ivy as Ivy's scream filled the hospital corridors.

The trauma of Murdy's relationship with Samantha kicked his PTSD to a whole new level. As much as he wanted to stay, he had to leave in order to survive. The military cleared him of any wrongdoing and released him from military duty. He was heading home.

After packing his bags, he made one last stop before leaving Salt Lake City. He drove to the hospital to see Samantha.

An overwhelming wave of anger and abandonment swept through him as he stood looking through the window into her hospital room. She was alone, and asleep. Part of him wanted to say "good-bye," but he couldn't, he just couldn't. He swallowed hard at the thought that she might blame him for everything.

Suddenly, an intense moment of loss, curiously mingled with bits of blissful joy, washed over him as his mind leafed back through all the good times he and Samantha had together. *I'll always remember you, Samantha.*

Then he wiped a tear from his cheek, straightened, and walked down the hallway, never looking back.

CHAPTER 87

Tired from a long day at work, Trace maneuvered home through heavy traffic, delighted when Olivia greeted him at the door with her hip jutted to one side, her right arm draped across her slender body, clasping her elbow. Her head tipped toward one shoulder, causing her curly hair to cascade down over her sweater.

"I bought your favorite pizza, BBQ chicken and mushrooms," she said with a smile as she followed him inside and opened the steaming box of pizza. "Come on; let's eat while it's hot."

Trace took a slice and they snuggled on the couch, feeding each other pizza, making jokes about the day and laughing at Bruno's puppy play.

Fumbling with the remote, Trace landed on a news channel. "The shooting on Darwin Street in Salt Lake City three days ago is now classified as a domestic dispute," the reporter said.

"That's just around the corner." Olivia moved in closer to Trace.

Trace put his arm around her.

The announcer continued, "The young female with a gunshot wound to the chest is still in critical condition in a Salt Lake Hospital. No arrests have been made. The mother and boyfriend of the young woman have been cleared of any wrongdoing."

"Wow...scary, way too close," Trace said, tightening his arm around Olivia. *What could have happened?* An unbidden thought slipped into his mind, making him shiver. *What if Olivia had been shot? How could he stand it if he lost her?* His life would be colder and uglier than a jail cell.

When Olivia pulled away from him, he asked with a trace of panic, "Where're you going?"

She gave him a searching look. "I'm just going to the kitchen to get us a couple of drinks, why?"

"I just miss you already," Trace blurted.

Olivia leaned over and slid her fingers through Trace's hair. "I told you before, I'm not going anywhere."

Trace pulled Olivia onto his lap and looked deeply into her eyes. "I love you, Olivia Owens. I didn't think I could ever say that to a woman again."

"I love you, too, Trace. The moment I saw you at the taco truck, I knew you were that kinda' guy I could fall for and I fell hard. Good thing you caught me."

As soon as Olivia disappeared into the kitchen, Trace's phone rang. "Hello?"

Olivia was alarmed by Trace's stricken expression when she walked back into the room. "What's wrong?"

"That was the police. The woman shot the other night over on Darwin was Ivy Greene."

"What? Isn't that the girl...I thought she lived in Meridian."

"I guess she moved here looking for me. She changed her name to Samantha Stout and she's been right around the corner from me all this time. I can't believe it. And the topper, it was my gun that shot her."

"How in the world did she get your gun?" Olivia looked bewildered.

"It was stolen from my apartment in Meridian a while back. They didn't give me any details about the shooting, but said she's the one who robbed my apartment. It all adds up. Eli lied for her. I knew he was lying. He even went to jail for her."

Trace stood and paced the floor. "She's been here all this time. I knew it…I felt it in my gut. The black car that kept following me and that girl, she looked just like Ivy. I knew it was her."

Olivia stopped Trace and wrapped her arms around him. "It's okay Trace. I'm here. I'm with you."

"She's in the hospital," Trace added. "I guess she's in pretty bad shape. She's might be charged with, I don't know, assault or something, as well as robbery, if I want to press charges.

"I don't know what to do. Why did she have to come back? They said my gun is evidence, but I can pick it up after they've closed the case." His gaze focused on Olivia. "I don't want it back, they can keep the damn gun. I don't want any part of my old life."

Olivia gave Trace a squeeze.

"You don't know how glad I am that you're my life," Trace said.

"I'm so glad you're in mine, too," she replied, relieved that he was calm again.

CHAPTER 88

The next day, Trace picked Olivia up from her work at a clothing store. "Get in Olivia; I have something I want to show you." *Your engagement ring, the one I hope you'll like. The shooting put my life in perspective. I want to be with you always, so I hope you say, "Yes."*

Olivia scooted in. "What are you up to, Trace? I know that look, you're up to something."

"Yes, I am, but you'll just have to wait and see." Trace leaned over and kissed her.

Just then, Olivia's phone rang. When she checked the screen, she said, "Oh my gosh...Trace, it's from the office of Dawson and Lorette."

"Well, answer it."

Olivia fumbled with her phone. "Hello?"

"Hello, Olivia, this is Marsha from Dawson and Lorette's office. Mr. Dawson and Mr. Lorette would like to see you. Don't worry, Olivia, its good news."

"Uh, okay, should I come now?"

"Yes, if at all possible. They're waiting for you, but if it's inconvenient, they'll reschedule."

"No, that's okay, give me a minute, I'm not too far away." Olivia hung up. "Trace, you've got to turn around."

"What happened?" Trace asked, checking his mirrors before making a move.

"Marsha said it was good news. Maybe it's about getting my job back. I can't think of what else it would be. They wouldn't call me if they weren't going to hire me back, right?"

"I don't know," Trace said. "Just be calm. You'll find out everything soon enough."

When he pulled up in front of her former office, Olivia climbed out of the car. She looked back at Trace with a worrisome pause, then walked into the building and rode the elevator to the 7th floor. When the doors opened, she held her head high and walked inside the law office of Dawson & Lorette.

"Hi, Olivia," Marsha said with a welcoming smile. "Go on in. You know where it is."

Dawson and Lorette looked up when Olivia walked through the door. "Please," Mr. Lorette said, "have a seat."

Olivia perched warily on the edge of a chair as Mr. Dawson folded his hands on his desk. "Olivia, are you familiar with the recent shooting of Samantha Stout? It's been all over the news."

What could that possibly have to do with Dawson and Lorette? Was it a trick question? She decided a direct, simple answer was best. "Yes, I heard about it, why?"

"We've been given some very interesting information from the detectives on the case. It seems that while examining Samantha Stout's computer, they found a letter written to our office accusing you of talking openly about our clients' private cases."

"It exactly matches the letter we received, word for word," Mr. Lorette added.

"They also found photos of the corresponding confidential documents on her cell phone. Marsha remembers her coming in, acting desperate for an attorney, on the same day we had technical difficulties. Marsha unwisely left her unattended for a moment to try and get help, so we assume she helped herself to the information left on Marsh's desk."

"So you've been proven innocent of any and all wrongdoing," Mr. Lorette said, beaming.

"Olivia, we would be honored to have you back on our staff," Mr. Dawson said.

"With a raise," Mr. Lorette added.

Olivia glanced from one attorney to another. "I'd be happy to come back, but I need to talk it over with someone else first, and to give notice at my other job."

"Of course," Mr. Dawson said.

"We'll draw up your employment agreement," Lorette said. "You let us know when you're ready."

Olivia shook hands and walked out of the office, so relieved and happy that she was all but certain she could grant wishes and even fly if she wanted to. *Was it legal to feel this happy?*

When she saw Trace waiting for her in the lobby, she rushed toward him. He grabbed her in a hug. What happened? Did they hire you back?"

"Yes, I can't believe it! It was Ivy Greene! She was the one who sent the letter to them. The police found it in her computer. I guess she came into the office and stole the information from a file. I'm still in shock."

Trace just stood without moving a muscle.

She pulled back far enough to look into his eyes. "I need to know if you're staying in Salt Lake City."

Trace moved his feet. "Why wouldn't I?"

Olivia's voice lowered. "Because that girl lives here in Salt Lake."

Trace reached out and brushed a finger down Olivia's freckled cheek. "You put her out of my mind, Olivia. You make me brave. I want to be with you everywhere, anywhere, here, if you like it best. Do you want to stay in Salt Lake City?"

Olivia nodded, not trusting her voice.

"Then I'm staying with you, wherever you are. Now, I was going to play this differently before you got that phone call, but I just can't wait any longer." Trace dropped to the floor right in the middle of the law office lobby, landing on one knee. Olivia gasped and grabbed his arm. "It's alright," Trace said, taking her hand. "Olivia, you're the best thing that ever happened to me. I promise to be honest with you always. Will you please marry me?"

Olivia clasped Trace's hand, and with tears of joy, replied, "Yes, yes, I would love to marry you!"

Trace jumped to his feet and gave her a warm, lingering kiss. When they pulled apart, he said, "I know this is where I'm supposed to put a ring on your finger, but I haven't bought one yet. I was trying to surprise you by taking you to look at a ring that I think would be perfect." He glanced down to check the time on Great Uncle Warren's watch. "The jewelry store's still open. Do you want to go with me?"

Olivia laughed in delight. "I'll go anywhere with you forever, Trace Aragon. I love you."

The End

A few excerpts from Ivy/Samantha's Notebook Journal entries:

I am Ivy Greene, I am beautiful, and I am amazing. I am the best thing that ever happened to my mother. I don't know my father; he chose to leave before I was born. I hope he burns in Hell!

Just so, you know...I am able to tell right from wrong and to distinguish between good and evil. In the pursuit of my own interests and causes, I choose to act wickedly. I don't care about anyone but myself. I guess you could say I lack empathy and I am rarely remorseful. If I do say, "I'm sorry" it's because there's something in it for me, because I really don't care. I feel entitled; exploiting others is second nature to me.

My childhood sucked. We always had to move. My mother only cares about herself. I was always looking for another family. I wanted a happy family. When I go to sleep, I am sad. I cannot go there. Tomorrow will be full of adoration, attention, and applause for me.

Poor Eli, he is so vulnerable. He has no self-esteem and lacks self-confidence. His parents never reported his abuse, and neglected to get him counseling. As a result, Eli will have a life of shame, feeling as if the violation against him was somehow his fault. He's grown up striving for acknowledgement, doubting his true worth, believing that nothing he does is ever good enough. His limiting beliefs made it easy for me to saturate him with more guilt. He eventually came to think that he deserves my abuse and it's O.K.

Chloe Holden gave me a ride home today. We became fast friends. Her friends will LOVE me too! We have so much in common. She's smart, beautiful and everyone loves her. It's like looking in the mirror. "Mirror, mirror on the wall, am I the fairest one of all?" Of course I am!

Today, Ted told me he cares about me. He's the greatest dad ever! Chloe doesn't know how lucky she is. I wish my dad would have stuck around to see how beautiful I am. I know it's my mom's fault. She ran him off by thinking only of herself. Soon Ted will look at me with more affection. Poor, poor Chloe.

Ted took the bait. He caressed my body with passion tonight. Chloe saw just how much her dad cared about me over her. Do I care if I hurt her or if she feels bad? Well, maybe a little, but tomorrow she'll have to face the truth about me and her dad.

Ted just thinks he can toss me aside. I don't think so...I have all I need to ruin him if he doesn't capitulate to my demands. Maybe I want him and maybe I don't. He's old anyways. Not my type for sure! I'll have him when I need him.

I used my crafted charm and intense flattery to make Tayla believe she had met her ideal friend. She believes I am devoted and loyal to her. She is too naive to recognize the malicious intent behind my smiling blue eyes. She should be wary of our "instant friendship."

Met Tayla's boyfriend Trace...he had his eye on me the whole time we were talking. The way he looked at me was, well, he couldn't keep his eyes off me. He's going to be my boyfriend! Tayla has to go bye-bye.

Meridian is the most boring place to live. Even the most exciting and varied routine becomes so dull to me after a while. Living in the same place, hanging out with the same stupid people, doing essentially the same things everyday- all qualify as BORING! Not for me. I will leave this place someday!

I deserve it! I feel it is my right - due to my intellectual superiority - to lead a thrilling, rewarding, kaleidoscopic life. People around me should yield to my wishes and needs.

Mom always told me, "If you want something, go get it." I have a new Gucci purse, and I did just go get it. Want it, got it! Easy in and easy out...no one even noticed the slip. Rules and laws are meant to be broken - that's how I win. Legal or not, makes no difference to me. Catch me if you can, Mr. Policeman!

I used a cycle of emotional manipulation and a variety of other tactics to destabilize Trace's feelings. I will convince Trace that he is unlovable and that I am the only one who really understands him. Trace will eventually believe that he is lucky to love me at all.

Am I a narcissist? I was called a narcissist today. Do I care? NO! Ever since I was five, I was smarter than everyone else. My skill of con-artistry has elevated my existence. By making friends with up and coming intellectuals, my reputation is gold!

People say I have no conscience or feelings for others and that the only thing that matters to me is my own selfish ego, coercing, and manipulations. I say to them "Too bad you're not me!" I enjoy causing chaos. It's stimulating and makes my life more interesting.

I flirted again with Trace today. He finds it impossible to digest my gorgeous, blonde, well-built, and sexually insatiable body. He's not a hermit to me but a beguiled boyfriend of Tayla's, with an inkling of interest in either sex or other carnal pleasures with me. I know he finds me desirable. Soon he'll be mine!

I've mastered my control over Eli. My snide comments and little lies were unnoticed in the beginning, but I continually remind him of his shortcomings with backhanded compliments, criticism, and subtle jabs so he'll feel that there's something wrong with him. I throw in a little praise now and then, making him question his view of reality and his own sanity. He no longer feels he can trust his own judgment or memory; he has become so grateful to have me in his life. My lies are his truth; he has no idea what are lies and what's the truth anymore. He would do anything for me. They call him my flying monkey.

Do I have this much power over people? Yes, I do...I only love them when they do what I want. I withdraw my love very easily. I give them the silent treatment to ensure their loyalty to me and to punish them for refusing to do what I tell them to do. Eli understands.

I cannot stand self-important, self-inflated, pompous, bigoted, self-righteous, and hypocritical people. They say I should look in the mirror. Please...do I see myself in them? I try to break the painful reflection of my own flaws in theirs. I force them to confront their mediocrity. I negate their sense of uniqueness. I reduce them to proportion and provide them with my perspective. I do so with mean intent and cruelty. I don't care about them. I have no compassion for any of them and I prey on their vulnerabilities. I expose their double-talk and deride their double standards. I refuse to play their games. They will play mine.

Finally, Trace and I had sex last night. His kisses and caressing hands all over my body warmed me inside and out. Should I tell? Should I write about it on these pages? Oh, I just couldn't. It's our passionate secret. <u>His love for me is real!</u>

He won't take my calls. I know he loves me but is afraid of Tayla. If he doesn't tell her about us, I will. I have no patience.

Tayla won't answer my calls either...screw her. I drove over to her house and had to follow her to the store. I cornered her and told her the whole thing. I told her Trace and I had sex. I think she's mad at me. Ha Ha...I have her boyfriend!

Trace's attempt to ignore me only sets me off for a short time. I will not allow myself to show any weakness. If he keeps up with his ignoring and avoiding behavior, he'll eventually realize that controlling me is not within his power. That's when he can expect me to lash out in a mean and hurtful way. He can't get rid of me that easy.

Everyone will believe he raped me! He'll have to learn the hard way. My finger dialed 911 today. I couldn't believe my eyes when Officer Ted Holden showed up to take my statement. He just about shit his pants when I opened the door. No doubt, he'll be doing just as I say.

Today Trace will realize how much I love him. I wouldn't be doing this if I didn't love him and I didn't know he loved me too but he just sits in the courtroom and tries not to look at me. I look very nice and innocent in my dress. The jurors will notice even if Trace doesn't.

All of Trace's friends and family showed up to court again. They think the jury will feel sorry for him. It's me they feel sorry for. I'm the victim!

I can look people straight in the eye and lie quickly and guiltlessly, even when I'm confronted with probing questions and evidence of deception. It's not my problem that real rape victims are often mistaken for false accusers and often don't get their justice. They say false accusers like me usually have identifying traits, such as narcissistic behavior, including a history of lies, but if the lies help me get what I want, then so be it.

My rape prosecution hinged entirely on my credibility. My testimony is the evidence. The judge and jurors think they are good at catching liars. Creating my believable dialogue wasn't difficult. I used my dubious, stereotypical descriptions of what Trace and I supposedly did and said to one another. I reported dialogue with Trace that was full of credible, seductive lines and manipulative tactics. While my memory for physical detail was a little lacking, maybe, my recall for words was impressive enough to help me answer the important questions convincingly. My act was flawless. As I explained the details of my rape, it was almost as if I was taking the jurors back to when it happened. I will convert them to my point of view. I put my hand on the Bible and swore I was certain Trace Aragon had raped me, and I wasn't about to change my story.

That stupid bitch of an attorney thought she could make me look bad in court. She's not even in my league. Her ugly blue pantsuit...it might as well be on a man. She keeps looking over at me as if she can rattle me or something. Shut the hell up, bitch. Yadda Yadda Yadda Nobody really cares what you're saying.

The juror on the end keeps looking at me. I know he believes me. I look at him, too, on occasion. He dressed nicer today than yesterday, probably for me.

My truth...It's what makes me strong. I am fully aware of the difference between true and false, make-believe and the invented. I am NOT crazy! My delusions are in the service of my own mind.

They all lied! Liars! ! ! Even Eli...I will show them all. If they think their prick of shame and humiliation has exposed my façade and deflated it, and effectively destroyed me, think again. The shame and humiliation may be a blow to my ego, but HELL hath no fury like mine.

Trace belongs to me. We're destined to be together. The details in my head about our romantic relationship do exist. Why can't he see that he loves me? Trace doesn't know I'm here in Salt Lake City yet, but I know where he and Ethan live. I waited for him to come home from work today...he looked so good. He didn't even notice me, but he soon will.

I consciously choose to adopt one version of my life, an exaggerated narrative, a fairy-tale existence, a "what-if" counterfactual life. It's mine if I want it to be!

ADDITIONAL INFORMATION:

Some people believe that narcissism is merely self esteem on steroids, but researchers found that narcissists consistently view themselves as better than other people, while people with high self esteem view themselves as just as good as others.

Evidence points to narcissists as being made, not born.

HOW NARCISSISTS ARE MADE:

A 2015 study conducted by Ohio State University and the University of Amsterdam <<u>https://news.osu.edu/how-parents-may-help-create-their-own-little-narcissists/</u>> showed that "narcissism in children is cultivated by parental overvaluation."

Some environmental and/or developmental factors that are thought to influence Narcissistic Personality Disorder (NPD):

Unreliable or unpredictable care from parents or caregivers.

Some traumatic childhood experiences, such as loss of a father figure, abandonment, or sexual abuse or emotional abuse.

A parent who is jealous of their child's accomplishments and claims ownership of their child's success.

A sense of betrayal created by mixed signals of punishment and approval from the person who is depended on to give love and security, but turns out to be the one who also takes it away with no reason the child can understand.

Parents who are threatened by a child's independence because they fear they won't be needed anymore. This fear leads to a lack of autonomy for children whose parents insist on controlling their children's lives.

Regardless of whether parents demonstrate narcissistic tendencies or not, those who over value their child, perpetually telling him or her how much better and more talented they are than other children, are not boosting self-esteem. Instead, they tend to foster narcissistic tendencies in children.

Research notes that parental overvaluation is not the only cause of narcissism, which, like other personality traits, can also be affected by genetics and individual children's temperaments.

This is not to say that children shouldn't be valued for accomplishments. Parental warmth is not associated with narcissism. Focusing on a child's best efforts with encouragement, rather than comparing them with others' performance, leads to healthy self-esteem.

Parenting is not a popularity contest. There will often be some anger and disappointment when children aren't able to get what they want, but a child's acting out behavior should not determine a "parents" response.

THE MAYO CLINIC'S SYMPTOMS OF NARCISSISTIC PERSONALITY DISORDER:
<https://www.mayoclinic.org/diseases-conditions/narcissistic-personality-disorder/symptoms-causes/syc-20366662>
- ❖ Have an exaggerated sense of self-importance.
- ❖ Have a sense of entitlement and require constant, excessive admiration.
- ❖ Expect to be recognized as superior even without achievements that warrant it.
- ❖ Exaggerate achievements and talents.
- ❖ Be preoccupied with fantasies about success, power, brilliance, beauty, or the perfect mate.
- ❖ Believe they are superior and can only associate with equally special people.
- ❖ Monopolize conversations and belittle or look down on people they perceive as inferior.
- ❖ Expect special favors and unquestioning compliance with their expectations.
- ❖ Take advantage of others to get what they want.

❖ Have an inability or unwillingness to recognize the needs and feelings of others.

❖ Be envious of others and believe others envy them.

❖ Behave in an arrogant or haughty manner, coming across as conceited, boastful, and pretentious.

❖ Insist on having the best of everything.

HOW TO KNOW WHEN A NARCISSIST OR NARCOPATH (narcissistic sociopath) IS LYING:

This a lot easier than you might think. If their lips are moving, they are probably lying. Plain and simple! It's a scientifically proven, fact-checkable, medically accurate, historical truth!

PROTECT YOURSELF FROM NARCISSISTS:

Although narcissists initially appear charming and highly concerned with another person's welfare, be wary of the signs of a narcissist.

BOREDOM - Because they're easily bored, a narcissist's sense of entitlement, being "above the law," means it's not unusual for narcissists to engage is socially unacceptable behavior.

CHEATING - Narcissists may view monogamy and marriage as average and mundane. With their sense of superiority, they feel the rules don't apply to them, so they are free to cheat, in many ways including adultery, and having extramarital affairs.

COLLECTING PEOPLE - Narcissists tend to rotate their time among different sets of "friends," but their ploy is to get attention, admiration, or information. Once they have what they want, they quickly disengage.

DEVALUATION/DEGRADATION/HUMILIATION - To keep themselves on a pedestal, narcissists employ methods to make people feel as if they were of lesser value than the narcissist with tactics such as verbally putting people down, intermittently withholding affection, disappearing from contact without explanation, blaming the target, or gas lighting.

DISCARDING - If a narcissist decides their target has lost appeal, they can orchestrate their victim's own abandonment by initiating emotional abuse until their target wonders how they could be cast out of such an initially loving relationship.

EMOTIONAL BLACKMAIL - Using a sense of obligation, guilt, and/or fear to control behavior.

FLYING MONKEY - Someone willing to do the narcissist's bidding, acting on their behalf to help abuse, bully and torment the narcissist's victims.

FRAGMENTED RELATIONSHIPS - Although many narcissists have few, if any, family or friends, they love to adapt to their victim's social interactions and enjoy scamming their friends to test loyalty. For example, if a disparaging remark about the victim elicits laughter, the narcissist pursues a closer relationship with this friend, sensing a "flying monkey" for future use against the victim.

GAS LIGHTING - Emotional and psychological abuse, which is implemented by manipulating the target into doubting his or her sanity by questioning their memory and/or perception of events. The gas lighting may include accusations of overreaction, followed by the abuser's own thoughts presented as truth.

GRANDIOSITY - A narcissist's need for adulation and admiration fosters their lack of empathy, which can lead to grandiose feelings and behavior to the point that they can live in a fantasy of their own making.

GUILT PLOY - Guilt and pity ploys used are by narcissists to play on a victim's compassion. Many punishments are used, such as ignoring the victim or threatening to leave, which are effective in guilting a kind and empathetic victim to cooperate.

IDEALIZATION - Early in a relationship, narcissistic targets can hardly believe their good fortune in finding their soul mate and being placed on a pedestal.

IRREGULAR REINFORCEMENT - This occurs when either a reward or punishment is not administered every time the desired response is given.

LOVE-BOMBING - A narcissist may attempt to create an intense atmosphere of adoration and affection, making the target feel like the most special person ever by smothering him or her with extravagant courting, vacations, promises of a blissful future, and high praise. This tends to disarm a person's natural sense of caution so they don't tend to question the speed of where a relationship is headed.

MANIPULATIVE MALIGNANT NARCISSIST - To keep anyone from knowing who they really are or what they're up to, narcissists lie. Seeking power, dominance, and control, one of their main ambitions is to keep others in the dark and second-guessing themselves.

MASKS - In order to get what they want, narcissists act out different roles. To hide the parts of themselves they don't want seen, they wear "masks." You may see someone you don't recognize when the mask slips. A narcissist will usually dump someone who glimpses his or her cruel or frightening persona.

MIRRORING - A narcissist mimics a target and agrees to everything said in order to falsely charm the victim and learn his or her strengths, weaknesses, and insecurities. In this way, they have a script to play against their victim, and helps determine what source of supply will be provided for them, from financial to sexual.

NAME CALLING – Calling names is a tactic narcissist use for someone who crosses them. Ironically, they names they choose are often ones they are: terrible parent, liar, cheat. This is usually claimed to be a joke, but escalates as they figure out what most hurts the person they're speaking to.

NO ACCOUNTABILITY - Narcissists don't accept responsibility for their actions or anything they say. Don't expect an apology, because they see it as "your fault," or the fault of their boss, ex, friend, or anyone else they target.

NO REGARD FOR RULES - Narcissists believe they are above the law. This gives them license to ignore restraining orders, speed, commit murder, or whatever else they please.

PERFECT PUBLIC IMAGE - Narcissists care what people think of them, and are very conscious of how others see them.

SMEAR CAMPAIGN - Narcissists undermine their victim's credibility by creating a series of lies, exaggerations, false allegations and half-truths about their victim's behavior. The victim may question his or her sanity, question trust in their friends, and lose their support system. The narcissist seeks to make them fearful, isolated, and unsure where to turn.

TRAUMATIC BOND - Cycles of intermittent reinforcement, both positive and negative, tends to form powerful emotional traumatic bonding. This unhealthy loyalty to a destructive person is extremely resistant to change.

TRIANGULATION - A narcissist seduces a target to do their dirty work for them by means of words and posturing. This "rescuer" then helps torment the victim under the delusion that they're protecting the narcissist from a bully.

UNAPOLOGETIC - Narcissists are never wrong, never accountable, and will never apologize.

HOW TO RAISE A NON-NARCISSIST CHILD:

The following behaviors can help a child feel good about themselves without encouraging narcissistic tendencies:
https://www.davidwolfe.com/1-parenting-trait-narcissistic-children/

• Connect: Make sure to tell your child you love spending time with him or her because you love him or her, not because of what the child does.

• Empathy: Children need to understand that their actions can help or hurt another person. By teaching children to be aware of other's feelings, you're giving them important social skills that will stay with them into adulthood.

• Encourage friendships: Friends will tell your child the truth, and let them know they don't have to be perfect to be liked.

• Be Gentle: At their root, most narcissists, and especially narcissistic children, have low self-esteem. Discipline is important, but approach it with respect. It's okay to make mistakes, and it's important to apologize. Teach them how to make wrong things right.

DON"T MISS THE WARNING SIGNS:

Staying educated about the signs of child sexual abuse is imperative nowadays. Sexual predators can be neighbors, family or friends. Internet predators are rampant. The statistics of reported child abuses are that 1 in 5 girls and 1 in 8 boys will experience some form of child abuse before the age of 18.

Always listen to your parental intuition.

FALSELY ACCUSED OF RAPE…WHAT NEXT?

Being accused of rape is an ugly reality that happens all too often. False accusations of rape are used as a way to gain an upper hand, get revenge, or otherwise harm another person. The results of such a charge can be devastating, even if the person wrongfully accused is ultimately acquitted. No one can feel or understand the heartache of these horrific rape allegations unless you've been accused. The silent pain and suffering are cemented in the victim's soul forever.

Hire an attorney before talking to the police!

If you have been accused of rape, the first thing you need to do is contact a criminal defense attorney, who will then respond to the allegations and defend you against the rape charges facing you. A criminal defense attorney will guide and assist you with the steps necessary to proceed against the rape allegations.

The site below is dedicated to the families whose college sons have been falsely accused of sexual misconduct. There is a lot of information and advice for anyone that has been falsely accused of rape.
https://helpsaveoursons.com/

Author's Note:

I am not a professional on this subject and I make no explicit guarantees about the accuracy of the information contained in this book. It's through my own experience and observation, the destruction, and horror left behind by narcissists that unraveled my inner soul. Inspired by true events and the broken people left behind, I entwined personal thoughts with research to create this book.

My heart aches every time I read or hear about someone else being abused by a narcissistic predator disguised as co-worker, friend, and even a family member. The day-to-day behaviors of narcissists are depicted in this book to help you to identify and protect yourself against becoming a victim.

I hope you will understand the point of view I've presented with an open heart.